OFF AND RUNNING

Byron Tennyson Wilder—better known as The Poet—made a living betting on horse races. A good living, because he was the best. But now he had been too good. He had hit three super longshots in a row, and if he couldn't find out how somebody was beating the odds at tracks all over the country, the Las Vegas big boys were going to put him out of the money for good. He not only had the mob on his back, he also had a beautiful chick on his hands, and a coast-to-coast trail of thundering hooves to follow. And unless he got wise in a hurry to a dust-in-your-eye deception being pulled off, there would be bone-crushing violence to worry about right up to the finish line. . . .

RINGERS

SPELLBINDING THRILLERS...
TAUT SUSPENSE

☐ **A REASONABLE MADNESS by Fran Dorf.** Laura Wade was gorgeous and gentle, with a successful husband and three lovely children. She was also convinced her thoughts could kill ... "A riveting psychological thriller of murder and obsession." *Chicago Tribune* (170407—$4.99)

☐ **THE HOUSE OF STAIRS by Ruth Rendell writing as Barbara Vine.** "Remarkable ... confirms (Barbara Vine's) reputation as one of the best novelists writing today."—P.D. James. Elizabeth Vetch moves into the grand, old house of her widowed aunt and plunges into a pit of murderous secrets 14 years old. "The best mystery writer anywhere." —Boston Globe (402111—$4.95)

☐ **SIGHT UNSEEN—A Novel by David Lorne.** Once Hollywood's top sound effects man, Spike Halleck has been forced to live in a world of darkness, after an accident took away his sight. Despite the odds, he sets out to save the life of a kidnapped little girl he loves. With a female officer acting as his eyes, he begins the strangest hunt a man ever made ... with the most shattering climax a gunshot ever ended.
(165349—$4.50)

☐ **BLINDSIDE by William Bayer.** "A dark and sultry *noir* novel."—*The New York Times Book Review*. Burned-out photographer Geoffrey Barnett follows a stunning young actress into a world of savage secrets, blackmail, and murder. "Smashing ... unstoppable entertainment." —*Kirkus Reviews* (166647—$4.95)

Buy them at your local bookstore or use this convenient coupon for ordering.

NEW AMERICAN LIBRARY
P.O. Box 999, Bergenfield, New Jersey 07621

Please send me the books I have checked above. I am enclosing $_____
(please add $1.00 to this order to cover postage and handling). Send check or money order—no cash or C.O.D.'s. Prices and numbers are subject to change without notice.

Name_____

Address_____

City _____ State _____ Zip Code _____
Allow 4-6 weeks for delivery.
This offer is subject to withdrawal without notice.

RINGERS

Tim Underwood

A SIGNET BOOK

SIGNET
Published by the Penguin Group
Penguin Books USA Inc., 375 Hudson Street,
New York, New York 10014, U.S.A.
Penguin Books Ltd, 27 Wrights Lane,
London W8 5TZ, England
Penguin Books Australia Ltd, Ringwood,
Victoria, Australia
Penguin Books Canada Ltd, 2801 John Street,
Markham, Ontario, Canada L3R 1B4
Penguin Books (N.Z.) Ltd, 182-190 Wairau Road,
Auckland 10, New Zealand

Penguin Books Ltd, Registered Offices:
Harmondsworth, Middlesex, England

First published by Signet, an imprint of New American Library,
a division of Penguin Books USA Inc.

First Printing, January, 1992
10 9 8 7 6 5 4 3 2 1

Copyright © Tim Underwood, 1992
All rights reserved

 REGISTERED TRADEMARK—MARCA REGISTRADA

PRINTED IN THE UNITED STATES OF AMERICA

Without limiting the rights under copyright reserved above, no part of this publication may be reproduced, stored in or introduced into a retrieval system, or transmitted, in any form, or by any means (electronic, mechanical, photocopying, recording, or otherwise), without the prior written permission of both the copyright owner and the above publisher of this book.

PUBLISHER'S NOTE
This is a work of fiction. Names, characters, places, and incidents either are the product of the author's imagination or are used fictitiously, and any resemblance to actual persons, living or dead, events, or locales is entirely coincidental.

BOOKS ARE AVAILABLE AT QUANTITY DISCOUNTS WHEN USED TO PROMOTE PRODUCTS OR SERVICES. FOR INFORMATION PLEASE WRITE TO PREMIUM MARKETING DIVISION, PENGUIN BOOKS USA INC., 375 HUDSON STREET, NEW YORK, NEW YORK 10014.

1

"You just want my goddamn job," Buck Brewster accused. With his petulant expression, his reddening features, and his crowning shock of curly silver hair, he looked like a peevish Santa Claus.

I didn't have time for this. I had work to do, a meeting to attend. Buck was trying to make his problems my problems and I was just plain tired of hearing it.

"Give me a break, Buck," I said impatiently. "Why would I turn the job down, recommend you, and then try to steal the job from you?"

"That was before *Vegasline* became a hit. You thought the show would bomb."

The waitress came around to refill our coffee cups. I put a hand over mine. Buck passed his cup to her and added cream to the fresh brew.

"I'm not gonna argue with you, Buck. I turned down *Vegasline* because I was afraid it *would* be a hit. If I wanted that job, all I'd have to do is let Sheline know."

Buck had no response. He knew it was true. His voice lost some of its strident tone. "Okay, okay. That was out of line," he conceded. "But I need some help here, Poet. Sheline's been on my case . . . you know, give the viewers some winners they can't get by reading the morning paper. Forty-percent winners aren't good enough. It's longshots he wants."

I shrugged. "So give him some long shots. What good are forty-percent winners when the odds are so low they produce a flat-bet loss?"

"It's not my thing, Poet," Buck insisted. "I'm conservative . . . a numbers cruncher. You're the one with the data base. You're the one who pulls long shots out of his ass.''

Out of my ass? I invest a small fortune in computer equipment and work fourteen hours a day to pull winners ''out of my ass''? There are two sure ways to piss off a professional handicapper: one is to refer to him as a ''gambler''; the other is to suggest that his winners are a product of ''luck.''

''Let me see if I understand you correctly, Buck,'' I said deliberately. ''You want me to give long-shot plays to you so you can go on television and relay them to every horseplayer from Aqueduct to Hollywood Park. Buck, we've been friends for three years and I'd like to help you, but you're out of your mind.''

''Not all your plays,'' he assured me, ''just a good one every now and then.''

I dropped a bill on the table to pay for the coffees. ''I gotta go, Buck,'' I said, trying to keep my temper in check. ''Look, I'll tell you what I will do. You pick the winners. You do the dog work. I'll go over your selections with you and let you know when I think you're out to lunch. If your long shots are reasonable, you'll win your share. Your viewers and Sheline can't ask for any more than that.''

Buck opened his mouth to press the argument. He looked so desperate, for a moment I was afraid he was going to beg. Instead, he nodded agreement and gave me a little smile of feeble gratitude, as though the degrading nature of his solicitation had suddenly dawned on him and left him embarrassed.

I gave Buck a ''hang-in-there'' slap on the back, waved to the waitress, and walked out of the coffee shop. When I looked back, Buck was staring into his coffee cup with the badgered expression of a hard-knocker who owes his bookie more than he can pay.

For the few dozen gamblers leaning wearily on blackjack and craps tables, 6:45 A.M. was late . . . the end of a long and stultifying night. Most of the tables in the Tiara's vast, sprawling casino were closed and covered. As faded and wrinkled as their evening finery, the players were obviously from out of town. Only visitors pounded the tables past the point of exhaustion, as though the casinos would disintegrate forever if they left. Last night they had felt youthful, on the verge of adventure. Now they were older, on the brink of defeat. The cocoon of the casino made the metamorphosis regressive, turning from a colorful, soaring butterfly to a more basic creature groveling along the ground.

The longer you stay, the worse it gets, I thought as I passed through. But I'd been there before, and these gamblers were beyond advice.

There was little sound—just an occasional bell from the slot machines followed by the metallic clatter of tokens falling into the tray and the listless monotone of the craps stickman. The players at the tables pushed chips from space to space mechanically, engaging in small talk with tired dealers who were waiting for the ends of their shifts. This was the hour when even the illusion of magic had vanished.

For me, 6:45 was early. I was fresh and rested, working on an extremely profitable winning streak. Even the troubling meeting with Buck couldn't destroy my feeling of well-being.

From the main casino, I crossed into the Tiaradome, the hotel's cavernous race and sports book. The Tiaradome had surpassed Caesar's Palace and the Hilton as the premier facility in Las Vegas for sports betting. More than a thousand bettors could witness and wager on major sporting events and horse racing under the arched fifty-foot ceiling. There were four television screens, each twenty by twenty feet, suspended high on the front wall above the area where a small army of dealers accepted bets. To the left of the screens was a scoreboard reflecting odds for the day's major league baseball games and the projected point spreads for the NBA playoffs currently in progress. On the side wall, digital totalizator boards reflected the "morning line" odds for the first races from Aqueduct in New York, Sportsman's Park in Chicago, Hollywood Park in Los Angeles, and Golden Gate Fields in San Francisco. On the weekends, particularly in the fall when football dominated the sports action, televised broadcasts of the games competed with simulcasts of the horse races to create deafening confusion. "They're at the post" overlapped "First and ten."

When the Tiaradome was cranked up, the atmosphere was intensely charged, electrifying.

On the opposite side of the Tiaradome, I reached the neatly camouflaged door with the discreet brass plaque which read "TURF CLUB—Members Only." The optical scanner accepted my membership card, the lock buzzed, and the door swung open to my touch. With a sense of anticipation which hadn't waned after three years of membership, I entered an inner sanctum so exclusive that the multitudes of Las Vegas visitors and most of its sporting residents were ignorant of its existence.

The club was dark. Aqueduct post time, the day's first, was at nine-thirty Las Vegas time. The club staff was due at seven-thirty and members would start trickling in between eight and eight-thirty. I groped along the wall near the door until I found the light switch and, one by one, the banks of fluorescent lights illuminated the room.

The Turf Club was a miniature version of the Tiaradome except that its wide-screen televisions and its totalizator boards were devoted exclusively to horse racing. The first of the club's several levels, the one closest to the screens, was furnished with comfortable swivel armchairs. These were reserved for the hotel's invited guests and were designed more for watching than for working. The second and third tiers were more businesslike. Two rows of twelve oak desks were separated from one another by low, sound-muffling partitions. Behind the desks, comfortable executive chairs were covered with the same dark brown leather as the guest chairs. The cubicles featured special reading lights, outlets for personal computers, and placards embossed with the names of the daily occupants. This was a state-of-the-art working environment, designed to rival the most modern business office.

On the highest level of the club were a conference room, an office for the club's executive secretary, a secured area for the dealers, whom the members persisted in calling "mutuel clerks," the rest rooms, and a small but tastefully appointed lounge. The bar in the lounge was staffed by a pair of waitresses during normal operating hours, but I was unwilling to wait until seven-thirty for service. I rummaged beneath the bar for coffee and filters and set the coffee maker to work.

While the coffee was brewing, I snapped on the reading lamp of the third-tier work station, where the placard read "Tennyson Wilder," and unloaded my portfolio. My normal equipment consisted of three regional editions of the *Daily Racing Form*, a sheaf of computer printouts, a legal pad, two felt-tip pens, and an abominable pair of reading glasses which my failing vision had forced me to adopt in addition to my contact lenses.

The Turf Club was the brainchild of a hotshot casino executive named Michael Bellisari. While I'd never cared much for Bellisari personally, I had to admire his Turf Club creation in both its concept and execution. Bellisari made the Tiara Corporation a ton of money and assured his own future within its management structure by reversing the typical casino mind-set of abhorring winners and loving losers.

A Las Vegas race and sports book is nothing more than a legal bookmaker. Unlike a racetrack, which rakes in a preset percentage of its parimutuel pools, a bookie or a Las Vegas race book is operating out of its own pocket. As long as losing bets add up to more than winning-bet payoffs, the book makes a profit, or is "in balance." Given this economic fact of life, a professional handicapper might expect to be about as welcome as a card counter at the blackjack tables—somewhere in between an outbreak of gonorrhea and a nuclear catastrophe.

This would certainly be the case were it not for the existence of a phenomenon known as "layoff bookmaking." Back in the old days before the advent of the parimutuel system, all racetrack wagering was conducted by bookmakers. Each bookie was an entrepreneur who set his own odds for each entry in every race. A bookie succeeded or failed on the strength of his knowledge of handicapping, his track intelligence network, the agility of his mathematical acuity, and the resilience of his nerve. The best of them succeeded handsomely.

Whenever a single horse was bet so heavily that its winning would create a "negative pool"—that is, losing bets would not be sufficient to cover the winning payoff—a bookie would typically protect himself by placing bets of his own with another bookie just to get back "in balance." This form of hedging was known as "laying off."

As long as the bookies were on the track grounds, adjacent to one another, laying off bets was no problem. However, as soon as the parimutuel system displaced them and bookmaking became an illegal enterprise, the logistics of laying off became much more complicated. To compound the problem, most bookies stopped computing their own odds and used track odds from the parimutuel system. This practice simplified the bookies' operations but increased both the chances of a negative pool and the need for a simple layoff mechanism.

Even illegal businesses are governed by the laws of supply and demand, and there evolved a business known as a "layoff bookmaker." The first really large-scale enterprise operated out of a modest storefront in Newport, Kentucky, under the name of Bobben Realty, after its owners, Bob and Ben Lassoff. Bobben Realty accepted layoff action from more than fifteen thousand illegal bookmakers throughout the eastern half of the continent. It was the "bookies' bookie." Using various names and under different managements, all of which had close connections to organized crime, the operation moved from Newport, to Montreal, back to Newport, to Miami, and, finally to Las Vegas in the form of the vast underground National Sports Book.

Las Vegas race books, including the Tiara, keep in balance by laying off bets with one another and with the National Sports Book. This has been standard operating procedure for more than forty years. Around five years ago, Mike Bellisari found a way to change the layoff game from a defense mechanism to a moneymaker by harnessing the talents of professional horseplayers.

A professional handicapper, like a blackjack counter, is not some kind of "supergambler" who wins vast sums by otherworldly flights of insight. Instead, like the counter, a professional is someone who is willing to work exponentially harder to create an "edge" which generates profit over time. A counter keeps track of the cards in a blackjack deck and increases his bets when the composition is in his favor. Similarly, a handicapper will wait patiently to bet only when his understanding of a race and the prevailing odds mesh to give him an advantage. Only the combination of strong feelings about a horse's chances and attractive odds can induce a wager. Mike

Bellisari reasoned that by attracting the very best resident handicappers in Las Vegas through an elite, luxurious club, and by using the Tiara's computer capability to track their "edge," he would then be in a position to lay off the best bets of the best bettors.

The system works beautifully. For example, if I bet $1000 on a 6-1 horse and if the wager falls within my "win profile," the Tiara lays off $2000 on that same horse. If I lose my bet, the Tiara's exposure is $1000 (the $2000 they laid off less the $1000 they won from me). If my bet is a winner, the Tiara returns my $1000 plus my $6000 winnings. In turn, the house collects the $2000 they laid off plus $12,000 profit. Simply stated, the house is betting with me instead of against me. In racing parlance, the Tiara gets the "ultimate overlay"—the selected action of twenty-four of the best handicappers in the world with half of its downside risk guaranteed. It's almost like a license to steal.

As a professional handicapper, the arrangement is much to my liking. I avoid the lines and the noise of the Tiaradome in favor of the comfort of the Turf Club; I bet amounts higher than the posted limits of the main race book; and I associate with the absolute masters of the craft. As for my downside, if my percentages fall, the Tiara will back away from my action. If a losing streak is prolonged, my membership is forfeited and another "hot hand" will claim my seat.

I stretched to relieve the tightness in my back and neck. Normally at this time of day I would be working out or playing racquetball at the Las Vegas Athletic Club, and my body was protesting the break in routine.

In truth, I was feeling a case of "the guilts." All my life I've fought a battle against a tendency to gain weight, suffering defeat in those blue periods when I neglect to care for myself properly, but winning in the times when high self-esteem provides the impetus for diet and exercise. For the past few years I've been winning, but not without hours in the gym and buckets of perspiration, all the while spurred by a relentless conscience which constantly whispers, "You're fat, you're fat."

An old coach used to point out that "some guys look better than they play; some guys play better than they look." In most things—beyond just sports and games—I'm one of the latter. I'm not tall enough (five-foot-nine) to make a dramatic first impression, and I'm too broad in the shoulders and thick in the chest and thighs to wear the latest fashions or look good when I'm dancing. I've been told I have rather striking blue eyes, but I'm so nearsighted I have to hide them behind thick glasses or use those stupid little half-glasses with my contacts just to read the small print in the *Racing Form*. Fortunately, I have lots of near-black hair (a feature I've come to appreciate, having reached an age when so many of my friends are losing theirs), and I'm able to hide deficiencies behind a thick beard touched with just enough gray to keep me from looking like a pirate or a brigand.

All in all, I tend to be somewhat stronger and a whole lot quicker than I look; I look better out of my clothes than in them; and I tend to be a little bit smarter than I sometimes feel. The combination leads to surprises—unpleasant for the hotshots with whom I play racquetball, pleasant for the ladies with whom I occasionally get naked, and just perplexing for my ego, with which I frequently lose touch.

Today was the monthly meeting of the Turf Club's board of directors. It was scheduled to begin at eight o'clock, but I needed to come early to review the *Form* and my printouts before the first post time. The meeting was mostly a waste of time. The Tiara administered the club with admirable efficiency. The directors met only as a formality to maintain the club's private status.

"Where would you rather be?" I asked myself aloud as I spread out the eastern edition of the *Form*. The question was part of a ritual I've used to begin every working day since the time I abandoned three-piece suits, schedules, and deadlines more than thirteen years ago. It's part superstition and part a realistic reminder that payday depends solely on my wits, concentration, and discipline. Handicapping horse races for a living is exceedingly difficult and full of financial traps which can suck up money faster than a black hole in space.

I worked for about ten minutes, comparing the information contained in the *Racing Form*'s "Past Performances" with that printed out from my computerized data base. Mondays were not particularly productive racing days. Most tracks were "dark." Only Aqueduct, Sportsman's, and Churchill Downs were running today and there were only three races on the New York program which held any interest for me. The other two tracks' cards consisted of low-priced claiming races full of indistinguishable contenders.

I went to the coffeepot and filled a mug with steaming brew. Standing on the highest tier, I surveyed the Turf Club as if it were a private domain. I felt an almost proprietary pride as well as just a shade too much self-satisfaction.

Alysheba had won the Kentucky Derby on Saturday, two days earlier, keeping alive my personal streak of big scores on Derby Day. The community of horseplayers in Las Vegas has a grapevine all its own, and already the word was out—"The Poet" had crushed the Derby.

"The Poet"—that's what they call me out here. The nickname is a Runyonesque play on the name my father gave me, after his favorite Romantic poets—Byron Tennyson Wilder. "Tennyson" was bad enough, "Byron" unthinkable. I could live with Poet. It had a certain mystique. In a town like Las Vegas, where everyone and everything is a little larger than life—or wanted to be—a little legend, like my Derby streak, or a little color, like my nickname, was useful.

Following an impulse, I located the television controls and played with switches until the faces and sound of *Vegasline* filled one of the screens. *Vegasline* is a sports show for gamblers. For fans who like their sports news and scores short but sweet, or for those who like the glitz and glamour of the big network productions, *Vegasline* is about as animated as the morning livestock report. But for those who bet their money on football, basketball, baseball, fights, or the horses, the program has all the import of the tablets Moses brought down from Sinai. Barry Sheline, *Vegasline*'s creator, producer, and host, had parlayed the programming freedom of cable television and the American public's insatiable desire to wager on almost anything into a veritable gold mine.

Horse racing was the backbone of the *Vegasline* format. Only football had more bettors, and football was not an everyday event. *Vegasline* originated live from the Tiaradome every morning in order to reach the East Coast horseplayers before they left for the track and to accommodate the Nevada handicappers who bet on eastern tracks in the race books. Gamblers in Central and Mountain time zones, and those on the west coast, viewed the show at a later hour on videotape.

The program's basketball expert, a horse-faced transplant from the East with the unlikely name of "Hoops" Farb, was just completing an uninspired rundown of the NBA playoffs. When he had finished, Sheline introduced Buck Brewster, and I settled back to watch.

Buck was one of those people for whom the television camera performs cosmetic wonders. His curly silver hair made him appear cerebral rather than fatuous, and his too-perfect dentures became the source of an authoritative but benevolent smile. The combination of makeup and technology transformed his normally florid complexion to a healthy tan. In short, the burly horse-racing expert projected the ideal image for TV.

One of the original members of the Turf Club, Buck occupied the cubicle next to mine. In his "former life," he had been the business manager for a large Chevrolet dealer in Chicago and a weekend race fan. Then, when he was in his early fifties and had been divorced for more than twenty years, Buck's passion for horse racing grew to the point where he decided to leave his job and Chicago behind and try his luck in Vegas.

I had come to regret having recommended Buck to Barry Sheline. Buck was not one of the heavy hitters in the Turf Club. He squeezed his profits from conservative handicapping and tight-fisted money management. My friend Cowboy called him "Scrooge McBuck." Still, he managed to grind out a profit and a comfortable living. While he never cashed in on an insightful long shot, as far as I know, he never experienced any prolonged losing streaks either. He did well enough to hold his seat at the Turf Club, and that was no small accomplishment.

Unfortunately, Barry Sheline had higher expectations. His legion of viewers tuned in to receive racing insight beyond what they might get from the public handicappers in the morning newspaper. Buck picked a high percentage of winners, but his selections went to post at poor odds. As a result, Sheline and Buck existed in a constant state of bickering, which they both brought straight to me.

True to form, Buck followed his usual procedure for the first three races at Aqueduct, recommending horses which were certain to be the public favorites. Favorites win a third of all races at every track. They finish in the money ninety percent of the time. However, because of their low odds, betting the favorite in every race is a certain path to bankruptcy. I could see why Sheline was disgruntled.

Then Buck surprised me.

"Turning to the fourth race at Aqueduct," Buck announced, "I particularly like the chances of the number-one horse, Luminescent. Ten days ago this filly went a mile and one sixteenth against forty-five-thousand-dollar claiming horses. She started out of the tenth post position and got caught four or five wide in both of the turns. Still, she contended for the lead until mid-stretch before dropping back to finish fifth.

"What makes this filly even more attractive today is that she's coming back against allowance company. Now, it may appear that she's moving up in class, but today's race is restricted to New York-bred nonwinners of two races. In her last outing, Luminescent faced multiple winners, so today she is really facing weaker opposition. Plus she's drawn the inside post position and should have no trouble making the lead while saving ground. I look for Luminescent to go wire-to-wire at a nice price.

"Moving on to the fifth . . ."

"Sonofabitch!" A curse from behind me interrupted Buck's monologue. "I gave ol' Buck that horse yesterday, an' damn if he don't broadcast it to the whole goddamn world. I don't mind givin' a guy a horse now and then, long as he's in Vegas and can keep his mouth shut. Now all them New York assholes will run to the track and bet that horse down to nothin'."

Toby "Cowboy" Waltham, former rodeo rider, high-stakes poker devotee, and professional horseplayer, was livid with anger. I could easily sympathize, since I had Luminescent as my best bet of the day. An axiom of horse-race betting is that the more people who possess a piece of information, the less valuable it becomes. Thanks to Buck's broadcast, a horse which should have gone to post at 8–1 or higher would now bring only 3–1 or 5–2. Buck had just sent a prime wagering opportunity "winging south," leaving Cowboy and me as pissed-off as if we had just lost a bet in a photo finish.

A gambler might ask, "If the horse is gonna win, why not bet it anyway?"

For a professional horseplayer, the proposition of Luminescent winning the race was not enough to bet on. There are no sure things. Luminescent, with perhaps a thirty- to forty-percent chance to win, yet going off at 8–1 or 10–1, was what we call "value." The same horse, with the same expectation, running at 5–2, was barely a break-even proposition with no margin of error.

"Goddammit," Cowboy swore, "situations like that horse are too hard to come by." He marched his wiry, bowlegged body to the nearest house phone. "Can you reach the *Vegasline* set?" he demanded when the hotel operator answered.

Cowboy fumed silently while the hotel operator put through his call. I remembered that there was a phone near the set which flashed a red light instead of ringing.

"Is this the *Vegasline* set?" Cowboy shouted to an innocent stage hand. "Tell Buck Brewster he's a no-good sonofabitch an' not to call me no more." He listened for a second. "What do you mean, 'Who is this?' This is God. Who the fuck do you think it is?" He slammed down the phone and came back to my desk looking immensely pleased with himself.

Cowboy is what's known as a "trip handicapper." In other words, he wins races by watching races. He watches carefully for horses who are caught wide in the turns or in blind switches, for speed horses burned out dueling for the lead in a blistering early pace, for victims of rider error, or for just bad racing luck. These horses, he knew, had the potential for vast improvement in their next outings if they benefited from an "easier trip." Best of all, the details of their previous losing efforts were not readily apparent to the hordes of readers of the *Racing Form*. Cowboy's selections usually went to post at attractive odds.

"Must be these show-bizness people," Cowboy continued philosophically. "Ol' Buck's turnin' into a major asshole since he became a star. He used to just take care of his own bizness but now he talks to everyone. 'Who d'ya like? Who d'ya like?' He sounds like a goddamn Hollywood Park railbird.''

I had to laugh at Cowboy's mincing imitation. The most common phrase in horse racing is the ubiquitous "who d'ya like." Whether a request for clarification of a difficult race, a desperate search for a winner by a chronic loser, an invitation for an argument, or a tacit plea for confirmation that another has observed the same equine virtues with the confidence to put his money on the line, the phrase is the essence of the unending search for an informed opinion which can be turned into profit. Among the Turf Club members, the solicitation of outside opinion in such a manner is considered highly unprofessional. If a bettor has no firm opinion of his own, he has no business betting the race. The advice of others, no matter how competent, is viewed as being confusing and counterproductive.

"You guys need anything?" June, the first of the club's waitresses to arrive, called to us from the upper level.

Cowboy's sour expression lit up. "Darlin,' " he intoned, sweeping off his ever-present Stetson with exaggerated country courtliness, "you're in a position to fulfill all my needs—and fantasies. But considerin' the time an' place, I'll settle for a big ol' coffee with cream an' sugar an' I'll hold the rest of my desires in abeyance."

June never seemed to know whether or not to take Cowboy seriously. She blushed and hurried off to fill his request. On the screen, Buck was finishing up his commentary with a few words about upcoming stakes races.

"Good," Cowboy grumbled. "Now maybe we can get this meeting bullshit over with."

"You're in a terrific mood this morning," I observed dryly.

"Tough night," the Texan admitted. "I played poker with that bunch down at the Horseshoe and couldn't draw a hand all night. Them boys got no mercy. Naturally I ain't been to bed yet. I was countin' on Luminescent to get me refinanced so I could take another crack at 'em tonight, but Uncle Buck just fucked that idea up royally."

I shook my head to express appropriate commiseration. Cowboy was the only professional handicapper I knew who seriously pursued another gaming avocation. "That bunch at the Horseshoe" he referred to were the big-time, no-limit poker players who earned national attention at the Horseshoe's annual World Series of Poker. Cowboy played cards in the kind of company where the absence of either iron nerve or good cards was tantamount to swimming with sharks while wearing a sirloin life jacket.

"Just between you and me, try Rattlestake in the sixth if the track is 'off,' " I suggested casually. He responded with a curious glance. "Rattlestake is a mud lark," I explained. "His only wins, in eighty-six, are too far back to show up in the *Form,* but they were both on muddy tracks. I punched up his lifetime record on the computer and all his wins have come on wet tracks at big prices. He's been entered twice in the last ten days but scratched both times when the track turned up fast. Looks like the trainer's got him ready and is just waiting for the right spot."

"What's the weather like in New York?"

"Rained hard yesterday," I confirmed conspiratorially. "They're supposed to get more today."

A big grin split Cowboy's craggy face as he visibly shook off his fatigue and became his usual animated self. "Hot damn," he chortled. Then, his eyes wide with complicity, he whispered, "Don't tell Buck." We both broke up.

"Let's go down and get this meetin' over with," Cowboy suggested. "This might turn out to be a good day after all."

2

The meeting of the Turf Club directors was always held in the coffee shop next to the main casino. Once a month we would meet for breakfast, hear the club's executive secretary, Lou Fine, report that everyone had paid his nominal dues and that the club's financial condition was sound. Of course, the club's financial condition was never a matter of concern. If any of the members had complaints, we passed them on to Lou and they were quickly and efficiently dispatched. As a rule, breakfast took longer than the actual business.

At the entrance to the coffee shop, Cowboy and I ran right into Buck Brewster and Barry Sheline. As I expected, neither looked very happy.

"Could I have a word with you, Tennyson?" Sheline asked while Buck glowered.

"I have a meeting, Barry."

"This will only take a minute . . . please."

"Go ahead and start without me," I told Cowboy and Buck. As the two made their way into the crowded restaurant, I could see the Texan's jaws moving tersely. Buck was, no doubt, getting an earful over his broadcast indiscretions.

"I wish you would reconsider and do *Vegasline* with me," Sheline said, coming directly to the point.

"No thanks, Barry."

"Look, we'll sweeten the offer—six hundred per show. Six hundred a day for a half-hour segment. That's three times what we're paying Buck."

"Sorry. I'm just not interested. Money isn't the problem."

"Shit," Sheline cursed. "Look, I gotta get somebody

else. Buck is just too conservative, and he lacks charisma. I got Pete Hanlon doing football, and Hoops for basketball, but racing is an everyday event. It's the backbone of the show. I need someone who has personality, someone who can pull long shots. That's you, Tennyson. Look what you did in the Derby."

I was a bit startled by the reference. Apparently the Vegas grapevine had been working overtime. "All I had was the exacta, Barry," I said in an effort to downplay the gossip. "I couldn't separate Alysheba, Bet Twice, and Cryptoclearance."

"But that's my point," Sheline insisted excitedly. "Your horses finished one-two-three and not one of them was picked by a public handicapper. That exacta paid over two hundred dollars for a lousy two-dollar bet, and what did you have, a grand on it? Do you have any idea what that kind of handicapping is worth to my viewers? Just name your price, Tennyson. I know we can work something out."

"I'm sorry, Barry. I'm just not interested in being a public handicapper. The betting strategy you're talking about is worth more kept to myself than anything you could afford to pay me."

"All right," he acquiesced at last. "How about someone else? What about Cowboy or Aaron?"

I laughed at the absurdity of the suggestion. "You can ask them," I said. "But you're talking about guys who only bet maybe three or four races a day, and neither one of them would tell his own mother which horse he liked, much less a national audience. Seriously, Barry, I think you should try to work with Buck. Everyone I know is just too secretive to go on television. Most of them are so afraid of the IRS, they don't even go by their real names. Most don't even have bank accounts. At least Buck is willing and he knows the game."

Sheline shook his head in resignation. "Think about it, Tennyson. There has to be someone out there who wants to be a star."

In the coffee shop the others were waiting. Along with Cowboy, Buck, and Lou Fine was the fourth board member, Aaron Friedman. "The Gnome" was one of the senior members of the Turf Club. He was sixty-three but he looked ten years older. Jockey-sized, but frail, with parchment skin, delicate hands, and Coke-bottle glasses, the Gnome was a study in contradictions. As far as anyone knew, he had no interests outside of horse racing, not books, music, other sports, politics, religion, nor sex with either males or females. He lived alone and always arrived at the Tiara by taxi. Yet despite his reclusive habits, he was always meticulously dressed in perfectly tailored suits of the finest fabrics with coordinated accessories from shoes to hat. He cultivated no friendships, but once, when a fellow club member had suffered a heart attack, Aaron's taxi had made a daily stop at the hospital. His manner in dealing with people ranged from terse to downright rude, unless the topic of conversation was horses. Then the Gnome became loquacious and eloquent, recalling racing lore and trivia which spanned five decades.

When I arrived, Friedman was exchanging barbs with Cowboy. Though they argued constantly, the Texan was one of the few people the Gnome actually liked. He completely ignored Lou Fine and Buck, both of whom he considered to be of no consequence. I was lucky. According to Cowboy, Aaron considered me an "up-and-comer." As a result he treated me with as much warmth as he could muster.

We ordered breakfast and got down to business. There were three minor items of old business and nothing new. By the time the food arrived, the formal meeting was over. The Gnome, as board chairman, declared adjournment and fell upon his sausage and eggs with an enthusiasm belying his slight stature.

With post time in New York only forty-five minutes away, we didn't linger over coffee. The work ethic is very strong among professional horseplayers. As we broke up, Lou Fine detained me.

"Mike Bellisari wants to see you, Tennyson," he said. The executive secretary, an employee of the hotel, was a sad-eyed, droopy little character who seemed ever anxious not to give offense.

I was surprised by the summons. "What does he want, Lou?"

"He didn't tell me, Tennyson," Fine answered evenly.

"He just said it was important and that you should come up after the meeting."

I had plenty of time before I needed to place my first bet. "What the hell," I answered. "I'll just stop by the men's room and go on up."

I walked out with Cowboy, hoping to avoid the inevitable confrontation with Buck. By now Buck's irrational fear that I was trying to steal his job would be gnawing at him incessantly. He would demand to know what Sheline had to say.

When we came out of the men's room, Cowboy nudged my arm. "Do you know, those two fellers over there."

"Where?"

"The two guys who look like Teamsters from Cleveland. Over there by Slot Rat Rosie."

I spotted Slot Rat Rosie lurking in her usual haunts among the slot machines. Rosie was a local character, a Las Vegas version of a bag lady. She lived in a rooming house not far from downtown and walked everywhere. She wandered from casino to casino, prowling the endless banks of slot machines, keeping her eyes on the trays and on the floor for lost change. She would judiciously watch the play and try her luck when she became convinced that a particular machine was "ready to pop." Cowboy and I usually kept an eye out for her and occasionally staked her to a few bucks on what she insisted would be a "partnership basis."

Rosie seemed to be trailing two men who wore suit pants with gaudy Hawaiian shirts. One was immense; his head, a square block, rested directly on hulking shoulders. The other was thin and ferretlike; his eyes shifted nervously from point to point, as if searching for prey.

"I don't know them," I told Cowboy.

"Well, they seem to be real interested in you," he said. "I saw them when we went into the coffee shop, and they ain't moved."

I could think of no reason why anyone would be watching me, and was prepared to dismiss the notion. At that moment the two men seemed to take note of our interest and abruptly broke off their play of a dollar slot machine and walked away.

Rosie watched carefully to make sure the two men had gone and then crept up to the slot machine they had just abandoned. After one last furtive glance, she tugged the handle to complete their play. She waited excitedly while the mechanical fruit turned over. There was nothing Rosie enjoyed more than a freebie.

Cowboy and I watched with amusement as the bell sounded and tokens began to pour into the tray. The payoff wasn't a jackpot, but it sounded like fifty or sixty dollars. Rosie jumped up and down gleefully in her high-top sneakers. Her brassy "movie-star" sunglasses slipped off her nose and her wide-brimmed flowered straw hat fell off her head.

Immediately she gained control of herself and again searched for the two men. Prompted by curiosity, Cowboy and I strolled over.

Rosie jumped when Cowboy spoke her name. She lowered her sunglasses and squinted up at us.

"Oh, Cowboy . . . and the Poet. You scared an old lady half to death. I thought you were those two nasties coming back."

"Do you know those guys, Rosie?" I asked.

She snorted contemptuously. "Of course not," she declared haughtily. "How would I know gangsters?"

"How do you know they're gangsters?"

Rosie stared at me like I had recently descended from Mars. "Everybody knows gangsters are everywhere in Vegas. I used to deal blackjack for Moe Dalitz at the Desert Inn. I certainly know gangsters when I see them."

Rosie had a selection of stories about her past which always included one of the famous early names in Las Vegas. In various versions, she claimed to have been a dancer for Bugsy Siegel at the Flamingo, a "hostess" for Ed Levinson at the Fremont, and even Nig Devine's mistress in the early days of the Stardust. Perhaps all of it were true . . . or none of it.

"Gangsters may be tough, but they sure are dumb," she cackled as she retrieved her tokens. "Imagine dropping three dollars in a machine and forgetting to pull the handle."

"Looks like you're hot today," Cowboy observed as he handed her a twenty-dollar bill. "Maybe you can catch a jackpot."

"Partners?" the old woman confirmed.

"Don't worry about it," Cowboy said.

"Wha'd'ya think I am, a charity case?" Rosie shot back indignantly. "Partners!" She marched off in her bright colored sundress with as much dignity as she could muster.

"One of these days she'll hit a progressive slot and dump a fortune on you," I told Cowboy.

"Maybe," he answered, skeptically, "but if she's like both my ex-wives an' all my ex-girlfriends, she'll take the money an' run."

I laughed, slapping him on the back. "I'm going up to see 'Mr. Big.' I'll see you at the club before the sixth race."

"Gangsters," he muttered, shaking his head in disbelief as he walked away. "Jesus Christ."

As general manager of the Tiara Race and Sports Book, Mike Bellisari had an office directly above the Turf Club. It was a spacious room, maybe three hundred square feet with a wall of one-way glass overlooking the main Race and Sports Book. On the other walls were Leroy Neiman serigraphs of races and athletic events. The furnishings were modern, with lots of Lucite, leather, and chrome.

Bellisari was about my age and deported himself like a man on the way up. He was over six feet tall, fashionably slender, and dressed in a sharkskin suit which had to cost over one thousand dollars. The Tiara Corporation had recently named Bellisari a vice-president, and very likely he would be its next casino boss, if not here, then in casinos owned in the Bahamas or Atlantic City.

While there was no denying his competence, he was a man I found difficult to like. Bellisari stayed behind his desk, offering neither a handshake nor small talk. I accepted his invitation to sit, feeling mildly apprehensive. The atmosphere, though not overtly hostile, was certainly not friendly.

"I'll come right to the point," Bellisari stated abruptly. "I want you to tell me everything you know about a horse called Picky Peaches."

The question took me completely by surprise and I had to think for a minute. "Picky Peaches is a three-year-old Kentucky-bred filly, as I recall, who broke her maiden about three or four weeks ago at Louisiana Downs."

"Surely you haven't forgotten, Mr. Wilder, that you

bet the horse and won, shall we say, at rather long odds?" Bellisari's tone dripped with sarcasm.

"No, I haven't forgotten. I had a win bet and I wheeled her in the exacta. It was a nice hit."

"Yes, I would say twenty-three thousand dollars and change is a nice 'hit.' Tell me, Mr. Wilder, how did you happen to select this horse?"

I was starting to become annoyed with both the line of questioning and the tone. Everyone hit long shots from time to time, and with the Turf Club's sophisticated system of laying off members' bets, the casino should have made more money on Picky Peaches than I did.

"Picky Peaches was obviously a spot play," I answered cautiously. "I would have to check my notes to be able to tell you what the angle was, but what's the problem here? Didn't you guys lay off this bet? I mean, if you passed, I'd have to say you made a mistake. Wouldn't you agree?"

Bellisari regarded me for a moment before speaking. "As a matter of fact, Mr. Wilder, the selection of Picky Peaches was so far removed from your win profile that we did pass." He shrugged elaborately. "That decision cost us twenty-three thousand dollars and change. As you say, our mistake, but I assure you, that's not the problem we're here to discuss." He shuffled through some papers on his desk. "Two weeks ago you bet on a horse named Calamatator at Santa Anita. Again, a maiden with an abysmal record."

"What? You guys didn't lay off on that one either?" I asked.

Bellisari looked up from his papers. "Oh, yes. This time we did." He glanced back at his papers. "Last week you had a filly named Winter Muffin. Again, a maiden, claimed in Detroit and stepping up in class in Chicago, and again, you won at long odds. I don't suppose you recall how you happened to select these horses?"

"Yes, I can," I shot back. "Calamatator and Winter Muffin have the same owner as Picky Peaches and they had the same pattern, stepping up off a claim and moving from a minor to a major track. Calamatator was claimed at Turf Paradise, and as you said, Winter Muffin was claimed in Detroit."

"I see. Here we have cheap maidens running at three

different, widely scattered tracks. Not one of them looks like it'll ever win a race. You've got three different trainers, and out of all the races you look at, you just happened to pick out the fact that they have the same owner? Out of the fifty-odd races a day you look at? Out of a couple of hundred horses?"

"Yes, that's correct," I insisted. "Well, I didn't actually pick it up. My computer did. That's the kind of thing I use it for."

Bellisari's expression left no doubt of his opinion of my veracity. "What do you know about Capricorn Racing Stables?" he demanded.

I shrugged. "Other than the fact that they claimed and won with each of the three horses you mentioned and I've got them tagged in my computer to watch, I know absolutely nothing about them."

"You've had no contact with any of the principals of Capricorn Racing Stables, Inc.?"

"That's right."

"Mr. Wilder, do you know a man by the name of Aaron Locklear?"

"No, I . . ." I hesitated. There was a familiarity about the name that I was trying to recall. "Let me have that name again, please."

"Aaron Locklear," Bellisari pronounced distinctly. "President of Capricorn Racing Stables, Inc."

"I've met an Aaron Locklear," I admitted cautiously. "Quite possibly, the man you're talking about, but I had no idea he had any connection with Capricorn Racing Stables. The fact is, I never gave it a thought."

"Then what is your connection with this Aaron Locklear?" Bellisari demanded, zeroing in on what he felt to be a key point.

"I met Locklear for a drink about a month or so ago, at his request," I said warily. I had a feeling that Bellisari already knew what I was about to say. "As a matter of fact, that meeting was right there at the hotel. Locklear called me and said he had a proposition he was certain I would find interesting."

"I'm sure he did," Bellisari interrupted derisively.

I bit back my anger and continued. "Locklear said he represented a group investors who were prepared to capitalize a betting consortium with a half-million dollars.

They were willing to put as much as fifty thousand dollars a day in action with me as the consortium's handicapper. In return I'd get ten percent of the proceeds with no investment or risk."

Bellisari's eyes flashed triumph. "And, of course, they would occasionally bring you a selection of their own for you to wager on their behalf," he suggested.

I shook my head. "We never got that far. I told him I wasn't interested, thanked him for the drink, and left. No discussion, no debate."

Bellisari did some rapid calculations on his scratch pad. "Just roughing the numbers against your winning percentage," he said finally, "the deal you say you turned down could be worth five or six million dollars a year to you by doing just what you're doing now. It could be two or three times that, if your connections could provide you with horses like Picky Peaches, Calamatator, or Winter Muffin on a regular basis. I have to wonder how you could turn down such a proposition. Perhaps you would care to enlighten me, Mr. Wilder."

I smiled, still suppressing my irritation. "Two reasons, Mr. Bellisari. One, I'm doing just fine without outside financing and, two, if I played the game with someone else's money, it wouldn't be fun anymore. I promised myself a long time ago I'd never again work at something that wasn't fun. Now, Mr. Bellisari, I think I have had just about enough of this interrogation."

Bellisari rose quickly to his feet. "Yes, I can see this isn't taking us anywhere," he agreed. "Lou Fine will retrieve your personal belongings from the Turf Club and I will call the casino cashier to prepare any funds you have on deposit here. You are no longer welcome at the Tiara, Mr. Wilder."

"What is this bullshit?" I shouted, aghast at the casino's action. "I haven't done anything illegal or unethical and you have no evidence that says otherwise."

"I don't have to have evidence, Wilder." He sneered. "The Nevada courts have been clear on the matter of the casino's rights as private property to exclude anyone we choose."

I recognized, as he spoke the words, that what he said was a fact. "All right," I said with resignation. "Fuck it and fuck you. There are other race books in this town who'd welcome a chance to lay off my action."

Bellisari uttered a short, derisive laugh. "You still don't have the picture, do you, Wilder? Someone took the race books in this town for a few million dollars on those three horses. Close to half-million in Reno and Tahoe. Unless you want to wear a disguise and bet nickels and dimes, or send in runners who'll eventually rip you off, you're finished in this town. Probably in this state. And that's not your only problem, my friend. There are a bunch of angry bookies, most of them with mob connections, who are very eager to find out how they managed to lose who knows how much money." Bellisari flashed a self-satisfied smile. "I would say you have problems, Mr. Wilder."

3

I was stunned when I came out of Bellisari's office. Stupefied. Almost in a trance, I went down to the casino level and stood in front of the cashier's cage to withdraw the money I had on deposit. Perversely, I refused to take a check and insisted they pay me in cash. While I waited, Lou Fine came by with my personal belongings from the Turf Club. The droopy little bassett hound offered no apology, no sympathy, nothing. Not even a "kiss my ass." He just handed over my possessions and walked away.

For reasons I still don't completely understand, I walked over to the Turf Club door and stuck my membership card into the scanner. Nothing happened. Whatever codes were programmed into that little strip of magnetic tape, they no longer unlocked any magic. That didn't take long, I thought helplessly. I was locked out, history. I resisted the almost overriding impulse to kick the door down and walked away, my emotions rocketing between despair and rage.

The feelings were familiar, I realized with a sinking sensation. I had felt this same helpless, frustrated, bewildered anger before. The first time, I was only ten. I had just learned that my father, a journalist, had been killed in Hungary. A Russian tank had leveled the building where he hid with a handful of hopeless revolutionaries armed with ridiculous wine bottles filled with gasoline and stuffed with rags.

The second time, I was a freshman at the University of Michigan. The university police broke into the dorm room where my two roommates and I were smoking marijuana. In 1965, an action which no one gives a damn about today was grounds for immediate expulsion. I later learned that a nerd from down the hall, who hated one of my roommates, had told the cops my roommate was a dealer. The asshole later had the nerve to tell me he was sorry he had gotten me in trouble.

The last and most recent time was fourteen years ago. Jenna Sonnier, my business partner and the love of my life, was killed in an automobile accident. A drunken driver.

The circumstances in each case were different and the degree of losses cannot be compared, but each served to throw my world into complete upheaval; each managed to shatter whatever harmony I had managed to achieve; each event had left me nauseous with helpless rage. And fear. The mind-numbing anxiety which stemmed from no comprehension of what I would do next, no idea of how I would go on and start over, controlled my life.

At ten I had sworn undying enmity toward the Russians, but the Russians were an abstraction and beyond my reach. At eighteen I vowed to haunt the nerd for the rest of his days until I ruined his life the way, I was certain, he had ruined mine. But he was just a kid and, by the time I got back from Vietnam, I had come to realize that my life was far from ruined, while he would remain a weasel through the rest of his. Revenge seemed redundant.

When I was twenty-eight, I wanted to tear the drunken driver to shreds. I resolved that nothing the law would do to him would be enough. But the drunk had died in the head-on crash that took Jenna. He, too, was beyond my reach.

I guess at forty-two I still hadn't learned much. Michael Bellisari went on my list with Russians and weasels and drunken drivers. And I still had no idea what I would do next.

I waited for my car and mentally tuned out the chatter of Ernie, the valet captain. Ernie was a horseplayer of great enthusiasm combined with marginal skill and little discipline. He sustained his passion only because running the valet stand at one of Las Vegas' flashiest casinos paid very well. But Ernie longed for the respect and admiration of the true professionals, the handicapper/investors like me.

Every morning for the past three years, Ernie had greeted me with a rundown of horses he liked and on which he expected to make a killing in the day's wagering activity. I always listened respectfully and, from time to time, added a useful comment. On the way out, invariably, Ernie would regale me with the excuses and hard-luck stories which explained his lack of success.

I was in no mood for Ernie's monologue. I was still seething with rage and all I wanted was to get as far from the Tiara as possible. I couldn't believe what Bellisari had told me—that I was barred from all Las Vegas casinos. Perhaps someone had beaten the race books for a fortune, but that someone was certainly not Tennyson Wilder. I had to get to the Athletic Club and find Jack Hanrahan. Hanrahan would know the whole story.

I was about to interrupt Ernie to ask what was taking the kid so long with the car, when a piercing shriek startled both of us. Rosie the Slot Rat screamed at a decibel level which belied her age and diminutive stature.

"Don't kill me! Don't kill me! You can have the money, just don't kill me!" she cried hysterically.

While I stood there gaping, a security guard, two valets, and Ernie rushed to the aid of the old woman. The objects of her fear, the two rough-looking men Cowboy and I had seen earlier, exchanged confused glances.

"Gangsters!" Rosie railed plaintively. "They're gonna take me for a ride!"

The security guard eyed the two men accusingly. The house-size one with the scarred brow and jutting jaw stared back blankly. The smaller, rat-faced man shrugged his shoulders and stammered, "I dunno. She's crazy. We never seen her before."

A crowd was forming and I noticed that for some reason both men kept glancing at me as they backed away from the old woman. They seemed to display more than the normal discomfort of the completely innocent caught in an embarrassing situation.

Two more security guards rushed up demanding to know what was going on.

"She says a couple of guys are tryin' to kill her," the first guard explained.

"What guys?" the supervisor shouted.

Still looking furtively at me and demonstrating a definite reluctance to leave, the two men began backing up in an attempt to blend with the crowd. I watched as they reentered the casino and disappeared. Rosie continued to carry on while the security people tried to calm her down.

Weird, I thought as my car arrived. The two men did look like they were up to no good, but old Rosie, with her mismatched getup and fantasized memories, seemed an unlikely victim. Satisfied that she had all the help she needed, I turned my attention to my own problems and drove away.

The Las Vegas Athletic Club was about two miles west of the Strip, off Tropicana Avenue. The facility was like a country club without a golf course, featuring a first-rate dining room and a more casual bar and grill. With eighteen racquetball courts, four squash courts, and both indoor and outdoor tennis, it was a rackets player's dream. A gym for basketball and volleyball, a weight room, a fully equipped Nautilus center, indoor and outdoor pools, and an aerobics program that seemed to rock and roll around the clock completed the attractions and provided something for everyone—except, of course, the golfer.

Jack Hanrahan, besides being the casino boss at the Frontier, was one of the top amateur racquetball players around. Hanrahan had won the state championship for the thirty-five-and-older age group for three consecutive years and expected to rule the division for time to come. But that was before I came to town. The two of us played at least twice a week, very close and hotly contested matches, and from the rivalry, friendship developed.

I knew where to find Hanrahan, because every Monday at noon, the casino executive worked out with Joe Grady, the club's pro, who was ranked in the top ten on the men's tour. I had always been amused by Hanrahan's efforts to gain an edge from his workouts with Grady. Though neither of us was a match for a touring pro, both of us actually knew and employed more competitive tricks. Joe Grady employed no tricks. He was twenty-four years old, quick as a cat, and hit the ball at 140 mph, forehand or backhand. Hanrahan's Monday lesson normally consisted of his watching the ball fly past and then walking over to pick it up.

Hanrahan was on one of the glass courts practicing by himself. When he saw me, he waved for me to come onto the court.

"Get your stuff on," he urged. "Grady went to San Diego for a tournament and he's not back yet."

"Five minutes," I answered, welcoming a chance to work off my frustration.

We played four very close games, each winning two. Our skills matched up well. I'm a back-court shooter and Hanrahan is a fast retriever—on one hand aggressive offense, and on the other, tenacious defense. The player who made the fewer mistakes invariably won. A small crowd of spectators gathered outside of the glass-walled competition court and, Vegas being Vegas, some money changed hands.

Afterward, outside the court, we flopped on the floor, exhausted, to rehash the critical moments of the contest. Among the spectators, I noticed three large men in street clothes. Two were big and bulky, carrying maybe forty pounds of excess weight over muscle. The third was genuinely obese, round in all dimensions. I recalled seeing the three of them around the club, but had no idea who they were.

"Nice game, gentlemen," the round man said with a broad smile. "You guys look like the pros out there."

"Thanks, Jimmy," Hanrahan replied. "Unfortunately, though, the pros play a different game from old guys like us."

"We haven't met," the fat man said, turning to me and offering a hairy hand with sausagelike fingers, offset by gold jewelry and a perfect manicure. "I'm Jimmy DeMaria."

Surprised by the power of the fat man's grip, I shook the outstretched hand. "Very nice to meet you. I'm Tennyson Wilder."

The fat man's eyes narrowed for an instant in recognition. "Tennyson Wilder," he said expansively. " 'The Poet.' I've been wanting to meet you for some time now. I'd like to talk to you if you have a few minutes."

I was a bit taken aback by a stranger knowing my name, much less requesting a meeting, and the morning's events had left me wary.

"Sure, I guess so." I shrugged. "But I have to talk to

Jack, here, for a few minutes. So if you don't mind waiting . . ."

"No problem." DeMaria beamed. "If you would be kind enough to join me in the whirlpool, I promise not to take up much of your time."

Hanrahan and I retreated to the relative privacy of the sauna.

"I presume my running into you here was no accident," Hanrahan offered as we let the 180-degree heat penetrate our bodies.

"That's right. Do you know what's going on?"

"Yeah, I know."

"Then, it's true. Somebody popped the race books for a bundle and I'm getting the heat for it."

Hanrahan sighed. "Tennyson, if you say you didn't have anything to do with it, I believe you. But the fact remains you did bet those horses and, therefore, yours is the only name floating around. Bellisari is under pressure because he laid off your bets on two of the three, so part of what he's doing is throwing the heat off him to you. Unfortunately, whether or not I believe you doesn't matter. When the word on someone goes out, all the casinos have to abide by it. It's an unwritten rule."

"Shit."

"Let me ask you. Where did you get those horses? From what I gather, it couldn't have been a handicapping play."

"No," I replied thoughtfully, "the first one was a tip from a friend, a guy who spends his winters in New Orleans and his summers in Detroit playing the ponies. A couple of years ago I loaned him some money when he was tapped out, and even though he paid it back, he still feels like he owes me. This was the third time he'd called me with a horse he was real high on. The first two were nice winners, so I played this one, even though it looked terrible on paper."

"How did this guy get the horse?" Hanrahan asked.

"He wouldn't say. All he said was, 'Trust me on this one,' so I did."

"What about the other two horses?"

"Well, you have to understand how I work. I keep track of patterns in my data base. The other two horses had the same owner as the first and they were both claims at minor tracks and moving up in class at a major track. I just followed the pattern and bet it. If all of this hadn't blown up in my face, I'd still be looking for that same pattern."

"So you don't know any of the people involved?"

"Well, that's the problem. Although I didn't know it at the time, I did meet with one of the owners." I went on to describe the fateful meeting with Aaron Locklear.

"God damn," Hanrahan swore. "That has to look bad. I suppose you told Bellisari about it?"

I nodded. "Seemed like he already knew. Don't ask me how."

"It sounds like this Locklear was setting you up."

That idea stopped me cold. Why would anyone want to set me up for this kind of problem?

"Maybe he talked to several people and one of them took the deal," I suggested, hoping to dismiss the "setup" theory. "All I know is that I didn't. But the big question is, what can I do? Every day I can't make a bet in Vegas costs me a fortune."

Hanrahan thought for a moment. "You know, Tennyson, one of the reasons I never believed that you were in on some kind of scam was that you are so goddamn innocent sometimes. You're sitting here worrying about a loss of income when there's a bunch of pissed-off wise guys out there trying to find out who took them off. Your name is bound to come up, if it hasn't already."

"What are you telling me?" I demanded incredulously, still unwilling to accept the fact that I was in danger. "Bellisari all but said that might be the case, but I thought it was just Italian swagger. Now you're saying I should take it seriously?"

"You should take it damn seriously, my friend. The big fear of anybody who books race bets, whether it's a legal casino or a bookie, is getting hammered by an insider. Once in a while is expected. The cost of doing business, you might say. But after three times in less than two months, by what looks like the same people, is not only financially damaging, but it smells rotten. If I were you, Tennyson, I'd take a vacation. Or, if you have to have some action, rent a furnished apartment in L.A. for cash and stand in line at the grandstand at Hollywood

Park. Give the people beating the bushes some time to turn up the real principals of Capricorn."

I sat staring at the walls of the sauna, the sweat pouring either from the heat or perhaps from the fear that gripped me as the realization of just how precarious my situation had become sank in.

"There's just one more thing," Hanrahan continued. "Jimmy DeMaria wants to talk to you. My advice is to tell him everything you've just told me."

I stared at the casino boss in surprise. "Who is this guy? Some kind of mobster?"

Hanrahan smiled. "Jimmy DeMaria runs the National Sports Book. You know, the big layoff operation."

"Perfect," I said disgustedly. "The mob. Right?"

Hanrahan shrugged. "Yes and no. Jimmy is wired in tight with the boys, but aside from the fact that his business is underground, he's not a gangster. I have no way of knowing for sure, but I'd guess that DeMaria handles more money every day than all the Vegas race books combined. For all I know, it could be many times that volume. It is a giant business and Jimmy's a sharp operator."

"And, one of the guys after my blood." I finished sarcastically.

Hanrahan shook his head. "If DeMaria wanted to do you harm, he certainly wouldn't have approached you here in front of me. Oh, I'm sure he got burned, but he's a businessman and what he needs most is an orderly market. He damn sure doesn't want a bunch of hoods running around rousting people. Go talk to him. If he believes you, he can deflect some of the heat. If he's hostile, you know what your options are."

Jimmy DeMaria and his two immense attendants were soaking chest-deep in the bubbling waters of the spa. They presented an eerie image. With the steam rising and the water swirling, they looked like a cannibal's delight: "fat-man stew."

DeMaria greeted me cordially, inviting me to join the group soaking in the hot water. After making some small talk about the temperature of the water and the healthful benefits of athletic-club membership, the topic turned to the business at hand.

I repeated my story on Picky Peaches, Calamatator, and Winter Muffin for the third time that day. DeMaria listened attentively, nodding occasionally, but saying nothing, except to insist he be called "Jimmy."

"Let me tell you what I think," he said when I had finished. "I think you're either a victim of circumstances or somebody has taken some trouble to set you up. Either way, your ass is definitely in a crack. Personally, I don't think you had anything to do with it, but I felt that way all along."

"Why's that, may I ask?"

"It's simple, really," the fat man continued. "You're a pro and you're kicking some ass in this town. Think about the numbers. There are better than ten million horseplayers in this country, but I'd be surprised if there were even ten thousand who actually make a living from it. To do that, you got to be disciplined and smart, too smart to get involved in something that could jeopardize your livelihood. Even if you did it, you wouldn't leave your signature all over the deal. Somebody hit the casinos and books for maybe four or five million dollars, and you're on record through your normal operation as having hit 'em for seventy-five thousand? Come on. Smart people, even smart egotists, don't do shit like that."

"Why can't you check out all the people who collected these bets?" I asked. "That's how all of this centered on me."

The fat man let out a short laugh. "That's all being done right now, but I can tell you in advance what they are going to find. Nothing. The typical bookie is going to check and find some regular customer, probably a steady loser who popped one. They're going to ask him and he's going to tell a story about 'some guy.' That's it, just some guy gave him the money to place the bet for ten percent. Here in the casinos, the exacta winners had to fill out some IRS forms. I guarantee you, the social-security numbers and ID's are going to be fake. The whole effort is a zero."

As complicated as the circumstances appeared to be, I felt profound relief that DeMaria believed my explanation.

DeMaria splashed some hot water on his face and on the back of his neck, rotating his head as if to loosen up his neck and shoulder muscles. I suspected that this was as close as the fat man ever came to working out. "Don't be too relieved just yet, my friend," he said, as though reading my thoughts. "I have some influence, but these people don't work for me. Most of them respect my judgment, but there are a few out there who will want to satisfy themselves that you had nothing to do with this, and that doesn't mean that they're going to want to sit down and have a friendly discussion. If I were you, I wouldn't hang around this town any longer than you absolutely have to."

"Yeah, but if I split, doesn't that make me look guilty?"

The two bodyguards, silent until this moment, looked at each other. One choked back a laugh while the other let slip a high-pitched "hee hee."

DeMaria raised an eyebrow. "Look, pal, we're not talking about cops and courts here. At this moment, you're fuckin' guilty. Taking off doesn't change that one way or another, it just keeps you healthy." DeMaria's expression brightened. "There's one thing you can do maybe," he said. "The guy who tipped you on the first horse. He obviously knows more than you do. If we could talk to him, that might deflect some attention from you."

I shook my head. "I'm sorry, Jimmy. I can't do that," I told him without hesitation. "The guy's a friend. What I will do, though, is talk to him myself. He's an honest guy who only bets at the track, but he must have seen something. If you give me a number where I can call you, I'll let you know what he says."

DeMaria sighed elaborately. "I guess that'll have to do," he said. "I think your position is a little crazy, but I respect you for it. Call me at my restaurant, Jimmy D's. Do you know it?"

I nodded.

"Noon is a good time to call. As you can see, I don't miss many lunches."

I had started to climb out of the spa when a thought occurred to me. "Jimmy, there is one other thing. Is there any indication that anybody cheated other than the betting pattern and the size of the payoffs? Has anybody talked to the trainers, that kind of thing?"

"Now you're getting into the really interesting aspect

of this whole deal," the fat man said with a laugh. "All three trainers, as you undoubtedly know, are respectable veterans with good-size public stables. The drug tests were all negative, the legitimate contenders all ran credibly, and in two races, the favorites ran their best ever final times, and still got beat by daylight."

"Ringers?" I suggested speculatively.

"Impossible," DeMaria insisted. "Everything checked out."

"So maybe nobody cheated, then."

"You bet your ass somebody cheated," the fat man shot back. "Somebody bet maybe a hundred grand per horse and spent a lot of money to stay anonymous. Now, if it's just a matter of having a long shot with hidden form, nobody bets that kind of money. A couple of grand maybe, on the outside. Nobody bets that kind of dough unless they're sure. And the only way to be sure is to have it 'handled.' These pricks cheated, all right. We just don't know how. But there is one thing you can count on, they'll do it again. They may wait a few months, but they cleaned up too good. They'll be back."

By the time I had showered and dressed to leave the Athletic Club, shock, dismay, and fear had given way to cold anger. Jimmy DeMaria's argument that somebody had to be cheating was indeed compelling. As a professional handicapper, I needed, first and foremost, an honest game. Otherwise, research, experience, and decision-making principles became useless. That I stood out as the number-one culprit further fueled my temper. The full impact of my situation was now painfully clear. Not only would I lose something like four thousand dollars a day by being shut out of Vegas, but I either had or soon would have a bunch of no-neck leg-breakers out looking for me.

The hell with it. Let 'em come. I might even do some damage myself.

"Bullshit," I muttered, deriding my flare-up of ferocity. Here I was acting like a hard-ass when it was time to start using my brain.

I had begun to unlock the car to drive home, but quickly changed my mind. My condominium was part of the same development project as the Athletic Club and, in fact, the club's dues were included in the condo's management fee. Instead of driving through the twisting streets of the condo project, I could cut through the outdoor pool area, which the club shared with the condos, and take one of the jogging paths for less than a half-mile to reach my back door. That way, I reasoned, I could elude anyone watching the condo.

On a second inspiration, I went back into the club and changed back into sweaty athletic togs. Following the jogging path, which meandered around the entire condominium project, I hoped to blend right in with the surroundings. Shirtless and at an easy trot, I picked up a little additional cover by falling in with three joggers, a man and two women, all three of whom I knew casually from neighborhood parties. I was in good shape from racquetball and some weight work, but I almost never ran for exercise. The slow, easy pace, which lent itself more to socializing than fitness, suited me perfectly.

As soon as the condo came into view, I spotted the car, a Ford Thunderbird, probably rented, containing two large men in sports clothes sweltering in the midday sun. I suppressed a twinge of anxiety as the group passed within fifty feet of the car, but the two men paid us no mind. The path swung around behind the buildings, and, with relief, I saw that no one was hovering within sight of my back door.

Waving to my unwitting camouflage escorts, I approached the back door slowly. The possibility that somebody was inside had to be considered, but common sense dictated that the two watchers would not roast in a car if they could maintain their vigil in relative comfort. I moved quietly and carefully, just the same. All the drapes and shades in the front of the condo were closed, so I had no fear of being seen from the street. Snatching a Diet Coke from the refrigerator, I went down to the study.

My condominium is a two-bedroom town house. The study, a twenty by thirty room, takes up most of its finished basement. The walls are lined with bookshelves containing hundreds of volumes collected over more than twenty years of voracious book buying. On one side of the room I had fashioned a desk using a four-by-eight slab of oak butcher block, supported by metal file cabinets. Next to the desk was a computer stand with an IBM

PC-XT, and on the shelves behind the chair were my most frequently used racing records and manuals.

The lounging furniture was selected for comfort and durability—a leather sofa and matching recliner—for this was the room I used, not just for work, but for watching television, listening to music, or just loafing. I lived in this space. The rest of the condo was mostly for guests.

Centered between the pieces of furniture was a coffee table which appeared to be a solid block of marble. The stone table had a very carefully concealed storage compartment where I kept backup computer disks, an emergency stash of cash, and some personal papers. I accessed the hidden compartment and removed three banded stacks of hundred-dollar bills, each totaling ten thousand dollars. In my portfolio was the proceeds of my deposit account from the Tiara, and the combined funds, I decided, should be adequate operating capital.

At the computer console I booted up my data base and called up all information relating to the three races which had become the source of my problems. Next I retrieved the past-performance lines of the three horses in question. The printer spit out a copy of all the data, which I stored in the portfolio, along with the cash and my address book. Satisfied, I leaned back in the swivel chair and thought back to my conversation six weeks ago with Kermit Golightly, my friend whose tip on Picky Peaches had precipitated this current hovering storm.

After Jenna was killed, I came apart, unraveling like a baseball with the cover missing. I lost interest in the advertising agency the two of us had started three years before her death. I set upon a self-destructive course of alcohol and gambling in a futile attempt to bury her memory. Our employees and clients, at first sympathetic, became increasingly frustrated and antagonized by my erratic behavior.

Gambling seemed to be the only thing that worked. The booze left me ill and shaking, though no less haunted, but I had always had a flair, an instinct for gambling, and at the point where my intuition took over and I was on a roll, I was, for an instant, free. Unfortunately, in my impaired emotional condition, my perverse inclination toward self-destruction overrode all other factors. On junkets to Vegas, in marathon poker games, and during afternoons at the racetrack, I would plunge ahead with flights of insight which others called brilliant, parlaying win on top of win until I gained an illusion of power over the universe. Inevitably I would lose, as I was subconsciously compelled to do. Everything I had won and everything I had started with would vaporize in the final parlay, the ultimate "big play" which I was convinced would set me free.

In time I accomplished what my underlying hurt and depression sought for me. I came to think of myself as a loser, that I didn't deserve to win, that Jenna's death was undeniably my fault because I had entrapped her and made her a victim of my own accursed luck.

Kermit Golightly reached into that emotional maelstrom and caught me before I was pulled under. He was just an old horseplayer I had met at the Detroit Race Course. By chance, we both preferred the same seating area and, one day, we struck up a conversation. Kermit was neither a therapist nor a philosopher, but, at the time, he was the only one around who seemed to care about me as a person rather than my "productivity" and "wasted potential." He had an unshakable belief that the solution to chronic losing was not abstention, but winning, and little by little he instilled a sense of discipline and self-worth in me.

In time I sold what remained of the business, paid my debts, and began a new life as a professional horseplayer. If the wounds of Jenna's loss didn't exactly heal, at least they scarred over, and if ghosts still haunted the nights, at least in my daily activity I was free and could function.

About two years before I moved out West, Kermit went through a cold streak that lasted nearly two weeks. The streak was very unusual, for Kermit was normally conservative and consistent. But throughout the period, he seemed both distracted and physically ill. Ignoring all urging that he see a doctor, he came to the track every day, his condition visibly deteriorating. Finally, as we were leaving the track one day, Kermit's appendix ruptured. I got him to the hospital, made sure that his bills were paid, and when he was released, loaned him enough money to get started again.

Before the end of the season, Kermit had repaid the money, but he considered himself eternally in my debt.

Whenever he had a "blue chip," when a horse he had been watching seemed to be ready to win at a nice price, he would call me in Las Vegas with the tip. I had bet on Picky Peaches without hesitation.

I remember questioning Kermit as to why he had been so high on a horse that looked so bad on paper, but the old man's answer was very evasive. In retrospect, I guess I should have been suspicious, but such secretiveness was completely consistent with Kermit's carefully cultivated air of mystery. I had not been put on guard. He, like every other gambler I knew, needed to maintain a certain "aura."

I was certain that there was no way Kermit could be involved in anything illegal. The organization of such an adventure was beyond his resources and scope of interests. He would be the first to admit that no punishment could be too severe for those who fix horse races. However, if Kermit came upon a situation where he knew the fix was in, his first inclination would be to capitalize on his perceptiveness by cashing a wager. He must have seen something, I speculated, perhaps during his customary observation of early-morning workouts. Whatever it was, I had to find out.

After packing a travel bag with a few essentials, and having discreetly checked both the front and rear of the condominium, I slipped out the back door and made my way back to the Athletic Club. Fortunately, the two goons were paying no attention to the jogging path; a jogger with luggage was bound to generate some suspicion. I stowed the bag in the car and went back into the club to shower and dress one more time.

As I stood in front of my locker, stripping off the sweaty clothes, I caught a glimpse of a wiry naked body scuttling in a bowlegged gait toward the steam room. Whenever the Cowboy planned to play high-stakes poker, he went through an elaborate ritual, part superstition and part serious preparation. He took a long steam bath in an effort to "sweat out the poison" in his system. He would then shower and relax with a half-hour massage from one of the staff therapists. From the massage, he went first to the whirlpool and then to the "quiet room" for a half-hour nap. After the nap, he would shower again, dress in his best Cowboy finery, eat what he would call his "training meal" in the dining room upstairs, and proceed, rested and ready, to the site of the game.

Confident that, by this time, Cowboy would have picked up at least some gossip, I followed him into the steam room.

"Well, I'll be damned," the Texan said with a smile, "I figured you'd be on your way to Mexico by now."

"I guess you heard, then," I prompted.

Cowboy tested the wall behind him for temperature and leaned back gingerly. "I heard some talk. The rumor has it you beat the casinos and bookies for ten or twelve million dollars on fixed races, that you've been barred from the Tiara, and every place else for that matter, and that bookies from New York to the West Coast want a piece of your ass in the hope of gettin' their money back. Ol' Uncle Buck is scared spitless that those same people are gonna be askin' him and me questions jus' because we're friends." He paused to peer at me with a cockeyed smile.

"Now you know how it is about rumors, son. I don't know how much of this is true, but that's what's on the streets."

I had to chuckle at the image of Buck's obvious discomfort. "Well, at least some of it's true," I allowed. "As of about nine-thirty this morning, I'm no longer welcome in the casinos around here. Probably Reno too. And there's evidence that some hard-nosed folks are looking for me, if the two big, ugly guys parked across from my condo are any indication. That wouldn't be so bad if the rest were true, but I don't have any ten million dollars. Somebody did win a bunch of money on what looked like fixed races. I doubt if it was ten million dollars, but it was plenty."

"How come they figure you for the culprit, Poet?"

Once more I recounted the whole story, including my conversation with Jimmy DeMaria.

"Mercy! You do have some grief," the Cowboy said when I had finished. "It's a damned good thing DeMaria believes you, 'cause he knew right where to look for you. So what are you gonna do?"

"I don't know, Cowboy. Maybe you'd be better off not knowing."

"Fuck them assholes," he shot back. "You're gonna need some help, and just maybe I can offer it."

"You're probably right, but I'd hate to see you come to grief on account of me."

The Cowboy shrugged. "Little late to be worried about that, don't you think?"

"What I'm gonna do is find the guy who tipped me on Picky Peaches and find out what the hell he knows," I told him, conceding the point. "After that, I'm gonna see if I can't check out the trainers and owners, past and present, to try to find out who cheated and how. I guess that's not much of a plan, but it's the only way I can think of to get off the hook."

The Cowboy nodded in agreement. "In that case, I think I know someone who can help you. You remember Peter T. Westmoreland?"

"Your buddy from Austin? The Texas Ranger?"

In fact I remembered Peter T. Westmoreland well. On his last trip to Vegas, Peter T., Cowboy, and I had set out on an adventuresome carouse of the city's nightlife that turned into a monumental drunk. We had played cards, shot craps, chased women, and consumed an endless flow of beer and tequila "solos." The end result was what the two Texans described as a "Boone and Crocket" hangover. The term bore no relationship to the legendary Daniel and Davey but, instead, referred to the Boone and Crocket who published the record book for hunting and fishing trophy records. According to Texas lore, a Boone and Crocket hangover was won only after dogged pursuit and hazardous adventure and, as such, was worthy of admiration and respect.

"He's some kind of private investigator now," I said as the recollection came back to me.

"Well, ol' Peter T. ain't exactly your average P.I.," the Cowboy answered. "He's got what you call a specialized practice. When he left the Rangers to set up his own business, he settled on an area where there was a lot of need and not much expertise. Peter T. investigates equine insurance fraud. You know, some ol' boy has cash-flow problems, so he knocks off his registered Arabian sire. 'Course he just happens to have the animal insured for a hundred grand."

"What?" I exclaimed, incredulous.

"It happens all the time," Cowboy assured me. "Don't matter if its race horses, breedin' stock, show horses, rodeo stock, cuttin' horses . . . owners kill 'em or have 'em killed to collect their insurance. Fires, poison, 'lectrocution, vandalism, suffocation, you-name-it."

"Jesus Christ! People get away with that?"

"Used to be easy to get away with," Cowboy explained. "The animals were the property of their owners, nothin' more. So it wasn't like nobody committed murder. In most cases, some country lawman would come out and take a look, scratch his ass, pick his nose, shrug his shoulders, and file a report. I guess it's kinda human nature not to care too much if some big insurance company loses money, but the insurance companies damn sure care. Particularly as the value of horses and the amounts they get insured for get higher and higher. So they started doin' some serious investigatin'. They got a few of their own people, of course, but there are just two independents everybody calls the best in the business. One's a fella from South Carolina called The Fatman and the other's Peter T. Westmoreland."

I failed to see what help Peter T. could be, and said so.

The Cowboy grunted derisively. "Have you thought about how tough it is to talk to stablehands, let alone trainers? I mean, how the hell you figure to get into the stable areas, just for starters?"

My blank expression obviously answered the questions.

"Didn't think of that, did ya?" he pointed out sagely. "Peter T. Westmoreland can walk onto any backstretch in the country and track security and the Thoroughbred Protective Bureau will roll out the red carpet. Breedin' farms, trainin' centers, the whole thing. He's helped design the security system for a good many of 'em."

"What makes you think he'll take my case?"

"Don't worry about that. Peter T. and me go back to the days when we was both rodeoin'. Matter of fact, let's give him a call right now."

Cowboy went to the phone in the men's lounge while I sat in front of my locker trying to figure out my next move. After a few moments, he returned.

"Peter T. ain't there," Cowboy explained. "But the

good news is, he's in L.A. I talked to his secretary, Wanda Jean. He's just finishin' up a case for an insurance company out there. She said she'd get a message to him to expect your call. He's at the Century Plaza. You can call him when you get there."

"When I get there?" I asked blankly.

"Tennyson," Cowboy lectured patiently, "you gotta get your ass outta Vegas. You didn't think you were just gonna go out to McCarran Airport an' fly outta here did you?"

Actually, I hadn't considered that possibility at all.

"Play it safe," he instructed. "Drive . . . just in case your friends are watchin' the airport. Los Angeles is as good as anyplace. You can meet up with Peter T. an' fly outta LAX or Ontario. Get yourself lost."

I had to admit, Cowboy was making sense. I had to start thinking clearly on my own, and I cursed my preoccupation.

"There's somethin' else you better oughta consider, son," Cowboy said finally as he stood there with a towel wrapped around him. "Follow me."

Padding to the next row of lockers, he opened his to reveal one of his specially tailored western-cut suits still in the dry cleaner's plastic bag, a pair of custom-made lizardskin boots polished to a high gloss, and a briefcase. The row of lockers was empty but Cowboy made a quick check of the adjacent row to make sure he could not be overheard. Reassured, he popped open the briefcase. Inside were a thick stack of hundred-dollar bills—his table stakes for the evening's game—and a well-cared-for automatic pistol. Cowboy picked up the gun.

"I'm gonna feel a little naked without this tonight, but I think you may need it more'n I do.

"Take it, goddammit," Cowboy growled when I recoiled from the weapon. "I know fuckin' well you know how to use it. The Marine Corps must've taught you somethin' in Vietnam. You got people out there that wanna put you in the hospital, or worse."

I found Cowboy's reasoning compelling and accepted the weapon without further comment.

"It's a nine-millimeter Beretta," Cowboy explained. "You can get ammunition about any place guns are sold. Like I said, I'm sure you know how to use it."

With the Marines in Vietnam, I had become proficient in all types of firearms, and although such weapons were supposed to be reserved for officers, I carried a .45 automatic when on patrol. The nine-millimeter was lighter but packed plenty of stopping power. Although nearly twenty years had passed since I had last handled such a weapon, I was mentally transported back to the time when its possession had made me feel less vulnerable. The pistol's effect on my confidence was the same.

The loan of the gun proved to be providential. I was leaning into the back compartment of the Corvette, transferring shaving kit, racket, and court shoes into the carry-on bag, when I felt a sensation which had not been present for almost twenty years. Back in my days in Southeast Asia, I had developed an uncanny ability to sense danger. Over there, almost anything could kill without warning—the enemy from ambush, civilians, even children, booby traps, deadly snakes: Vietnam had it all. Virtually everyone who fought over there and survived had the sixth sense to some degree, but, perhaps from pure fear or as a by-product of constant vigilance, my ability to sense danger before the actual signs could be seen was acute.

I had just taken the gun out of the gym bag and was trying to decide where to store it when the sensation came upon me. I jacked a round into the chamber, stood up without turning around, flicked the safety off, still using my body to shield the gun from sight. Over my shoulder I could see two men crossing the parking lot no more than twenty feet away, and with astonishment I realized that these were the same two men who had startled old Rosie in front of the Tiara. Jesus Christ, my mind shouted, they had been following me even then. I turned to face them, keeping the gun out of sight behind my hip. The pair separated slightly and stopped.

"Tennyson Wilder?" the rat-faced one inquired.

I nodded, trying not to show any signs of concern.

"Some friends of ours would like to talk to you," Rat-face continued. "Would you come with us, please?"

"Who are your friends?"

"You'll find out soon enough. Let's go."

"Well, if you put it that way," I said with a smile, "I think you and your friends can all go fuck yourselves."

Ratface sighed and looked at his companion with a weary expression. "Look, pal," Ratface said, "we'd just as soon not have any trouble, but one way or the other, you're goin'."

The pair started to take a step forward, but stopped abruptly, eyes widening, as I leveled the pistol.

"I would say that my previous answer still stands," I said, deriving no small amount of pleasure from the surprise on their faces. Ratface and Neanderthal, apparently, were so accustomed to intimidation working that effective resistance left them speechless. "Now, where's your car?"

The rat-faced thug nodded toward a white Lincoln Town Car. Checking to make sure no bystander was observing the action, I marched the two hoods to their car. Pointing to the trunk, I ordered, "Open it."

The trunk was big, but not big enough for both men. I decided that the bigger man represented the most immediate threat.

"Get in," I told Neanderthal. The big man hesitated. This time it was my turn for a weary sigh. "You guys are probably wondering if I would really shoot you right out here in front of God and everyone," I continued evenly. "At this moment, I figure I got to keep you from following me. The fact is, I probably wouldn't kill you, but I'd put one through your knee cap without even thinking about it. Of course this is a nine-millimeter, so the damage might be rather extensive. So, how do you want it?"

Neanderthal looked at Ratface, who nodded. Without changing expression or uttering a word, the more formidable of my would-be abductors took himself out of the game by climbing into the trunk. With a good measure of relief, I slammed the lid and put the keys in my pocket. I was reasonably confident that I could handle Ratface one-on-one. That assumption nearly cost me my life.

Ratface didn't look like much, but he moved with lightning quickness, the switchblade appearing in his hand as if by magic. Gambling that I would hesitate to shoot, he attempted to settle the issue with one fast, incapacitating stroke. A veteran knife fighter, who had honed his skill in the custody of the Illinois Department of Correction's "graduate school of crime," he almost made it.

The knife point grazed my rib cage, but Ratface had underestimated my own reflexes and had bet everything on that single thrust. His momentum left him wide open when I managed to twist away, and the weight of the pistol thundered against his jaw with a sickening crush of bone. Ratface went down like a rock and lay still.

My heart racing, I felt the blood on my shirt but somehow determined that the wound was not serious. Frantically I looked around the parking lot in search of possible witnesses. There was no one in sight. From inside the trunk came a thumping as the Neanderthal pounded on the deck.

I dragged Ratface to the side of the car, opened the back door, and dumped the knife-wielder on the back seat. Ratface made no sound, but a pulse was evident in the vein in the man's neck. The asshole would be eating through a straw for a while, but I was relieved that he hadn't croaked.

Two at the condo, these two . . . I wondered how many more were on my trail. I was not about to hang around to find out.

4

In the rest room of a combination service station and convenience store, I attended the wound inflicted by Ratface's knife thrust. The cut, about three inches long, was not deep and had stopped bleeding. The most painful part of the treatment had been removing my shirt after the blood had dried.

I washed the cut thoroughly, applied an antiseptic salve, and covered the wound with gauze and surgical tape to keep my shirt from chafing the injury. Back in the store I bought a six-pack of diet cola, a small Styrofoam cooler, some Life-Savers, and a road atlas. Securing these purchases on the passenger seat and the floor of the Corvette, I settled down gingerly to examine the map of southern California. With Las Vegas and the confrontation with Ratface and Neanderthal a half-hour behind me, the adrenaline surge had worn off, leaving me fatigued to the point of exhaustion.

The service station was off Interstate 15, just east of the California border. After the incident in the Athletic Club's parking lot, my only thought was to put some distance between myself and Vegas. Now that I had come this far, I had to begin making decisions.

After another painful struggle to climb out of the car, I made my way to the open telephone booth. From Directory Assistance I obtained the number for the Century Plaza. Peter T. Westmoreland had not returned to his room.

I drove back onto the freeway heading west and set the cruise control. I retained some skepticism over whether Peter T. could really help me, but I had no better ideas. I would keep trying the Century Plaza until I reached the detective. If everything worked out, I would meet him tomorrow in L.A. before catching the first available flight to Detroit. Having made a decision, I discovered that a plan, as opposed to mindless flight, improved my sense of well-being.

Air conditioning kept the Corvette's interior comfortable, and the powerful car whispered along, eating up the highway. Outside, the late-afternoon heat shimmered off the desert surface and, in the distance, dry, barren mountains glowed red and purple like banked coals heating an inhuman crucible. The Devil's Playground. Was I escaping from it, or plunging into it? I put the operation of the vehicle on a mental "automatic pilot" and turned my attention to my predicament.

Though perceiving myself as lucky was difficult under the circumstances, I had to admit that good fortune had at least brought me this far. Ratface and Neanderthal had been on my tail at the Tiara and, had strange old Slot Rat Rosie not started screaming, they would have taken me well before I had even realized there might be danger. Warnings from Jack Hanrahan, Jimmy DeMaria, and Cowboy had frightened me enough to take precautions and to arm myself. Otherwise I might have blundered into the trap waiting at the condominium or I might have been abducted with ease by Ratface and Neanderthal.

I was grudgingly grateful, but I knew that the same kind of blind luck could not continue. I reminded myself that I was no tough guy, nor was I a detective. What, then, could I possibly hope to accomplish? Peter T. Westmoreland might be a seasoned investigator, but could he be expected to know much about race fixing? For that matter, what did I know about race fixing?

"Stop!" I said aloud. "Think things through." What else could I do but go home and wait? Say, "Here I am boys. Come get me." Should I hide out and hope the whole thing would blow over? Small chance. Almost by force of will, I brought my concentration to bear. There had to be salient facts, some place to start.

Since the time when the first hairy men domesticated their first hairy horses, the compulsion to establish, through competition, who owned the best and the fastest has been part of man's heritage. If prostitution is truly the "oldest profession," or at least the oldest of man's vices, the fermenting of alcohol from grain and betting on horse races must vie for second place among the ancients.

Throughout the millennia, there have been countless attempts by the unscrupulous to fix the outcome of horse races to ensure the profitability of their wagers. The clever Roman who first affixed blades to his chariot wheels to gain an edge in the Colosseum races can be viewed as a relative newcomer to race fixing.

In modern racing, I knew, there were still attempts made to fix races. However, there were so many safeguarding security measures and regulatory overviews that fixing a race was difficult to accomplish and even more difficult to get away with. I had heard, for years, the common loser's lament that all races were fixed, but the accusation was nothing more than sour grapes. More than ninety-nine percent of all thoroughbred races, on every program and at every track, were run honestly.

Picky Peaches, Calamitator, and Winter Muffin had each won at odds ranging from 28-1 to 35-1. Before their victories, each had displayed, in its running lines, the classic profile of a career nonwinner. The horses had begun their careers at major tracks in races designated Maiden Special Weight. This is the highest-class level for horses which have never won a race. Over the course of as many as a dozen poor performances, the horses had been entered at progressively lower levels until they reached the lowest maiden claiming event at minor tracks, the proverbial bottom-of-the-barrel type of race where every entrant may be purchased for a predetermined claiming price as low as two thousand dollars.

At this nadir, in stepped Capricorn Racing Stables with a claim. So why, I wondered, would anyone want to claim these horses?

In the instance of a rare claim at this level of racing, the reasoning of the claimant, or purchaser, is usually based on some measure of breeding value overshadowing the horse's lack of racing ability. On even rarer occasions, one trainer may see some latent promise which another's mishandling has failed to bring out. None of the three horses had pedigrees which suggested a future in the breeding shed and, in fact, Calamitator was a gelding.

Still, Capricorn made three successive claims of this sort, each in a different area of the country. What I found even more astounding was that Capricorn then moved their new acquisitions up in class at major tracks and won in the horses' first appearances. These dramatic form reversals were accomplished in three divergent locales utilizing three different trainers. Amazing. One such claim would be considered by experts to be fortuitous . . . three for three, impossible.

Why hadn't I noticed this before? That's easy, I answered my own question, I look at the running lines and past performances of as many as four or five hundred entries per day. I'm not looking for evidence of cheating, but for opportunities to make money. Yet somebody, or some agency, had to be looking for what I had missed. The combination of the form reversal and the long-shot odds, I felt certain, would trigger the intense scrutiny of the racing authorities. Yet no evidence of cheating had been uncovered.

A rest stop was coming up. Though my traveling supplies were in good order, I gave in to an impulse and took the exit. I stood at the door of a convenience store identical to the one in Nevada and reconsidered my decision. Fuck it, I thought, in the next few days I might get shot. With that resolution I went inside and bought two packs of ultra-low-tar-and-nicotine cigarettes.

This time Peter T. Westmoreland answered his telephone.

"If it ain't the king of the horseplayers," the Texan crowed. "Who d'ya like at Hollywood Park tomorrow?"

I had to laugh at Peter T.'s banter. The detective, as I remembered him, approached life with uncommon good humor, ever ready with a laugh or a joke of his own.

"I talked to Toby already," Peter T. informed me in a more serious tone. "He says you got some trouble."

I gave him a brief synopsis of the situation and waited for a response.

"I might be able to help," he allowed. "Depends on what you have in mind. Why don't we get together an' talk about it. If nothin' else, I might be able to put you on to the right people in the racin' community. You gettin' in here tonight?"

"Yeah, but it'll be late. Let's have breakfast in the morning."

"Fine with me. Will you need a room?"

"No. I think I'll stop on this side of L.A. You name the time and I'll see you at the Century Plaza in the morning."

We settled on nine-thirty in the coffee shop. I got back on the road feeling just a little bit less alone. After a few seconds' hesitation, I set fire to the first cigarette I had smoked in two years. Look at yourself, I berated with cynical amusement, a little pressure and you're addicted again. The cigarette tasted wonderful even if my self-esteem had a faint aftertaste of bile.

"So who looks for evidence of race fixing?" I voiced the next question of my logic sequence. The stewards. Every track has three. Two are employed by the track and report to the National Jockey Club, while the third is a representative of the state racing commission. Collectively they enforce the rules of racing. In the cases of the long-shot wins of my three horses, the stewards would have automatically reviewed the race with particular attention to one of that group's primary responsibilities, corruption by riders and trainers.

Rider corruption is one of the oldest forms of race fixing. A crooked jockey may not be able to cause a bad horse to win, but he can certainly cause a good horse to lose by employing any number of tactics which might appear as poor racing luck or simple misjudgment. When a long shot wins, the stewards' first action is to review the videos of the race to make certain that the beaten favorites were ridden fairly. Should they find anything suspicious, the rider of a beaten favorite will likely be called before the stewards to explain his actions in the race. In the same instance, trainers might also be called to account for a losing performance by a favorite or a dramatic form reversal for a long-shot winner.

I resolved to review the *Daily Racing Form* Results Charts at length when I stopped for the night, but from my brief examination earlier, one fact stood out in each case. The betting favorite in each race ran second or third and completed the races in respectable times. Picky Peaches, Calamitator, and Winter Muffin had not been handed first place. They had totally blown out their respective fields.

What else could a corrupt jockey do? I considered and rejected the possible use of a battery, a "machine" in racing parlance, to shock a horse to the limit of its physical capabilities. Such instances were exceedingly rare, and the devices were of questionable value. Too remote a possibility to dwell on, I decided.

I lit another cigarette. This one tasted as good as the first, with the remorse growing fainter still.

Drugs? Time and again horsemen, from the corrupt to the desperate, had adopted the Du Pont slogan of "Better Living Through Chemistry." There were drugs which could improve the performances of slow horses and drugs which could stop a fast horse in its tracks. There was an ongoing technological race between modern pharmacology developing new substances and the evolution of new testing devices and procedures to detect them.

The Thoroughbred Protective Bureau, in its role of providing track security, and the state racing commissions, who supervised the drug-testing procedures, formed the vanguard in the prevention of illegal drug use. The key elements were sophisticated laboratory testing, usually performed by a state university, strict limitation of access to the stable area with even tighter security surrounding horses on race day, and the concept of trainer accountability, whereby a trainer has the ultimate responsibility for the actions of anyone connected with his horses. Should a horse be discovered to have run on an illegal medication, the trainer was automatically at fault. Legal medications could only be administered by duly licensed veterinarians, and even the possession of a hypodermic syringe by a trainer or one of his employees was grounds for suspension.

I could not bring myself to dismiss the possibility of illegal drugging to account for the horses' performances. There were always new substances being developed and, lately, I had heard stories of legal medications being used to mask illegal drugs. The problem was too complicated to discount. At the same time, the racing authorities had a far greater chance of uncovering such activities than I. My own efforts would be better spent focused on the people surrounding the horses.

RINGERS

Ringers? Impossible. Of that I was certain. The practice of fraudulently substituting a superior race horse for a less capable look-alike was, at one time, a fairly common racing tactic, but thoroughbreds are now registered and tattooed with an identification number on their lower lips to prevent such maneuvers.

I could recall the last ringer incident I had heard of and remembered that the events were more than a little comical. Back in the early eighties, two hustlers from Indiana gained possession of the tattooing equipment used by the TPB for applying registration numbers. They then went to Agua Caliente, in Tijuana, and purchased a fast sprinter who bore a resemblance to an impossibly slow horse the pair raced in Ohio and Kentucky. The Mexican horse, complete with its newly altered tattoo, was entered against three-thousand-dollar claimers at River Downs in Cincinnati. The horse won easily at odds of over 30–1 and the two hustlers congratulated each other as they cashed bets worth over one hundred thousand dollars.

But the two Hoosiers were by no means home-free. For one thing, the "Tijuana Special" had been too good, drawing off to win by nearly twenty lengths in a time just a few ticks off the track record.

Even more troublesome was the fact that the hustling Hoosiers had not done a thorough job of their homework. The tattoo is not the only means of horse identification. It merely serves to expedite the process. On their legs, above the knees, horses have a small callus called the chestnut or night-eye. For the purposes of identification and verification, photos are taken of them. They function in the same manner as human fingerprints. The Hoosiers were nailed.

The story lost its humorous touch when one of the fundamental implications of race fixing was considered. The Hoosiers were convicted of a felony under Ohio law, and spent some time in prison. The Mexican horse was disqualified and the purse for the race was forfeited and redistributed among the losing entries. Just the same, the race had been declared "official" within minutes of completion, with all the testing and verification having been completed several days later. All parimutuel wagers were paid based on the "official" outcome of the race.

The people who had bet on the losing, legitimate horses were the ultimate victims, even though the order of finish was later adjusted. There are never refunds once the "official" sign is posted.

I was stumped, at least for the time being. Perhaps I was a fool to think I could uncover something that the racing authorities had missed. But then again, I had no idea whether the authorities were even looking beyond their normal procedures. I did have Kermit, at least. The old horseplayer had certainly observed something out of the ordinary. If Kermit didn't actually know how the fix had been accomplished, he could at least set me in the right direction.

Taking some heart from this ace in the hole, I settled back to make the most of what was becoming an interminable drive. I punched up a cassette of Segovia performing his classical guitar magic, popped open a can of soda, and lit a cigarette. This time I gave no thought at all to my lapse of abstention.

Hours later, in a cheap motel in the eastern suburbs of Los Angeles, I rolled and tossed fitfully before giving up any attempt at sleep. Despite my physical exhaustion, I knew that sleep would continue to elude me. I got out of bed, turned on the television, and immediately turned it off again. The insomnia was back again, as it always was in times of stress. In the best of times, I am an erratic sleeper, subsisting on four or five hours per night in two- or three-hour stretches broken by a period of wakefulness. At the worst, I barely sleep at all. In these sleepless periods, my mind simply refused to shut down and kept me prowling and cogitating until, at last, my depleted body and nervous system would manage to steal an hour or two just before dawn. The sleep was so fleeting, I would barely notice it had occurred.

Disgusted, I dressed and crossed Ontario Boulevard to an all-night liquor store. There I bought a bottle of Sauza Gold and a handful of fresh limes. I have never been much of a drinker, but I hoped that the tequila would settle me and allow me to relax.

I left the motel room dark. The bathroom light, through a six-inch crack of the door, provided sufficient illumination. I poured two inches of tequila into a cheap plastic motel glass, added a squeeze of lime, and lit a cigarette. Sipping the drink, I settled back in my chair and allowed my mind to drift. It drifted, as it always did in times like these, to thoughts of Jenna.

I had returned to Michigan from the Marine Corps and Vietnam in 1971. From the experience I had gained a few stripes, a number of scars, a couple of medals, and a strong desire to leave that period of my life behind. After immediately reenrolling at the University of Michigan, I quickly completed the baccalaureate program that military service had interrupted. In my final semester, like most college seniors, I made the rounds of the campus recruiters in hope of landing a career.

There had been plenty of opportunities. The recruiters were willing to overlook their requirements for technical or business degrees to consider a presentable, decorated combat veteran, older than the average college kid, who was about to graduate summa cum laude. I made several expense-paid trips to various headquarters. After due deliberation, I accepted a position with one of the country's largest advertising agencies and was assigned to the Detroit office, to a team working on a major automotive account.

The account, as might be expected, was one of the agency's largest, and the team included a supervising vice-president, a senior creative director, and what seemed like a legion of writers, artists, media buyers, and administrators. The most junior members of the team were a "creative specialist" named Jenna Sonnier and I.

I soon came to wonder if, perhaps, I had made a mistake. My job was little more than acting as the account supervisor's gofer. "Account services" was the job description, and the duties consisted of delivering gifts, playing golf with the client's executives, as well as general wining and dining. I participated in no significant decisions or strategy developments, my opinion was never sought, and, in short, I did absolutely nothing worthwhile. The client's people liked me, I looked okay, and I did nothing to embarrass the firm. That was enough.

Jenna had her own problems with the senior creative director. There was little that was "creative" in the automotive advertising of the early seventies. The mandate was, give the buyer an image of how he—most definitely "he"—would look in the car. Let the styling sell the car. Such features as quality, performance, reliability, utility, and, most especially, economy were ignored. The agency collected its percentage of enormous advertising billings and did its best not to rock the boat.

Jenna had chafed under this creative bridle. She was full of energy and ideas. The closest automotive advertising came to appealing to women, for example, was the image of the family station wagon. Jenna knew that the ranks of women in the work force, single women professionals, women as heads of households, were growing rapidly, but if the ads were any indication, they simply didn't exist to the car makers. The concept of auto safety was an inconvenience, Ralph Nader a pain in the ass. Small cars were regarded as "second cars" and almost as a necessary evil in the product lines.

Disillusioned by well-paid, supposedly glamorous jobs, Jenna and I had become confidants and, inevitably, lovers. We shared our frustrations over the waste and complacency, and we worked on ideas of how things should be done. We actually worked harder together, off the job, roughing out entire strategies and ad campaigns, and we waited for the chance to show what we could do. Then came the Arab oil embargo and the ensuing energy crisis and Tanaka Motors.

Tanaka Motors, a huge Japanese automaker, was looking to follow Nissan, Toyota, and Honda into the American market. Tanaka executives came to the States looking for advertising and marketing expertise. They listened to presentations from all the major agencies, but were unable to find the touch they were looking for. With Jenna providing the impetus, the two of us literally "crashed the party," and, miraculously, persuaded these dour executives to take a look at our ideas. Even more miraculously, they liked what they saw. The firm of Wilder and Sonnier was launched.

I stood up and paced the floor. Goddammit! Leave it alone, I railed silently. What good can come from picking at old wounds? I drained off my drink and poured another. In an effort to block Jenna from my mind, I sorted through my papers until I found the next day's

Racing Form. It was the only thing that helped, solving the mysteries, the perplexing questions, of a horse race.

With the *Racing Form* spread out before me, I considered, once again, the wisdom of just letting the whole thing lie. I could make a comfortable, and anonymous, living handicapping the southern California racing circuit. I could even go to Tijuana. Agua Caliente wasn't much of a track, but it was a hellacious race book. Who needed Las Vegas?

But where else would a professional horseplayer go to hide? I asked myself. To a major racing circuit? An off-track betting facility? And how much time would elapse before Ratface and Neanderthal or some equally disagreeable bastards showed up? For five or six million dollars, they wouldn't give up easily.

At forty-two years old, the prospect of starting over again was daunting. I liked Las Vegas, and the opportunity to make money had turned out to be beyond my wildest expectations. I had to do something to keep what I had gained, even if those efforts were hopeless and dangerous.

5

Peter T. Westmoreland did not fit the Hollywood image of a Texas Ranger, six-foot-six, whipcord-thin, Old West lawman type, in a western-tailored khaki twill suit and custom-made cowboy boots, with a big white Stetson to top off the ensemble. The boots were the only aspect of the image he favored.

The man who sat across the table from me was about five-foot-seven, a couple inches shorter than I. He wore khaki slacks, pressed to a sharp crease, and a blue oxford-cloth short-sleeved shirt, carefully tailored to fit the wide pair of shoulders which would have been more at home at an NFL training table than in a trendy Beverly Hills hotel coffee shop. No Stetson, perhaps because Peter T. Westmoreland disliked hats, but perhaps because the manufacturer made no size to fit his massive head. In overall physical configuration, Peter T. had the short muscular legs of a rodeo rider and the upper body of a football player. He looked like he could walk through a wall.

Peter T. had indeed ridden bulls in the rodeo in high school and had continued after he had enrolled at the University of Texas. Attracted by the abundance of beer, girls, and good times, Peter T. had been much better at rodeoing than studying. He had gone to college to stay out of the service, but academic life had not been to his liking. He flunked out in his second semester and Uncle Sam came knocking.

By some inexplicable process of the military machine, he was assigned to an MP unit and shipped out to Vietnam in the Criminal Investigations Division. He spent his tour in Vietnam as an undercover operative, investigating theft of supplies, black-marketeering, and drug dealing by U.S. military personnel.

His military obligation complete, Peter T. joined the fabled Texas Rangers, and after training, was assigned as a district officer for a sparsely populated county east of El Paso. Most of the crime in the district centered around drug smuggling and the importation of illegal aliens. Peter T. was constantly frustrated by what seemed to be an inexhaustible flow of both. Eight years went by, throughout which Peter T. found himself becoming increasingly jaded as his sense of accomplishment eroded.

Finally, one day while Peter T. was catching up on some paperwork, an old desert rat wandered into his office. The old man lived by himself in a shack well off the main highway and had driven to town to report finding a dead horse lying on the prairie near his home. Peter T. was not especially interested in the old man's story until the wizened loner persisted: the horse looked like a "damned fine" animal, and besides, it had been shot between the eyes.

His curiosity aroused, Peter T. checked the recent police reports and found that a champion quarter horse had been stolen just twenty-four hours earlier from a ranch owned by an El Paso auto dealer. Investigation at the scene revealed that someone had trailered the horse out into the middle of the prairie and killed it. The horse was later identified as the missing quarter horse reported stolen by its owner.

The whole affair seemed very strange to Peter T. Why would anyone go to the trouble and risk of stealing a valuable race horse, only to drive it some sixty miles away and shoot it? If the horse thief had a grudge against the auto dealer and could gain access to the horse, why carry it away? The answer became clear when Peter T. learned that the horse had been insured for a quarter of a million dollars. Further investigation revealed that the auto dealer was experiencing some financial difficulty. He had a couple of notes coming due with banks and was "out of trust" in his floorplan financing with the manufacturer. The $250,000 in insurance money would bail him out.

Officially, Peter T. Westmoreland was not the investigator of record when the auto dealer was brought to trial for insurance fraud. But the insurance company recognized the value of his efforts and he was invited to visit company headquarters in Lexington, Kentucky, for a serious discussion about his future. There he learned that the business of equine insurance was undergoing some dramatic changes.

Insuring horses had always been a profitable venture, earning premiums commensurate with the risks of catastrophic injury and illness that valuable horses face constantly. The insurance company was becoming increasingly concerned, however, because the values for which horses were being insured, particularly racing and breeding stock, were escalating drastically. A top thoroughbred, for example, might earn hundreds of thousands of dollars in purses from racing and later produce offspring worth, collectively, millions of dollars. For a top thoroughbred sire to be insured for multiples of millions was not unusual. With the world being what it is, circumstances under which the horse might be worth more dead than alive were occurring with increasing frequency. The auto dealer's quarter horse was a case in point.

The insurance company was impressed with Peter T.'s record as a law-enforcement officer and also with his earlier background working with livestock in the rodeo. For his part, Peter T. felt he was ready for a change, and so began his career as an equine insurance investigator. After a couple of successful years as an employee, he opened his own agency and established his reputation as one of the very best in the field. Along with earning a comfortable living, he felt a definite sense of accomplishment from his work. His only frustration came from the fact that the penalties meted out to the culprits were not severe enough.

"Anyone who would murder a helpless and trusting animal to collect the insurance has to be among the lowest forms of life," Peter T. declared emphatically. "I take some pleasure in messing up their game, but I'd feel better if we could put 'em away for a long time."

We finished breakfast and small talk before turning to my case.

"Waltham says you're the top dog out there in Vegas,"

Peter T. began, all business now. "And now you got yourself some serious trouble."

I spent the next hour providing as much detail as possible. While he took no notes, I sensed that the investigator was mentally recording and storing everything said. I included the details of my conversation with Jimmy DeMaria and a description of the scene in the parking lot of the Athletic Club.

"These two goons," Peter T. interrupted, "what else can you tell me about them?"

"Other than what they look like, not much. If Bellisari, Hanrahan, and DeMaria are to be believed, they work for bookies. From their dress I'd say they weren't from Las Vegas, but beyond that, they could be from anywhere, for all I know."

"Maybe I should stick with you for a while, just in case more of 'em are beating the bushes," he suggested.

I disagreed. "I think for now we can cover more ground separately. These people don't have any idea of where I'm headed, and I'm not using credit cards or anything that would leave a paper trail. I think I'll be all right."

"All right," Peter T. agreed with some reluctance. "How do you want to handle this?"

"Well, first off, let's deal with the hard information. Capricorn Racing Stables as a corporation must have some legitimate structure. Their front man, Aaron Locklear, is a real person. Otherwise, licensing would be impossible. We need to find Locklear and see if he's legitimate. Also, we should see who else is in the Capricorn organization. Can you get access to racing-commission records?"

The Texan nodded. "The insurance companies I represent carry a lot of clout. It won't be a problem."

"Good. Track security also has photo I.D. requirements, so if you can connect there, maybe we can come up with a picture of one or more principals. While we're looking for Capricorn people, let's see if we can work backward. For the time being, I'm reasonably convinced that the trainers who have these horses now are solid citizens. Maybe we can't eliminate them outright, but I think we have some more promising areas of investigation. The trainers who had them when they were running badly, for example, were listed as the owners of the horses they trained. We need to know how they came to acquire the horses and what they think about the sudden form reversals. This is a list of the three trainers and the past performances for each of the horses before they won. These guys are all small-timers, so almost anything is possible."

"Let's check with the National Thoroughbred Registry," Peter T. suggested, "and trace the ownership of these horses from the time they were sold as yearlings right up till now."

The Texan leaned back in the booth and lit a cigarette, a quizzical expression on his face. "Suppose we find something, Tennyson. Then what?"

"Good question," I answered. "Yesterday I would have said I'd use any information we turn up any way I could to get myself off the hook. And I damn sure want to do that. I don't like the idea of being the object of a mob search. More important, every day I can't play the horses in Vegas costs me serious money. But I'd also like to get enough hard facts to go to the racing authorities. I'm an investor and the racetrack is the market I play. I'm willing to accept the risk, but I need an honest game. Otherwise I can't depend on the information I gather and the decisions I make based on that information. Whoever these people are, they've pulled off something very, very slick and they'll keep doing it unless somebody catches them."

"Seems to me it's gotta be some kinda drugs," Peter T. declared. "Somethin' that doesn't show up on the drug tests as they do 'em now."

"That's certainly a possibility," I allowed. "I keep coming back to it myself just because nothing else seems to fit, but something just doesn't quite ring true about drugs."

"You mean these trainers are honest men?" Peter T. interjected with just a hint of skepticism showing.

"There is that," I acknowledged. "But under the right set of circumstances, almost anyone could be corrupted. No, it's that the horses themselves just don't seem like drug prospects."

"I don't follow you."

"Okay. Let's say you are Peter T. Westmoreland, all-pro football player, a wide receiver. You're six-foot-three, you weigh two hundred pounds, and you can run the forty-yard dash in 4.3 seconds. For season after season you can get deep and catch the long bomb. Then one day you get your knee torn up, you undergo surgery, a rehabilitation program, and you're back in the lineup. Only for some reason now, you don't have that deep speed anymore. Maybe the knee hurts and you're just a step slower because it hurts, or maybe you're afraid to really test it.

"Or, another possibility is that the injury itself has curbed your intensity. You're no longer trying to win, you're just trying to stay in one piece. In this kind of circumstance, you can be drugged so that you don't feel the pain or you can be drugged to remove inhibitions and restore your intensity. Under medication you can run that 4.3 forty again, because you've always had the physical capability.

"Now, by comparison, I'm Tennyson Wilder, former high-school halfback. I'm five-foot-nine and weigh 185 pounds, and on my best day I might have run that forty yards in 4.7 or 4.8, only now I'm twenty-five years older and twenty pounds heavier. You can give Tennyson Wilder the same dosage of the same medication and he will never perform that 4.3 forty. The physical ability isn't there and never was. Do you see what I mean?"

The Texan nodded.

"The kind of horse somebody drugs," I continued, "is the horse that somewhere along the line showed the ability to run fast. He gets drugs so that the old injuries don't hurt, or so his desire to race is restored. None of the horses we're talking about have ever showed any ability. Calamatator, when he woke up and won at Santa Anita, ran six furlongs in a minute, ten and one-fifth seconds. No other horse came close to that time until the feature race. Some of the best sprinters on the West Coast ran a 1:09.4, just two ticks faster. Calamatator was running in a twenty-thousand-dollar maiden claiming race, the bottom of the barrel in Southern California, and he runs just two-fifths of a second slower than some of the fastest horses on the grounds? If we looked at his past performance and workout lines, you would be willing to bet that Calamatator couldn't run five and one-half furlongs in 1:10.1 even if they stuck a rocket up his ass."

"It's hard to believe that it's the same horse," Peter T. observed, looking up from the printout of Calamatator's running lines.

"You got it. If the remotest possibility existed that such a thing could happen, I would swear that they had to bring in a ringer."

"And you're absolutely convinced that it couldn't happen?"

"It would be like a guy with a prison record finding a way to change his fingerprints," I declared emphatically. "As far as I know, crooks haven't figured out a way to do that yet."

"Okay," Peter T. summarized, "we're gonna do a little traveling to see if the racing authorities have anything useful and check out the previous trainers. What else?"

"Well, it's like I told you. I bet the first horse, Picky Peaches, on a tip from a friend, an old-timer named Kermit Golightly. If Kermit follows his regular pattern, he will have been in Detroit for a little more than a month. I'm going up there to find him. Something caused him to be damned sure that a horse which looked terrible on paper was going to win big. We need to know what it was. After checking the trails of the horses, I want to get back to Vegas and try to get a handle on the 'smoke.'"

"The smoke?" the Texan quizzed.

"'Smoke' is a Las Vegas term for smart money, insider wagering. It's what gives race book managers nightmares. Insiders with a live long shot bet all their money off-track so that they don't move the track parimutuel odds at all. So a horse that should be five or six to one ends up 20-1 or 30-1. The race books, who pay off at track post-time odds, get creamed."

"Don't the race books get suspicious when they get a bunch of action on a long shot?" Peter T. asked.

"Sure they do, but a lot of times, the action is hidden until it's too late. In other words, if I walk into Caesar's or the Tiara and try to bet ten thousand dollars on a 50-1 shot, there's a good possibility they won't even take the bet, unless they know me to be an idiot loser who throws money away. Then they'll gladly take my money. But, if

I spread my ten thousand dollars out a hundred or two at a time over a lot of books, I can probably get it down. The other thing is, if I bet too early and the books begin to see a big aggregate on a long shot, they'll sense that something is up."

"Yeah, but by that time you've got your bet down," Peter T. noted.

"What they do then is hold up payment," I explained. "You know, if you bet a long shot at the track, the bets get paid off as soon as the race is declared official. The tracks don't give a shit. It's not their money. Later, if it turns out that the horse was drugged or some other fix was in, they disqualify the horse and redistribute the purse, but the parimutuel payoff is history. The race books, on the other hand, are playing with their own money, so they hold up payment on tickets and wait for any official ruling if it seems obvious some hanky-panky has been going on."

"But they didn't do that in this case," Peter T. said.

"No, they didn't. Whoever handled the smoke spread their action around and bet within fifteen or twenty minutes of post time. In other words, they never gave a clue that something was up."

"You have to cover a lot of ground to do that," Peter T. suggested.

"Yeah, that's just it. If you waited until fifteen or twenty minutes to post time, you would be hard pressed to get in and out of a couple casinos, and you would only be able to get down a few hundred dollars. In this case, these guys bet as much as a hundred grand per race, so whoever handled the smoke had to be big and well-organized."

"Difficult, but not impossible. Is that what you're saying?"

"Actually there are people who make a handsome living spreading smoke," I replied. "They run betting services for out-of-towners or sometimes for people who live in town but want to be anonymous, if you know what I mean. I would venture a guess that every trainer who runs at any track Vegas makes book on knows somebody out there who will get his money down."

"Is that legal?"

"Well, it's against the law to book bets without a license in Vegas, and that's technically what they're doing. They're taking the bet from an out-of-town trainer, pocketing a percentage, and laying off the rest at a race book. If the bet is a winner, they get another percentage before they send the proceeds to their customer. Usually, if the customer is real reliable, they'll get some of their own money down too. It is a very lucrative business, from what I'm told.''

"Don't these betting services have the same problem when it comes to spreading out the action?" he asked.

"They use runners. 'Beards,' they call them. As I understand it, they are usually senior citizens."

"No shit!"

"Yeah, think about it. You have a large group of people who need to make an extra buck without taking much risk. They're in and out of the casinos by the thousands, but no one pays any attention to them. They just kind of wander through the casino, play a few slot machines, make a bet on a horse, watch the race, collect the money, and wander on out. Nobody ever notices them."

"Damn, that's pretty slick. And there are guys who make a business of running these ol' folks around all over Las Vegas?"

"You better believe it. As far as the casinos are concerned, they are the most hated people in Vegas. Even if casinos know who they are, they never see the actual moneymen anywhere near the race books, and if they throw out one of the old people, there are a dozen more to take his place. I know where one of the biggest services in town is located. Maybe, with a little luck, I can get some kind of handle on how the money moves around."

Peter T. looked troubled. "Suppose we're able to locate the betting service. What good is that gonna do us? Surely this guy isn't gonna give us the name of his client or how he delivered the money. I mean, I hope you don't think we're gonna go around beating answers out of people and things like that."

"No, of course, not," I answered quickly. Such a notion had never occurred to me. "But right now the casinos and the bookies all think I'm the guy who spread the smoke, that I'm the betting service. As long as they believe that, they won't look too hard for anyone else.

They'll just send muscle after me. If we can learn about the flow of money, maybe the worst we can do is present Jimmy DeMaria with a plausible alternative scenario. I got the impression that DeMaria doesn't believe I'm the one who took them. If we can give him something to work with, maybe he'll help."

The Texan smiled with understanding.

"Obviously, you're the key man in all of this," I continued. "Your access to official sources and the ability to go places where I can't go is vital. The job will be to work at the track and stable level—the street level in Vegas—to put together the pieces of what really happened."

Again Peter T. nodded in agreement. I dug into my portfolio and came up with a banded stack of hundreds.

"Here's ten thousand. Hopefully, that will cover your time and expenses for the next week or so. Obviously, I don't work the same way your insurance companies do and I don't need an itemized statement. Don't hesitate to buy information, and let me know if you need more money."

I could see that Peter T. was uncomfortable dealing with me about financial matters. While he had no qualms about billing an insurance company for his fees and expenses, he thought of me as a friend, and his personal code in that regard made him hesitate perceptibly.

"Look, Peter T.," I admonished, sensing the detective's unease. "It's worth a lot of money to me to clear this thing up fast. You're a professional, and a professional is what I need."

"Okay," the Texan agreed decisively as he stuffed the money into the inside pocket of his jacket. "We got the business out of the way. Let's get to work. Since we're this close, what d'ya say we go on out to Hollywood Park and see what we can see?"

"I don't know," I objected. "I feel like I should get to Detroit and find Kermit."

"Why don't you just call 'im?"

I laughed. "You gotta know Kermit," I explained. "He's got a little house in New Orleans where he lives with his widowed sister, but when he's in Detroit he stays in the cheapest kitchenette motel or furnished apartment he can find. The dumps are lucky to have electricity, much less a telephone."

"He's that cheap?"

"More like he just doesn't give a damn. He calls his sister every day and sends her money every few weeks. He figures if anybody else wants him bad enough, they know where to look for him." I smiled to myself, picturing Kermit with his half-glasses hanging on the end of his nose, sorting through the piles of paper and cartons of files which made up his "mutual data base."

"Here's an idea," Peter T. offered. "It's already after two o'clock Detroit time. The earliest you could get there, even if you could get a flight within the hour, would be this evening. Why not get an early flight in the morning or even the red-eye tonight?"

"Not a bad idea," I conceded. "I'd have to find Kermit at the track tomorrow anyway."

"Good. It's settled. Let's go look at some ponies."

Hollywood Park is in Inglewood, between Los Angeles International Airport and Watts, more or less next door to the Forum where the Lakers routinely take apart their NBA opponents. A huge, multistory structure, the track lacks the beauty of Santa Anita or the resort atmosphere of Del Mar, the other two major tracks on the Southern California circuit. Still, in this bustling inner-city setting, some of the most important racing in North America takes place.

We ignored the main entrances to the grandstand and clubhouse and I followed Peter T.'s directions to the gate serving the stable area. Peter T. showed his identification to the guard, who directed us to a parking area. There we were met by an agent of the Thoroughbred Protective Bureau, who introduced himself and treated Peter T. with deference. As the agent escorted us to the security office, I began to realize just how useful Peter T.'s contacts could be. My chances of being admitted to this highly restricted area by myself were precisely zero.

Peter T. introduced me as an "associate" and explained briefly what we were investigating. The TPB agent, Al Hodak, perked up his ears when the name Calamatator was mentioned.

"I'll be damned," he said wonderingly. "DeGuerre was right. There is something going on with this horse."

I wanted to jump out of my seat, but a look from

Peter T. restrained me. "Who's this guy DeGuerre?" he asked casually.

"Luci DeGuerre," Hodak answered pointedly. "She's an investigator for our Chicago regional office." He searched his desk until he came up with a legal pad covered with handwritten notes. "DeGuerre called me yesterday asking for the same information you're looking for. Everything we've got on Calamatator, Capricorn Racing Stables, the race itself, and Isaac Turner, the horse's trainer at the time."

"Did she say why she wanted this stuff?"

"Sure. A horse in Chicago owned by the same outfit won at a big price. DeGuerre says the word on the street is that someone made a huge killing off track, like a seven-figure killing. Vegas, so I'm told, got hit for a bundle."

Peter T.'s face remained impassive, while I did my best to keep my mouth shut. "So what can you tell us, Al?" he asked. "Is there anything to it?"

Hodak scratched his head. "I'll tell you what I told DeGuerre," he said. "We went through our normal routine when a long shot turns around so suddenly. There were no drugs involved, not even legal medication like bute or lasix. The horse was clean.

"The stewards studied the videos of the race, but nothing unusual happened during the running. Riders playing games doesn't happen much here. The jocks make too much money to mess around. We looked at the tapes ourselves and concurred with the stewards' opinion.

"All prerace and postrace identification procedures checked out. The horse was unequivocally the animal duly registered as Calamatator. In short, we found nothing to support the notion that the fix was in."

"So you're satisfied, then?" Peter T. speculated.

Hodak shrugged. "Let's say, we're 'officially satisfied' that every apparent possibility has been explored."

"In other words, your ass is covered."

Hodak bristled at the suggestion. "The Bureau doesn't think in terms of covering its ass, Mr. Westmoreland," he declared tersely. "To be honest, there are some aspects of this thing which make us, well, uncomfortable. We just haven't found anything to work with. Remember, there are hundreds of race horses stabled here, with dozens more shipping in and out every day. It's not like we've got nothing to do."

"Oh, I know." Peter T. held up a hand in agreement. "I didn't mean to imply you boys were ignoring anything. I'm curious, though. What are the things making you 'uncomfortable'?"

The agent sighed, obviously wishing he hadn't opened his mouth. He held up his fingers to tick off the items. "First, there's DeGuerre," he said. "I don't know her personally, but her reputation is first-rate. We have to take her interest seriously.

"Second, even though rumors out of Vegas tend to get inflated, there was obviously tremendous off-track action on this horse. The Chicago horse too. That fact in itself says something.

"Third. The guy on the Capricorn license is a bad actor by the name of Marcel Larrance, a downright scary sonofabitch. We got nothing on Larrance, but his brother, Armand, was involved in one of the biggest race-fixing scandals in modern racing history about ten years ago in New Orleans. Nobody ever implicated Marcel, but even so, he's not exactly squeaky-clean in our book.

"Fourth. About three days after the race, this Marcel Larrance gets into a knockdown, drag-out fight with Isaac Turner, the trainer. Right there in the stable area. We handed out fines and both of them got a few days' suspension, but neither one of them would say what the fight was about. Right after that, Calamatator got moved to another trainer's barn and, later, was sold. As a matter of fact, Capricorn Racing Stables is officially out of business. Marcel Larrance departed for parts unknown. Peculiar, isn't it?"

Peter T. allowed that is was, indeed, peculiar. "You got a file on this Marcel Larrance?" he asked.

Hodak rummaged through a file cabinet and handed Peter T. a folder.

The detective grimaced when he opened the file. "Jesus," he muttered. "He's an ugly sonofabitch. What the hell happened to his face?"

"War wounds, so I'm told," Hodak replied. "Vietnam."

Peter T. read silently for a few moments before passing the file over to me. The face that stared up at me from the five-by-seven photograph was the stuff of nightmares. Marcel Larrance was totally hairless, with hideous burn scars covering half his face. One ear and part of his nose and mouth were disfigured as though they had been eaten away. What was left of the mouth was twisted into an evil sneer. At the center of his great dome of a head, two dark eyes burned with bloodcurdling hatred.

I passed the file back to Hodak without comment. Normally I could view a fellow veteran, so scarred from his experience in Southeast Asia, with nothing but sympathy seasoned by anger at the waste and a small measure of relief that my own scars were less visible. For this man I felt no compassion. Early indications were that Marcel Larrance was probably an enemy. From the photograph alone my mind saw him as the devil himself.

"That it?" Peter T. asked Hodak.

"Not quite. DeGuerre asked us to help locate a trainer by the name of Anselmo Calderon. He's the guy who trained Calamatator in Arizona before Capricorn claimed him. The guy loaded his horses when Turf Paradise closed its season in Phoenix, and hasn't showed up at another track yet. His usual circuit brings him over here to Los Alamitos, but he hasn't appeared there or anywhere else in California."

"Where can we find this Isaac Turner?"

"His horses are stabled in barn thirty-two." Hodak checked his watch. "This time of day you can probably find him at the track kitchen unless he has a horse entered on today's card."

Peter T. stood up. "You've been a big help, Al," he said, shaking the agent's hand. "I think we'll get out of your way and go see ol' Isaac."

"Good luck," Hodak offered. "You will keep us informed should you learn anything?" Peter T. nodded. "Oh, there is one other thing," Hodak said as we turned to leave. He consulted his notes. "Here it is. DeGuerre asked us if we had anything on a Las Vegas gambler by the name of Tennyson Wilder."

I was halfway out the door when I stopped short. I felt Peter T.'s grip on my arm as he stood between me and Hodak. Slowly Peter T. turned and said, "Never heard of the guy. What's he got to do with this?"

Hodak shrugged. "According to DeGuerre's sources,

this guy cashed some big bets in Vegas. Could be our race fixer."

"Perfect," I muttered between clenched teeth, once we were out of the building and walking through the shedrows. " 'Las Vegas gambler.' Jesus Christ." If there is any label a professional handicapper hates, it's to be called a "gambler." Irrationally, I was more annoyed at the description than at finding out the TPB had taken an interest in me.

"Take it easy, son," Peter T. cautioned. "We're doing real good here. Ol' Al may know your name, but he damn sure don't know what you look like. Just stay cool."

Forty-five minutes later we were sitting in the track kitchen drinking coffee and shrugging off our disappointment. Isaac Turner, we had learned, was in San Francisco saddling one of his charges to run at Golden Gate Fields. There was nothing more we could do.

Around us the track kitchen buzzed with activity. At any track the kitchen serves as the social center for all backstretch personnel. In the past, track kitchens were open to the public and, with Kermit, I had frequently breakfasted at the facilities of the Fair Grounds in New Orleans and of Detroit Race Course. Now, due to stricter security regulations, most track kitchens were restricted to licensed personnel.

The kitchen at Hollywood Park was a long, low, block building with a concrete floor and durable rather than decorative furnishings. Along one wall, plain but uniformly tasty food was served in large portions at uncommonly low prices. At the tables, stablehands, their rubber boots caked with a combination of mud and horse excrement, ate in close proximity to jockeys whose pictures adorned magazine covers, famous trainers whose words were sought by reporters as though they came from "on high," and multimillionaire owners who vied with Japanese, Arabs, and Europeans for the privilege of spending millions for year-old race horses who might never run.

"It's no big deal," Peter T. was telling me. "You can take the red-eye, like we planned, and I'll stay here and see Turner. They said he'd be back tomorrow."

"Oh, yeah, sure," I answered distractedly.

"What's the problem, ol' son?" he inquired.

"I'm sorry, Peter T. I was just thinking what a mess this has turned out to be. The TPB can't find anything, but of course they think I'm involved. Capricorn's out of business, so there goes another lead. Then we got a guy who looks like he's right out of a monster movie out there somewhere, but where?"

"He does look pretty awful," Peter T. agreed goodnaturedly. "But look on the bright side. We've only been at this for a few hours, and look what we found out."

My only response was a disgusted grunt. What we had found out gave me not one second's satisfaction.

"Wait a minute, son. You see that guy in the silk sport jacket?"

I turned to follow his gaze. "Sure." I shrugged. "That's Sandy Presser, the director. He's at the Tiara a couple times a month. The girl with him is Dina Conklin, the jockey." I didn't add the "so what" that remained on my mind.

"I know Presser," Peter T. explained. "One of his horses busted out of the paddock at his ranch. Got hit by a truck out on the San Diego Freeway. The insurance company sent me out to check out the claim." The "so what" must have been visible in my expression. "Just for the hell of it," he went on patiently, "let's go see if he knows anything about Capricorn or this guy Larrance."

I didn't think much of the idea, but I followed him to the director's table. Presser had a friendly, relaxed manner and insisted we join them for coffee. I was happy to meet Dina Conklin, who had just recently become the all-time leading female jockey in history. Conklin was a pixielike twenty-eight-year-old whose engaging grin and ragamuffin mop of blond hair disguised the fact that she was arguably the toughest ninety-pound female on the face of the planet.

As I had expected, Presser knew nothing of either Capricorn or Larrance. We were about to leave when Dina Conklin spoke up.

"I know who Marcel Larrance is," she said in her munchkin voice. But her eyes had lost their playfulness and she looked less like a millionaire rider than a frightened child. "The asshole followed me home, or I should say back to the hotel, one time in Chicago. I've taken spills in traffic that scared me less."

"What do you know about him, Miss Conklin?" Peter T. inquired gently.

"I don't 'know' anything," she replied, failing to suppress a shudder. "The only thing I do know is that he wasn't following me to ask me to dinner." She raised her eyes to meet Peter T.'s. "Ask around the backstretch," she challenged. "The women, that is. They know who Marcel Larrance is."

6

The first leg of the Los Angeles-to-Detroit journey was not bad at all. It was the 747 red-eye special which leaves L.A. at midnight to arrive in Chicago at about six A.M. local time. I would have an hour layover in Chicago before connecting to Detroit.

The first-class cabin of the jumbo jet was about two-thirds full. The combination of the bargain fare and what was becoming an almost desperate need for sleep induced me to put aside a deeply ingrained aversion to first-class travel. Never mind that I could afford it, I had always considered the premium a ridiculous overcharge by the airlines. The business schedule which, years ago, had me flying more than one hundred thousand miles per year had left me with an antipathy toward the airlines that time and infrequent flying has not dispelled. I can still recall Jenna's response to the profuse apologies of a ground hostess for a particularly bizarre series of screw-ups. In a tone so casual the barb almost went unnoticed, she said, "We are experienced business travelers. We're accustomed to bungling."

I actually slept for a few hours, though not for any extended restful period, but in fitful naps of, perhaps, a half-hour's duration. These brief intervals were haunted by alternate dreams of Jenna lecturing me on what she considered the "unhealthy isolation" I had made part of my life since her passing, and the glaring, sneering image of Marcel Larrance reveling in the fear and loathing he inspired. By the time the plane landed in Chicago, I felt as though I had been trampled. After the past two days, trampled was a bit of an improvement.

The aircraft for the Detroit leg of the flight was a DC-9.

The jumbo jets have always given me the illusion of staying in one place while everything else moved. A passenger boards the massive structure, which could not possibly fly; the machine vibrates while he eats, drinks, and naps; and when the doors open again he is at his destination. The machine doesn't move, it just grinds up time and space. The smaller plane and daylight conspired to remind me that I was soon to be really flying.

I have never been a comfortable flier. Even in the days of business travel, I was tense on takeoffs and landings and heard every strange noise the aircraft made. To complicate matters, I always seemed to have the worst luck in seating. Invariably the adjacent seats would draw the nervous first-timers, the aggressively talkative, the airsick-prone, or, worst of all, squalling infants.

With a seat at the rear of the cabin, I was among the first to board the Detroit flight. A businessman claimed the aisle seat, promptly removed some documents from his briefcase, and began reading. So far, so good, I thought hopefully. I felt a twinge of dismay as a sweating three-hundred-pound woman eyed the center seat next to me before moving on. The flow of boarding passengers was steady. Morning flights between the two Great Lakes industrial centers were nearly always full.

An extremely attractive young woman in a business suit boarded among the latecomers. She was neither tall nor petite, nor was she what I would necessarily call beautiful. Some of Cowboy's showgirls were conventionally beautiful, but this young woman did not have that carefully cultivated look of women for whom their appearance was their livelihood. She looked like someone who worked at a career rather than on herself. Nevertheless, there was something about her that appealed to me. Perhaps it was her athletic grace, her watchful blue eyes, her cute, turned-up nose, or the little lines that appeared at the corners of her mouth and eyes when she smiled. Whatever it was, she radiated an unusual combination of warmth and competence.

The young woman checked her boarding pass and located her seat on the aisle a few rows ahead of me. I allowed myself a faint smile of disappointment and resignation, convinced that my luck at airline seating was likely to continue.

The businessman on the aisle worked on, making his margin notes and shaking his head over occasional corporate inanities, oblivious of the movement around him. For a moment I allowed myself to hope for the best—a vacant center seat—but I was conditioned to expect the worst. The "worst" began moving down the aisle. A couple, each carrying a child. The man was huge, both in height and girth. The woman was somewhat shorter, though no less broad, clad in a shapeless frock designed by Omar the Tentmaker and sold in the thousands by K Mart. The man had a wide mustache. The woman's was only slightly less full.

I looked around the coach compartment with growing despair. There were only a few empty center seats, including the one next to me. Once again I vowed to reconsider my attitude toward first-class air travel.

The family stopped in the aisle next to the young woman who had attracted my attention. The man indicated to his wife that she should take that seat. I knew in my heart where the man would sit. In my mind I could already smell his sweat, feel his elbow poking me in the ribs as his bulk spilled over the seat to crush me against the window.

Then the miracle happened. The young woman stood to allow the wide-bodied female to crowd past and, wonder of wonders, offered her adjacent seat to the man. The couple beamed gratefully and the man exchanged boarding passes with the young woman. I could have kissed her right there.

The young woman retrieved her carry-on articles, checked the boarding pass, and took possession of the center seat between the businessman and me. As the children of the obese couple sent up a howl of protest over the rigors of air travel, I smelled the young woman's perfume, admired the firm line of her jaw, and silently blessed her courteous heart.

"Christ," I heard the young woman mutter under her breath with a hostile glance forward at the caterwauling children. So her unselfish exchange had been less courtesy than self-preservation, I thought wryly as my estimation of her character rose a notch.

Chicago to Detroit is the type of flight where the aircraft climbs rapidly to thirty thousand feet and then almost immediately begins to descend. A passenger swallows hard in an effort to clear his ears, finally adjusts to cabin pressure, and then repeats the procedure. The flight's only redeeming characteristic was brevity.

The young woman squirmed in the narrow seat, trying hard not to disturb her neighbors as she reached for her briefcase stowed under the seat in front of her. She had so little room that she had to unfasten her seat belt to reach her case. She removed a file and settled back to read. The businessman on her left brought out a lap-top computer and began entering data using terse abbreviations. I paged through my copy of the *Thoroughbred Record* and feigned concentration.

For some reason my thoughts went back to the earlier dream of Jenna. Along with accusing me of avoiding "meaningful relationships," the dream-Jenna maintained that I never dated blonds. Never blonds? I had never consciously avoided dating blonds. Had I? And if I tended to compare the women I dated with Jenna, was that so unnatural? Jenna had been the love of my life, my best friend, an alter ego. A man was lucky to find one such romance in his lifetime. To find another was asking too much. Of course the dream-Jenna has passed too fleetingly through my fitful rest and I had been unable to make these perfectly logical arguments.

The young woman next to me was blond and I found her most attractive, I decided, resting my case. What was I doing here? I wondered. Conducting a mental argument with a dream? Were lack of sleep and stress turning me into a basket case?

I found myself wanting to talk to the woman, to introduce myself, and get to know her. I tried to think of a way to open conversation, but abandoned the idea. She would probably think I was trying to pick her up. No, to attempt to prove something to the dream-Jenna, who entered and left my subconscious unbidden and never on invitation, was more than foolish. I had things to do, problems to solve. The timing was all wrong. Besides, I rationalized, this woman was too young for me, and probably engaged to a linebacker or had a silly voice or loved heavy-metal rock-and-roll. I picked up my magazine and tried to read.

As the plane began its final descent, I resigned myself

to the fact that I had been reading the same page of the same article for the past half-hour. I tried to attribute my lack of attention to the lingering effects of alcohol or simply general fatigue, but I recognized that I was troubled beyond the current crisis. Somehow in the stress of my narrow escape from Las Vegas, in the insomnia attack, or in the admonitory words of Jenna's apparition, I had come to focus on my personal life. Or lack thereof. Had I really become little more than a solitary creature of routine like Aaron Friedman or even Buck Brewster? Why was I flying around the country trying to decipher how a group of horse races had been fixed and by whom? For vindication? Maybe what I needed wasn't a detective, but a good lawyer. Sue the hell out of the Tiara—become so visible that the bookies couldn't touch me. Create such a furor that the racing authorities would have to mount an investigation to answer these compelling questions.

I stole a furtive glance at the young woman beside me. Maybe I would be better off behaving like a solid citizen rather than a fugitive. A normal person with normal relationships.

The young woman was reading some kind of report. I read over her shoulder in hope of finding a clue to her occupation. Perhaps I could uncover a means of initiating conversation. Suddenly I sat upright in my seat, a surge of adrenaline gripping my guts. On the pages in front of the young woman I had just read my own name! Calming myself, I looked over the magazine at the pages in front of the woman. It was some kind of report, like a credit report or government dossier. Incredible. The woman beside me was reading my life history while I speculated over her love life and struggled to find a clever opening line. What would she have done had I introduced myself, clapped me in handcuffs or reached for a gun?

What was she? Some kind of cop or private investigator? Surely she wasn't a hit man—a "hit person"—like Ratface and Neanderthal. She had boarded in Chicago, a bad sign. The Chicago bookies had been hard hit by the scam. Ratface and Neanderthal could easily have come from Chicago.

Whoever she was, she was among those searching for me, I concluded. Sitting right beside me on an airplane, reading my history—incredible. How could they, whoever, "they" were, have picked up my trail? I hadn't used my name to book the flight and I hadn't written checks or used a credit card.

The jolt of the landing gear touching down brought me back to reality. The next few minutes would be critical. If the young woman's confederates were waiting at the gate, the game was over.

Every second of the interval during which the aircraft taxied and docked at the gate, every delay caused by the deplaning passengers, recorded itself on my racing mind. The businessman seemed to take forever to pack his equipment. The overweight family plugged the narrow aisle, as they retrieved both children and overstuffed shopping bags, as neatly as a cork stopper in a wine bottle. The three-hundred-pound woman, still sweating profusely, barged past, glaring in preemptive challenge and pinning the young woman and me in our row. The young woman smiled and shrugged helplessly as we waited for the next break in the flow of bodies.

Finally in the aisle, moving at last, I made my way to the front of the plane. The flight attendants smiled mechanically and made their good-byes as if all the passengers in their care had become fast friends over the duration of an hour's flight. I knew better. Passengers were always "The Enemy." I cleared the jetway and, finally, the departure lounge, the young woman ahead of me. I had an image of her being met by a squad of no-necks and she would turn and calmly point me out.

There was no one waiting in the concourse. The young woman turned her head to look at me, and then, as though embarrassed to have been caught staring, gave me a faint smile and moved on. I started to breathe more easily at this perceived show of empathy, but I caught myself. Just because you're paranoid doesn't mean somebody isn't after you, I thought in admonition.

Of course they wouldn't be at the gate, I thought. They couldn't clear security with their weapons. I had a fleeting recollection of Cowboy's Beretta now resting under the seat of the Corvette parked at LAX. Feeling completely helpless, I went into the men's room, waited my turn for a urinal, disposed of my most urgent need, and finally splashed cold water over my face.

There was nothing to do but go on. I would watch at the security station. Should the young woman be waiting with her retainers, I would retreat, wait until the last minute, and then book passage on the first departing flight. A reasonable plan, I decided, irrationally encouraged by what I took to be mental acuity.

The only people in evidence in the main concourse were part of a small army of relatives of the obese family, weeping with joy and smothering the newly arrived with wet kisses. I had visions of a welcoming feast which would create food shortages throughout the Midwest. The young woman was nowhere to be seen.

I wasted no time questioning this piece of good luck. I exited the terminal from the upper level and took the first available taxi to the nearest of the type of car-rental agencies which feature well-worn used cars. A hundred-dollar bill to the manager ensured my anonymity in renting a battered Cadillac Fleetwood of early 1970's vintage. For the automotive capital of the world, Detroit has an astonishing number of near-junk cars on its streets and freeways. I would blend right in.

The facade of Detroit Race Course always suggested more than a patron actually received. I remembered the first time I entered this track as a teenager, and recalled, just as vividly, why I had abandoned this venue in favor of Las Vegas.

In the 1960's and early '70's, Detroit had been a major stop on the Midwest racing circuit. Then DRC and its sister track, Hazel Park, had been acquired by a partnership which managed to antagonize horsemen and fans alike. Michigan thoroughbred racing went into a decline to the point where the two tracks were often referred to by horseplayers as the most crooked tracks in the country. I had found the dubious nature of the racing, along with the preponderance of races restricted to horses bred in Michigan, to be intolerable and moved on to the race books of Nevada. Even Kermit Golightly, a stickler for routine, considered relocating his summer operation to Chicago.

In 1985, an aggressive, though controversial, racing commissioner invoked a long-ignored state law prohibiting more than one track to be owned by a single interest and thereby forced the partnership to divest itself of one of its track holdings. The partners retained Hazel Park and elected to specialize in harness racing. Detroit Race Course was then acquired by Ladbroke, the British gaming conglomerate. Under Ladbroke's management, the DRC physical plant underwent renovation and the stable area was expanded and improved. The track rejoined the Thoroughbred Racing Association, security was restored to industry standards, and the trend of thoroughbred racing in Michigan improved dramatically.

Kermit Golightly spent November to mid-April in New Orleans handicapping the races at the Fair Grounds, the principal track of the Crescent City. Every April, he moved north to make DRC his base. Before the decline of racing in Detroit, this was a normal circuit for a large number of Midwest horsemen.

I had no idea where Kermit was living this season; there were too many kitchenette motels within a few minutes' driving time from the track. It didn't matter. It was a racing day, and I knew exactly where to find him.

I felt strange walking into a racetrack without a *Racing Form* and binoculars. I passed by the sellers of programs and tip sheets and took the escalator to the second floor of the clubhouse. There were more than fifteen minutes to post time for the first race, and relatively few bettors were lined up in front of the second-floor parimutuel windows.

Kermit never bet a race until he had seen the horses on the track, so I went through a doorway and up another, shorter escalator to a seating area I knew Kermit favored. He wasn't in his usual seat in the first row high above the finish line. I checked the clubhouse dining room, the bar, and even the outdoor box seats, all to no avail. As post time drew near, Kermit did not appear in the parimutuel lines. I figured that he must have found another place to sit, and hoped fervently that he had not moved to the much larger grandstand area.

I went back down to the ground level of the clubhouse and checked the parimutuel lines there. Again, no success. The clubhouse featured a new teletheater complete with three wide screen TVs and seating for about three hundred fans. I had a hard time imagining a traditionalist like Kermit opting to watch races on television, but I checked the teletheater anyway. I watched the first race with a vocal and enthusiastic crowd, and while some of the faces looked familiar, Kermit's was not among them.

I had just about resigned myself to a long search of the grandstand area when I spotted "Boog" lounging against the wall that enclosed the paddock. Back in the late '60's, Buford "Boog" Wilson had been something of a terror as a defensive tackle for Tennessee A & I. Despite the relative obscurity of the school, the NFL has an uncanny ability to find unheralded college athletes with size, strength, and quickness. Boog had been drafted in one of the later rounds by the Detroit Lions and had been the surprise of their summer camp in 1970. Only the fact that Boog was a lineman on a less-than-mediocre team kept him from being rookie of the year in the NFL, but the consensus had been that Boog Wilson was a potential all-pro. Instead of realizing that potential, Boog suffered a career-ending knee injury in his second year as a pro.

Having majored in football as a collegian, like so many athletes before and since, Boog found himself with little in the way of marketable skills. He got a job selling office equipment for an employer who hoped that his name would get him in the door. For a time, his name was, in fact, something of a door opener, but Boog really didn't like the life of a salesman and he lacked the self-discipline to do the dog work that most good salesmen hate, but handle. Most of all, Boog couldn't cope with the lack of supervision, the perceived freedom that came with the job. He spent more time "goofing off" and "hanging out" than he did working. Fortunately for Boog, one of the places he hung out was the racetrack and, while his work habits were to cost him his job, they also put him on the path of his life's work. At DRC one summer, Boog met Kermit Golightly.

They were as strange a pair to strike up a friendship as one could possibly imagine. Kermit, physically small and unathletic, almost reclusive in his habits, contrasted with Boog, whose weight had blossomed past the three-hundred-mark and whose outgoing, party-loving nature was almost totally undisciplined. Something had clicked between them, however, and Kermit had become the big man's mentor. For his part, Boog treated Kermit with a respect that bordered on worship, absorbing racetrack wisdom as if it were prophecy from a saint.

By the time I met Boog, the big man was no longer a student, but a professional in his own right, with some skills of his own to teach. The principal area in which Boog excelled, perhaps more than anyone I have since encountered, was his ability to interpret the body language of horses. He earned his living at the paddock and during the post parade, separating horses who were physically fit and ready to run their best from those who were tired, sore, or otherwise distracted.

As was his habit, Boog wore a brightly colored running suit (today's selection was lime green), athletic shoes, and a baseball cap advertising Sportsman's Park. When he saw me, Boog straightened to his full six-foot-five and a wide grin spread across his face.

"The Poet Man, sure as I'm born," he crowed, engulfing my hand in a paw that would have done justice to a grizzly bear. Boog had picked up on "The Poet" nickname when he had made a trip to Vegas over the winter. He had been impressed with the race book, in general, and with the luxury of the Turf Club, but the unavailability of horses for on-site scrutiny was not to his liking. "What are you doing here? They finally run you out of Vegas?"

Boog had no way of knowing how close to the truth he had come, but I didn't bother to explain. "Good to see you, Boog," I said, retrieving my hand before it sustained major damage. "You're looking trim and fighting fit."

As the big man laughed, his immense bulk shook and he allowed that his training currently consisted of lifting chicken and rib bones from his plate to his mouth. "They're not very heavy," he chuckled, "but I do lots of reps."

"I'm trying to find Kermit. Have you seen him?"

From the look that clouded the big man's features, I knew that I wasn't going to like the answer.

"Kermit's in Sinai Hospital," Boog answered slowly. "He's in a coma and he isn't doing well. Some guys beat him up. Real bad. Right there in his motel room."

"Jesus, when did all this happen?"

The big man shook his head sadly, "Few days ago.

Johnny Lanchek found him right after it happened. Saved his life, that is if Kermit makes it. I find the men who did it, they won't end up in a hospital.''

"What was it? A robber?"

Boog shook his head, "Kermit's been carryin' some heavy bread. He says he made a big score on a long shot down at the Fair Grounds before he come up here. But all his money was there, man.''

My mind reeled with the news. That the attack on Kermit was, in some way, connected with my troubles was unmistakable. Now an old friend was in a coma and whatever information Kermit had was unavailable.

"Terrible thing," Johnny Lanchek muttered as he spread horseradish over a roast-beef sandwich. I remembered the things as being a tough and tasty as a boiled tennis shoe, but Lanchek had never been too discriminating. "Christ, I've never seen anything like it. We were going up to the bar, you know the old place up on McNichols, and I was running a little bit late picking him up. Maybe if I'd been on time . . .'' He barked a sarcastic laugh. "What am I talking about? I would've gotten the shit kicked out of me too." He shook his head disgustedly and tore a huge bite out of his sandwich.

Johnny Lanchek was in his mid-fifties, but he looked ten years older, a scrawny little man who chain-smoked Camels and spent his evenings in shot-and-a-beer bars. Lanchek played the horses on a daily basis, but unlike Boog or Kermit, he was by no means a professional handicapper. He could read the *Racing Form* and had a rudimentary understanding of handicapping fundamentals, but he had an inability to see beyond the obvious, and most of the time ended boxing the program favorites in perfectas and trifectas. If the track handicapper was hot, so was John, but when the converse was true, he would tap out two or three times a year.

Going broke was not so big a problem for Johnny Lanchek as it might have been for other people, for Johnny was an exceptionally skilled tool and die maker. Even in the worst of times, he could find work easily. He would simply work for a few weeks, until he was recapitalized, and then he would be back at the track.

"Johnny, do you have any idea who could have done this to Kermit? Or why?" I asked.

Lanchek shook his head in disgust. "I don't have a clue," he declared, "but I can tell you what I think. I think whoever did it went to that motel room looking for Kermit and nobody else. And I believe they intended to kill him. Like I said, I don't know who they might be."

"But why, Johnny? Kermit was about as anonymous as a man could be. Why would someone seek him out and beat him early to death?"

"I don't know for sure," Lanchek answered slowly, "because Kermit never talked much, but I think he knew somethin' he shouldn't have known." Lanchek sat back in his chair and looked around, perhaps checking for eavesdroppers.

I leaned across the table, "Johnny, for whatever it's worth, I agree with you. I'm not going to tell you why I agree, because I think you're better off not knowing, but I need your help."

The Michigan Mile Room was full of people, all studying *Racing Form*s, rehashing the race just finished, or discussing expectations for the race soon to be run. Johnny Lanchek, as avid and intense a bettor as they come, was strangely oblivious of all that went on around him. He pushed the remnants of the sandwich aside and fired up a cigarette.

"A couple of weeks into this race meeting, I tapped out. You know how it goes." Lanchek smiled sheepishly and shook his head in self-mockery. "No big deal. Hell, it happens all the time. But this time, Kermit's givin' me a ration of shit about it. We're sittin' up at the bar and we both had a few and Kermit offers to loan me a thousand dollars, provided I stick with him and learn how to handicap the races right. I tell him no thanks, because first of all, it isn't any problem for me to get some money, and second, Poet, I couldn't see myself doing the things he does. He'll sit all day and bet one race. Me, I get bored. I've got to have the action, you know what I mean? So I tell him this and he gets hot, you know?

" 'Johnny,' he says, 'in all the years I've known you, you never made a nickel at the races and, goddammit, the way you play the game, you never will. Sure you score some big trifectas every now and then, but you throw it away like you're pissing on the floor and the track soaks it up like a big sponge. What're you gonna do when you can't work anymore? Your hands get shaky or your eyesight goes?''

Lanchek paused to light another cigarette. "He got to me, Poet," he continued. "It's not like I haven't known for a long time that what he was saying was true, but hearing it from him, just that way . . . hell, I'm fifty-five years old, I know I've got emphysema from smoking these things, and about all I have to show for myself is the money in my pocket.

"So I take him up on his offer. Every day I'm following him around like a puppy and I only bet the way he tells me to bet, when he tells me to do it. He even got me up at five o'clock in the morning to go watch workouts. One day we sat through a whole program and didn't make a bet. Fucking unreal.'' He stubbed out his cigarette and stared hard at me.

"But we were making money, Poet," he declared emphatically. "No spectacular killing, just steady profits and I'm feeling good about it. I'm going to the track every day expecting to win money, instead of hoping to get lucky.''

I understood exactly what Lanchek was saying and told him so: Kermit had been performing the same task with chronic loser Johnny Lanchek that had turned my own self-destructive slide around.

"I pissed and moaned," Lanchek continued, chuckling at the recollection. "Jesus Christ, up in the morning watching workouts, five hours at the track in the afternoon, studying the *Racing Form* at night. I never worked so hard in my life, I'm tellin' you. And all this looking at horses. Hell, I mean to me, they all look alike, you know. But that Kermit, he wouldn't let up a bit. He kept saying, 'You gotta keep your eyes open. There's bullshit going down here all the time and if you watch, you can be on the winning end of it.' ''

I smiled as the same words echoed in my memory.

"You know, he's telling me this and I'm tired and I'm bored, because shit, betting on races is fun. This is work. I'm doing a lot more working than betting and Kermit says to me, 'John, what do you want? You wanna quit? Quit! Go cut some tools and bring back some more money to shovel through the windows,' He's really pissed and he takes out his notebook and shoves it under my nose and he says, 'See that?' And, of course, I can't see shit because he's got it right up under my face. 'Twenty-four thousand dollars. One bet, and not some half-baked trifecta where the three longest shots on the board come first, second, and third. One bet, one thousand dollars at 24-1 and I never had a doubt when I made it.' ''

Lanchek smiled wryly and lit up another cigarette seconds after putting out his last. "Naturally, he's got my attention, but he just shoves the notebook in his pocket and he won't say anything more about it. He just tells me to keep my eyes open and don't piss away my bankroll and be ready when it happens."

He paused long enough to watch a race being run on the television monitor. Lanchek watched the race closely, but without visible emotion. He had nothing wagered on the outcome. The announcer's voice intoned, describing the positioning and repositioning of the striving horses, and the tension in the room increased, both palpably and audibly, as the race drew out toward its conclusion.

So Kermit had made a big score, I thought to myself. Picky Peaches at 24-1, no doubt. Johnny Lanchek believed that Kermit was not a victim of random violence, and certainly in Lanchek's mind, at least, that big score must be related to Kermit's current condition. I stifled my impatience with some effort and waited for Lanchek to resume his narrative. The race was posted "official" and the din subsided.

Lanchek chuckled sarcastically. I couldn't tell if his amusement was self-deprecating or derisive. "There, you've seen it with your own eyes, Tennyson," he said after a moment. "When have you ever seen me pass a race?" He dragged deeply on the unfiltered cigarette as though the smoke was his first after long abstinence rather than his third or fourth since the two us had been sitting together.

"Johnny, you said that you believe that the attack on Kermit was planned," I prompted. "You mentioned this big score he made, but Boog said his money was still there." The question brought Lanchek back to reality and the fear returned to his face.

"It wasn't the money, Tennyson," he said flatly.

"Hell, we made another big score later. Flew to Chicago to do it."

Damn, I swore silently, Kermit knows everything and he can't talk.

"The money figures in," Lanchek continued. "But that's not all of it. You see, there was this guy. We were watching workouts early one morning, just drinking coffee and shootin' the shit with the clockers. Kermit sees this guy leading a horse to the track and he turns white as a ghost and he shuffles around behind some other people so this guy won't see him."

"Who was this guy?" I asked eagerly.

Lanchek shook his head. "I asked Kermit, and he kinda mumbled somethin'. Sounded like a name, but then he caught himself and told me I didn't want to know. No doubt about it, this guy was bad-lookin'. Big, maybe six-two or six-three, and built like one of those bodybuilders, but as strong as he looked, it was his face I'll never forget. He was totally bald, not even a stubble, and his face was mangled. You know, scars, almost no nose, and half his mouth looked like it was just gone. The scars looked like he had been in a fire. You know what I mean? Burn scars."

Marcel Larrance! There could be no mistake.

Lanchek thought for a minute and then shook his head mournfully. "I just don't remember any name, Tennyson. I remember how he looked and that Kermit was scared shitless of him, but the name? I'm not even sure I heard it. Anyway," he went on, "we moved away from the clocker's stand while that monster was hanging around. The guy waits while the horse steps off a slow half-mile and then he collects her and heads back for the barns."

"So this guy is a trainer?"

"Nah. After he left, we went back and asked the clocker who the horse was. The filly had shipped up from Kentucky, and that kid Tarpley was her trainer. The scar-faced guy must have been a groom or stablehand of some kind."

"What was this horse called, John?"

"Winter Muffin," Lanchek answered without hesitation. "She worked a half-mile in :52 and change or something like that, came back a couple days later, and went five furlongs in 1:07. A week later, she ran six furlongs with five-thousand-dollar maiden fillies, the real bottom of the barrel, and ran tenth in a field of twelve. A regular piece of shit, or so it looked. I just about crapped when a couple of weeks later Kermit shows up with two plane tickets and we fly to Chicago to go to Sportsman's. This same filly, Winter Muffin, is entered with sixty-five-hundred-dollar maidens, and that's who we was going to bet. I thought Kermit had lost his mind."

"Except Winter Muffin won?"

"Bet your ass. Paid fifty-eight dollars, can you believe it?"

"Nice price," I agreed. There was no reason for Lanchek to know that I had bet on Winter Muffin too.

"Hell, she shoulda paid a hundred," Lanchek insisted.

"Somebody put a ton of money on that horse."

"You see, Tennyson, that's what I think the problem was. Kermit and I pushed about a grand apiece through the mutuels on Winter Muffin, and even on a Saturday in Chicago, that amount of money popped the odds pretty good. I think the jokers betting Winter Muffin were expecting to get 35 or 40-1 on her, and we drove the odds down ten to fifteen points. I think that really pissed 'em off."

"But, Johnny, how could they know it was you?"

The look on Lanchek's face was so pitiful, I thought he was going to cry. "It was my fault, Tennyson," he admitted sorrowfully. "We made a bunch of twenty-dollar win and place bets and we were going to spend the rest of the day cashing them one at a time at different windows. Kermit wanted to make damn sure we didn't attract any attention to ourselves, but you know how it is. Old habits are hard to break. I wheeled the horse in the perfecta. 'Exacta,' they call it over there in Chicago. Another fucking long shot ran second and damn if I didn't have to fill out IRS forms. So I'm standing in line filling out the papers and hell, I don't know any bullshit's goin' on. So, while I'm standing in the IRS line, this guy behind me, real friendly, starts talking to me and he asked me how the hell I ever picked that horse and I say, 'My buddy Kermit picked the horse,' and like a fool, I even point him out standing at another window cashing a win ticket. The guy just smiles and says, 'Nice hit' and I didn't think any more of it. I didn't say anything to Kermit about the exacta. I knew he'd be pissed. Then, later on, I see this same guy, you know, the guy in line, and who do you suppose he's talking to, looking our way?"

"The scar-faced guy," I answered flatly with not a doubt in my mind.

Lanchek nodded ruefully. "Shit, Tennyson, I didn't know anything like this would happen. How could I?" he pleaded, as if my absolution would somehow mitigate his guilt.

For what it was worth, I gave it to him. "There was no way you could have known, Johnny. Kermit never warned you that the deal was dangerous."

We sat quietly for a moment, Lanchek lighting the ubiquitous cigarette, no doubt berating himself silently. "There is one thing, Johnny," I said, finally. "I know how Kermit handicaps, and this one is a little unusual. What did he see that made him want to go to Chicago just to bet a cheap maiden?"

"I don't know." Lanchek shrugged. "He didn't say, and every time I asked, he just changed the subject. But I can tell you what I saw. The horse I saw in Detroit that morning was dull. She worked out like she was half-asleep and trotted around the track in a slow time. The horse I saw in Chicago was the same dark chestnut, two white feet, the same white blaze on her forehead, but everything else about her was different. Her head was up, her ears perked, and she was prancing, you know like they do. Now, I know it's pretty much impossible to bring in a ringer anymore, what with the tattoos and stuff. But all I can say is, somebody did one hell of a training job to get that animal that sharp in so little time."

I had thought that my conversations with Boog and Johnny Lanchek had prepared me for seeing Kermit. In fact, I was shocked by the sight of the devastation rendered upon my old friend's body. One leg and both arms were in plaster casts, and some kind of contraption braced his neck and held his head immobile. Both of his eyes were blackened, most of his face either stitched or bruised, virtually all of his front teeth missing.

Boog had described Kermit's condition. "Nothing but

plaster and tubes. He's even got a tube in his dick so he can piss," Boog said mournfully. Indeed, the description was no exaggeration. Oxygen, I.V., heart monitor, catheter, all the props of modern intensive-care medicine. I stood in the corridor leaning against the wall of the ICU, shaking with shock and rage. I could remember sitting in a bar with Kermit more than thirteen years ago. I had been drinking tequila, straight, as was my too-frequent custom at the time. I had known Kermit for about a month, having struck up a conversation with the older man over the miserable task of extrapolating a winner from a field of cheap claimers. My horse had run third. Kermit had passed. To Kermit, I had been another homeless puppy, like Boog, who needed a guiding hand.

"I was married once," Kermit had declared out of the blue as we sat at the bar. "I'd known the girl all my life—loved her since high school. I was working as a bookkeeper for a shipping company out of New Orleans, and all I thought about was making her happy.

"I lost her, son, just like you lost your lady. Not an accident or anything like that, but maybe worse in a way. Booze took her. She drank all the time. Oh, she'd cry and say she'd quit, but then I'd come home from work and she'd be passed out cold on the sofa, a bottle still dangling from her hand.

"I stuck with it for ten years. I just couldn't forget the woman she used to be. But I got so I couldn't take watching her kill herself. That's when I started going to the track regularly.

"The horses saved me, son. And what I'm telling you is, they can save you too. Nothing's gonna bring your lady back, boy. You know that without me saying. But you, son, you got the brains and intuition to be the best, better'n I ever thought about being. Why don't you put that greaser whiskey away and learn how to play the game right? Give yourself a chance to put your life back together."

That was the beginning. Patiently Kermit had instilled his knowledge and experience in me with the patience of a mother spoon-feeding a baby with colic. And, if the wounds left by Jenna's death didn't exactly heal, at least they scarred over. The horses, and Kermit Golightly, had indeed been my salvation.

A doctor came by as I stood in the hospital corridor trying to pull myself together. We spoke for a few moments, but the doctor's prognosis only confirmed what my own eyes had seen. In all likelihood, Kermit's life had come to an end on the floor of a grubby motel room strewn with yellowing *Racing Form*s and cryptic handwritten notes.

As I spoke with the doctor, I became aware of a hospital employee hovering nearby. The worker was a skinny black kid from the housekeeping department who was going through the motions of running an electric buffer over the corridor floor. He had been buffing the area in front of the ICU when I went in to see Kermit and he was still going over the same spot when I came out. Instead of concentrating on the floor, he kept glancing at me.

I told the doctor to see that no effort was spared in Kermit's care. I would be responsible for any medical bills. The doctor escorted me to the nurse's station, where I provided my name and address—to hell with avoiding a paper trail. I needed to be satisfied that no reasonable treatment would be withheld because Kermit had no insurance or obvious funds. The kid had followed, still operating the buffer over a spotless floor, moving closer, as if to monitor my instructions.

I walked down the hall to the elevator, and when I looked back, the kid was leaning over the nurse's counter talking to the duty nurse. The buffer stood by itself against the wall.

When I got off the elevator on the first floor, I spotted the worker immediately, coming out of the door of the stairway. That the kid was observing me, tailing me, was no longer just a possibility.

I didn't feel threatened. Having seen Kermit, I welcomed the chance to lay my hands on anyone remotely connected with his condition. This was just a skinny kid in his late teens or maybe early twenties. Unless he had a gun, he was no danger.

Giving no indication that I had noticed the kid, I walked out the front door and headed for the visitors' parking lot. The kid followed, by no means inconspicuously. Instead of going directly to the car, I ducked behind a van so that the view from the hospital would be obscured. Seconds later, the kid followed. At that instant I grabbed him by the scruff of the neck and shoulders and slammed him into the side of the van. The kid hit the van hard and crumpled to the pavement. His hand went quickly to his back pocket and came out with a sharpened steel comb, the kind designed to open like a switchblade but legal to carry. I kicked it out of his hand. The kid howled and brought his damaged fingers to his mouth, his face contorted with pain.

"You broke my hand, man," he complained after a moment. "I haven't done nothing."

"Sure thing, pal," I agreed, trying to put as much menace in my voice as I could. "I suppose you were just gonna comb your hair?"

"Wasn't planning nothing. Man's gotta protect himself."

"All right. Enough bullshit," I barked impatiently. "Why were you following me?"

"Wasn't following you, man. I was just going to my car," he responded, trying to summon some righteous defiance.

I picked the kid up by the lapels of his white hospital uniform and slammed him against the van again. I didn't want to brutalize the kid, but I had to find out what was going on.

"Let me make sure you understand your situation," I said slowly. "We're behind this van where no one can see us. In just a few seconds I can make you a patient in that hospital rather than an employee—an emergency patient. You are, what you might say, in considerable jeopardy here. Answer my questions and you walk." I didn't know what I would have done had the kid continued to hold out. Fortunately, the boy believed my threat.

"Dude paid me, man. He give me fifty bucks to keep track of who came to visit that old man during my shift. Said he'd give me another twenty for every name I bring him."

"What's this guy's name?" I demanded.

"Don't know his name. Big, mean-looking dude, face all scarred and shit."

Marcel Larrance! Why wasn't I surprised?

"C'mon, man," the kid pleaded, "I was only trying to see what you was driving. I only popped the blade when you attacked me. I thought you were gonna kill me or something."

"Okay, let's assume I'm dumb enough to believe that crock of shit. How were you supposed to get that information to the scar-faced man?"

"He said he be at Frankie's Bar, about a block down from the hospital, every night about eleven o'clock after I get off work. He said if he's not there, come back the next night."

"What about his phone number?"

The kid shook his head. "He didn't give me a phone number. I'm just supposed to go to Frankie's. So far, I ain't got shit outta this deal, except the first fifty dollars and a busted hand."

I leaned over and read the name on the kid's I.D. badge. "Leon White." I stared hard at the kid for a minute, wondering if he knew anything else, but finally decided the boy was too dumb to know much more and too scared to hold back if he did.

"All right, Leon," I said at last, "pack your ass, but don't show your face at Frankie's for the next few nights or you can end up with some serious hurt. Understand?"

"Yessir," the kid said sullenly, scuttling away. After one backward glance, he was in a trot toward the hospital entrance.

A cheap motel on Telegraph Road, cash in advance for the room, no identification necessary. The place could have put up a sign that said "John Smith slept here ten thousand times." There was no phone in the room, but Michigan Bell had an unvandalized pay phone hanging on the wall near the office. Eight o'clock in Detroit, five in L.A. Peter T. Westmoreland answered my call on the third ring. After an exchange of pleasantries, we got down to business.

"Turner didn't want to talk," Peter T. said flatly. "He's been knocking around the tracks for more'n twenty years an' he's tough as boiled owl, but Marcel Larrance has him plenty scared."

"So you didn't have any luck?" I inferred.

"I didn't say that, son." The Texan sounded mildly offended that I would assume the worst. "Tell the truth,

I got lucky. Ol' Turner remembered the Symphony Seven case."

"You're the one who broke the Symphony Seven case?" I interrupted, surprised that I hadn't made the connection. Symphony Seven had been a smallish colt of undistinguished breeding but blessed with an uncommon turn of speed. As a virtual unknown two-year-old, the colt had shocked the racing community by winning the prestigious Hollywood Juvenile Stakes, thereby establishing himself as one of the "winter book" favorites for the Kentucky Derby.

Symphony Seven had wintered in Florida at a farm rented by his owners, a pair of New Jersey real-estate developers. There the colt came to a tragic end. While grazing in a pasture, he was bitten by a rattlesnake and died.

Later the papers reported Symphony Seven had been killed deliberately so the owners could collect the $2.5 million he was insured for. The brilliant and determined efforts of an insurance investigator had foiled the plot.

The case received some national media attention, but within the racing community it was a scandal of major proportions. Until that moment, I had not connected Peter T. with the case.

"He's was 'a game li'l sumbitch,'" I observed, using the words a famous trainer quoted in a *Sports Illustrated* article.

"That he was," Peter T. agreed. "Anyway, Turner remembered the case an' musta figured I wasn't about to let him alone. He don't know much, but he sure has his suspicions. The fight with Marcel that Hodak mentioned came when Turner told ol' Ugly to get his goddamn horse outta Turner's barn."

"Sounds like Turner's got more than suspicions."

"Maybe. All he would say was, he knew something wasn't right."

"Shit," I cursed, "We already know something isn't right."

"Take it easy," he cautioned. "There's more. Turner claims there's an exercise rider, name of Pedro Estrella, who knows a lot more. He told me where this Estrella spends his evenings. I'll check it out tonight and fly out in the morning."

When my turn came, I recounted the day's events, beginning with Boog's delivering of the news about Kermit and culminating with my encounter with the Sinai Hospital orderly. Peter T. listened carefully as I reconstructed Johnny Lanchek's story, and his interest peaked when I expressed my conclusion that Marcel Larrance had stalked and attacked Kermit. When I stated my intention of going to Frankie's Bar that evening, he balked.

"Oh, that sounds like a great idea, son," he said sarcastically. "What were you plannin' to do? Walk into this Frankie's, get this boy out behind the building, and beat some information out of him?"

"Well . . ." I started to protest.

" 'Cause if that's what you had in mind, you're probably not going to like your end of that deal."

"All right, all right," I conceded. "You've made your point, but we've got this guy connected with Winter Muffin here and in Chicago, and we may also have him in L.A."

"Why don't we do it this way," Peter T. suggested. "I'll talk to this Estrella and catch the red-eye. Then we'll have all day to check out the situation and go to this bar together."

"But that puts us one more day behind," I objected. "This guy is clearly linked to two of the horses. Plus there's no reason on earth for him to pay someone to keep track of who visits Kermit in the hospital, unless he was the one who put him there. If he takes off, we're screwed. We've got nothing."

"Don't be stupid. If he takes off, we'll find him again. It's not like the sonofabitch is inconspicuous-looking! He's bound to turn up wherever the horses are."

Everything that Peter T. was saying was true, but I had no interest in hearing rational arguments. Peter T. may have had the patience of a trained investigator, but I had the urgent perspective of a potential victim.

"Let's compromise, Peter T.," I offered finally. "I'll go there tonight just to make sure he shows up, and I'll take somebody with me for backup. There's no reason Marcel Larrance would know who I am, but, if for some reason he does, I think my friend Boog would give him plenty of reason to keep his distance. If everything's cool, we'll follow him and find out where he's staying here in town. When I pick you up at the airport tomorrow, we can decide what to do."

Peter T. continued his protest, but finally gave in grudgingly, after I promised that, under no circumstances, would I confront the scar-faced man and that I would absolutely have a 350-pound ex-football player as a backup. The Texan hung up and then called back five minutes later with his flight schedule, once again repeating his admonitions. I placed one more call to Johnny Lanchek to confirm that Boog still lived in the same place and then set out to organize the night's activity.

Boog kept an apartment in the once-fashionable Palmer Park area in northwest Detroit. The building was well-maintained and Boog's spacious one-bedroom apartment was neat and comfortable. He paid the rent on the place year-round, even though he spent the winter months in Florida.

Boog had expensive taste in home furnishing: chrome-and-leather furniture, a high-tech entertainment center with the newest vintage stereo components, television, and VCR. His bedroom, however, looked like it came out of Arabian Nights. What he didn't have was a telephone—not because he couldn't afford one, but because of his need for total anonymity.

Like Kermit, Boog settled all his obligations in cash, maintained no bank accounts, and of course filed no tax returns. He had arranged for all his utilities to be included with his rent, which he paid several months in advance in cash. His landlord carried Boog's apartment on his books as a model apartment and pocketed the rent payments. The system worked neatly for all concerned, except for someone like me who needed to contact Boog in a hurry.

As I feared, Boog wasn't home. I left a note indicating that I had a line on the guy who had beat up Kermit and asking Boog to meet me at Frankie's between ten and ten-thirty P.M. I was confident Boog would show up—if he got the message. Once again firing up the old Caddy, I drove a couple blocks east to Woodward Avenue and about a mile south to Uncle Johnny's Louisiana Kitchen. Since Boog was a regular at Uncle Johnny's, there was a reasonable chance he would put in an appearance. Besides, I was hungry and Uncle Johnny's turned out some of the best food in the city.

I spent the next several hours shooting the breeze with Uncle Johnny Rosier and his son, Bill. When Boog failed to make an appearance, I decided, against the advice of my friends, to explore Frankie's alone.

"I promise I won't do anything stupid," I assured the Rosiers. "Just send Boog if he shows up."

"You'll already be doing something stupid if you go to Frankie's by yourself," Johnny Rosier told me with great certainty. "You think you're bulletproof or something?"

I checked Boog's apartment one more time. The note was still in the door. Good judgment told me to heed the advice of Peter T. and the Rosiers. I knew very well how dangerous the Detroit inner city could be even without the specter of the scar-faced man. But the thought of Kermit lying comatose dispelled all caution. This thing had gone beyond vindication.

7

One look at Frankie's gave me reason to pause and rethink my hastily formed plan. While I certainly had been warned, I wasn't totally prepared for what I saw before me. The flashing pink neon sign outside the building proudly announced "Topless Entertainment" and it featured little silhouettes of nude women in dancing positions. The building was free-standing, with a parking lot next door. The little hut intended to house a parking-lot attendant was empty. Apparently its purpose was to provide just the illusion of security.

Having seen the place, I was even more uneasy about having failed to make contact with Boog. Even if the scar-faced man were not present, Frankie's was likely to be dangerous. A stranger alone, in no way intimidating in either size or demeanor, would very likely look like a victim to a fair number of the bar's patrons.

I gave some serious consideration to driving off, to wait for Peter T. Westmoreland and Boog. The place looked that bad. What the hell, I thought, rehashing the same arguments I had given Peter T. on the phone, I'm here, let's see if our man is here. If he doesn't show in the next half-hour, pay up and leave.

Clutching the frail straw of hope that Boog had checked in at Uncle Johnny's and was now on his way to back me up, I parked and locked the old Caddy and went inside. The interior of Frankie's fulfilled the exterior's promise of grime, crime, sloth, and sleaze. On one side of the room was a bar with seating for around twenty customers. Most of the stools were occupied by patrons who paid no attention to the stage opposite the bar. There a slightly overweight white woman in high heels, G-string, and what looked like a cut-off T-shirt, was gyrating half-heartedly to rock music.

There was a low counter surrounding the stage, designed for up-close viewing of the entertainment. Only one of these seats was occupied, by an obese white man, complete with scraggly beard and tattoos, slobbering into his beer like an overweight bulldog. The rest of the seating consisted of uncomfortable chairs clustered around postage-stamp-size tables. As my eyes adjusted to the darkness, I discerned that a few were in use.

Behind the stage were mirrors, intended no doubt to enhance the view of the dancer. While the mirror did reveal the heart-shaped tattoo of the dancer's ample buttock, there was little enhancement to be had. The rest of the walls were covered with some kind of red and black flocked wall covering, no doubt someone's idea of what a Victorian brothel might have on its walls. The carpet's once-red color had long given way to dirty footprints and streaks of grease.

There were fewer than thirty patrons on hand, all of whom looked as though their careers covered the full range of the Michigan Criminal Code, with nothing but needle tracks, jagged scars, and a couple of centuries of jail time to show for their efforts. In its own way, Frankie's was a "workingman's bar" with pushers coming off shift, burglars waiting to go on, and muggers, pimps, and armed robbers on break.

For a Detroit inner-city bar, Frankie's had an exotically diverse racial mixture among its clientele. The club's location placed it in an area where the city's black majority overlapped an already large and growing Arab population. As if that combination were not explosive enough, Frankie's had a large contingent of big biker types, complete with Nazi insignia and Aryan Brotherhood tattoos.

There had to be something beyond the handful of dumpy dancers to attract these volatile factions to the same place, I reasoned. What it might be, I could only guess, and none of the hypotheses gave me any reason for comfort. Despite the almost laconic atmosphere, this was hardball, Detroit style, where unreasoning violence would erupt in the blink of an eye. All I could be sure of was that Death was open for business at Frankie's seven nights a week.

I was almost relieved that the scar-faced man wasn't present. Inquiring about him from the crowd at Frankie's seemed a singularly bad idea, so I found a seat at a table near the door. Reminding myself of the allocated half-hour time limit, I sat down to wait.

After a moment a tall, well-built black woman, obviously a dancer awaiting her turn onstage, strolled over and sat down at my table. Adopting her most flirtatious manner, she offered both a drink of my choice and company while I drank it. Although I knew that a drink for her would be overpriced and mostly water, I reasoned that the expense would, for a time at least, afford the protection of hospitality. Allowing a paying customer to be hassled would be bad business.

The dancer, "Vanessa" she informed me, returned and collected four dollars for my bourbon and water and eight for her champagne cocktail. She pulled her chair close enough so that I could smell the combination of her perfume and sweat on her well-constructed body, laid a playful hand on my thigh, and launched into her standard "customer-entertainment" spiel aimed at encouraging additional drink purchases with the promise of undefined intimacies yet to come.

I played along, fabricating a story that undoubtedly matched up with tales she had heard hundreds of times before. Vanessa's company quickly cost me around thirty dollars in drinks and tips, but it served its purpose as I blended into the "scene" at Frankie's. No one paid me undue attention.

I was about to give up the surveillance when the scar-faced man walked in. He hesitated a moment at the door, as if to survey the premises, before taking a seat at the bar. The bartender placed a beer and a glass in front of him without being asked and without offering any greeting. I got the impression that the scar-faced man was familiar, but not exactly welcome.

"Do you know that guy?" I asked when Vanessa gave off an involuntary shudder as the scar-faced man passed the table.

"No," she answered emphatically. "An' I don' wanna know him either. Man is bad news."

"He is pretty fierce-looking," I agreed.

Vanessa shook her head. "It ain't just his looks that's bad. My friend Leslie, she's a dancer here too. She went out with him two days ago. I ain't seen her since. I know that motherfucker did something to her. I know it." Vanessa suddenly looked less like a painted and perfumed seductress and more like a frightened child. I saw the same almost hypnotic horror that tough little Dina Conklin had displayed when talking about Marcel.

"No shit?" I tried to sound casual. "Did you call the cops? File a report or anything?"

"You kiddin'? Man, you work in a place like this, you don' be callin' no cops for nothin'."

"What about the management? Don't they give you girls any protection?"

"Usually they do, you know, but Marcel's got them scared or somethin'. They don' fuck with him at all. Kenny, he's the bartender, he pretty bad, but he don' fuck with Marcel, no way."

I could readily see why Kenny the bartender didn't want any part of Marcel. Johnny Lanchek's description didn't do him justice. The scar-faced man was built like a professional wrestler—six-foot-four or so, maybe 240 or 250 pounds to go with his fearsome visage. He had the arms and shoulders of someone who worked out regularly with weights, and his hands, scarred like his face, were huge and powerful-looking. Inflicting the damage that Kermit had suffered would have been child's play to Marcel. I could only imagine the range of atrocity this walking nightmare might have performed on Vanessa's dancer friend.

"He looks like someone to stay away from," I said as casually as I could manage.

"You got that right," Vanessa said distantly, repeating the shudder.

I bought Vanessa two more drinks and we carried on with what a friend of mine called "tit-bar flirtation." All the while I studied the scar-faced man. My chair was positioned so that I could observe Marcel without attracting his attention. Marcel, in turn, downed several beers while watching the dancers with interest. He seemed to have taken no notice of me.

"I have to dance now," Vanessa informed me as she

stroked my leg. "You gonna stay awhile?" She was no doubt earning commissions on the drinks I was buying and she didn't want to lose a "live one."

"Sure. I'll be around for a while. I'm looking forward to watching you dance."

"Good, 'cause I'll come back after my set and maybe we can talk about some serious things."

The implied promise of "serious things" was almost comical, but I suppressed amusement and simply smiled in agreement. There had been, probably still were, some go-go clubs in this town where the dancing was nothing more than an "advertisement" for prostitution. Most of these, however, did not serve liquor and the dancers performed totally nude. Frankie's served alcohol, so topless was as far as the entertainers could go, and the scrutiny of liquor-control-board and law-enforcement agencies was tighter. The odds were less than even money that Vanessa was hustling anything more than drinks.

In my case it didn't matter. I would act like any other customer who became enamored of a dancer—buy drinks, try to cop feels, and otherwise act like a complete fool. Then, when Marcel left, I would stagger out like any other drunk, and, with luck, follow the scar-faced man to wherever he was staying. Simple, I thought. Brilliant.

Though I had paid scant attention, I had somehow noted that the dancers performed a set consisting of three songs. In the first, they removed no clothing. About halfway through the second, they wiggled out of their tops. The third was topless from start to finish. This routine did not vary from dancer to dancer. In fact, the records played varied little regardless of the performer. Same act, same music, same lack of enthusiasm—the whole show has as much sex appeal as Lawrence Welk reruns.

Vanessa, to her credit, at least put some animation into her act. I could see that she was a good, albeit untrained, dancer. Perhaps her enthusiasm could be attributed to the fact that she had already attracted the attention of a paying customer and wanted to ensure that the ardor would be maintained. Whatever the motivation, she did get across the impression that she enjoyed dancing.

Marcel, who had been watching the somewhat dumpy, tattooed white dancers with interest, turned away from Vanessa's act with what seemed to be unconcealed contempt. Since Vanessa's act was the first I had seen remotely approaching sexy, I had to conclude that Marcel had considerable revulsion for blacks. Common sense would dictate that such a prejudice would best be kept private, given the company with whom Marcel shared the bar, but Marcel made a show of it in a manner that could only be perceived as an open challenge. Even so, if anyone found his attitude offensive, no one protested the point. Marcel clearly had the patrons of Frankie's buffaloed.

Once again the image of Kermit, in his plaster and tubes, filled me with a cold rage. I felt a foolhardy temptation to challenge the scar-faced man, despite the complete awareness that I would have no chance against the monstrous Marcel.

Somehow these thoughts must have projected themselves, for I found myself staring directly into Marcel's eyes, receiving first a look of pure malevolence followed by one of amused contempt. In places like Frankie's, silent confrontations like these frequently led to bloodshed, yet I could not, would not drop my gaze. The instant stretched to an eternity and I knew I would soon hear, "What the fuck are you lookin' at, asshole?" Even worse, I recognized that I was on the verge of issuing challenge myself.

I felt arms encircle my neck, lips pressing close to my ear, a voice whispering urgently, "Are you crazy? Look at me, man."

Vanessa, having finished her dance and having observed the interaction between Marcel and me, had acted to save me from what was likely to be certain destruction. She had no reason to care what happened to me, but, inexplicably, she did. The tension flowed out of me and the heat of the moment subsided. I returned her caress as if my only interest had been her return.

"You got some kinda death wish or somethin'?" she whispered. I could hear the relief in her voice. The music was playing again and another dancer had taken her place on the stage. "I thought you were goin' after Marcel. Man, he'd kill you."

I couldn't deny that she was probably right, and as the rush of the moment passed, I felt a faint wave of nausea. A waitress brought two more drinks. I paid and tipped the waitress, and in the process, peeled off a hundred-dollar bill, folded it twice, and stuck it in Vanessa's garter.

"Wait a minute, man," she protested, "I don' do—"

I held up a hand to cut her off. "Of course you don't," I agreed gently. "It's just that I may have to leave suddenly and I want you to know that I've enjoyed your company. Take the money and do something nice for yourself."

She stared at me with an incredulous look on her face. "You goin' after Marcel, aren't you? Man you're crazy. What you gonna be tanglin' with him for? You'll just get yourself killed. You a cop of somethin'?"

"No, I'm not a cop," I assured her, certain that she knew I was not a policeman. Cops do not hand out hundred-dollar bills as gratuities to topless dancers. "Let's just say that Marcel and I have something of a score to settle."

She shook her head. "You'll be dead if you try to settle with that dude, unless you got a gun, an' I know you ain't got no gun. Forget that motherfucker an' hang around till I get off. Keep me company instead of gettin' your ass kicked."

As unlikely as it seemed, I sensed that her offer had nothing to do with the hundred-dollar bill or the promise of more to come. Perhaps the apparent hopelessness of my confrontation with Marcel had stimulated some protective instinct in her, or maybe the fact that I had treated her as something other than a piece of meat touched her in some way. Whatever her reasons, I believed her concern was genuine and it warmed me.

"Don't worry, Vanessa. I'm not as crazy as you think. I just have to find out where he goes from here and where he's staying. That's all." As I said the words, I believed them. But Vanessa wasn't buying it for a minute. She said no more, but her expression revealed the depth of her experience with the idiocy of men.

I ordered another round, grateful that Frankie's did not pour an honest drink. Vanessa relaxed and Marcel seemed once again absorbed with the dancers. The bikers mumbled together in some indecipherable code, perhaps relating to drugs or women. I remarked on their presence to Vanessa without any real curiosity.

"This is business to them," she observed seriously. "They own a couple of clubs over on the east side and I hear that they're lookin' to expand." She followed with a succinct and surprisingly knowledgeable account of the structure of the topless-entertainment business in Detroit, including the involvement of Arabs, bikers, and the Mob. As I suspected earlier, many of the joints were fronts for prostitution and drugs. When I observed that it was obviously a complicated and dangerous business, she merely shrugged. It was the best living she believed she could earn, hazards notwithstanding. Where Vanessa came from, life was complicated and dangerous.

Vanessa was onstage for the second time when the scar-faced man left his seat at the bar and went down a narrow corridor toward the rear of the club. The men's room, I assumed. I glanced at Vanessa on the stage and could tell from her anxious look that she, too, had noticed Marcel's movement. I waited impatiently for Marcel to resume his seat, hoping fervently that I would not have to follow him through the narrow hallway and out a back door. But somehow, I knew Marcel had not gone to relieve his bladder, and after waiting longer than I knew was reasonable, I followed.

The men's room was down the corridor, but Marcel was not inside, as I had known all along he would not be. A dusty but still legal exit sign marked the back door at the end of the hall. Suddenly all I could think of was Marcel escaping undetected. Our best connection disappearing while I sipped whiskey in a sleazy go-go joint. I hit the back door on the run. Marcel was waiting and I could not have made things easier for him.

I sensed rather than saw the blow coming, and made a belated effort to duck. Marcel's shot missed the back of my head, but landed full force at the point where my neck and shoulders came together. I never saw what Marcel had in his hand—a sap, a blackjack—but the blow sent me sprawling, stunned, and gasping for breath.

When my vision cleared, Marcel was standing over me. And the scar-faced man had company. I had come to rest with my back up against a filthy dumpster, my limbs unwilling to respond. Marcel's devastated face was twisted into his version of a malevolent grin. Beside him, looking considerably more dangerous than the skinny kid

I had handled so easily that afternoon, was Leon White, accompanied by two of his friends. Leon looked especially glad to see me, but not in a way that gave me any cause for hope.

"Mr. Wilder's playin' detective," Marcel drawled. "I thought you were goin' to be a hardass back there until the bitch came back. Might have been interesting, but I doubt it." For sport, he leaned over and backhanded me with a short snap of his wrist. As casual as the blow had been, the man's strength was awesome and my head rocked back against the steel dumpster. I nearly passed out again.

"Well, you found me, detective. Ain't you lucky? Oh, yeah, I did kick the shit outta your buddy, that old fart, just so you know." The memory seemed to give him some pleasure. "I guess maybe the question is, 'who's been found?' I understand some people been looking for you." Marcel glanced slowly at Leon White and his friends, checking to see if they were appreciating his sense of humor. Apparently they found him sufficiently amusing, for Marcel turned back to me.

"They're gonna find you, most likely in the same hospital as your friend," Marcel continued. "I'd like to stick around and participate in this little party, but I'm afraid I might get carried away. Besides, old Leon here has been pining for a chance to renew acquaintances with you. I guess you sort of embarrassed him a little this afternoon. I won't be seeing you again, railbird, but that's the last piece of luck you're gonna have in this lifetime."

Marcel turned his back and walked about twenty feet to a battered pickup truck of indeterminate age and color. Climbing in and starting the engine, he called Leon over to the truck, where he issued final instructions, inaudible over the engine noise. As Leon turned to go, Marcel grabbed him by the scruff of the neck. "Don't fuck up," Marcel warned loud enough for me to hear. Leon tried to look tough and cool, but the fear he held for the scarfaced man was evident.

My breath was returning by then and I used the brief respite to assess the situation. Unfortunately, Leon's buddies both looked bigger and stronger than the skinny hospital employee. While one tapped a leather sap in his palm, the other fitted a set of brass knuckles on his right hand. I moaned as if I were still dazed, and moved my legs into a better position to get to my feet. I knew my only hope was to get in the first lick and keep moving. On my back, I was a piece of meat for their punching pleasure.

Leon rejoined his accomplices as the battered pickup drove away. Having Marcel out of the game was some small consolation. I recognized that my chances against these three, even armed as they were, were better than against Marcel by himself.

The two accomplices looked expectantly at Leon. "Let him come around a little bit," Leon instructed. "I want him to know what hit him. On your feet, buddy, it's show time."

I struggled to stand, exaggerating the slowness of movement and feigning considerable pain. Leon's overconfidence was good fortune. While I had no great illusions of overcoming all three, I knew that I was going to get some licks in. With luck, I could get a couple of shots at Leon himself.

As I got to my feet, the three started to close in. I doubled over as though I were going to throw up. Instinctively my would-be assailants stopped short, thereby giving me the opening I needed. Wheeling to my left as I straightened up, I caught the kid with the brass knuckles with a hard right to the jaw. The kid's head snapped back and he went down hard. Leon, in the middle, reacted too slowly and my backhand blow landed squarely on the side of his head. Leon backpedaled a few steps but did not go down. Recovering his balance, he shook his head, brought up the sharpened comb, and advanced cautiously.

The kid with the sap took a wild swing which missed scrambling my brains but did glance off my left shoulder. The force of the blow was mostly spent, but my left side went numb. The kid circled warily, putting distance between himself and Leon so that I couldn't attack both of them together. A veteran of previous muggings, I thought wryly.

In the meantime, the third assailant was struggling to his feet and I was again facing three against one. I considered the kid with the sap the most dangerous, so I shuffled away from him to attack "brass knuckles" while he was still groggy. My left arm throbbed, tingled, and hung uselessly at my side. Still, I knew my only hope was to maintain the offensive.

The bright lights of a car froze my attackers in place. There was just a moment's hesitation as the trio looked at each other in indecision. As if some instantaneous signal had been passed, the three turned and bolted into the darkness of the alley.

I heard the report of a gun and a high-pitched and frightened command. "Hold it right there!" There followed only the pounding of six running feet, which faded to leave only the thundering of my heart. I sagged against the side of the building in pain and exhaustion. My unknown savior remained obscured behind the car door as the vehicle's bright lights blinded me.

I reeled away from the building and took two steps toward the car.

"Stay right where you are!" the voice ordered. A feminine voice.

I staggered backward in confusion. I could see a small form crouched behind the door and I could make out the pistol leveled at me. I tried to raise my hands, but my left shoulder was still numb. The movement threw me off-balance and I sat heavily on the ground. Fuck it, I thought, disgustedly.

"My God, it's you!" the voice exclaimed. The figure, clearly a woman, slammed the car door and rushed to my side. As she moved into the light and her features became clear, I recognized her. The woman from the plane.

I tried to struggle to my feet, but my body wouldn't respond. Here was another unnamed pursuer, but there was nothing I could do. She must have been following me all day, and now she had me.

"Shit," I muttered in pain and confusion.

In the moments following the encounter in the alley behind Frankie's, I had assumed the young woman had been following me since my arrival in Detroit. I had no doubt she intended to finish the job Leon White and his friends had started. I was just too exhausted to resist. Then, as I regained my senses, I realized that she was white as a ghost and quaking with fear. I remember thinking that this, certainly, was no "hit person."

She had been no less confused. The shock of recognizing me from the plane, followed by the realization that she had come very close to shooting a human being, was too much for her. She turned her face away and let the tears flow. Baffled by the turn of events, I struggled to my feet to comfort her.

"Who are you?" she demanded after the tears subsided. "What the hell are you doing here?"

"Who am I?" I exclaimed, now thoroughly confounded. "What're you talking about? You've been following me all day."

"Following you? Are you crazy? I was following . . . I was following someone else."

"Who?" I demanded, not believing her.

"It doesn't matter," she answered, dismayed. "He's gone."

"Who?" I insisted.

"Marcel Larrance, for whatever it's worth."

The revelation was too much for me on top of everything else. None of this made sense. I could only respond with uncontrollable laughter.

After we both regained our composure, she helped me into her car. Her intention had been to take me to a nearby hospital for treatment, but I convinced her that a strong shot of caffeine was all I needed.

As we sat facing one another in a booth in an all-night coffee shop, emotion gave way to indignation.

"Who are you?" she demanded. "And what was going on back there?"

"You mean you really don't know?" I asked, incredulous.

"What are you talking about?"

"You were reading my dossier on the airplane. I thought you were following me. I'm Tennyson Wilder."

This time she stared in disbelief. Then the humor of the situation overtook her and she mimicked my earlier reaction, laughing hysterically until more tears flowed.

"I don't believe this," she said finally, when her laughter subsided. "When I saw you on the airplane, I was trying to figure out what you did for a living. It's a game I play. The only clue I had was *The Thoroughbred*

Record, so I made up this fantasy that you were a big-time gambler on his way to a betting coup. I remember thinking: Wouldn't it be a hoot if this guy were really Tennyson Wilder?"

"Then you weren't following me?"

"Hell no. I was . . . Wait a minute. What were you doing at that miserable place?"

I thought about my answer. "The same thing you were doing," I said at last. "Following Marcel Larrance."

"Marcel Larrance!" she nearly shouted. Heads in nearby booths turned in our direction.

"Don't you think it's time you told me who you are and why you're carrying around my dossier?" I prompted.

"My name is Lucinda DeGuerre. I'm an investigator for the Thoroughbred Protective Bureau. I'm investigating a case of possible race-fixing."

This was the mysterious DeGuerre Al Hodak had mentioned when Peter T. and I had explored Hollywood Park. Up until that point, I had thought she would be some kind of relentless harpy to be avoided at all cost. Instead I found her an attractive woman of uncommon courage—perhaps an ally rather than an enemy.

We talked far into the night, consuming endless cups of coffee and finally a gargantuan breakfast. I told Luci the whole story, from Kermit Golightly's first tip right up until that afternoon when I had found Kermit in a comatose state, a victim of Marcel Larrance. I explained Peter T. Westmoreland's involvement and what the detective had learned in California.

In turn she told me of her investigation into what she had considered suspicious races. By the time we had compared notes, neither of us was any closer to solving the mystery, but Luci was prepared to agree that I was a victim rather than a participant. Right now, Marcel Larrance was the key link to the real conspirators.

"What were you doing when I came through the back door of Frankie's and Marcel nailed me? I mean, if you were following him, why didn't you intervene then?"

She nearly choked on a sip of coffee and blushed profusely. "If you must know, I had to pee. There was no way I was going into that sleazy joint. There was a Burger King down the street."

"So you rescued me, not even knowing what was going on?" I noted. "That can be pretty dangerous in a town like this. Hell, it could have been a drug deal gone sour . . . anything."

"Seemed like the thing to do at the time." She shrugged. Then she favored me with an irresistible grin. "It's a good thing I'd just been to the bathroom, though."

"And now Marcel is gone," I said, feeling the loss.

"But I know where he's staying," Luci countered with a glint of triumph in her eyes.

"Jesus Christ! Why are we sitting here?"

We detoured long enough to pick up the Caddy from Frankie's parking lot. I followed Luci to the doughnut shop where she had spent the late afternoon and evening staking out Marcel's motel room. Marcel's truck was not in the motel lot across the street.

"It's four-thirty in the morning," Luci complained. "Where can he be?"

"In a town like this, he could be anywhere," I speculated. "A red-blooded American ghoul like Marcel is probably in a graveyard someplace trying to dig up a piece of ass."

Luci chuckled, glancing at me out of the corner of her eye. "What if he's checked out?" she asked, voicing her concern.

A call from a nearby phone booth reached a surly clerk, who, after cursing in protest, confirmed that Marcel was still registered.

"What if he just left?" Luci was still not satisfied.

"One way to find out," I suggested.

"Wait a minute. You're not thinking of breaking in?"

"Beats the hell out of sitting here all night. We'd feel pretty stupid if Marcel's on his way to who-knows-where."

"But that's illegal," she protested.

I merely rolled my eyes. "No problem," I said. "You stay here and sound the horn if he drives in. I'll check out the room." I opened the door and stepped out.

"Shit," Luci muttered. Then she jumped out and followed. "You're crazy if you think I'm just going to sit there by myself." We scampered across the street.

By the number of cars in the lot, I guessed that the motel was about half-full. This joint made my own no-tell motel look like a Hyatt Regency. The area in front of Marcel's door was illuminated by an unprotected one-hundred-watt light bulb. I jumped and gave the bulb a twist. The heat from the bulb scorched my fingers, but the pain in my shoulders and neck made me dizzy.

I extracted a credit card from my money clip. "This always works on television," I said doubtfully. I fumbled for a few moments while Luci looked on with amusement. I straightened up, cursing with exasperation and wondering how much attention we might attract if I kicked the door in.

Without a word, Luci relieved me of the credit card, and within seconds the door swung open. She answered my questioning stare with a look of feigned innocence as she handed back the card.

"Tennyson, what if he comes back?"

"Do you still have that gun?"

She nodded.

"If he comes back, shoot him."

Marcel was not coming back. A matchbook advertising Frankie's was the only evidence he had ever used the room. In fact, the room was cleaner than it probably had ever been.

Despite the room's almost spotless condition, we could feel Marcel's presence. The malevolence was palpable.

Something terrible happened here," she told me with conviction, without knowing why she felt so strongly. Her expression was the same as that of Dina Conklin and Vanessa.

I considered telling her about Vanessa's missing friend, but decided she had seen enough for one night. Wordlessly I led her from the room, back to the cars.

8

Back at my motel room, I placed a series of phone calls which finally penetrated the airline bureaucracy and left a message for Peter T., now en route from the West Coast. I wanted him to stay in Chicago instead of boarding the Detroit connection. An hour later, his call awakened me from a dead-to-the-world sleep.

I had to hustle to shower and meet Luci at the Detroit airport, so I promised to explain everything later. I asked him to rent a suite at the Hyatt Regency near O'Hare Airport and told him I would see him in a few hours. I hung up and stumbled off to the shower.

Three hours later, when Luci and I deplaned in Chicago, Peter T. was waiting by the gate. After I introduced Luci, the Texan led the way to the nearest concourse cocktail lounge. Without consulting either Luci or me, he ordered three Bloody Marys and carried them to our corner table.

"It's a tradition," he explained. "I prefer beer most of the time, but I always have a Bloody Mary whenever I survive air travel. If you don't like these, I'll get you something else and drink these myself, but if you don't mind my saying, you two look like you can use one."

Luci allowed that a Bloody Mary would be just fine. I was too tired to be discriminating.

"I've been looking forward to meeting you for a long time, Mr. Westmoreland," Luci said. "I really admired your work on the Symphony Seven case."

"Darlin'." Peter T. beamed broadly. "I only answer to 'Peter T.' Mr. Westmoreland has been my daddy for as long as I can remember, an' he ain't ready to give up the title. You know, you're the second person to mention

Symphony Seven in the last day or so. I'm startin' to feel famous."

"I don't know about famous," Luci responded, "but the case certainly made the rounds at our office. Just tell me one thing and I won't bother you about it anymore."

"What's that?"

"How did you know? I mean, what made you suspicious that the snakebite had been administered intentionally?"

Peter T. was by no means indifferent to the attention of an attractive woman. He propped a booted foot up on an empty chair, sipped his drink, and eyed Luci speculatively. I found myself mildly jealous of Luci's obvious interest in the detective and, recognizing my agitation for what it was, experienced a degree of consternation.

"Darlin,' it was mostly common sense," Peter T. recounted expansively. "Horses do get bit by snakes now and then, but they're so big the bite rarely kills 'em. They have to get bit in a really vulnerable spot, like the neck, to die from snakebite.

"Now, I don't know if you ever been to central Florida, but the land is flat as a pancake an' that pasture had no rocks or trees or anyplace that snake could get up on to bite Symphony Seven on the neck. The owners explained that the horse must have been grazing when the snake got him, but only a Yankee would come up with a story like that."

"What do you mean?" I asked, intrigued by the story.

"See what I mean about Yankees?" The Texan smiled to Luci. Luci, in turn, was pleased not to have been included among the "Yankees," so she nodded without really knowing what she was agreeing to.

"See, the ol' Poet here knows all there is to know about race horses, but he don't know shit—pardon me, darlin'—about horses in general. See, the chances of a horse going on calmly grazing with a six-foot diamondback within striking distance are slim to none. Horses hate snakes and give 'em a wide berth. Snakes aren't all that fond of horses either."

"But why would they do that?" Luci asked. "If Symphony Seven had continued to develop, he could have been worth much more than the insurance face value. He could have run in the Kentucky Derby—maybe even won it."

"Why, indeed, pretty lady?" Peter T. drawled. "I asked myself that very question. That's when I ordered an autopsy on the horse and a financial check on the owners. Turns out that Symphony Seven was lame. Bowed tendon. They could have brought him back to the races, but he'd never be a champion. And as a breeding prospect, without some big-stakes victories, he wasn't worth all that much.

"Then we found out the owners were in trouble. They were building a big apartment complex that was way over budget and way behind schedule. Once we had those facts, the rest was just dog work. The insurance company was pretty happy, though."

"But the owners were convicted of insurance fraud, weren't they?"

"One to five." Peter T. shook his head sadly. "Out in nine months. Small justice."

Peter T. got up from the table and was headed for the bar when I stopped him. "We've got work to do, Peter T., and if you get us started on the whiskey, we'll never get it done. Luci's office is just a few minutes from here. Let's sort some things out and then we'll hit the streets."

Peter T. was just getting started, but he sighed regretfully and allowed himself to be led away from the cocktail lounge.

The Midwest regional office of the Thoroughbred Protective Bureau occupied ten thousand square feet of expensive floor space in a high-rise building about a mile from O'Hare Airport. Luci escorted Peter T. and me past the receptionist, directly into the office of her boss, Melvin Gendler. The director of investigations was a bear of a man with a gruff expression and a rough, growling voice.

"Don't mind Mel," Luci had forewarned us. "Deep down he's a pussycat."

This "pussycat" looked like he would tear your leg off and beat you over the head with it. His office looked more like a lair. The hulking ex-police lieutenant had littered the room with stacks of files, loose paper, and computer printouts. The air was fouled from the smoke of his ever-present cigar, which coated everything around him with a layer of gray ash. The expensive wall covering was defaced where Gendler had taped or pinned memoranda and cut out news paper articles. Intended to be a well-appointed executive of fice, the room had been trashed by a world-class slob.

Despite his intimidating presence, Gendler greeted us warmly, and his manner made clear his high regard for Luci.

"You get all the good stuff, Frenchy," he told her enviously with a wave of disgust at the chaos where he worked. "Administration is a pain in the ass. You get to run down interesting cases while I get to sort through this nonsense."

"It might help if you'd let the cleaning people straighten up in here," she countered, brushing aside cigar ashes before she sat down.

Gendler stared at her with unfeigned astonishment. "Are you kidding? How would I ever find anything."

Gendler excused himself, with apologies all around, to attend a previously scheduled meeting of department heads. Before he left he expressed his concern over the magnitude of the cheating scam and promised the bureau's complete assistance.

At Luci's suggestion, we moved from the lair of the beast to a spotless conference room. She went to her own office and returned with a stack of files. One of them yielded an old I.D. photo of Armand Larrance. The man I knew as Aaron Locklear had shaved his beard and his hair was now shot with gray, but Locklear and Larrance were clearly one and the same.

"This is Marcel Larrance's older brother," Luci explained. "I'm convinced that this man is the brains behind whatever is going on." I noticed that Luci DeGuerre's eyes gleamed fervently when she talked about the Larrance brothers.

I recounted the details of my meeting with Locklear in Las Vegas as Luci scribbled furiously on her legal pad. Then she booted up the computer terminal and started typing in commands.

"There is some political action going on now in Washington for a uniform nationwide licensing procedure," she explained. "But right now, every state does its own licensing. If a trainer licensed in Illinois wants to run his horse in Detroit, he has to go through the paperwork of applying for a license there, or have a local trainer stand for him as trainer of record. The states pretty much reciprocate, so they don't do much more than make sure the original license is in good standing—that the guy isn't under suspension and that his bills are paid up. But racing commissions are like any other government bureaucracy, the paperwork takes time."

She paused to type in some responses to the computer's queries. "Our data base is on line with all the states, so we can track the movement of licensed personnel from jurisdiction to jurisdiction," Luci continued. "There are some people out there whose licenses are in good standing, but that doesn't mean that we trust them, if you know what I mean."

"Marcel Larrance, case in point," Peter T. offered.

"Exactly. We can't bar Marcel from the grounds if the racing commission has accepted his license, but we damn sure want to keep an eye on him. Let's try something here." She typed in a couple of abbreviations and symbols, followed by the name Armand Larrance. After a second's hesitation, the screen filled with information. The word "ATTENTION" was flashing prominently followed by the words "THE ABOVE SUBJECT IS UNDER PERMANENT LIFETIME SUSPENSION IN THE STATE OF LOUISIANA PENDING HEARING ON MULTIPLE RULES VIOLATIONS AND MULTIPLE CRIMINAL CHARGES. THE SUBJECT IS WANTED BY THE FBI, THE DEA, AND THE NEW ORLEANS POLICE DEPARTMENT. ACCESS TO GROUNDS DENIED. DETAIN IF POSSIBLE."

Instead of paging up to view the rest of the file, Luci punched up the name of Aaron Locklear. The computer responded with the words "NO DATA AVAILABLE."

Luci muttered, "I thought we might get lucky. Larrance hasn't applied or held a license under the Locklear identity. I was hoping we would get something, maybe even just a stable pass, that would give us a current address."

"What did Armand do to get banned for life?" I asked.

Luci took a deep breath and began, "About ten years ago, Armand Larrance was a moderately successful trainer on the Louisiana circuit. He was good and probably would have made it to the big time eventually, but Armand wasn't the type to pay his dues. So he set up a neat little package. Armand became the principal backstretch drug connection at the Fair Grounds and Louisiana Downs.

"He sold drugs to people—mostly stablehands, grooms, exercise riders, a few jockeys—and he doped horses. What made the whole thing work is that he never doped his own horses. He'd get some stable employee, someone he had hooked on drugs, to slip the needle to another trainer's horse. Armand didn't give a damn if the drugging was later uncovered. He just wanted to cash the bets."

"In the meantime, the other trainer takes the rap," Peter T. observed.

"Exactly," Luci agreed bitterly, her expression grim. "The trainer of record is always responsible. Some good people got ruined by Armand's scheme."

"So how did they catch on to him?" I asked.

"His main connection got busted," she replied. "A low-level mafioso was Armand's main supplier, and the guy got taken down with enough cocaine to put him on a Louisiana prison farm for twenty years. The guy made a deal, giving up Armand in the process.

"Problem was, a crooked cop Armand had been paying off tipped him, and Larrance took off. He had plenty of cash stashed away, and he just disappeared."

"I know it happens all the time," I said, "but how does a guy like Armand Larrance, wanted by all these law-enforcement agencies, just take up a new identity and wander around?"

Both Peter T. and Luci laughed. "People always think of relentless detectives pursuing fugitives to the ends of the earth," Peter T. explained. "What really happens is that most people who get caught are nailed at the scene of the crime, or at one of their usual hangouts before they think anyone is looking for 'em. Or they get caught where they're hiding out because somebody tips off the police. If the crook can get out of the immediate jurisdiction undetected, he's gone until he gets caught for something else.

"What usually happens is, the crook runs out of money with no way of getting it legitimately, so he reverts to what he does best for a living, robbing, mugging, whatever it is, and eventually he's busted again. A guy like our boy Armand split with a nice chunk of money, so he can avoid the attention of the authorities for a good long time. Besides, he's not the kind of guy to go out and knock over a Seven Eleven so he can buy breakfast. But, here we are again. He's into something."

"Yeah, and maybe this time we can make him take a fall," Luci put in.

"Where did Marcel fit in back then?" I asked.

"Marcel got out of the army in 1975. He was in one of those special units that were the last out of Vietnam. We tried to get his record from the army, but all we could get were the dates of service and the fact that Marcel was discharged honorably. Everything else was classified."

"So he was one of those. It figures," I noted. Seeing the questioning looks from Luci and Peter T., I continued. "The CIA ran some special units in Vietnam. They did assassinations, counterterrorism, that kind of thing. My Marine unit was a recon team and sometimes we'd run into some of these guys out in the bush. More than a few of them were downright crazy. It's not hard to imagine Marcel as one of 'em."

Luci's fingers were busy on the computer keyboard again. This time the screen flashed with information on Marcel Larrance. Once again, there was a warning code. This code told track security that they needed to keep an eye on this guy. He was not under suspension and could not be ruled off, but the Bureau considered him trouble.

"Here, look at this." She continued paging up data. Marcel's movement from track to track followed Picky Peaches, Calamatator, and Winter Muffin exactly. "This is how I got on to Marcel. His license is as a groom and assistant trainer, and here it says 'owner's representative Capricorn Racing Stables.' I went to Detroit because he had checked through track security at DRC the day before yesterday."

Luci reviewed her findings on the complex corporate structure of Capricorn. According to her initial search, Capricorn was a Delaware corporation whose headquarters turned out to be the offices of an expensive law firm. All of her questions for additional details were met by polite refusals. All she was able to learn from her computer search was that Capricorn was a wholly owned subsidiary of a Cayman Islands company called Bellestar, Ltd. The corporate office of the offshore company, which turned out to be a bank, was the same sort of dead end as the Delaware law firm.

"Unfortunately, all this means is that there's something fishy going on," she complained. "We knew that to begin with. When they closed down Capricorn, we were dead in the water."

"Maybe not so dead," I suggested. A glimmer of an idea was starting to form. "This law firm in Delaware is almost certainly one with impeccable credentials. It probably doesn't do anything more than receive and disburse funds, but those funds certainly wouldn't include any gambling takes. Chances are the Caymans are the ultimate destination for the gambling proceeds. We need to find out the identity of the Bellestar shareholders."

"You're probably right," Peter T. conceded. "But what good will that do us?"

My mind was spinning as I sorted the possibilities. "First, we have three horses who experienced dramatic form reversal and their identity checks." I turned to Luci. "The Bureau is satisfied on those points. Correct?"

"That's right." She nodded. Peter T. looked like he wanted to interrupt, but the Texan held his peace.

"We have three different trainers who won with the horses. All were men of good reputation, not likely to be involved in anything down and dirty." Again, nods of agreement from Peter T. and Luci. "Then we have Marcel Larrance, a known asshole, who both handles the horses and obviously serves as muscle. Now, I was prepared, up until we got into the corporate structure, to put Armand Larrance at the top of the pyramid, the brains behind his brother's brawn. But when I did that, the size of the operation bothered me. I could give Armand credit for a betting coup in the tens of thousands. But I have a problem with the numbers I was hearing in Vegas. They were talking about possibly five or six million. And now we have a corporation fronted by an expensive lawyer and owned by an offshore corporation." I fumbled for a cigarette, shaking my head. "The whole thing is too rich for Armand," I declared as I lit up. "It's too sophisticated, too polished, for a crooked horse trainer and dope dealer."

"So you think there's somebody else pulling the strings?" Peter T. suggested.

"Seems to me there has to be."

"Then where does Armand Larrance fit?" Luci demanded, a faint overtone of protest in her voice. I shot her an inquisitive look but she merely stared back with tight-lipped resolution.

"Armand is in this up to his neck," I assured her. "Call him the operations manager, for want of a better term, but to have it all, you have to look beyond Armand. There's definitely somebody else."

We refilled our coffee cups while Luci and Peter T. digested this bit of speculation. Peter T. propped one ostrich-hide custom-made cowboy boot up on the conference table and sipped his coffee thoughtfully.

"I have some information I picked up in California yesterday that's left me a little puzzled," he said after a time. "Ol' Isaac Turner didn't want to say anything at first. He's a tough ol' boy, but I think the ass-kickin' he took from Marcel scared the hell out of him. Then, too, I think he was worried about bein' mixed up in somethin' dirty.

"When he finally came around to talkin' to me, he put me onto this exercise rider named Pedro Estrella. They call him Petey. Seems this Estrella used to be a jockey until he had trouble makin' weight. For the last four or five years he's been just gettin' by as an exercise rider.

"Estrella came to L.A. from Turf Paradise in Phoenix."

"Calamatator!" Luci and I exclaimed in unison.

"That's right. Estrella worked out Calamatator in Arizona when the horse was getting beat by anything with feet. He came to L.A. just in time to see Calamatator beat the hell out of a decent field.

"Now Estrella and Turner go way back to Estrella's jockey days, and he figures he owes the trainer a favor or two. So what do you suppose he tells Turner and me last night?" Peter T. paused for effect. "The horse he rode in Arizona ain't the same Calamatator he saw in California."

"Impossible," Luci objected. "You might be able to fake a tattoo, but the night-eye photo is conclusive."

"That's what I said, darlin,'" Peter T. replied, unperturbed, "but the boy was certain. Turner told me that Petey Estrella has been ridin' horse for more than thirty years. When Petey told him the story, he went straight to Marcel and told him to get the horse out of his barn. That's when the two of 'em got into it."

I was still pacing the room. Recollecting that long drive between Las Vegas and Los Angeles when I first speculated on the possible ways the cheating could have been accomplished, I had felt then, as now, that something important was eluding me. As I rehashed the Bureau's testing and verification process and tracking the movement of the horses along with Marcel Larrance across the country, an idea was beginning to take shape.

Once more I turned to Luci. "Can your computer access the National Jockey Club data base?"

"Of course," she answered, and checked her watch, "but not until tomorrow. They're closed for the day."

"Shit."

"Peter T. regarded me intently. "What are you on to?"

"I'll tell you tomorrow after I've looked at the registry of these horses from the time they were sold as yearlings."

"You've figured it out," Peter T. accused.

"Let's just say I have a theory."

We had dinner at a steak house in Old Town, one of the few places left which serves a big porterhouse steak, char-grilled, au poivre, smothered in onions, any way that pleases. Peter T. and I watched in awe as Luci DeGuerre put away a twenty-ounce porterhouse covered with sautéed mushrooms and accompanied by a salad, baked potato, and vegetables du jour. When the waitress brought coffee, Luci was ready to see the dessert tray. Peter T. speculated that she had consumed ten percent of her body weight in one sitting, an estimate which she disputed heatedly.

As if by agreement, the topics of investigation—the Larrance brothers, Capricorn Racing Stables, Bellestar, and the rest—were avoided. Still, conversation flowed easily and, for me, the tension of the investigation abated. I found myself increasingly drawn to Luci, with an attraction I hadn't felt for many years. Even more startling was the realization that I had not once compared her to Jenna.

Over conversation, coffee, and after-dinner drinks, exhaustion caught up with all three of us at the same time. We piled into Luci's Bronco II and headed west toward O'Hare International. Driving into the city to have dinner in Old Town had seemed like a good idea at the time. The return seemed interminable.

Luci dropped us off at the Hyatt Regency, where Peter T. had rented a two-bedroom suite in his own name. The cost of the suite was outrageous, but I was fed up with cheap motels and felt an abiding need for a health spa and laundry service. As she bade us good-bye, Luci handed me a copy of the next day's *Racing Form*.

"Several copies come into the office every day," she explained. "I assume we'll nose around the track tomorrow. Maybe you can find us a winner while we're at it."

As tired as I was, I had trouble sleeping, though not from the feverish and frustrating insomnia I'd grown to expect. The idea that possessed me in the TPB conference room kept resurfacing, and at three o'clock in the morning I was up and pacing. I pulled on a pair of jeans, bought a diet cola from the hotel vending machine, and settled down in the sitting room with my feet up on the coffee table and the familiar *Racing Form* in hand. After scanning the articles, I turned to the Sportsman's Park Past Performances.

Over the years, I have developed a habit of scanning the Past Performances before settling down to a race-by-race analysis and bringing the computer into play. Frequently something would leap off the page and capture my imagination—perhaps a rider change, a distance change, a familiar trainer shipping from track to track, or a surprising turn of early speed never before shown. Sometimes there would be no apparent reason for a horse to catch my eye, and my mind somehow bypassed both logic and handicapping fundamentals. Whatever this chemical reaction in the gray matter might be, I had long since learned to trust it. The winning percentage on these intuitive plays was too strong to ignore.

Perusing the *Racing Form* at three o'clock in the morning was having exactly the effect I had hoped for. I was having trouble focusing on the numerals and symbols making up Sportsman's Past Performances. Having caught myself a couple of times nodding off, I had that familiar feeling of knowing I should give up and go back to bed, yet not being able to force myself to move. Now and then I would jerk awake, turn a page, and try to concentrate on a horse's running line.

Peter T. found me sleeping on the sofa, the *Racing Form* spread over me, like a bum on a park bench. A room-service waiter knocked on the door and delivered a thermos of coffee, and Peter T., in jeans and a T-shirt, tipped him. The Texan laced his coffee liberally with cream and sugar, eyeing me with a glint of humor.

"Son, you look like something that should be covered up with kitty litter," he observed dryly as he handed me a cup of coffee.

"Only way I could feel worse is if I was bigger," I rasped. I accepted the hot liquid gratefully, hoping that a dose of caffeine would get my brain, if not my body, working.

"You want the shower first or you want to work at gluing your eyeballs open?" Peter T. asked.

"You go ahead," I answered. "I need a quick workout and maybe ten minutes in the sauna."

After a half-hour in the exercise room, I was beginning to function. Accustomed to hard exercise daily, I was feeling the effects of a few days' layoff and the reps came hard. I was sitting in the sauna when the name Thurgood came to mind.

Millions of scholarly words have been written on the workings of the human subconscious. I have no clinical knowledge of how the name had stuck in my mind, any more than I am able to explain my occasional intuitive reaction to horses from a quick scan of the *Racing Form*. But somehow, while I nodded and blinked over the *Form* the night before, the name of a horse stuck with me. Thurgood. I had no recollection of why I had been attracted to the name and I couldn't even remember which race the horse was entered in, but I saw the name clearly in my mind imprinted in the bold type of the Past Performances.

In a rush I burst out of the sauna and ran through the weight room to the elevators. Peter T. was still in the bathroom when I reached the suite. Pouring the last cup of coffee, I sat down and paged through the *Form* until I found Thurgood.

When Peter T. emerged, he found me in sweaty athletic togs, laughing uproariously.

"Got the motherfuckers," I said gleefully.

9

Luci tapped the commands into the computer terminal to call up information from the data base of the National Thoroughbred Registry in Lexington, Kentucky. Peter T. and I sipped coffee and looked on. After a moment the terminal screen lit up:

PICKY PEACHES—Ch f by Pick Me Up—Shesa Peach by Just Peachy

—Br. Silverhill Farm, Cynthiana, Ky.

—Yearling purchase by private sale, $12.5K Astral Stud, Inc.

—Unraced 2YO season

—Acquired, private purchase by owner/trainer Guy LeBlanc 11-86

—First entered, MSW, FG, 1-3-87

—Claimed 3-31-87, $2500, 2nd race DD, Capricorn Racing Stables, Inc.

—Purchased 5-6-87, private sale, owner/trainer Sydney Reese

"Let me see Calamatator and Winter Muffin," I told Luci. I had a good idea what we would find.

The computer responded as directed, drawing the data from the National Thoroughbred Registry. I grinned triumphantly when Calamatator's vital statistics appeared, and by the time Winter Muffin came up, Peter T. and

Luci had caught on. Two names appeared prominently in the records of all three horses—Astral Stud, Inc., as the original purchaser and Capricorn Racing Stables as the eventual claimant.

"See what they have on Astral Stud," I directed, but Luci had already anticipated me. The video screen confirmed what we all three suspected: Astral Stud was listed as a subsidiary of a certain offshore corporation, Bellestar, Ltd. After the obligatory whooping and hollering, we sat back to digest this information. We all knew we had discovered something important, but what did it mean?

Peter T. spread cream cheese liberally over a salted bagel. "Seems like what you have to do," the Texan suggested between mouthfuls, "is to ask that thing for all the horses purchased by this Astral Stud outfit."

"Good idea," I agreed.

Luci shook her head. "I tried that already," she said. "But the Jockey Club and the Registry data bases aren't organized by purchasers. Racing and breeding stock are maintained up-to-date, but you have to know the horse's name to retrieve this kind of data."

Peter T. cursed, but I was not at all disappointed. "Just for the hell of it, try this name," I prompted. " 'Thurgood,' spelled just like the Supreme Court justice."

The screen filled with the data. We crowded around the screen with great interest.

"You sonofabitch," Peter T. exulted.

According to the graphic, Thurgood had been purchased as a yearling by Astral Stud and was sold as an unraced two-year-old. After a series of miserable performances, he was claimed by Orion Racing Stables out of a $3,500 maiden claiming race at Turfway Park in northern Kentucky.

"See what your licensing information has to say about Orion Racing Stables," I suggested, by now confident of the result.

Luci exited the National Thoroughbred Registry data base and reentered the TPB's own. As expected, Orion Racing Stables was shown to be a corporation and a wholly owned subsidiary of Bellestar, Ltd.

"You have this figured out, don't you, Tennyson?" Luci demanded.

"I think he had it yesterday," Peter T. agreed, "and he held out on us all night."

I shook my head and paced the room, trying to organize my thoughts. "Not until this morning," I said finally. "In the sauna, back at the hotel ... that's when the whole thing started to make sense."

"So? Let's have it."

"Let's talk about ringers for a minute," I began. I told them the story of the Indiana hustlers and their Mexican horse. They laughed at the obvious humor and agreed that this was the way a ringer scam could be expected to work.

"Okay, here's the way I see it. Luci, some very smart sonofabitch has found the 'hole' in the system."

Turning to Peter T., I continued, "Yesterday you told us that Pedro Estrella thought Calamatator was a ringer. We all agreed that was impossible, but an exercise rider with Estrella's experience would make that observation based on more than just the horse's appearances and physical condition. A rider would recognize things that maybe even a trainer wouldn't see. Things like the animal's stride, his gait, the way he holds his head when he runs, his 'action.' I have to believe that the Calamatator who won in L.A. was not the Calamatator Estrella rode in Arizona."

"But the night-eye photo," Luci protested. "Calamatator checked out. Period."

"That's right," I agreed. "So what does that contradiction suggest?"

"The records got switched," Peter T. offered. "They had someone inside the security system."

"Luci?"

Luci shrugged. "It's hard to imagine. They'd have to get to more than one person."

"What about the guy who confirms the night-eye photo?" Peter T. was unwilling to give up the notion.

"Same thing," Luci insisted. "The prints are verified by more than one source."

"Let's not dismiss either idea totally," I said. "We may have to check out both theories. But for now, let's assume Luci's correct and the verification system is secure. Where does that leave us?"

Luci and Peter T. made no response.

"The only other possibility, the one scenario we failed to consider all along, is that the *losers,* the horses which lost so miserably before the Capricorn claims, were ringers."

Both investigators looked stunned by the suggestion. They both sat silently, considering the proposition.

Peter T. spoke first. "Nobody checks the losers. That right, Luci?"

"Standard procedure, when a horse is entered in a race, is that the entry documentation includes a description and photograph. The tattoo I.D. is checked in the paddock at race time. After the race, blood and urine samples are taken from all horses who win purse money—usually one through six, not just win place and show. When something unusual happens, like a well-bet horse running poorly, the stewards may request samples and even order an investigation."

"So if a loser matched the photo and had the proper tattoo, he would skate by?" My question was more a statement. "That is, if the horse was a long shot and not much was expected of it?"

"Yes," Luci acknowledged, "but it doesn't make sense. I mean, why bring in ringers to lose?"

"You have to think like a horseplayer rather than a track security expert," I explained. "The underlying principle is that the worse a horse's record looks on paper, the higher the parimutuel odds against him winning. It's common practice among trainers, especially trainers of cheap claiming horses, to hide a horse's improving form to maximize the betting odds when the horse is ready to win. The practice is deceptive, but perfectly legal. More than ninety percent of all racing stables couldn't survive any other way. They have to cash bets to make a profit. This scheme is an illegal variation of the same concept, with a much bigger and more secure payoff."

"My family has been in racing for a couple of generations," Luci said. "I understand 'darkening' a horse's form, but the idea you're suggesting eludes me."

I recognized that neither of my listeners was a handicapper and I struggled to make a better arcane concept understandable.

"The backbone of thoroughbred racing is the concept

of claiming races," I began. "It's what keeps people from entering Secretariat against 'Dog Food' just to win a purse. If a horse worth one hundred thousand dollars can be claimed for ten thousand dollars, it would be foolish to risk losing him. The claiming system keeps the races competitive. That's why more than eighty percent of the races carded at any track in the country are claiming races.

"The typical five-thousand or even ten-thousand-dollar claiming horse is, on average, a pretty sorry animal. He has chronic physical ailments which require medication—legal medication—to make it possible for him to even run, much less win. What's more, he doesn't win enough purse money over the course of a year to pay for his oats, upkeep, and training.

"But his trainer, who is almost always his owner or part-owner, loves him, feeds him, and nurses his ills as if he were as valuable as Secretariat. Why? Because he's what we call a 'money horse.' Once or twice a year, when the nagging injuries are cleared up, when he's breathing right, when he feels good, he can beat a field of similar sorry nags and produce a fifty-dollar mutuel payoff. The winner's share of the purse might be a few thousand, but the betting proceeds might keep the stable going for the next six months."

I paused to make certain my friends were following this narrative and, also, to rein in my enthusiasm. The scenario I had just recounted was the essence of the racing game for most horsemen as well as the very heart of the challenge for the handicapper.

"All this is standard practice," I continued. "It drives the fans crazy when impossible horses win at long odds, but it happens all the time. It's why you hear losers complain that all races are fixed. In their minds, the only way this money horse could win is through a fix.

"But there are risks and limitations to the game when it's played honestly, and no one gets rich on the system. Horses like these are competitive only at certain levels. Our five-thousand-dollar money horse may run spectacularly when he's ready, but he's unlikely to win his next race at five thousand dollars, much less move up to the next class and compete. His form and condition are too fragile.

"There's also the risk that the trainer may misjudge his readiness and the horse may run well but lose. Or everything might be just right, but some other trainer's money horse is just a little bit better. Then the trainer gets blind-sided just like the racing fan. Either circumstance is a major disaster because the stable loses its betting money and the next time out the odds on the horse are much lower because the good race makes him look better on paper. The point is that legitimate 'darkening' of a horse's form is, by no means, a sure thing."

"And a race fixer like Armand Larrance has to guarantee a sure thing," Luci put in.

"For the kind of money they're betting and winning, as a guy I met in Vegas would say, 'they have to have it handled.' "

I resumed my pacing. "Bear with me, now," I instructed. "This gets tricky, but here's how I think it works. Astral buys good, sound yearlings. Not Kentucky Derby candidates, but solid yeoman breeding. Looks like they pay a range of twelve thousand, five hundred dollars to seventeen-five for their horses.

"The yearlings are shipped to a training center and start learning how to be race horses. Again, Armand would be the key man here. He was a good trainer once.

"In the meantime, our boys buy unregistered thoroughbreds—probably in Mexico or South America—which closely match the physical descriptions of the legitimate horses. These ringers are tattooed and entered in races by small-time trainers like Guy LeBlanc or Anselmo Calderon. Chances are, these guys have no more complicity beyond the hidden-ownership angle."

"Hidden ownership is illegal, but it's practice for subsistence trainers," Luci added for Peter T.'s benefit.

"That's right," I continued. "Now, the new owner/trainer takes the horse to a major track on whatever circuit he works and enters him in a Maiden Special Weight race. That's the highest maiden class. First-time starters rarely attract much betting attention unless they're sent out by top trainers or unless they're 'live' on the tote board. No one would be surprised when the horse runs poorly. Over a series of races, running badly each time, the horse drops down through the maiden claiming ranks, gets shipped to cheaper tracks, and, when he finally reaches the bottom, Capricorn, using a legitimate trainer, claims him."

"They claim their own horse?" Peter T.'s question was a statement of disbelief.

"Sure. They invest another couple grand to make everything look good. It's probably part of the deal with the guy fronting for them. Theoretically he makes a few bucks so he's happy."

"And if he ain't, Marcel comes to visit," Peter T. noted.

I refilled my coffee cup before continuing. I sipped the brew thoughtfully and lit a cigarette.

"Now that Capricorn has the horse, the animal is shipped to a legitimate trainer's barn at a major track. At this point the legitimate trainer probably hasn't even seen the horse yet. The major track is important for three reasons. First, the fans there have a natural contempt for horses coming from a cheaper track. Second, the mutuel pools are large enough to absorb some fairly substantial action without dropping the odds too much. And, the most important reason is that Las Vegas and major bookies take action on the major track."

"Also, none of the jockeys has ridden the horse," Peter T. observed astutely.

"That's true, and very important," I agreed. "We got very lucky with Pedro Estrella.

"The horse is entered at a higher maiden claiming class," I went on, "but this time the real horse is the one who runs. He ships in from the training center, fit and ready. On paper, he looks like he has no chance, like he doesn't even belong in the race. But the real horse is capable of winning at an even higher level than this. He's a mortal lock and he's one hundred percent the real thing. No drugs, no nothing. What's more, he's capable of moving up off the maiden win and winning again at long odds. The horseplayers see those bad races against cheap maidens and write his win off as a fluke."

"Picky Peaches beat $6,500 maidens after being claimed for $2,500," Luci read from the papers in front of her. "She came back two weeks later and beat $12,500 claimers at 16-1 odds."

"That's what I mean," I said. "That second race was restricted to nonwinners of two races, so what looked like a big jump in class was really a race against lesser animals."

Peter T. looked troubled. "This idea is clever, I guess," he allowed thoughtfully. "What bothers me is, it seems like too much time and money invested with no guarantee of success. You know damn well that people spend millions on yearlings who turn out to be dogs. These guys buy a horse, buy a substitute, feed, train, and race 'em both—damn, how much would they have invested by then?"

"At least fifty, sixty grand per horse by then. Maybe more," I estimated.

"So they got a hundred and a half, at least, in these three before the real horse hits the track." He shook his head disbelievingly. "That's a lot of front money."

"It's probably more than that," I concurred. "As you said, they had to have bought some dogs along with the good horses.

"But think about the return," I insisted, "I won over seventy thousand dollars by betting just one thousand dollars per horse. How much do you think these guys bet, knowing they had a lock?"

This time Luci spoke up, raising a key question. "How could they hope to get away with it?" she asked. "We're on this. The bookies have their muscle out. Surely they couldn't think the kind of money we're talking about would go unnoticed."

I smiled ruefully. "Obviously, they considered that contingency too. They used 'beards' with the bookies and a betting service in Nevada. They've already closed down Capricorn and all three of these horses belong to new owners." I paused to stare at Luci and Peter T. in turn. "And then they've got me. The bookies are looking for me. The TPB figured me for the culprit. The casinos have already taken action against me. These guys have everyone looking in the wrong direction. That can't be an accident."

"You're saying you were set up," Peter T. stated flatly.

"Has to be," I replied. "In that alley in Detroit where Luci saved me, Marcel could have killed me quickly. Instead he said that the 'people looking for me' would find me in damaged condition. He even called me by name and referred to me as a 'railbird.' How else would

Marcel know any of this unless it was part of the plan? Hell, I think Kermit was set up too."

"This is getting very crazy," Luci said in disbelief. "I mean, why you? How could they possibly do it?"

"I think Picky Peaches is the key. That's the first horse in the cycle and she started out in Louisiana. Kermit knows everybody on the Louisiana circuit. He eats at the track kitchens, hangs out in the bars the racetrack people frequent—it's all part of his system. My guess is, these guys arranged, through their interim trainer, to tip Kermit."

"Guy LeBlanc," Luci read from the computer printouts. "Maybe we should talk to LeBlanc."

"If we can find him," Peter T. said, unconvinced.

"Let's try something," Luci suggested. "My uncle, Etienne, has been a trainer in Louisiana for forty years. I'd bet a week's pay he knows LeBlanc."

Peter T. and I watched as Luci dialed and engaged her uncle in an animated conversation interspersed with family gossip and punctuated by phrases in Cajun French. At a point near the end of the call, her expression lost its gaiety and her eyes widened. She listened for a while longer, thanked her uncle, and hung up.

"Guy LeBlanc is dead," she responded to our unspoken questions. "They found him in his car in the bayou. There was an empty whiskey bottle on the seat next to him."

"Shit," Peter T. cursed. "So much for that idea."

"What else?" I prompted Luci gently.

"Uncle 'Tienne doesn't believe it," she answered in a soft voice. "He knew LeBlanc for almost forty years and never saw the man drink anything but wine." When she looked up, her eyes were hard. "They murdered him. You were right, Tennyson. LeBlanc, somehow, tipped Kermit, and the Larrance brothers got rid of him to cover their tracks."

"Wait a minute," Peter T. objected. "How could they be sure Kermit would tip you? It seems like we're stretching here."

"How, indeed?" I concurred, the answer leaving me chilled.

"Only one way," Peter T. said emphatically, answering his own question. "Someone who knows you well, knows about your relationship with Kermit, is in on it."

There was no mistaking the conclusion. Peter T. was right on the money and I knew it. "Excuse me," I said, and left the room, leaving Luci and Peter T. staring at each other, not knowing quite what to say.

I walked purposely through the corridor to the men's room. Peter T. had voiced the thought which had been nagging me all morning. I knew that there were relatively few people who could have provided the information the crooks obviously had, and that notion filled me with dismay. Who? Boog? Cowboy? Buck? Lanchek? Hanrahan? All unthinkable.

I splashed cold water on my face and the back of my neck before toweling off. We had just run together a long string of suppositions. There was time enough to track down the betrayer, but first we had to make certain we were right.

If a horseplayer learns one thing from his craft, he develops the ability to rebound from a serious misjudgment and push on. I squared my shoulders and rejoined the investigators who had become my friends and allies. They both looked at me with visible concern, but neither vocalized that big question. For Luci DeGuerre, this was becoming the biggest case of her career. For the veteran Peter T., the complexity of the circumstances challenged his skills and intellect. The natural instinct for both was to jump all over the potential lead. But they held their questions to allow me time to sort things out myself. I was grateful for their solicitude, a concern that went beyond professional courtesy.

I regarded my friends with mock severity. "What are you sitting around for?" I demanded. "We've got to get moving."

"Where?" Luci asked.

"Thurgood's running in the fourth race at Sportsman's," I answered. "Let's go to the races!"

10

There were some preparations to be handled before we could leave for the track. Luci reminded Peter T. and me that she was "undercover" at Midwest tracks and could not appear as an agent of the TPB. She shuffled through her desk drawer and extracted a picture I.D. badge identifying her as an assistant trainer. In jeans, T-shirt, and cowboy boots she could go anywhere on the backstretch without arousing curiosity.

For Peter T., she came up with an owner's badge and spent a few minutes producing the photo to go with the identity. From the standpoint of "cover" they were all set. We could take no chance that one of the Larrance brothers, if they were present, might recognize me. Peter T. and Luci would tour the backstretch to examine the activity and people around the horse Thurgood. I would meet them in the clubhouse.

"Thurgood runs in the fourth race. Locate him and see what you can find out before they take the horse to the holding area," I instructed. "Whatever you do, get back to the clubhouse by the end of the third race."

"Why is the timing so critical?" Luci demanded.

"How are you guys fixed for money?" I asked instead of answering her question.

" 'Bout a thousand in cash," Peter T. responded.

"Fifty or sixty dollars," Luci said, her expression still questioning.

"No problem," I said. "I'll loan you some. You can bet all you want on Thurgood. You'll be able to buy yourself a mink coat when the race is over and we'll manage to cost our friends a few bucks in the process. That's why you have to get back by the end of the third race."

"It's no sweat," Luci explained. "Sportsman's has advanced wagering. You can use the time while we're in the stables to get bets down with no hurry."

"No good," I countered. "If we get down early, the tote-board odds will open too low, the crowd will get excited, and the bad guys'll probably stiff the horse. We have to wait until the last minute, when their money's down and it's too late to do anything."

"We're talking about a 'sure thing' here, aren't we?" Peter T. observed with just a touch of excitement in his voice. "I've never had a tip on a sure thing. I think I'm going to enjoy this."

"This is the proverbial 'hot tip,' " I concurred. Turning to Luci, I asked, "How much do you want?"

She bit her lip. For someone who had been around the track for years, Luci was not much of a betting person. "How about one hundred?" she said with a flinch.

"C'mon, big-timer," Peter T. derided, laughing. "You don't get shots like this every day."

"Here's five hundred," I prompted gently. "When the time comes, I'll tell you how to bet it."

The normally assertive Lucinda DeGuerre was visibly nervous as she reluctantly accepted the "loan." "If we lose, I can't pay you back right away," she cautioned.

"Don't worry about it," I reassured her. "If we lose, it's my fault. But I consider the chances very slim. Thurgood will have to do something weird, like lose his rider or get knocked down, to lose. It can happen, but I think it's reasonable to expect our boys to be very careful."

By eleven-fifteen A.M., we were on our way to the track. Post time at Sportsman's is one-thirty, so we had plenty of time for the two investigators to explore the stable area. Luci had a list of the licensed personnel employed by trainer Norm Culver, so one of their objectives was to identify any others in Thurgood's entourage.

Luci and Peter T. were both visibly excited during the drive to the track, singing "Camptown Races" as Luci weaved her way in and out of traffic with considerable skill. I was amused by the behavior of two professionals on a "business" mission as the prospect of a betting coup overrode all other considerations.

As we traveled east on I-94, I began to consider one more maneuver which involved some personal risk. By the time Luci exited the freeway for Cicero and Sportsman's Park, I had made up my mind.

"Before we go in, find me a pay phone," I told Luci. The absence of public phones in racetrack grandstand or clubhouse areas is a tradition originally designed to prevent the practice of "past posting," that is, betting a race with a bookie after it has been run. Modern communications technology has rendered the tradition obsolete, and the lack of phones is no more than an inconvenience. Luci gave me a questioning look, but pulled into the next service station. I had no change, but decided that using my credit card presented no increased risk. The nature of the phone call would reveal my location. I could only trust that Jimmy DeMaria would keep it to himself.

The number that DeMaria had provided after the meeting at the Athletic Club rang several times before a rough-voiced man answered. He informed me that Mr. DeMaria was unable to come to the phone and offered to take a message. I assumed this was standard procedure. DeMaria was unlikely to spend much time talking on telephones.

"Ask Mr. DeMaria if he will speak to Tennyson Wilder," I instructed. "It is a matter of urgency with some financial consequences to Mr. DeMaria." The "telephone thug" grudgingly agreed to check, and put me on hold for what stretched into several minutes. Finally DeMaria came on the line.

"Mr. Wilder. Nice to hear from you," he said cordially. "What can I do for you?"

"Actually, I'm going to do something for you," I answered. "You are aware that I'm taking some chance in making this call?" A murmur of assent came from the other end of the line. "Have there been any changes in the situation since we last talked?"

DeMaria was cautious. "As I indicated in our last meeting, I remain skeptical. But some of my associates are, shall we say, 'adamant.' The employers of the two men you, uh, 'met with' are particularly displeased."

DeMaria's response was not unexpected, but I didn't enjoy hearing it. "I'm going to do you a favor," I said after a moment's hesitation. "I hope you will view it as a sign of good faith and react accordingly. In the fourth race on today's program at Sportsman's Park, a horse called Thurgood is entered. I believe that if you check the wagering activity, you'll find substantially more action than seems logical on a horse who appears to have little chance."

"Why are you telling me this?" DeMaria demanded.

"Because I believe I've learned a great deal about what's been going on. And, of course, I have nothing to do with this activity."

"I see," DeMaria responded thoughtfully. "You understand, I will need more information than this to be in a position to help you?"

"Of course. I'll contact you when I have everything put together. In the meantime, I thought you and perhaps a select few of your colleagues might want to protect your interests on this one. The only thing I ask is that you don't lay off at the track itself. It's important to me that track odds are not adversely affected."

"I understand and will take appropriate precautions. Thank you for your consideration. This information is most interesting. I'll look forward to hearing from you in the near future." DeMaria hung up.

I replaced the receiver absently, reflecting on the conversation. I had a momentary vision of a platoon of hit men combing Sportsman's Park, but quickly dismissed the thought. DeMaria had been sympathetic in our first meeting and, if he had wanted me, why had he warned me? I relaxed in the belief that my location was safe for a time at least.

Luci and Peter T. asked no questions as I climbed back into her car, but I explained anyway, since there was no reason to keep my actions secret from my only allies. Peter T. expressed concern about revealing my location, but accepted my assessment of the potential for danger. Luci, who wanted to bust the crooks through legal means, was unhappy about the involvement of someone like DeMaria and said so.

"Hey, I agree," I offered. "I'd rather do it your way. Just the same, if we reach a point where there's nothing more we can do, where the law is helpless, I'm going to tell Jimmy DeMaria everything I know and hope that it gets me off the hook. I hope you can understand my position."

Her expression softened. "I know what you have at

stake, Tennyson, and I know that you're not just using me and the Bureau to get information. It's just that I want these guys—Armand Larrance especially—more than I can tell you.'' She seemed so intense, I feared she might burst into tears.

Peter T. acted to restore the mood of adventure. "Hey, we're doing good here, darlin'. We'll nail ol' Armand and ol' Ugly while we're at it. Let's go to work here and win ourselves a vacation in Monaco."

"A Mercedes Benz," Luci insisted. "The two-seater."

"Make it an American car," Peter T. argued. "How 'bout a Corvette?"

"Diamond earrings."

"A Caribbean cruise."

"An emerald necklace."

" 'Camptown race track five miles long . . .' "

" ' . . . Do dah . . .' "

I had always thought of Sportsman's Park as a blue-collar track. The impression was based on just a few visits over the years and was, I acknowledged, unfair. Some of Sportsman's image is due to location—not some fancy suburb, but Cicero, Illinois. Sportsman's Park and its sister track, Hawthorne Park, are virtually side by side. I suspected there was some logical or historical reason for two major racing facilities to be located in such proximity, but I was unaware of it. About a mile north of Midway Airport, the tracks are surrounded by aging industrial facilities and run-down neighborhoods.

About halfway between downtown Chicago and O'Hare International, and about at the point where the major commuter arteries begin to converge on the downtown area, accessibility is the key feature of both tracks. They do draw racing fans—for thoroughbreds in the afternoon and standardbreds, harness racing, at night.

Chicago offers what is arguably the highest quality racing in the Midwest. The people in Kentucky would argue loudest and with some justification. The brief spring and fall Keeneland meetings are almost on par with the New York and Southern California tracks in terms of quality of racing stock, despite lower average purses. However, while Turfway Park, Churchill Downs, and even Ellis Park, assisted by the proximity of the Kentucky breeding industry, offer exciting and ever-improving racing, the Chicago tracks would have the edge day in and day out.

Sportsman's and Hawthorne's images are a bit dowdy, mostly because they occupy comparatively little land. To me, racetracks should have something of a pastoral setting. Even Aqueduct and Hollywood Park, completely surrounded as they are by urban sprawl, manage to achieve a wide-open appearance. Sportsman's is so boxed in that it seems much smaller than its actual size.

The track at Sportsman's is a five-eighths-mile oval, a "bullring" in racing parlance, instead of the usual one-mile thoroughbred track. This bullring aspect of Sportsman's Park is the true source of my antipathy toward the place. The most common race presented in thoroughbred racing is the six-furlong sprint. At the typical one-mile track, the starting gate is on a chute off the backstretch and the horses have a fairly long straight run, circle a single turn, and then finish in another straight run down the homestretch.

The six-furlong chute for a bullring extends from the homestretch in front of the stands and the horses run around two turns to complete the three-quarter-mile distance. The straight runs are comparatively short, the horse's position in the turns is vital, and times are slower. One of my favorite plays in handicapping has always been to back a horse shipping from a bullring track to a one-mile oval. The shipper always appeared "on paper" to be slower than he really was.

Luci and Peter T. dropped me at the clubhouse entrance on their way to the parking area reserved for horsemen. I paid the admission charge and followed the growing crowd up an escalator to a higher level. There I purchased three reserved seats overlooking the finish line and not far from a bank of mutuel windows. Because the thoroughbred meeting at Sportsman's ran from February to late May, much of the seating was behind glass, a feature which detracted from the view of the races and the overall atmosphere, but was nonetheless a necessary frostbite preventive.

The crowd at Sportsman's seems to reflect the personality of the city, boisterous, businesslike, and harboring little patience for pageantry or fashion. A Saturday afternoon at the track includes a beer and a bratwurst rather than champagne and pâté. Hats and gloves for the ladies are out of fashion. In fact, appearances would indicate that the "ladies" themselves are "out." Women are in a distinct minority. The men wear baseball caps or snap-brims and shirts imprinted with the names of sponsors for softball or bowling teams. Cigars of all shapes and sizes are the tobacco product of choice. I couldn't help thinking that if the races were for dogs rather than horses, Chicago fans would prefer pit bulls to greyhounds. It's a tough town.

The first three races for cheap claiming horses, each with several contenders of fairly equal ability. I couldn't make a strong enough case for any single horse at the odds offered, so I killed the time handicapping later races and people-watching. The contentiousness of the first three painfully reminded me of just how tough the handicapping game was becoming for horseplayers restricted to a single track.

As a Las Vegas handicapper, I would throw out the races which were too contentious, the races where all horses were so bad that any outcome might be possible, and the races where a single overwhelming favorite went to post at prohibitively low odds. The Turf Club allowed me to maintain this high degree of selectivity, since I would still have plenty of betting opportunities gleaned from four or five different racing programs per day. The "on-track" handicapper is stuck with whatever nine, ten, or eleven race program his local track presents. He must develop an "iron ass" to have any hope for a profit, sitting patiently through race after race, waiting for what often might be a single wagering opportunity on the entire card.

For most, such mental discipline is nearly impossible, and I have seen competent handicappers tap out for lack of it. The need for action overcomes the profit motive, bad luck becomes a losing streak, and suddenly they are transformed from "investors" to "gamblers." I am more selective than most, but I shuddered at the thought of going back to a daily regimen of Sportsman's Park.

I managed to imitate an iron ass through the first three races—a task made easier by prospects for the fourth. Short-priced favorites held off halfhearted contenders in the first two, completing a fourteen-dollar daily double.

A 5-1 shot who should have been 10-1 was the winner in a photo finish in the third. I was glad I'd stayed out.

By the time the third race went off, I had decided how to bet the fourth. Thurgood was matched up in an eleven-horse field with three- and four-year-old maidens running for a $7,500 claiming price. Thurgood, who had run poorly for $3,500 in his last race, appeared to be way outclassed. Fair odds, based on past performances, should have been at least 80-1, perhaps higher. I knew from experience that Thurgood would be bet down to 25-1 or 30-1 at best.

My goal was to hurt the payoff for the Larrance brothers and their partners, to hit them in their pocketbooks, but only enough to let them know that someone was on to them. I wanted them to react, to suspect one another, to worry about an outsider, and to wonder if the bookies had caught on. To do this I had to bet like they would—at the last minute and at least in part in the exacta pool.

When the third race was declared official, I left my seat to keep an eye out for Peter T. and Luci. They, too, would have to watch their timing carefully. I caught sight of them as they stepped off the escalator.

"We found the horse and he looks terrific," Luci announced without preliminary. "All the people around him were Norm Culver's regular hands except one, Marcel Larrance."

"That is one bad-lookin' hombre," Peter T. put in. "He was checkin' the horse out from head to toe and I 'bout expected him to pick the horse up so he could look underneath. It's a good thing he left you to those boys back in that alley."

"I noticed something else too," Luci said. "There seems to be some friction between Marcel and Norm Culver. They don't like each other very much."

"I expect ol' Marcel would be pretty hard to like," Peter T. observed.

"There might be more to it than that," I wondered aloud. "You said Norm Culver is a trainer of good reputation around here?"

Luci did not hesitate. "From everything I've heard. He's been at it for something like twenty years with what I'd say is a medium-size public stable. He's got a good nucleus of owners who have been with him for years.

One of the things I've heard is that he won't bullshit an owner about a horse's ability or chances. Most of the people who stay in the game appreciate that."

"That fits the pattern. In L.A., there was a physical confrontation between Marcel and Turner. Here we have some obvious friction between Marcel and Culver. A good, honest trainer has to recognize that something's wrong, and most would at least be uneasy about it."

"But Marcel scares 'em into playin' along," Peter T. said.

"Marcel provides a little intimidation," Luci put in, "so they keep their suspicions to themselves."

"They probably run a Mr. Hard/Mr. Smooth game," Peter T. offered. "Armand, or somebody with a little cool, reassures the trainer that the horse is absolutely legitimate and his poor record is due to mishandling by an incompetent. Marcel backs up the reassurance with outright intimidation. Then they sweeten the game by selling the trainer this 'killer' at an attractive price. The trainer decides that his ass is covered and his interest is best served by keeping his suspicions to himself."

"Bingo," I agreed. "But the idea isn't foolproof. Isaac Turner didn't buy it, so they had to go to a new trainer. It's a good bet that Culver's uncomfortable and we should talk to him before Marcel gets physical." I glanced at the tote board and noted that post time was ten minutes away. "We need to get moving," I prompted. "We have to time our bets to the last minute. Peter T., you go over to the grandstand. Luci, take the next floor up. If anyone notices one of us betting, they won't see us all. Luci, bet three hundred dollars on Thurgood to win. He's number four on the program, so just tell the clerk, 'three hundred to win on four.' Then tell him, 'twenty dollars exacta key, four . . . all.' That gives you Thurgood on top of all of the other ten horses in the race. If something long runs second, we hit big. If the favorite runs second, we lost a little of our return. It's worth a shot. You got that?"

Peter T. nodded and Luci repeated the instructions. They may have been more familiar with the betting technique than I presumed, but I was leaving nothing to chance.

"Get in line about five minutes to post time. If there are still two minutes on the clock when you get to the front, let someone go ahead of you. Try to get your bet down with a minute or less to post." Once again I looked at the tote board. The odds on Thurgood were holding at 85-1. "The horses are on the track with no action showing," I continued. "It's too late for them to change their instructions to the jockey. Watch out for Marcel. Don't be standing in line in front of him or next to him. We'll meet back here after the bets are down."

They dispersed to carry out the plan. I watched the tote board as I took my place in line. The odds on Thurgood still had not moved much. I considered the possibility that the crooks might not be going for the win that day, but rejected the idea. Marcel was not there to supervise a loss, I reasoned. The line moved fairly well, and with two minutes to post, I let the guy behind me go ahead. The odds on Thurgood started dropping—65-1, then 50-1, then 45-1. The clock showed one minute. The guy in front of me was betting all kinds of numbers on the trifecta. He had a heavy foreign accent and the clerk was having a hard time understanding him. I was amused that in none of the man's combinations did he include Thurgood, but I was beginning to worry about being shut out. Finally, with less than a minute left, the man completed his bets. He had over one hundred dollars bet with all his combinations. I had become annoyed enough to be pleased that the man was going to lose.

I placed my bets—six hundred to win with a forty-dollar exacta wheel—just before the bell sounded. I walked over to a TV monitor just as the horses left the gate. Luci joined me as the horses completed the first quarter-mile in a rather leisurely time of twenty-three seconds flat. Thurgood was running easily in about eighth place, approximately ten lengths from the leader. The leader, the favorite, opened up about a three-length lead on the backstretch with a half-mile time of just under forty-eight seconds. This was slow, even for a bullring. Thurgood had moved up to about the middle of the pack and was running easily, but I felt a twinge of fear that his rider might have misjudged the pace. Luci shot me a worried glance.

With a quarter-mile to run, Thurgood had six or seven lengths to make up, and so far, everything seemed to be favoring the front-runner. With an easy lead, he was likely to have energy left for the finish. The crowd, having heavily backed the favorite, was cheering wildly, but the elation was short-lived as Thurgood accelerated sharply on the final turn. He caught the leader near the top of the stretch and blew by him. Luci started to jump up and down as Thurgood widened his lead. Not wanting to attract undue attention, I had to take her arm to calm her down.

Thurgood won going away, and the demoralized favorite dropped back to third. A steady running 17-1 shot ambled home for second. Belatedly I checked the tote for the final odds on Thurgood and noted with satisfaction that he had gone off at 20-1. Thurgood would pay good price, but we had cost the Larrance brothers eight to ten odds points—at least a hundred grand when the off-track bets were collected.

All around, the bettors were grumbling. I whispered to Luci, "You just won yourself ten or twelve 'large,' depending on what that exacta pays." She stayed cool, but took my arm and squeezed. My guts did a little flip-flop. The big win had not provided near the charge as the touch of this clearheaded, gutsy female. I looked around sheepishly to see if my consternation was visible, but Luci's eyes were riveted on the tote board.

Peter T. joined us as Thurgood was led into the winner's circle. "Winner, winner, chicken dinner," he said evenly, his expression revealing his elation only to Luci and me. The race was posted "official" and the payoffs flashed on the board. Thurgood paid $42 to win with the exacta pegged at a healthy $540.

"Lookit that," a stranger standing next to me moaned. "The horse hasn't done a thing in his life and he goes off at 20-1?"

"They stiffed that goddamn six horse," his buddy agreed. "Took him right out of the exacta, the cheatin' sonofabitches. Lookit that . . . five-forty . . . should have paid two thousand dollars. I don' know why we keep fuckin' around with this crooked bullshit." The two horseplayers tore up their tickets and stalked off.

Every time a favorite loses, people grumble about cheating. Normally I felt no sympathy for horseplayers who bet the "chalk" as though it were a sure thing. But this time the complainers were right. The favorite had not been stiffed, but they had been cheated.

"Those guys would be pleased to know that the Thoroughbred Protective Bureau is on the case," Peter T. teased, giving Luci a pat on the back. Luci responded with a dark look just to remind him of the seriousness of the situation. But Peter T.'s sense of humor was irresistible and she broke into an embarrassed laugh.

Turning to me, she asked, "The exacta payoff is too low, isn't it?"

"Yeah. Two thousand may be too high, but a thousand to fifteen hundred would be more like it." I did some quick mental calculations. "With a twenty-percent track takeout, a fair return for a 20-1 horse over a 17-1 horse would be right around eleven hundred dollars."

"How do you know that? Are you a mathematician?"

"No," I answered. "Just a professional. I have to know those things just like you have to know the rules of racing or accepted security procedures."

"We won ourselves some money. How 'bout we go get it?" Peter T. suggested.

"Hold on," I said, placing a restraining hand on his arm as he turned for the mutuel windows. "We have to exploit this situation. When Winter Muffin won here, Kermit Golightly and his buddy Johnny Lanchek did just what we've done, cut into their payoff. Lanchek went to the windows right away and told a stranger what a great handicapper his friend Kermit was. Two days later Kermit's in a coma."

"In other words, they're hoppin' mad and they're watchin' to see who cashes in," Peter T. filled in.

"So we should wait to cash our tickets?" Luci asked.

"Not exactly," I answered. "We want to stir them up some, or we've accomplished nothing. What I'm suggesting is that I'll go cash the tickets. They already know who I am."

"I don't like it," Peter T. declared. "History shows that they're goin' to come after whoever got into their pockets. You're payin' me to investigate this case, so I oughta be the one they come after."

"The logic doesn't quite follow, but I appreciate the thought. Our advantage is that they don't know you or

Luci. We're ahead, and I'm probably safer if you're backing me up rather than the other way around."

Peter T. finally agreed that the idea made sense and we quickly formulated a plan. I would cash all tickets. This would take some time since the combined winnings amounted to nearly fifty thousand dollars. No single mutuel clerk would have that much cash. If Marcel's men were watching for big winners, they would have plenty of time to summon their leader. Under the plan, I would get the cash and go straight to the cab stand outside the clubhouse entrance, take a cab to Midway Airport, and get out at the "departures" area.

Peter T. would watch to determine if I were being followed. If Marcel or his people followed me to Midway, Peter T. in a second taxi would pick me up at the "arrivals" area on the lower level of the airport. If I were not being followed, Peter T. would get out at "departures" and then we would return to the track together to meet Luci at her car. We would then attempt to follow Marcel when he left the track.

"I have another idea," Peter T. said. He turned to Luci. "Right now, all the postrace testing and shit is going on for Thurgood, right?" She nodded. "Would they be doing anything special?"

"Probably not too much," she responded. "A longshot winner with a beaten favorite triggers an automatic investigation procedure that's pretty thorough. It's routine, but careful, if you know what I mean."

"What happens if they suspect something fishy? Get a tip or something?"

"They do the same things, but everything gets more intense. There's more security around the horse and they start interviewing the trainer and stablehands. Sometimes the stewards initiate a formal inquiry and the trainer has to explain the form reversal for the record. Normally, none of that happens unless they find something."

"I see what you're driving at," I said. Peter T. had found a way to turn up the heat.

"While we're playing chase, why don't you get to the Bureau people?" Peter T. continued. "You know what to tell them. If we're right that Norm Culver is uneasy with Marcel and company, an investigation that goes beyond routine could make him real nervous."

Luci agreed with enthusiasm and we scrambled to take up our respective roles. The lines at the mutuel windows were still short with fifteen minutes remaining before the fifth race. I stepped up to a window and presented the winning tickets.

The mutuel clerk ran them through the optical scanner without first looking at them. When the amount of the payoff came up on the digital readout, he muttered with disgust. The large payoff would cause extra work and tie up his window until well past post time.

"I don't have that much cash, sir," the clerk grumbled. "I'll have to get a supervisor."

As I stood there waiting, several bettors got in the line behind me. Each time I warned them that the clerk had a problem with his machine and each time they glared me as though the problem were my fault before moving to another line. Repeating this warning was beginning to bore me, but the strategy had been to attract some attention. I was certainly doing that. Marcel was nowhere in sight, but as time passed, I began to feel confident that I had been observed.

Finally a supervisor arrived with the still visibly annoyed clerk in tow. After clearing the tote machine, he took my winning tickets and the payoff receipt issued by the tote machine and directed me to a small office adjacent to the mutuel area.

I was admitted by a buzzer lock and found myself in the presence of the mutuels supervisor and another man in a lightweight suit and a neat haircut. Security, I thought to myself.

"It will take a few minutes to issue a check in this amount," the supervisor explained. "I thought you might be more comfortable waiting in here. This is Mr. Canfield, by the way." He did not explain Mr. Canfield's position.

"If you don't mind, I would prefer cash," I said calmly.

The supervisor was somewhat disconcerted. "Sir, normally we issue a check for payoffs in this amount."

"But you're required to pay off in cash if I demand it?"

"Well, yes, but carrying that much cash is dangerous.

This is a rough town. I assure you that any bank will honor our check."

"I don't want to give you a hard time," I explained in mild apology, "but the banks don't open until Monday and I have a plane to catch tonight. I appreciate your concern for my safety and I promise to exercise caution."

The supervisor was clearly unhappy, but could see that I was not about to give in. "I'll have to call down to the main cashier," he said. "It'll be a few minutes before the cash gets up here."

"So you're from out of town?" Canfield finally spoke up, observing the obvious.

"Yes." I offered no further explanation. I had no real reason to annoy Canfield, but the man's manner rankled me. None of the payoffs required forms or withholding for the IRS, so I was under no legal obligation to give him any information.

"You really hit a big one here," Canfield said, trying to be affable. "That Norm Culver really brings in some long shots."

I responded with a blank look. "Who's Norm Culver?"

"The trainer," Canfield replied incredulously. "You mean you just won almost fifty thousand dollars and you don't know who trained the horse? How did you happen to pick this horse?"

I shrugged. "Just luck, I guess."

"Did you like his breeding? Did he look especially sharp to you? Did someone give you a tip? How did you pick him?"

"I liked his name," I answered, trying to look a bit embarrassed by my good fortune. "And four is my lucky number."

Canfield was getting frustrated. "You bet, let's see, two thousand dollars on this horse, and in several different bets too. All this because you liked his name and number? I can't quite believe that."

Again I shrugged. "I got a strong hunch and went back and bet more."

"That's a lot of money for a hunch."

"Depends on your point of view. I have a lot of money."

The mutuel supervisor arrived with four banded stacks of one-hundred-dollar bills, ten thousand dollars to a stack. He counted out an additional eighty-eight hundred. Canfield looked on, fuming.

"What about the exacta?" Canfield demanded. "You actually had two long shots. How did you happen to pick that combination?" Canfield clearly thought he had me on that one.

"My birthday is April 8," I lied with a smile. So far I had cited every mindless hunch play I could think of. "I always play my birthday in the exacta." I picked up the money. I had spun a tale which was highly unlikely, but not impossible. Canfield was fairly certain that I was not a rich idiot, but there was nothing he could do. I turned for the door. "Thank you very much, gentlemen," I said over my shoulder.

The mutuel supervisor looked pained, but Canfield just glared. "By the way, I didn't catch your name," he said as I turned the doorknob.

"Bill Smith," I answered with a grin, and the door slammed behind me.

11

I was faintly amused, having had a laugh at Canfield's expense, but my mood quickly changed when I walked through the door and into the mutuel concourse. Marcel Larrance was leaning against the wall across from the office, conducting a whispered conversation with a sleazy-looking little weasel of a man. Though I had expected to see him, I was unprepared for the rush of fear and hatred that swept through me at his sight. I had been in combat, in life-threatening situations, but even through the worst, the most insane moments, I had never experienced a feeling so primitive and gut-wrenching. I was chemically primed to flee or attack, and for a split second I had no control over which it would be. The sensation passed almost instantly, but I knew I would never forget it.

My next reaction was a nearly uncontrollable urge to laugh. Given the opportunity, I might have been willing to exchange the $48,800 in my portfolio for the look on Marcel's face. Even the dome of Marcel's hairless head turned bright red with confusion and rage. His entire body shook with fury and frustration. He saw me, knew I saw him, and in a room half the size of a football field and full of horseplayers, there was nothing Marcel could do about it. I gave him the finger.

At the clubhouse entrance I got in the first cab in line. The driver, who spoke very little English, was evidently hoping for a fare downtown or the O'Hare area, for he was visibly disappointed when I requested Midway as a destination. With an exaggerated reluctance, the driver started the meter and peeled away from the curb with a screech of tires, thereby costing himself a ten-dollar tip.

I didn't see Marcel following as the cab pulled away. Peter T. was nowhere in evidence either. I kept glancing to the rear during the short trip to the old airport, but I detected nothing unusual. The fare was four dollars and I gave the surly driver a five. Cheerful service, under the circumstances, would have been worth a good deal more.

Peter T. pulled up in a second taxi as the cabbie further wasted his tires in an expression of anger at the small fare and modest tip. I piled into the Texan's cab and in seconds we were on our way back to Sportsman's Park.

"God damn, son," Peter T. swore. "For a minute there, I thought you were going after that sonofabitch."

"Had you worried, did I?"

"Shit, no. I was worried about my money." We both laughed, the tension flowing out of us all at once.

The taxi driver explained politely that he could not take us to the horsemen's parking lot. Track rules stated that passengers could be dropped only at the clubhouse or grandstand entrances. The grandstand was a long walk and the clubhouse was too visible, so we had him pull into the cab stand halfway between the clubhouse entrance and our preferred destination. I gave the guy a twenty—more for the good manners than the service.

Luci was already in the Bronco, sitting with the windows down and smoking a cigarette. Neither of us had seen her smoking in the time we had known her. She caught my questioning look and flushed like a teenager caught smoking in the school rest room.

"I quit two weeks ago," she explained. "I know it's bad for me, but today has just been too much."

"You don't have to explain to us, darlin'," Peter T. said, lighting up.

"Shit," she cursed, and threw the butt out the window. "I'm not embarrassed about smoking. I'm pissed that with a little stress, I need to."

"Maybe this will ease your stress," I suggested, removing the stacks of hundred-dollar bills from my case. I gave her a banded stack of ten thousand dollars, plus an additional twenty-four hundred. She counted out the five hundred dollars I had loaned her and handed it back.

"I have to confess, I'm a little uncomfortable taking this money after I've had a chance to think about it," she said with a troubled frown.

"Better us than Marcel and his friends," Peter T. shot back philosophically. "You can't give it back to the people who lost it, and if you could, they'd just find another way to lose it. What do you want to do? Turn it in to the Bureau?"

Luci stuffed the money into her purse, but I could tell that the issue still bothered her.

"Peter T.'s right," I said. "Why don't you just hold on to the cash for a while? I think by the time this is over, you're going to feel like you've earned it. If not, donate it to a worthy cause."

"I guess you're right," she agreed finally. "God, it's no wonder people become compulsive gamblers. When Thurgood was pulling away from the field, nothing else in the world mattered. All I could think of was how much money we'd won. I can't believe you do this every day. How do you keep your sanity?"

"Where'd you get the idea he was sane?" Peter T. quipped.

"The wins aren't often that big, but I know what you mean." I had seen people go out of control from betting on horses, and there had been times when I, too, had felt a little crazy. "To do what I do, you have to treat it like a business. You don't fall in love with a horse any more than a commodities trader gets emotional over soybeans."

"Maybe so, but races are a lot more exciting than soybeans." She looked skeptical. In fact, I had no real answer. I liked to watch and did get excited about horse races. Solving the puzzle often took precedence over profit potential, as my annual obsession with the Kentucky Derby proved. I felt compelled to bet the Derby and, unlike my day-to-day activity, I was willing to lose money on an unsure proposition rather than pass. As Luci observed, remaining completely dispassionate was impossible.

I felt Luci watching me carefully, waiting for further elaboration. I had always been content with the investor/trader spiel because it had a ring of truth while maintaining an air of mystery and inside knowledge. Strangely, this time I felt the need to make her understand, and I struggled to find the words.

"Here he comes." Peter T. broke the spell. Lucky

that someone was paying attention to business, I thought. Marcel had just passed the guard shack at the entrance to the stable area and was making his way between cars in the lot.

"He drives a beat-up old pickup. I don't know what make," I explained, easing down in the backseat.

"That's great," Peter T. muttered sarcastically. "This lot has more pickups than a cowboy bar on Saturday night."

Indeed, Marcel was headed in our direction, and beat-up trucks made up maybe sixty percent of the vehicles in the horsemen's lot. In near-panic, I noted that the truck parked next to us could have been the one Marcel drove in the alley behind Frankie's.

"He still looks mad," Luci observed.

"That's how he always looks," I told her. "You should see him when he really gets pissed."

"Oh, we did," she responded accusingly. "Giving him the finger was a great idea."

Marcel stopped two rows in front of us and unlocked a brown Ford pickup. Without so much as a glance in our direction, he backed out of his space and drove away in a shower of gravel. The races were still in progress, so traffic leaving the track was sparse. Luci maneuvered the Bronco to follow at a discreet distance.

Marcel turned north on Cicero Avenue, driving aggressively, cutting in and out of traffic. Luci, showing considerable skill, stayed with him. We were hoping that Marcel would lead us to his Chicago hideout so we could keep track of his movements and visitors.

Marcel took the westbound entrance to I-290, the Eisenhower Expressway, and quickly accelerated to almost seventy miles per hour. The old truck looked incapable of much more. After five or six miles, he took the northbound entrance to I-294.

"Shit!" Luci cursed, groping for her purse. "This is a toll road."

"Just drive," Peter T. cautioned her. Between us Peter T. and I came up with a handful of change and Luci followed Marcel through the exact-change booth, breathing somewhat easier. The lines at the manned booths had been just long enough to give Marcel enough time to get away. Ten minutes later, Marcel took the I-190 exit for O'Hare Airport.

Luci pounded her fists on the steering wheel in frustration. "Goddammit, he must have spotted us."

Peter T. was the essence of calm. "I don't think so. As far as he knows, Tennyson left the track in a taxi, and no one else has reason to follow him. I bet he's flyin' somewhere."

"So now what do we do?" she demanded impatiently. Just as I had planned to lose pursuers at Midway, Marcel could easily disappear in the crowds of O'Hare.

Peter T. was undismayed. "If he's flyin' out, he'll park in the garage closest to the terminal he needs. If he's pickin' someone up, he'll try for a space in a metered lot." Our expectations soared. If Marcel was meeting a flight, we might get a look at another player in this game.

No such luck. Marcel pulled into the parking garage serving the terminal housing American and Delta, among others.

"Quick, let me out here," Peter T. ordered, almost bailing out of the moving vehicle. "Park some ways away from him and follow. Don't let him see you." He ran across two lanes of traffic to the terminal entrance.

In the dim light of the garage, Luci and I caught sight of Marcel's brake lights just after he had pulled into a parking space. He was taking a small carry-on bag from the front seat when we cruised past like travelers looking for a place to park. We found a place about fifty yards further on, parked, and followed the arrows to the elevator. We could hardly get on the same elevator as Marcel, so we waited at a distance until he boarded before we hustled down four flights of stairs in time to catch sight of our target crossing the street to the terminal.

Out of the gloom of the garage, we had to maintain a greater distance. Marcel crossed the baggage-claim area and took the escalator to the main floor of the terminal. We let him reach the top before boarding.

On the main floor, Luci and I looked at each other in dismay. Marcel was nowhere in sight. Hundreds of people milled around, lining up before ticket counters and checking the flight-information monitors.

"American," Peter T. stated flatly, coming up behind us. Marcel was standing in front of the ticket counter checking the information on the screen against the contents of a red-white-and-blue ticket wallet in his hand.

"Go ahead. The H-K concourse," Peter T. ordered urgently. "I'll stay with Skinhead. Don't let him see you."

Luci and I cleared security and reached the point where the concourse split. American had gates in both sections.

"Terrific," I muttered.

Luci was watching the corridor behind us. "Shit! Here comes Marcel. He's bound to see us!"

Reflexively I nearly turned to look when Luci threw her arms around my neck and kissed me. At that instant Marcel could have been aiming a cannon at us and I wouldn't have cared. I returned the kiss with more enthusiasm than Luci was expecting, but she responded with an intensity that made me dizzy. When we broke, Marcel was gone and Luci was regarding me with a quizzical expression.

"Jesus Christ, let's move it," Peter T. griped as he continued his pursuit. Luci and I looked at each other and laughed. We followed Peter T. along concourse H, only this time Luci took my arm. Perhaps she was only carrying out the cover, but I knew that something had passed between us which merited further examination at a better time and place.

Ahead, Peter T. had come to a stop. About fifty feet further, Marcel was presenting his ticket to a gate agent and obtaining a boarding pass. Luci dropped my arm and walked on past the gate while I went in the other direction and found a seat at the bar of a small cocktail lounge.

In a few moments, Luci returned. From her expression I could see that she was clearly unhappy. "He got his boarding pass and went straight to a phone. Peter T. is waiting for a phone to open up so he can hear what Marcel's saying."

"Where is the flight going?"

"Dallas."

"Damn!"

Peter T. came in and ordered three beers without preliminary. The bartender served them up immediately, in the normal accelerated service characteristic of airport bars.

"He's boarding now," Peter T. informed us after draining off half his beer directly from the bottle.

"Did you pick up any of the telephone conversation?"

He shook his head. "All the phones were taken and I couldn't get near until he was almost done. He said, 'Okay, okay, I'll see you tonight,' and hung up just as I got to a phone. All I can tell you is that he wasn't passing a pleasant time of day with someone."

"You think they're feeling the heat?"

"I think you could say that." Peter T. waved to the bartender for another beer.

I fumbled in my pockets and came up with a cigarette. Luci went to her purse with the same idea in mind and I lit hers and then my own. "From Dallas he can connect to anywhere in the country," I said finally.

"Maybe," Peter T. agreed absently, "but you can fly anywhere from here too. Why fly to Dallas for a connection?"

"So you think his destination is Dallas?"

"Somewhere in Texas, anyway. I guess we'll have to find out." He got up from the bar with some effort. "I'll be right back."

Luci looked at me with a question in her eyes. "I don't know," I said with a shrug. "Maybe he has a contact with the airline."

"Where do you think Marcel is going?"

"If Peter T. is right about Texas being his final destination, he's probably headed to wherever they keep and train their horses. Texas would be a good choice. It's wide open and it's centered between all the tracks where they've raced."

"If we could just find out the location of that farm," Luci speculated. "We'd have them, ringers and all."

"That's the key," I agreed, "but how do you find a single horse farm in Texas when you don't know where to start?"

We sat there for a time, sipping our beers without much interest in the beverage. I wanted to tell her that I had enjoyed the kiss more than I could describe, but for some reason I continued to have a problem expressing myself in her presence. I noticed her looking at me strangely, out of the corner of her eye and behind lowered lashes, but she, too, remained silent.

I weighed desire against fear of rejection and began, "Listen I . . ."

"What's the matter with you guys?" Peter T. demanded, resuming his seat at the bar, oblivious of his timing. "Y'all look like your dog died. We've got these assholes on the run. Oops, 'scuse me." We laughed at Peter T.'s irrepressibility, but we reminded him that Marcel had quite literally "flown" and, even though pressure was being brought to bear on Norm Culver, chances were that the trainer knew nothing of value.

Peter T. remained undaunted. "We'll pick up Marcel's trail. I've got a friend of mine meetin' that flight. We'll at least find out whether he stays in Texas or makes a connection somewhere."

"Suppose he stays in Texas?" Luci asked. "Suppose Tennyson is right and they have their horses there? How will we ever find them in a giant state that has as many horses as people?"

"We don't have all that many thoroughbreds," the Texan insisted. "If their operation is based in Texas, we'll find it." Peter T.'s confidence was unshakable, but I remained skeptical and said so.

"Son, this is where I start earning my money," he declared. "If I can't find a thoroughbred training center in Texas, I'm in the wrong business."

"No false modesty in our boy, Peter T.," Luci teased.

The Texan forcefully set down his empty beer bottle with an emphatic nod of his head. "Everybody's got to believe in something, darlin'. I believe I'll have another beer."

Luci and I were watching a movie on HBO and eating pizza while Peter T. talked to his Texas associate in one of the suite's two bedrooms. The timing of the call suggested that the news was not going to be good. A flight from Chicago to Dallas takes just under two hours. That the Texas contact had called about two and a half hours after the flight departed seemed to indicate that Marcel had changed planes and continued his journey, or that he had deplaned in Dallas and subsequently eluded Peter T.'s operative.

Peter T. completed his call and joined us. "Marcel got off in Dallas. There was a guy waitin' for him. A

Mexican. My man followed them into the parking garage and got the license number of the Mexican's truck. A Texas plate with a Harrison County sticker—that's out around the Longview/Marshall area, closer to Shreveport than Dallas. Obviously, Donnie couldn't follow beyond the garage, but I'd say we did all right with what we got."

"All right!" Luci whooped. "If we can trace the plate, maybe we can narrow the search some."

"Let's hope we get lucky," Peter T. agreed.

"So what do we do now?" I asked.

"I think you two should follow up here with the testing and verification of ol' Thurgood. I don't think these boys are gonna screw up, but you never know. I believe I'll go to Texas tomorrow."

"To Longview?"

"No, Austin. We need more than a license number before we start centering on any location. I can get more done from home at this point."

"Peter T., just as a matter of professional curiosity, how will you go about finding this training center?" Luci asked.

Peter T. stared briefly at Luci, mentally debating whether or not to reveal a trade secret. "Thoroughbreds eat better than ordinary horses," he began seriously. "I'll just scout around for oat-rich horse turds."

Luci started to ask another question before realizing that the Texan was putting her on. When Peter T. and I burst into laughter, her Cajun temper was aroused and she looked around for something to swing or throw.

Peter T. held up both hands in surrender. "It's almost like that. Honest. Race horses do eat more oats and less hay. They get special vitamins and medication. I know most of the big feed dealers, but chances are they pick up their feed rather than have it delivered. A better shot would be vets. The horses would have to get treatment now and then, but I think I can do better than that." Peter T. paused long enough to capture and open another beer. He seemed capable of consuming almost unlimited quantities of beer without displaying any ill effects.

"Farriers," the Texan continued. "It's a lost art and there aren't but two or three dozen in the state, maybe a couple hundred in the whole country."

"Farriers!" Luci exclaimed, admiration in her voice. "Horses need shoes and race horses need special shoes. But how do you find them?"

"The computer age, darlin'. Tennyson keeps his records on computer and so do I. I might not have 'em all, but I have enough to make our chances damn good."

Earlier that day, I had considered finding a secret horse farm in Texas an impossible task. Peter T. was making it sound almost easy. I knew that he was oversimplifying somewhat, perhaps unwilling to volunteer all of his trade secrets, but every day I was feeling more confident. Now I was prepared to agree with Peter T.: we had them on the run.

Luci and I turned back to the movie and Peter T. retrieved a beer from the ice bucket. On the table, where the hotel's maids had left it neatly folded, was a day-old edition of the Detroit *News*. I had purchased the paper before Luci and I left for Chicago and had forgotten to throw it away. Peter T. leafed absently through its pages while he drank.

"God damn! Take a look at this," he nearly shouted, interrupting the film once more.

The item Peter T. referred to occupied just a couple of columns at the bottom of the second page of the Metro section. The modest headline read: "DANCER'S BODY FOUND."

The story went on to describe the discovery of the beaten and sexually assaulted corpse of Leslie Pilarcik in a dumpster in northwest Detroit. The police were "seeking information."

"Wasn't Frankie's the place where you got your ass kicked and Luci played Annie Oakley?" Peter T. suggested. His teasing smile faded when he saw my ashen face.

I walked away from the table and sat down hard in a chair, my hands shaking. "Jesus," I murmured.

"What is it, son?" Peter T. urged.

I told them about what Vanessa said about her friend "Leslie" and Marcel.

"At least this Vanessa can give the cops a lead," he said.

I shook my head. "She won't talk," I said sorrowfully. "She'll be too scared of Marcel and too scared of the police. They'll never hear about it."

"Oh, yes they will," Luci growled as she snatched up the paper. Furiously she punched numbers on the face of the telephone, reaching, in turn, Directory Assistance, Detroit Police Headquarters, and finally, the Sixteenth Precinct detective mentioned in the newspaper report. Without identifying herself, she suggested that the police interview a dancer at Frankie's named Vanessa about a certain Marcel Larrance. She even gave them the name and room number of the motel where Marcel stayed.

She was still quaking with fear and rage when she put down the phone. "I told you something terrible happened in that motel room," she said, her voice heavy with emotion. I took her in my arms and held her until she settled down. I had seen Marcel's rapt attention to the dancers at Frankie's and I had witnessed Vanessa's revulsion. There was no doubt in my mind that Luci's conclusion was correct.

12

The sun was just starting to make me drowsy. I had made myself as comfortable as possible in the outdoor grandstand seats of Sportsman's Park. My feet were up on the seat in front of me, the *Racing Form* resting on my knees. By the time the afternoon's racing began, the grandstand would be completely shaded, but now the sun, moving toward its zenith, caught this section of stands and warmed it softly.

Luci was attending the stewards' inquiry into the running of the fourth race on yesterday's program. I had no expectation that the stewards would find anything untoward, nor had I any hope that the procedure would unnerve Norm Culver. Even if Culver had his suspicions about Thurgood, he had to know that he was in the clear if only he were to play dumb.

The Capricorn/Orion ringers were somewhat removed from my thoughts as I watched a handful of horses complete their morning workouts. I went over the past twenty-four hours. Lucinda DeGuerre. Something was developing between us that both thrilled and threatened me.

Luci, Peter T., and I had worked until nearly midnight devising a system for maintaining communication and setting forth contingency plans. The exhilaration from the big win with Thurgood, the intensity of the pursuit of Marcel Larrance from the track to O'Hare Airport, and the numbing discovery that the scar-faced man was very likely a murderer, had combined to leave us emotionally drained. We decided to call it a night. Peter T. had an early flight and Luci volunteered to pick him up in the morning.

"No need, darlin'," Peter T. had insisted. "The hotel has a courtesy car. You guys get some rest."

"Sounds good to me," Luci acquiesced.

"I'm not likely to sleep in," I confessed. "I'm starting to get desperate for some exercise. Even this joint's Universal Gym is beginning to sound good."

"Why don't you work out at my club?" Luci suggested. "I'll pick you up in the morning, we'll drop Peter T. at the airport, and you can work out while I drum up a racquetball game."

That she played racquetball seemed too good to be true, and we confirmed the date. According to plan, we would hit the courts, grab some breakfast, and still get to the track in plenty of time for the stewards' inquiry.

"Fitness maniacs," Peter T. muttered in mock disgust.

Over her protests, I had walked Luci to her car. She got the Bronco unlocked, but hesitated before climbing in, as if she had forgotten something. Abruptly she turned and, with precisely the same move she had used earlier at the airport, kissed me with the same passion. Like a teenager on a first date, I was dazed and awkward at her touch. Without another word she climbed into the truck and drove away.

Earlier that morning the "battle of the sandbaggers" had taken place. Luci was a graduate of Memphis State University, one of a handful of colleges where racquetball is taken very seriously. She had competed at the intercollegiate level and, one year, had been a semifinalist in women's doubles at the national tournament. In other words, she was very good at the game and was an expert at taking overconfident men by surprise. While she was outgunned by professionals and semipros, she was more than a match for the average club A player.

Luci had retained a slight advantage in that she knew, from the dossier she had read, that I was a quality player. Nevada might not have been as deep in talent as Chicago, but a senior-division champion could be expected to be a challenge.

The equipment Luci carried and the way she warmed up had tipped me off to her game. Casual players did not spend the money for $150 oversize rackets with customized grips. Her warmup was precise, designed to test a variety of shots and establish a rhythm in her footwork. One of my frequent playing partners in Las Vegas was a lady once ranked on the women's pro tour, a hundred-and-ten pounder with an angelic smile and wrists of steel. Luci, I noted, had the same look of intense concentration and the same stylistic strokes. I was certain I was intended to be her next victim.

I loosened up carefully, revealing nothing of style or strategy. I knew nothing of the dossier's revelations and hoped that she would believe she had nothing to worry about.

"Loser buys breakfast," Luci had suggested innocently.

We played a tournament-style match, best three out of five games to eleven points. Luci came out firing and won the first game, while I experimented and analyzed her strengths and weaknesses. Her strategy was solid. Recognizing that she couldn't match a man's power, she concentrated on not making unforced errors while she invited her opponents to gamble and show off. Then with her deft quickness, she would gobble up mistakes and put the ball away to score.

I had seen these tactics before, having employed them myself against younger, faster opponents. In the next three games I refused to take the shots she wanted me to take and reversed the strategy, making her come to the back court to shoot, thereby negating her quickness. In a contest of skills, we might have been evenly matched, but experience lay clearly on my side. I earned both her respect and a free breakfast.

"I feel a little guilty monopolizing your time like this," I told her at breakfast. "I mean, this is your hometown and I'm probably interfering with your plans. For all I know, you're engaged or have a steady boyfriend who's wondering where you've been." I couldn't believe how moronic I sounded.

"Tennyson," she interrupted my awkward babbling, "will you stop it. Honestly, how can a man of your . . . experience . . . aha, you thought I was going to say age . . . how can you be so dumb? I mean, can't you tell when a woman is attracted to you?"

In retrospect I realized that my expression must have

betrayed my surprise and it must have been ridiculous, for she had laughed uproariously.

"You don't think a man of my, ah, experience is too old for you?" I had asked, voicing my worst fears.

Her grin was full of mischief. "I guess that remains to be seen, doesn't it?" Her expression grew more serious. "I have to admit, you've taken me completely by surprise. When I read your file, I had this image of a professional horseplayer in my mind. You can imagine what I mean, someone wild and independent, accustomed to a fast life-style. Hot cars, hotter women, diamond pinkie rings, the whole stereotype. Then, instead of coming on strong, you seemed reserved, almost shy." She gave me a sly smile just to let me know that my bumbling hadn't been completely overlooked.

"After we started working on this thing, I became impressed with the way your mind worked. Those wheels seemed to be constantly turning and I was even becoming slightly intimidated."

She held up a hand when I started to protest. "What gets me—every time I think I have you figured out, you show me some other side of yourself. Christ, you even beat me at my favorite sport, and you outfoxed me rather than overpowered me. You're a fascinating and complicated man, Tennyson, and I want to get to know you better." The mischievous grin was back. "There," she declared with an emphatic toss of her head. "We're officially past the 'awkward stage.' Now let's just see what develops."

Yes, something indeed was developing, I thought, as stablehands led the last horses back to the barns and the ground crew fired up their tractors. I was in the midst of a very serious and threatening situation, yet the Chicago sunshine could have been like the beach at Maui, the breeze off the Cicero factories blew tropical and fragrant. You're too old, I warned myself, to be so infatuated. My experience with a serious relationship had been too full of heartache to allow me to be so full of hope. I tried to summon thoughts of Jenna and found her memory to be just a bit more remote, the wound of her loss slightly less tender.

Shaking off cautions and contrition, I let my thoughts

drift forward to the evening . . . dinner at Luci's apartment. No business. No horses, no ringers, no cheaters. Just the two of us. Completely relaxed and flushed with anticipation, I dozed off in the sunlight, thinking about my newfound luck.

A sharp blow to the rib cage jolted me awake and dispelled any further dreams. Ratface, his broken jaw wired and his eyes venting hatred, glared down at me. His partner, Neanderthal, held a gun, complete with silencer, to my temple. Frantically I looked around for possible assistance, but there was no one in this section of the stands. Ratface jerked his head in a silent indication that I was to rise. There was nothing to be done but to comply. They could have shot me as I slept and escaped undetected.

Once inside the betting concourse, I saw that the track was beginning to fill up with fans. Neanderthal kept the gun hidden under his jacket as I walked, bracketed between the two thugs. The track early birds, absorbed by the task of selecting winners, paid the three of us no attention. My eyes were constantly moving, looking for a possible means of escape or a source of assistance, but I saw no security guards or cops.

I cursed myself for a fool. DeMaria must have revealed my location to the Chicago bookies. I'd been stupid to trust the fat man and even more stupid to come back to the track today. Nothing like making it easy for them, I lamented silently. On the open mezzanine above me, I saw the TPB agent Canfield come out of a room in the company of other men in jackets and ties. A few seconds later, Luci came out by herself. She paused at the rail overlooking the concourse where I walked with my two captors. Desperately I willed her to look my way. In moments we would be out of the building and I would be out of reach of any help.

At that moment, she looked my way and our eyes met. Her expression grew quizzical. What's going on? her eyes asked. I looked first at one of the men, then at the other, and finally raised my eyes back to Luci. She must have understood my silent message. She whirled and checked the mezzanine, but found it empty. I watched her break into a run in the opposite direction and my spirits lifted slightly. My captors had not noticed her. Luci had seen and understood, I told myself. I might have a chance if only I could get free of Ratface and Neanderthal.

Ahead in the concourse, between the three of us and the exit, a large black man was heading our way. He was walking slowly, his attention riveted on the *Racing Form* rather than on the people around him. My captors and I were about fifty feet from a gate and racing fans were now entering in a steady stream. I figured that if I could break for the gate and reach the parking area, Neanderthal might hesitate to use the gun in a crowd.

As we passed the big horseplayer, I faked a stumble and bumped Neanderthal directly into the man.

"What the fuck," the black man growled indignantly as Neanderthal crushed his *Form* and knocked his program from his hand. In that instant of confrontation I straightened and threw a ragged punch at Ratface. It was a glancing blow, but it caught Ratface on his previously broken jaw and he howled in pain. The black man shoved Neanderthal and I was off and running.

I could hear shouts behind me as I crashed through the gate. The entering horseplayers voiced their outrage as I plowed through. Their protests grew even more vocal as Ratface and Neanderthal followed on my heels. There was a collective gasp of astonishment as Neanderthal leveled the gun, and the people in front of me scattered to get out of the line of fire.

The shot never came and I dodged between cars, hoping to get a line of busses between me and the two thugs. I glanced over my shoulder to gauge the pursuit and almost got run down as the Bronco slid to a halt in a shower of gravel. Luci had anticipated that Ratface and Neanderthal would try to exit the track and had hustled to her car. I scrambled into the passenger seat, urging her to go. Behind us Neanderthal leveled the gun once more, but Ratface held him back with a hand on his arm. With his free hand, Ratface was motioning frantically. At first I couldn't see the object of his signal. Then a black Cadillac limousine detached itself from the curb and sped to the two thugs.

Luci glanced nervously into the rearview mirror. Our progress was slow, impeded by pedestrians. All of the gates to the grounds were set up in a receiving mode. We were struggling against the grain. Our only salvation was that the limo was obstructed by a bus which was even then unloading passengers.

Finally Luci broke clear and we were out on Cicero Avenue. The traffic inbound to the track was heavy, but the limo bulled its way past the bus and was soon on our tail. Just a few cars separated the limo and the Bronco. The entrance to I-55, the Stevenson Expressway, loomed ahead, and Luci seemed inclined to take it.

"No," I shouted, "not the expressway." The big limo was undoubtedly capable of a higher top speed and our pursuers could use its bulk to force us off the road or come alongside and bring their guns to bear.

Luci ignored the warning, taking the westbound ramp and increasing her speed. The little truck was more agile than the limo and we opened a little distance on the ramp.

"Trust me," Luci said calmly. The limo began gaining ground as we merged onto the expressway. Its driver swung wide into a passing lane and I could see heads and arms come out of the open windows. I expected Luci to change lanes also, but she stayed in the extreme right. The limo gained inexorably and Ratface's features became clear, as did the shotgun trained out the window in our direction. Luci swerved, appearing to be panicked with indecision. Ratface caught the movement and grinned his steel-wire grin.

As the limo started to draw alongside, Luci, no longer indecisive, cut sharply to her right, cutting in front of the traffic exiting the expressway at Central Avenue. I saw Ratface's head snap back as the limo braked sharply to avoid passing the exit. Behind us horns sounded indignantly as the limo forced itself into the line of exiting cars. We had gained as much as ten car lengths but now they were mired in the traffic headed back toward the track.

Luci's strategy became evident, and I grinned in admiration. In the thick snarl of cars, the maneuverability of the Bronco was now a clear advantage. The goons in the limo apparently didn't think so as they edged out, little by little, into the oncoming lane, waiting for a break in traffic. My heart sank as I realized their intention, but Luci remained unfazed.

"C'mon, assholes," she muttered between clenched teeth. To the right of the Bronco were the empty grounds of Hawthorne Race Course, the sister track to Sportsman's Park. There was nothing but a long run of chainlink fence. We had nowhere to go, but Luci actually smiled as the limo wheeled out into the oncoming lanes to overtake us.

As coolly as a brain surgeon, Luci jumped the little truck over the curb and traveled along a sidewalk just wide enough for it to pass. In the line of cars, racetrack patrons gesticulated angrily at what they presumed to be a brazen attempt to ditch the traffic. The limo slowed, its occupants oblivious of the chaos created by its presence in the lane heading the wrong way. There was a solid line of cars between the Bronco and the limo as it attempted to parallel our flight.

We came to a break in the Hawthorne fence, a gate with a guard shack and a barricade. Luci made a hard right, sending the barricade flying, and, ignoring the irate guard, she sped across the open parking lot. There was no way the limousine could follow. The maneuver was slick, but I was puzzled. We seemed trapped in the empty Hawthorne Park, but Luci was unperturbed.

We reached the stable area, where another guard, this one almost apoplectic with anger, confronted us. Luci cut him off with a flash of her identification and the guard scrambled to lift the gate to the stable area. With a sigh of relief, she slowed to the service road's posted fifteen miles per hour. To my surprise, the stables were not empty but were bustling with activity.

"Half the horses running at Sportsman's are stabled here," Luci explained. "The service drive lets out on Cicero. We'll be out of here before they can circle around."

In a matter of minutes we were back on Cicero Avenue heading south away from the track. We went west on the Stevenson Expressway with no destination in mind, but with the simple desire to put distance between ourselves and Sportman's Park. After about ten minutes on the road, the narrowness of the escape began to hit me and I slumped in my seat, gulping great drafts of air. Luci looked on with concern and took the first exit from the expressway. We parked in front of a shopping center and smoked quietly, trying to collect our thoughts.

"Looks like your friend DeMaria pulled the plug on you," Luci offered after a moment.

I shook my head before the words came to me. "Not DeMaria," I croaked. "Had to be the Larrance brothers."

"Could be," she agreed, "but why not DeMaria?"

"DeMaria knew where I was soon enough to have grabbed me at the track yesterday. With his connections, a couple of phone calls would have been enough. Besides, I think DeMaria wants me on the loose, particularly now that I've fed him some information. He has nothing to gain if the local boys grab me."

She seemed to take time mulling this idea over. "Okay, let's assume DeMaria is still neutral. What do we do now?"

"I'm not sure," I confessed. "Why don't we just drive while I get my act together."

We continued on our aimless course while I examined our options. There was no question in my mind that we had to get out of Chicago. Marcel had gone to some location in Texas, and Peter T. Westmoreland was on his trail. Nothing but the threat of capture remained in Chicago. We could link up with Peter T. in Texas, but our presence there would be superfluous until Peter T. managed to locate the training center. I was determined to do something constructive rather than wait for Peter T. to perform. The logical choice was Las Vegas.

"Las Vegas!" Luci exclaimed when I told her. "You barely got out of Vegas in one piece and now you want to go back?"

"It's the last place they'll expect to find me," I argued with more confidence than I felt. "We'll stay in one of the big hotels under a different name. They won't even be looking."

"But why Vegas?" she demanded, unconvinced.

"We can't stay here and Peter T. doesn't need us to find the training center. At least in Vegas we can try to track the movement of money. Who knows, maybe we'll get lucky. At least we'll be doing something."

"All right," she agreed, "let's swing by my place to get a few things and catch a plane. We can call for reservations from there."

"Too risky. There's a good chance they picked up your

license number and have your place watched by now. No reservations either. We'll pay cash and give the airline a false name. Let's just go to O'Hare and hope they're not watching the airport."

"But I don't have any clothes . . ." She broke off her protest abruptly. "Sorry. That was dumb. This isn't a vacation."

"We have plenty of cash," I agreed. "You can get a whole new wardrobe once we arrive."

However tough and competent Lucinda DeGuerre had revealed herself to be, she was entirely feminine in her enthusiasm for a shopping spree. Her expression brightened at the prospect, and the tension of the past hour faded. I stared at her, marveling at her resilience, recognizing that she had saved my ass a second time. Had things gone a bit differently, I might have been hanging from a meat hook in some deserted Chicago warehouse.

We were lucky. There was a flight leaving for Las Vegas in a half-hour with seats available. With a few minutes to spare, I dialed the Turf Club's number and, disguising my voice as much as possible, asked for Cowboy. A few feet away, Luci was on another telephone checking in with her office.

Cowboy readily agreed to my requests. He would rent a suite in his name at the Hilton, hire a car, and meet our flight. Though Cowboy was among the people who knew of my relationship with Kermit, I dismissed the possibility that the Texas could be the betrayer. I had to trust someone.

Luci finished her call a few minutes after mine and joined me in the departure lounge. She placed a hand on my arm.

"Those guys kinda messed up our evening," she said somewhat wistfully. When I didn't respond, she continued, "I did something when I had Mel on the line. I hope you approve."

"What's that?"

"I can't get that dancer out of my mind. You know, the one from Frankie's."

"What about her?"

"I realize we can't be sure Marcel had anything to do with her murder," she began, but her expression showed that she was not in the least unsure. "Let's face it, Marcel's a maniac, probably a murdering maniac. People who commit sex crimes tend to repeat their actions. Do you know what I'm saying?"

"You think Marcel's killed other girls," I confirmed.

"Right. Anyway, I asked Mel to run a check through the police departments for unsolved murders of young women in the same towns where our horses ran. I know it's a long shot, but maybe there's a pattern." She paused for a moment for emphasis. "I also asked him to check for the same thing in Texas."

I turned sharply to stare at her. If Luci turned out to be right, if Leslie Pilarcik was not just an isolated case, a similar murder in Texas might pinpoint Marcel's location.

My stare must have revealed my unconcealed admiration. She took my hand and squeezed it gently. The theory might be a long shot, but it was the kind of long shot, based on information and intuition, which appealed to my horseplayer's instinct. I would have bet a bundle on it.

13

I watched Luci sleeping and thought wistfully about our evening that Ratface and his no-neck friend had screwed up. Instead of drinking wine and enjoying her cooking, I was picking at a tasteless airline meal; and instead of holding her close to me, the best I could do was watch her curl up beside me in a first-class seat. I hoped Ratface's employer had strung the goon up by his thumbs for losing us back in Chicago.

I never have been very good at sleeping on airplanes—or anywhere else for that matter—and I used the time to sort out our next moves. Initially Las Vegas had been a destination of impulse, but I was beginning to like the choice more and more. We should be safe enough, I thought. The Hilton was hardly my favorite hotel, but it was huge and off the Strip. More important, I knew none of the casino or race book people and doubted that they would know me by sight.

Just before our flight had boarded, I reached Peter T. Westmoreland at home, explained the latest developments, and provided the contact information. Peter T. would have preferred that we come to Austin, where he could assure our safety, but after discussion, he agreed that Vegas made some sense. He had reacted to Luci's idea of the police inquiry with great enthusiasm. According to our plan, while Peter T. worked to uncover the training center, Luci and I would try to locate the trail of betting money and follow it to Armand Larrance.

As the 727 crossed plains, mountains, and drylands, I considered how, exactly, this task could be accomplished. It made sense that the elusive Armand was in Vegas. Substantially more money was being bet off-track than on, with the majority going down in the legal race books. Someone had to be supervising the operation. Armand had put in at least one appearance in Las Vegas, as I knew well. I had an idea of where to start looking, and with that thought in mind, I fell into a fitful doze.

I came awake as the plane began its final descent, my body perceiving the change before the cabin lights came on. Luci awoke moments later as the flight attendant delivered hot towels. Rubbing her eyes, trying to come alert, she looked younger and more vulnerable than I had seen her before. I felt a fleeting desire to keep her secluded in the hotel suite with an armed guard to protect her, but I recognized as soon as the thought occurred that she would refuse to stand on the sidelines.

As soon as she was awake, excitement took over. Luci had confessed that she had never been in Las Vegas, had never had a desire to visit, but the town's magic was starting to grip her as it did virtually every tourist who flew in to "play with fire" for the first time. By the time we stepped out of the jetway, she was wide-eyed and nearly jumping out of her skin. I had to hustle her past the slot machines in the concourse, for she had heard the old rumor that the slots at the airport paid off better than the slots in town.

"I'm serious," she insisted. "I've heard that they do it to get you primed for the casinos when you come in and to get you leaving with a good feeling so you'll come back."

I'd heard that rumor hundreds of times. "Sweetheart, if that were true, this place would be so packed with slot rats, no one could fly anywhere." She was unconvinced and glanced wistfully at the one-armed bandits as we rolled through the concourse on the moving walkways.

Cowboy was waiting, as planned, at the baggage claim and, as I had expected, charmed Luci with his good-humored banter.

"A lady cop!" Cowboy exclaimed in amazement when I made the introductions. "Okay, a lady horse cop. Why, darlin', you're just a little bit of a thing, a jockey, an exercise rider, but a sure-'nough pistol-packin', crook-catchin' investigator of the TPB. I believe if I was a horse doper, I'd flat surrender. You ever been to Vegas before, Miz Luci?" Cowboy inquired with what could have passed for pride of ownership. "No? Well, my dear, you have arrived at paradise on earth, the proverbial money tree. All you have to know is how and when to harvest."

Luci raised a skeptical eyebrow in my direction, but I could tell she was enjoying Cowboy's courtly bullshit.

"Say, have you tried your luck at the slot machines yet?" Cowboy continued, welcoming a new and fresh audience. "They say that the slots at the airport pay off better than anywhere in town." She gave me a triumphant look as Cowboy pretended not to notice my baleful stare. I threw up my hands in surrender.

"Where can I get a roll of nickels?" she demanded, and I knew she would not be denied.

"Nickels! Darlin', you're in Vegas, not the Thibodaux American Legion." Cowboy was putting on his favorite act, but he had not missed the traces of Louisiana in her accent. He grabbed a passing change girl, but before he could flash his habitual roll of hundreds, I handed the girl a twenty and received a roll of dollar tokens.

Cowboy gave me a dirty look behind Luci's back before assisting in the selection of the appropriate machine, and explaining how to deposit coins—three at a time, of course. About halfway through the roll, three plums came up and the one-armed bandit obligingly spit out sixty coins, complete with bells and flashing lights.

To her credit, Luci neither screamed nor fainted. She recognized that, despite all the sound and fury, she had hardly broken the bank. Instead, like a true slot rat, she dug into the pile of coins to play again.

This time, Cowboy stopped her. "See how easy it is, darlin'?" he said, sweeping her winnings into a small plastic bucket. "You just have to know how and when to harvest, and when to walk," he added pointedly.

Since Cowboy obviously knew a great deal more about gambling than I did, she refrained from protest, accepting his assurance that there was plenty more where that came from. With the dignity of someone who routinely accepted winning as her due, she marched off arm-in-arm with the "Pride of Abilene." I handed the bucket of tokens, which Cowboy had somehow managed to stick me with, to the change girl and claimed Luci's winnings.

When I caught up with them, Cowboy was explaining one of his favorite gambling philosophies. " 'A man should make at least one bet every day,' " he drawled, paraphrasing a quotation generally attributed to the famous trainer "Plain Ben" Jones. " 'else he could be walkin' 'round lucky and not know it.' "

Cowboy escorted Luci and me up to the suite he had signed for earlier. We had bypassed the valet parking and entered through a side door. Our only luggage was the two satchels we had carried out of Luci's racquetball club. Mine contained the records of the investigation and cash. Luci's contained only her sweaty court clothes, racquetball gear, and a small makeup kit.

True to form, Cowboy showed us the accoutrements of the suite in considerable detail. "The bathroom even has one of them bidets"—Cowboy pronounced it *"bee-*day"—"and your very own telephone, 'case you get an important phone call when you also get the call of nature."

He finally bade us good-bye. "And in case you get bored with ol' cheap, here," he cautioned, giving her a friendly kiss on the cheek, "you know where to find the real action."

"I won't forget," she assured him. "One of Tennyson's most endearing qualities is that it seems his friends all come from Texas."

The door closed behind Cowboy and we were alone in the suite. Not one of those two-story jobs with a Jacuzzi, it was two standard rooms converted into a bedroom and a sitting room. Efficient and flexible from the hotel's point of view, it was comfortable enough.

"Is he always like that?" Luci asked, referring to Cowboy.

"Yes and no," I answered after a hesitation. "He keeps up that 'country comedy' routine most of the time, except when he's playing poker. No one has more fun that Cowboy, but some of it is an act that invites people to underestimate him. I'm one of the few people who know that Cowboy holds a master's degree from Rice University. He's smart as hell and all the time he's talking a mile a minute, his mind is recording unimaginable detail."

"Like the 'Thibodaux American Legion,' you mean." Luci missed very little herself. "You know, I've been to dances at the American Legion in Lake Charles, Louisiana, not Thibodaux, but I didn't think the accent was noticeable enough to be identifiable." She seemed perplexed by that idea.

"It's not," I assured her. "You have to remember that a gambler, particularly a poker player like Cowboy, has been everywhere, and when he's on the road, he talks to everyone. Being able to identify regional dialects is something of an edge. Around a poker table, he can separate the locals from the imports. That knowledge might make him some money or save him some."

She thought about that for a moment. I was beginning to follow how her mind worked and I could see her evaluating that piece of intelligence, applying the concept to her own work, and deciding that, if the concept worked for a gambler, it could be useful for an investigator as well. "Do you know what I want to do?" she asked finally. "You're gonna think I'm crazy. I want to go down to the casino and try my luck. Do you mind? I mean, will you go with me?"

The Las Vegas allure had worked again, just as intended. "If that's what you want, that's what we'll do. But, given my advanced age, I need a quick shower to wake me up. We have two bathrooms, so you have your choice. I warn you, however, don't let me see you partially unclothed or the casino will have to wait until tomorrow."

She smiled, giving the proposition fair consideration. "Later," she promised, presenting me with a quick kiss before ducking into the bedroom and closing the door. Ah, Las Vegas, I thought.

The shower brought me back. Las Vegas worked on me too, I realized. It always had. I stood staring at my reflection in the mirror. Good sense dictated that we lie low, avoiding the risk that someone in the casino might recognize me. I should claim fatigue and let her go down by herself, I thought. My reflection stared back as though wiser, acknowledging before I comprehended myself that I would take her anywhere she wanted to go just to keep her in my sight. The fatigue of what was now a twenty-hour-day slipped away. I paused for just one last minute before stiffening my resolve, then carefully shaved off the beard I had worn for the past five years.

Luci was waiting when I finally emerged from the second bathroom. Her eyes widened with shock. Then my heart sank as she burst into laughter.

"I'm sorry," she said, touching my clean-shaven cheek. "It's just that you look so different . . . younger, for one thing. The only gray hair you have is in your beard." Then she kissed me, a long, slow, and promising kiss that nearly made the lure of the casino fade away for both of us. "C'mon," she said huskily. "It's time to teach me to be a gambler."

A Sunday night in May is not exactly prime time for Las Vegas casinos. A casino as immense as the Hilton's seemed all the more empty with more tables closed than open. Still I had the sensation that everyone was staring at me and my now-naked face. I glanced right and left as we strolled between the deserted blackjack tables.

Luci sensed my discomfort and gave my arm a squeeze. "I guess I'd better get some tokens."

"I thought you wanted to learn how to gamble?"

"I do, but the slots are the only thing I know how to do."

"Over the long haul, you'll save work and pain by just sending them a check," I explained. "The slots are a grind." I steered her away from the rows of machines and we walked through the group of open tables until I found what I wanted, a double-odds craps table with a five-dollar minimum. There was another craps table open with a few tired players gathered around it, but the table was so obviously cold that this unoccupied crew seemed a better prospect.

When she realized my intent, Luci held back. "I can't do this," she protested.

"There's nothing to it," I insisted. "You just roll the dice when it's time. I'll take care of the betting." Still she resisted, frightened. "Look," I explained patiently, "you're in my element now and I'm a firm believer in beginner's luck. Just relax and think: 'Mind over matter.' If we don't get rolling, we'll quit and try something else."

Casinos, as a rule, make a great deal of money by doing a nearly flawless job of inducing people to take risks with money they would not otherwise take. Where the industry falls short is in taking the intimidation out of the games. In Luci's mind, craps was an intricately complicated game reserved for sporting men in loud suits, to be conducted in the back rooms of bus stations, back-street bars, and bordellos. With difficulty, she choked back her nervousness and stepped up to the table.

The craps pit crew was glad to see us. An empty table makes for a long shift and certainly generates no tips. The boxman nodded, the dealers smiled, and the stickman raked over around a dozen dice for my ultimate selection.

"The lady is the shooter," I informed the stickman as I passed the nearest dealer five one-hundred-dollar bills. The pit crew was perceptive enough to sense Luci's nervousness and they went about their "coming-out" preparations with polite friendliness.

At the craps table, I always bet in units of three, making the dealer's task of handling odds bets easier. I placed three chips on the "Pass" line and backed them up with a smaller side bet. "For the boys," I said to the boxman, acknowledging the crew's courtesy in not spooking my brand-new shooter.

"Thank you, sir."

"Just toss the dice so they strike the other end of the table," the stickman instructed in a friendly manner. When Luci turned awkwardly to shovel the dice with an underhand throw, he stopped her and patiently showed her the simple backhand toss which assured that the dice would traverse the table in the prescribed manner. She glanced at me for approval and, receiving it, swallowed hard and let the dice fly.

Craps is not my favorite casino game. I prefer blackjack or poker, where I feel more sense of control over the outcome. However, I was serious about my belief in beginner's luck. What followed was a run which exceeded even my imagination. Luci held the dice for forty-five minutes of magic. She never really understood what was happening as I systematically increased our bets while she rolled the numbers. Though her confidence and excitement increased as she continued to win, she stayed cool and methodical, "willing" the dice to perform just like the jaded high roller.

When she finally sevened out, I had more than two

thousand dollars on the table. She watched with momentary horror as the house raked in the chips.

"I'm sorry, Tennyson," she said forlornly, and looked genuinely shocked when I burst into laughter. The crew was beaming, for my side bets had made a dull night rewarding.

"Tough shooter," the stickman acknowledged as he raked the multiple dice to the next person at the table. I shoved a couple black chips in the direction of the boxman, who shook my hand as a dealer sorted our winnings into wooden chip trays. The other players, who had gathered as word of Luci's blistering hand spread as if by jungle drums, gave her a round of applause as we left for the cashier's cage.

"I guess we won something after all," she said, brightening.

"We didn't do badly," I admitted blandly.

"How much did we win?" Curiosity overcame her.

"Take a guess."

"Five thousand?" she suggested hopefully. I surmised that five thousand was a number sufficiently large to make her feel better about what was left on the table on the last roll.

"I think we did a little better than that," I told her as we reached the cage. The cashier accepted the trays, measured and counted the stacks.

"Thirty-two, five-seventy-five," the cashier announced when the process was complete.

Luci blanched. "I have to go to the ladies' room," she stammered, and bolted in the direction I pointed.

When she returned, she was not only calm, she was radiant. In the few moments she spent in the ladies' room, she had somehow come to grips with winning and liked the feeling. She had cleared what was perhaps the largest hurdle to becoming a competent gambler. Anyone can handle losing, for it seems like the natural order of things, anguish and even ruin notwithstanding. But to take a serious win in stride, without arrogance, guilt, or intensified avarice, requires an element of class which cannot be acquired.

Without a word, I led her to the nearest cocktail lounge and ordered two Bloody Marys. "Are you okay?" I asked, beaming at her proudly.

She nodded and then chuckled. "I can't quite believe what I just did. Not at the craps table, in the ladies' room. They have an attendant in there, passing out towels and things. I used some of her mouthwash. Believe me, I needed it. So, naturally, I needed to tip her. When I opened my purse, I didn't have anything small, so I gave her a twenty. Can you believe it? Who do I think I am, Diamond Jim Brady? I hope she didn't think I was putting her down."

Winners who can't handle winning are big tippers in absurd situations, not from generosity, but to remind themselves and others that they are winners. Luci had recognized on her own that the extravagant gratuity was less than cool. I raised my glass. "You're a class act, Lucinda DeGuerre."

"I'm glad you think so," she replied softly. She gave me a strange look. "You're spooky. You know that, don't you?"

"What do you mean?"

"I mean this is not real. Yesterday we won a small fortune. Today I win a year's salary in forty-five minutes. I know it's not like this, that most people lose, but you always win. Spooky."

"You're right about one thing," I replied carefully. "Casinos are not real. But I don't always win. In fact, at the tables I lose more often than I win. I know the game and the percentages better than most, but I'm playing with fire in here just like everyone else. If I had to make a living in here, the casino would grind me up just like Bill Buffoon from Buffalo."

"But you live here. You're a professional," she protested.

"I'm a professional handicapper, not a professional gambler," I explained. "My skill and experience, the records I keep, the way I manage my bets, gives me an edge with the horses. I know that over time I'll earn a certain amount on every dollar I wager, and I check my records daily to make sure my return is holding up. Good days, bad days, the 'PC,' the percentage, is there.

"In here, the house has the edge in everything. These people know they'll keep eighteen cents out of every dollar that gets bet. They don't give a damn that you just beat them for thirty grand. If you come back, they'll get it back. If you walk, they'll get it from somebody else. They have the PC."

"But you still play."

"Hell, yes," I sighed. "But not often, and with some hard rules, and with plenty of fear in my heart. You see, unlike the guy who flies in here from Milwaukee, I know I can't beat the casino. Not too many years ago, places like this busted me. I've learned the hard way the best I can hope for is to 'sting' it every now and then. So once in a while I gently test my luck by risking a small stake. If I lose it, I walk away with a minimum of damage. If I hit a streak, I press my bets till it ends. Just like tonight. When a streak ends, it's over. The hot hand won't come back just because you don't want to stop. You walk with your winnings. That's the only way to make the money your own. Once in a while, like tonight, a hot streak adds up to some serious money, but I guarantee you, there isn't another one just waiting for us. We take the money and run."

"That's what we're doing, isn't it?" Her eyes were full of understanding. I nodded.

"Then I think it's time we turned our attention to more important things, don't you?"

The sun comes up in Las Vegas in sepia and neon. As a transplanted Midwesterner, I had come to appreciate what green—grass, trees, shrubs—does for sunrise. I had never been sure whether my habit of rising early was a matter of preference for the dawn or merely a by-product of chronic insomnia. I tended to think that the latter enforced familiarity with the sunrise and the preference was acquired.

Luci slept on. She was a serious sleeper for whom my thrashing and tossing presented no obvious distraction. For me, however, the presence of this new and cherished body in my bed definitely interfered with slumber for both real and imagined reasons. For one thing, I held her in genuine wonder, unable to refrain from touching and stroking her. For another, I suffered from an irrational fear that in sleep I might snore or otherwise prove to be an innocently obnoxious bed partner.

Mystery, excitement, flight from danger, and the winnings of serious sums of money seasoned and flavored our lovemaking. The circumstances we had encountered together had revealed a great deal about our respective characters, had helped to overcome the awkwardness of the first physical joining. We'd had time to develop a certain admiration and complicity of purpose, making our coming together in bed a natural, unhurried evolution we both wanted but wouldn't rush.

I had started this investigative project as a desperate attempt to save my livelihood and, probably, my life. Fleeing Las Vegas and seeking out Peter T. Westmoreland had been purely defensive reactions, rooted in the fear of my pursuers and an even greater fear of starting over one more time in my life. The brutal beating of Kermit Golightly had seasoned the quest with the tang of revenge. Marcel Larrance had to pay.

Now, however, the project had taken on a new perspective. I was no longer alone. The feeling of complicity, of partnership, had been absent from my life since the days when Jenna and I had started our business together. I had forgotten how good it felt. This had ceased to be "my" investigation.

The memory of Jenna brought to mind the fragility of relationships. With Jenna, I thought I was as the luckiest man alive, sharing a thriving business and an exciting life-style with the love of a lifetime. There had been nothing dangerous then, I reflected, with a twinge of agonizing loss. Not like now, with Mafia goons and Marcel lurking on the fringes of happiness. Yet Jenna had been taken by pure chance, the wrong place at the wrong time. I knew I couldn't bear that kind of loss again. Beyond the threat of physical danger, I had to wonder whether this relationship could survive after the completion of the investigation. Once the excitement and shared experience had passed, would the difference in our ages, the distance between our home bases, or our wildly divergent occupations become more apparent and interfere with what might be?

I stubbed out my cigarette and shook off the cloying pessimism like a soiled shirt. When Kermit had dragged me out of that bar and away from the edge of self-destruction, I had accepted the proposition of "one day at a time" in the same manner as a recovering alcoholic.

That pragmatic philosophy would have to serve me for the present.

I slipped on a pair of jeans and a T-shirt and went downstairs. I needed some coffee and the *Racing Form* without having a room-service waiter pound on the door at such an ungodly hour. Fortunately, the giftshop/newsstand was open and I was able to get all three editions of the *Form*. The coffee shop wanted to send coffee up to the room, but a generous tip assured that things would be done my way. Eccentricities were tolerable, in fact normal, in Las Vegas.

My immediate needs attended, I put aside the imponderables of love and larceny in favor of the familiar and comfortable. Scanning the Eastern edition first, I made some notes on some interesting possibilities at Aqueduct. In the Midwest, only Churchill Downs was open on Monday and the pickings were slim. I found a three-year-old first-time starter, entered by a favorite trainer who, I knew, liked to pop with long shots the first time out. This one was a bet.

The major West Coast tracks were dark, so I contented myself with catching up on the results of the weekend stakes and feature races. I had my feet up on the table and had poured my third cup of coffee when Luci emerged from the bedroom, wearing only my shirt and rubbing the sleep from her eyes. I needed no other inducement. I swept her up and carried her back to the bed. She laughed, and then she moaned softly, and then we were lost in one another.

I slept like a baby. Luci, freshly showered and completely dressed, woke me with a lingering kiss. "Let's go, Rip Van Winkle, it's ten o'clock."

"Shit." I never slept that late. I stretched, groaned, and almost distracted her enough to catch her and pull her back into bed, but she skipped away.

"No you don't, wise guy," she admonished. "We have things to do and the shops are open." She gestured to her outfit, the same one she had worn the day before. "Remember, I have nothing with me. The shops here are expensive, aren't they?"

"Ridiculously so," I replied, forcing myself out of bed. I found my jacket, retrieved last night's winnings from its various pockets, and handed the money to Luci. "No problem. You're loaded. Finding some things you like will be a bigger problem than the price."

"My God, you have scars!" she exclaimed as she unself-consciously examined my body for the first time in daylight.

I had always felt fortunate that the scars were neither deep nor disfiguring, but they were prominent enough. "Souvenirs of Southeast Asia," I explained. "Nothing but scratches."

She put her arms around my neck. "And you are going to tell me how you got them," she stated with conviction. "I want to know all there is to know about you." We held each other without talking until finally she pushed me toward the bathroom.

"Go. Get dressed. I'll be back in an hour."

I watched the door close behind her and thought of how her presence endured her exit. Despite my protestations of professionalism, analysis, and control, I was by no means indifferent to the matter of luck. The Chinese perceive luck as cyclical, three years of bad luck followed by seven years of good. My own belief is that luck is largely a matter of random events and circumstances, and an individual's attitude and personality determine any cycle. For some, a catastrophic event or a deplorably bad decision destroys positive perceptions about life and self, adversely affects subsequent decisions and actions, and precipitates a series of negative events, in other words, a streak of bad luck. I had seen it and experienced it.

Some people are psychologically or emotionally unable to exploit opportunities. I once had sat at a blackjack table with a friend who won twenty-two consecutive hands. During the course of the streak the man played the cards sensibly, but he never once increased his bet above the minimum of five dollars. At the end he had won just over one hundred dollars in something like fifteen minutes. Winning twenty-two straight hands, even with the limits imposed by a five-dollar table, a professional would have won over five thousand dollars. I remembered asking my friend why he hadn't pressed his bets.

"I was afraid that if I changed the bet, my luck would change," he answered seriously.

I knew I had been incredibly lucky. Getting barred in Vegas was a catastrophic event, but then, I could have been killed had I been captured in the parking lot of the Las Vegas Athletic Club or in the alley behind Frankie's. Who knows what would have happened had I been taken by Ratface and Neanderthal at Sportsman's Park.

Instead, I was riding an incredible winning streak at the track and at the craps table last night. I had solved the riddle of a complicated cheating plot in which I was the intended scapegoat. And, miraculously, I had fallen in love in the process.

Random events, fortuitous decisions. How long could the winning streak hold? There was, of course, no way to know. Luck is a fragile commodity.

14

The "Center" was on a side street between St. Louis Avenue and Charleston Boulevard, maybe a half-mile outside of downtown, a mile or two from the Strip. A hand-painted sign labeled the place "Fremont Social Center."

Luci and I were parked about fifty yards away, on the opposite side of the street, watching an unhurried parade of senior citizens come and go. There was no shade, and even with the windows down, the rental car was starting to heat up to baking temperature. Luci, in her newly purchased miniskirt and light silk, sleeveless pullover, seemed impervious to the heat.

"You haven't explained what we're doing here," she complained mildly. "This is a senior-citizens center, isn't it?"

"Yes and no," I answered, and explained.

The Fremont Social Center is a private enterprise, ostensibly nonprofit, but not supported by any government or charitable organization. It's owned and operated by one Louis Rubenstein.

The Center provides a hangout for seniors where they can socialize, play cards, and purchase simple meals at cost. There is no membership fee, but not everyone who wanders in off the street is made welcome. The senior citizens who patronize the center look like seniors anywhere, but few collect Social Security or other pensions. The clientele of the Fremont Social Center are retired or semiretired participants in the vast underground economy of hookers, gamblers, grifters, and strong-arm men. Lou Rubenstein does not provide this valuable service out of the goodness of his heart. Behind its innocuous facade, the Center is an enormously profitable underground service business.

"What kind of service?" Luci asked.

I explained the working of a Las Vegas betting service.

"So if you're Capricorn Racing Stables and you have a hot horse . . ." Luci speculated.

"You got it. Lou, using his very own 'gray panthers,' will spread out your action and collect your winnings."

"All those anonymous old folks." Luci shook her head in appreciation of the simplicity of the Fremont setup. "Now I won't be able to pass through a casino without wondering which ones are walking around with inside information.

"Will Lou Rubenstein tell us whether Armand Larrance has been here?" she asked speculatively.

"Not a chance. We'd be more likely to get an account number for Martin Bohrman from a Swiss banker."

"So we wait until Larrance shows up," she said, not at all happy with her conclusion.

"That might take forever," I said, to her relief. "But there's an old horseplayer who hangs out at Churchill Downs on the Strip when he has money and here when he's broke. He's broke most of the time. There's a chance he may have seen Larrance here."

Spending an afternoon in a car in the Las Vegas sun is not my idea of fun, but I knew of no other way to find "Mosey." I had no idea where Mosey lived or even his real name. I only knew that Mosey sometimes worked for Lou. I decided to wait another half-hour before trying the race book, Churchill Downs.

Mosey showed up fifteen minutes later, shuffling along the street in the seemingly aimless gait which had earned him his nickname. Mosey would never walk, trot, stride, or march with purpose under any circumstances. He just "mosied" here and there.

I touched Luci's arm and we jumped out of the car to intercept the old horseplayer. Mosey showed a flash of fear at being approached on the street by strangers. When I called his name, Mosey peered myopically before finally recognizing me.

"Jesus Christ, Poet," he sputtered. "Ya tryin' to give an ol' man heart failure? God damn, ya shaved yer beard too."

Over the past few years I had staked Mosey to a few bets when he was broke. Once in a while I gave the old man a winner when he looked like he could use one. The old man owed me and I intended to collect.

"Had lunch yet, Mosey?" I asked, knowing the answer. We drove to a coffee shop on the Strip and after the waitress delivered bacon and eggs for Mosey, a soft drink for Luci, and coffee for me, I got down to business.

"Yer puttin' me on the spot, Poet," Mosey protested. "Lou don't like nobody shootin' off their mouth." He rubbed his face nervously. "I ain't hit a decent winner in a while, ya know. I can't afford to get on his shit list."

"Cut the bullshit, Mosey. You know I'll make it worth your while."

"I know, I know. An' I ain't forgettin' I owe ya." He mopped up the last of his eggs with a soggy piece of toast and chewed thoughtfully. "I remember them horses. Real fleabags, at least on paper. I knew something was up an' I was tempted to get twenty down myself."

"But that's against Lou's rules?" Luci noted.

"Nah. Fuck him. 'Scuse me, pretty lady. I just didn't have the twenty." Luci and I laughed, and Mosey, looking pleased with his humor, joined in.

Mosey closely scrutinized the photo of Armand Larrance. "This guy ain't been 'round," he declared finally.

"You mean you haven't seen him?"

"I mean he ain't been 'round, goddammit, Poet."

"Could he have set something up with Rubenstein outside of the Center?"

"Maybe."

"Maybe? Just 'maybe'?" I was getting exasperated. If Mosey had not seen Armand Larrance around the Center, I had no other ideas on where to look.

"Look, Poet," Mosey continued patiently. "I never heard of Lou doin' bidness outside of his office, but that don't mean he don't. I'm jus' a 'beard.' Lou don't tell me what's goin' on. The guy with the briefcase, I seen. This guy, I ain't."

"What guy with the briefcase?" I demanded, my interest renewed. "You never mentioned a guy with a briefcase."

"Ya never axed me about no other guy, jus' this slick-lookin' fucker. 'Scuse me, lady. A day or two before these horses ran—I can't be real sure of the timin'"—this guy came in the Center carryin' a briefcase. A day or two later he was back."

"What did he look like?"

"I dunno. Just a guy. Tall, thin, three-piece suit, dark glasses. What can I tell ya?"

Luci and I stared at each other, recognizing the same fact. Armand Larrance was not supervising the Las Vegas end of the operation. "All right, Mosey," I said, slipping the old man a couple of bills, "you've been a big help. Can we drop you someplace?"

"Nah. With this money I'm back in the game. The Frontier is jus' across the street. I think I'll mosey over an' see what's runnin'. Got anything ya like?"

I glanced at the clock. "You still have time for the ninth at Churchill. There's a first-time starter named Blooie entered. You might give him a try."

Mosey nodded his thanks and "mosied."

"Now what?" Luci asked.

I shrugged. "About Larrance, I don't know. Right now, I suggest you follow Mosey across the street and get this five hundred dollars down on Blooie. I can't go in there, so I'll wait for you here."

She shook her head in wonder, but after the last few days, she needed no more urging. I watched her cross Las Vegas Boulevard in her miniskirt and new crocodile pumps. So much for not attracting attention, I thought wryly.

Perhaps a quarter of an hour passed and Luci had not returned. I assumed she had stayed long enough to watch the race and maybe collect the bet as well, so the elapsed time didn't worry me. What did worry me was the guy in the baggy sport coat and jeans who walked directly to the table and sat down uninvited. There was no way he could be a messenger of good news.

"Time to go, Mr. Wilder," he said without preamble.

"I don't think so," I responded as coolly as possibly. We were, after all, in a public place. What could the man do? Enough, as things turned out.

"Think again." He turned toward the window and my eyes followed his gaze. A black limo had pulled up and a driver and a front-seat passenger in dark glasses and suits stood alongside. Next to the passenger, looking pale but in control, was Luci.

My heart sank at the sight. I had been prepared to take my chances, but now making a break was out of the question. The winning streak, apparently, was about to run out.

"Look," I attempted to negotiate frantically, "I'll go with you, no problems. Just let the lady go."

The man looked at me with exaggerated patience. "I don't think so," he mocked.

There was nothing else to say. The man left a bill on the table to cover the check, and escorted me out. A hundred thoughts raced through my mind as we passed the counter and cashier, into the afternoon sun. It was unlikely that anyone had spotted us the night before, and not enough time had elapsed for Mosey to have let slip my presence in town, much less for anyone to have reacted to the information. That left Cowboy, I thought with stunning realization and revulsion. Our captors must have been with us all along, just waiting for an opportunity. Cowboy must have told them where Luci and I would be.

"I'm sorry, Tennyson," Luci apologized as the limo got under way. The two guys in suits had stayed in front; the man from the coffee shop rode in back. "They told me you sent them for me. I should have known better."

"Not your fault," I muttered. "They've been with us since we left the hotel, so they'd have got us sooner or later. I'm afraid Cowboy sold us out."

"No," she objected forcefully. "I don't believe it."

"Had to be," I said with resignation. Ever since our meeting in Chicago, when the circumstances pointed to a betrayal by a close friend, I had been unable to concentrate on the question of identification. When I made the call to enlist Cowboy's aid, I had considered and quickly rejected the possibility that the Texan might be the betrayer. Not Cowboy, I had thought at the time, certainly not Cowboy. Now we were caught because of my stupidity and I had put Luci in dire jeopardy. Asshole, I railed at myself bitterly.

There was nothing to be done but to see things through. Overpowering these three was out of the question. Our only chance was to tell our captors everything and hope they believed it. I was surprised at how calm I felt now that the options were narrowed to one.

The limo made its way through commercial districts and into the suburbs, finally reaching an area where the homes were spread out on expansive acreage. Some were closer to estates. At last we turned onto a blacktop drive which ran between two steep sandstone formations screening the house from the road. The house, when it came into sight, was a sprawling ranch of Spanish architecture, nestled among the hills and rock formations. The limo stopped at the front door and the man riding shotgun moved quickly to let us out of the back. The two men in suits remained with the car while the spokesman in the sport coat ushered Luci and me through the spacious house.

Toward the rear of the house we came into a bright screened-in sunroom. Two men in sports clothes had their backs to the room as they kept an eye on two others seated under a bright umbrella on the patio. The two men turned and my stomach twisted with anxiety. Ratface and Neanderthal.

The big man looked on impassively, but Ratface seemed beside himself with malicious glee. He moved closer, hooting a menacing laugh between his wired jaw, his eyes glinting with ferocity. He stopped just two feet from me, turned as if to say something to his hulking partner, and wheeled to slash a backhand across my face.

"Hey!" the man from the restaurant shouted in protest as I reeled from the blow. "Cut that out."

Ratface held up both hands, his eyes wide as if to apologize. Then he turned his attention to Luci, leering obscenely as he reached to touch her. The action was too much for me and I stepped forward. Ratface re-created his magic with the knife, just as he had in the parking lot of the Athletic Club. He stared at me, daring me to come on, a thin and vicious seven-inch needle of steel waving menacingly in his hand.

Ratface expected that the sight of the blade would cause me to back off. But I'd had enough. With Ratface involved, I didn't think much of our survival chances anyway, and I came to the instant decision that I had little to lose. Ratface's eyes widened as I stepped inside his defense and seized the wrist of the knife hand with my left. Pivoting sharply, I drove my right elbow into the side of Ratface's head with a force which produced a sickening crunch. Ratface's eyes rolled back in his head. As the knife wielder started to go down, I retained his wrist in my grip, brought my right hand to bear, and brought my knee up swiftly to meet the downward thrust of my hands. There was a loud snap as the bone gave way. Ratface would be out of the thug business for some time to come.

All this occurred before Neanderthal had time to react. The big man seemed astounded by the speed and savagery of my response. Before he could come to his partner's defense, the man from the restaurant had a gun out.

"That's enough! Back off!" he commanded, including both me and Neanderthal in the warning. "He had it comin'," the man told Neanderthal. "We said no rough stuff."

The hulking thug held up both palms in acquiescence. His face showed no emotion. He turned his head to regard me with new respect, as if to say that he had no problem with my action.

"All right. Now, everybody relax," the man from the restaurant ordered. "This is a business meeting. No more bullshit." I felt a mild sense of relief at the term "business meeting." "You," the man said to Neanderthal, "sit down."

"He's gonna need a doctor," the big man pointed out.

The man backed to the doorway; his eyes never left Neanderthal or me. "Bobby!" he called into the next room. One of the men from the limo appeared in seconds. "Get Mickey and get this guy some medical attention. Tell 'em he fell down the stairs. You wanna go with 'em?"

Neanderthal glanced over his shoulder at the men at poolside, who, so far, had demonstrated no awareness of the events in the house.

"I'll help you get him to the car, but I better stay here."

Neanderthal and Bobby gathered up the still-unconscious Ratface as gently as possible and carried him out.

"I apologize, Mr. Wilder," the man said. "He did that all on his own. If you're ready, we'll go out now."

I looked at Luci, who had stood wide-eyed through the exchange of violence. "Are you okay?" I asked. She gave me a faint smile and a slight nod.

I was still breathless from the encounter and confused by the apology. Maybe this wasn't as bad as I had feared. I took Luci's arm and followed in the direction the man indicated.

We emerged from the house, which was much bigger than its outside appearance indicated, onto a spacious patio equipped with the largest swimming pool I'd ever seen in a private residence. Two men in bathing suits sat talking under a huge umbrella while a third swam laps. The two at poolside broke off their conversation when we approached. They were both in their fifties, dark and tough-looking in spite of too many excess pounds. Neither looked friendly.

"Thank you for joining us, Tennyson." A voice I recognized came from the pool and I felt a measure of relief as Jimmy DeMaria heaved his immense bulk to the deck without the assistance of a ladder. I was still marveling at the fat man's agility when DeMaria offered his hand.

"Thanks, Al," DeMaria said to our escort. "I thought I heard some noise. Everything okay?"

"Yeah. One of Kosinski's guys, the weird one, had an 'accident.' Bobby an' Mickey took him to the doc's."

DeMaria raised a questioning eyebrow, but decided to put his curiosity on hold. I introduced Luci as the fat man led us to the table under the umbrella. Despite the warmth of DeMaria's greeting, his two companions still appeared hostile.

"We were just enjoying a cold margarita," DeMaria explained. "Will you join us?" He poured two without waiting for an answer. "This is Jerry Kosinski from Chicago," he continued, indicating the larger of the two men, "and Bert Wallech is from New Jersey. Bert and Jerry are in the off-track-betting business."

Neither bookie offered much in the way of a greeting and I found their presence discomfiting. DeMaria had seemed sympathetic from the start, but I knew that his affable manner was no more than a facade. DeMaria did business daily with Kosinski and Wallech; he owed me nothing.

"Jerry and Bert learned that you were in town the same

time I did, Tennyson," he explained. "Under the circumstances, I thought a meeting would be prudent. What I suggest you do, if you don't mind, is tell Jerry and Bert everything you told me on the phone the other day."

I had not told DeMaria much over the phone, but the message was clear. For the time being, DeMaria was still supportive and was giving me a chance to sell his skeptical "associates."

Apparently he had persuaded Kosinski and Wallech to hear me out. On the other hand, I suspected that DeMaria was prepared to back their judgment should they choose to disbelieve me. The outward hospitality notwithstanding, this was more of a trial than a meeting.

I exchanged glances with Luci. Her eyes told me that she was frightened, but that she had confidence in me. Gutsy, I thought, admiring her fortitude.

"Gentlemen," I began, "I believe I understand your position and I know that it's not your custom to discuss such matters so amicably. You've shown me a courtesy and I appreciate it."

DeMaria nodded approvingly and the hostility of the others abated slightly.

For the next thirty minutes I laid before them everything we had uncovered, including the identity of Aaron Locklear, the background of Armand and Marcel Larrance, and the corporate infrastructure of Capricorn, Orion, Bellestar, and Astral. All of this information I backed up with photographs and computer printouts from my portfolio.

"Where did this stuff come from?" Kosinski demanded.

"From the files and data base of the Thoroughbred Protective Bureau, for whom Miss DeGuerre is an investigator." When I outlined the ringer scam itself, the two bookies burst into prolonged cursing. DeMaria was a bit more restrained, but his amazement was unconcealed.

"How did you tumble to this setup?" Wallech asked warily. "I mean, you made a nice chunk of change on these horses, yet you claim you had nothing to do with the deal. I find that a little hard to swallow."

"Someone took pains to make sure I would bet on these horses. Armand Larrance, as Locklear, carefully set up a public meeting with me to make it look worse."

I went on to explain about Kermit, including his present condition.

"So there's no way to find out from your friend who tipped him in the first place," DeMaria observed.

"At least not right now," I agreed. "We believe it was Guy LeBlanc, the interim trainer of Picky Peaches, but there's no way to confirm, since LeBlanc is dead and Kermit's in a coma. I doubt that information would help us much. We know about the Larrance brothers and how the ringer switch works. What we don't know is how many ringers they have or where they are. And we don't know who's running the show or who made the linkup from LeBlanc to Kermit to me." I had intentionally left out the involvement of Peter T. Westmoreland and his search for the training center. "Perhaps if one of you gentlemen has some influence with Lou Rubenstein, we might be able to obtain the identity of the organizer."

"Not a chance," Kosinski stated flatly. "Lou does business with everyone. He's protected, sort of like neutral ground." He turned to DeMaria. "I think we need to talk about this."

Wallech nodded his agreement.

"There's just one thing, guys," DeMaria prompted. "Tennyson here has been very forthcoming and I, for one, believe him. I don't think it's fair to leave him and Miss DeGuerre hanging."

The two bookies thought this over. "Yeah, you're right, Jimmy," Kosinski said finally. "I guess I believe him too, for now. Besides, that was a good turn he done us on that Thurgood horse." He stared at me with menace. "If this turns out to be bullshit, mister, I guarantee you'll hear from us again."

DeMaria rose ponderously and escorted Luci and me toward the house. "Al will take you back to your car. These boys will leave you alone now." The affable-fatman act disappeared momentarily. "You did very well there, and the information you provided is impressive. That and the fact that you saved them, maybe, a half a mil apiece makes them want to believe you, but you know I'm out on a limb on this one. If all this is a clever smoke screen, Kosinski and Wallech will be the least of your worries." The smile returned and he clapped me on the back heartily. "Relax. We'll find these Larrance brothers and clear this whole thing up. Nothing to worry about."

"That's it?" I asked, not quite believing that I was off the hook that simply. "I mean, what about the casinos?"

"Give it twenty-four hours for the word to get out," DeMaria said. "Go home and lie low. Day after tomorrow you can walk into any place on the strip like nothing ever happened."

Al escorted us through the house. Neanderthal still lingered in the sunroom. When he saw me he shrugged his shoulders as if to say, "No hard feelings, it's just a job." Just the same, I was sure Neanderthal would have broken every bone in my body with the same equanimity.

"He's not such a bad guy," Al said in a friendly manner. "Don't say much, though. But his buddy, now there's a looney tune."

I wondered momentarily what it was like to live in a world where Neanderthal wasn't "such a bad guy" and a vicious man like Ratface could be classified as merely "a looney tune."

Luci and I said nothing during the ride back to the Strip, but something about her body language made me uneasy. We picked up the rental car and drove back to the Hilton, where we packed up our belongings and checked out. I was tempted to stick Cowboy with the hotel bill, but I settled it in cash. Cowboy's probable involvement troubled me more than I could articulate. I had intentionally left that detail out of my account to the bookies, even though I recognized that Cowboy might very well hold the key to the identity of the organizer. There had to be a better way. The bookies would certainly take decisive action with dire consequences for Cowboy, and there was still the possibility that I could be wrong.

Not until I unlocked the door to the condo and ushered Luci inside did I begin to feel jubilation. I could live like a normal human being, resume my business endeavors, regrow my beard, everything. I was once again the Poet, high-tech handicapper par excellence. I felt a heady sense of accomplishment which even Luci's dispirited demeanor could not completely dampen.

Luci clearly did not share my exhilaration. She toured the condo with polite detachment, refusing refreshment.

When we reached my lower-level sanctum, she paced the floor, her mind working furiously. My euphoria evaporated and I watched her pace, waiting for the explosion.

"Tennyson, what will happen to the Larrance brothers now?" she demanded, turning to me with flashing eyes.

"I don't know. Probably Kosinski, Wallech, and the people they work with will start looking for them like they were looking for me. We may never know what happens to them, but it won't be anything they don't deserve."

"What you're saying is that now that you're off the hook, you don't give a shit." The words sounded more like an attack than an observation.

I considered her words and had to admit to myself the element of truth in what she said. "Luci, I know you wanted to bust them legally," I argued defensively. "If I had my way, they would have been all yours. But what could I do? We could have ended up in a trench in the desert."

I was entirely satisfied with the logic of my argument. The bad guys had us and I had to convince them to let us go. There had been no choice at the time. Busting the Larrance brothers would have been an enormous coup in Luci's career, but a "ride" in the desert would have been more than just a setback.

Instead of accepting my logic, she squared off with the same competitive look she gave me on the racquetball court. I could see that she was getting ready to argue, to accuse me of backing down. Suddenly her ferocity crumbled and she sat heavily on the sofa, burying her face in her hands. I came around the desk to her side and she pressed her face to my chest, crying silently.

"I'm sorry, Tennyson," she said after she had gained a measure of control. "You're right, of course, we could have been killed. I've never been in a situation like that and it scared the hell out of me. Gangsters are for TV, not real life."

She got up from the sofa, fetched a tissue, and blew her nose loudly. The trumpeting was so incongruous that she laughed through the tears. Then she resumed her pacing.

"When Armand Larrance was dealing drugs and fixing races, he ruined a lot of people," she explained calmly. "One of them was my brother, Tony.

"Tony was six years older and I idolized him. Starting as a teenager, he worked his way up from stablehand to hot walker to groom to assistant trainer. He was just starting to go it alone as a trainer. It was tough getting started. His age worked against him. He only had a few horses and not very good ones at that. You have to be a winner to get good horses.

"The bills were piling up, but the training fees and purses weren't rolling in. Armand Larrance stepped in like the Devil with a contract and Tony was ready to sell his soul. First, Larrance got Tony hooked on drugs. Then he had him doping horses. His own, another trainer's . . . it didn't matter. Judgment was not one of Tony's strong points at the time. Naturally he got caught, officially suspended, but finished as far as racing was concerned.

"Six months later Tony was dead, stabbed to death in a fight in some dive in Algiers. He'd been hanging out in the honky-tonks across the river, trying to score drugs and scrounge a living. Maybe he was just in the wrong place at the wrong time—random violence, the cops called it. No one ever connected Armand or Marcel to the stabbing, but Armand Larrance killed my brother as sure as if he'd put a gun to his head. I was eighteen at the time."

Furiously she paced the room, stopping occasionally to dab her eyes or blow her nose. The pent-up anger and frustration poured from her as she finished her story.

"Larrance disappeared as all kind of stories came out. My brother died and that bastard walked with a ton of money. I finished my education working summers at Evangeline Downs back home in Lake Charles. I hoped all along that I would hear some word about Armand Larrance. When I graduated, I joined the TPB, figuring that if Larrance surfaced, it would be somewhere around a track. I was almost beginning to believe it would never happen when Marcel's name surfaced in this investigation. I knew Armand had to be involved somewhere.

"Don't you see, Tennyson, even if those gangsters track them down and they get what they deserve, I'll never know about it. To me the Larrance brothers would always be out there."

She turned her back, struggling to maintain control. I was stunned and embarrassed by my own stupidity as I put an arm around her and led her back to the sofa. Nailing the Larrance brothers was hardly a career coup for Luci. I had been so wrapped up in my own problems that I had never acknowledged that her interest in Larrance was far more intense than her obvious professionalism would normally allow. The signs had been present; I had blindly ignored them.

I poured her a brandy. She sipped, grimaced at its potency, and drank it down with a shudder. The stress of the earlier danger and the torrent of emotion had left her exhausted. I led her upstairs, helped her undress, and tucked her in my bed, but when I turned to leave, she held me. We made slow, tender, revitalizing love. Afterward she slept.

I was still on the phone in the den when Luci came down two hours later engulfed in a robe she had found in my closet. Her color had returned and the light was back in her eyes. She crossed the room and stood behind my chair, resting both hands lightly on my shoulders while I finished the call.

I had been busy while she slept. I had talked with Jack Hanrahan about moving to the Frontier's version of the Turf Club and had received delighted approval. I had then spent an hour on the phone with Peter T., advising him of the day's events in considerable detail and catching up on his activities. A couple of quick calls followed to make airline reservations and to a UNLV student who did some part-time computer work for me. The student, Rick Siefer, agreed to fly to LAX to retrieve my car, promising to stop by within ten minutes to pick up keys and expense money.

"I'm starving," Luci declared when I hung up. Her spirits had definitely improved.

I realized, feeling hunger pangs of my own, that neither of us had eaten since breakfast. I picked up the phone again and ordered a gargantuan Chinese dinner. "In a few minutes a skinny college kid will ring the doorbell.

Give him this envelope—and no flirtation. I'm going to fetch our dinner."

When I returned, Luci and Rick were drinking beer in the kitchen, the youth clearly captivated by the gamine in the oversize robe. Luci grinned at me mischievously, as if to remind me of my admonitions about flirtation. I hustled Rick out, overcoming the youth's reluctance by telling him he could hold on to the car for a few days until I got back in town.

"He's cute," she observed as I unpacked the meal. We had barbecued pork, egg rolls, shrimp in a spicy pepper sauce, sliced tenderloin with Chinese vegetables, a seafood lo mein, and what seemed like a gallon of rice. "You certainly have enough food there to have invited him to dinner."

"You have to understand about us old guys, babe. We don't like having young studs around when we're entertaining ladies. It makes us self-conscious about lines and scars and sags and flagging energies."

She hooted derisively. "I haven't noticed any flagging energy. This looks terrific," she added, as she reached in the kitchen cabinets for plates and bowls. "Where shall we eat?"

"The den," I answered. "We still have some work to do."

I had thought there was enough food for an army. As it turned out, there was little left after Luci unleashed her prodigious appetite. Using the chopsticks the restaurant had supplied, she shoveled in the food as adroitly as a Hong Kong fishwife.

"I did some thinking while you were sleeping," I told her. "If you remember our little meeting this afternoon, I didn't tell them anything about Peter T. and Texas."

"I remember," she allowed, her eyes narrowing.

"If we get to work, we have a shot at finding the Larrance brothers before 'the boys' do."

"Won't that make DeMaria and his friends angry with you?"

I shrugged. "Maybe, but if the law has the Larrance brothers in custody, what can they do? Besides, if Kosinski, Wallech, and the rest want them, I doubt that jail will put Armand and Marcel out of reach."

"What are we waiting for?" she exclaimed excitedly.

"We have to call Peter T." She began pacing the room. "We need to get flight reservations . . ."

"Relax." He laughed. "It's handled. I talked to Peter T. while you were sleeping. We have an eight-o'clock flight to Dallas in the morning. Peter T. will meet us there."

She plopped back down on the sofa. "God, I'm stuffed," she moaned. "I guess we could use a good night's rest. And you, you have to be exhausted. And here I am, wide-awake."

"I know just what you need," I said, crossing to the sofa. I kissed her, tasting the spicy food on her lips. Without breaking the kiss, I lifted her off the sofa and stood with her in my arms.

She chuckled. "Up two flights of stairs? Some old guy."

"Two flights of stairs, my ass," I replied, crossing the room. "You want me to have a heart attack? There, can you reach that doorknob?"

The inside of the tiled room was full of steam, for I had set the whirlpool to heat up while I made my calls.

"Oh, you are a magician," she said when she had taken in the comforts of the room. The spa had cost a small fortune to install when I bought the condo. I had hoped that the comforts would help cure my chronic insomnia. While its efficacy in that regard remained in doubt, its soothing effect on the spent muscles of an aging jock made it worth every penny. There was a dry sauna just large enough for two next to the hot tub which occupied nearly half of the room. The wisps of steam were rising from its now-calm surface. The combination was guaranteed to relax aching muscles, cure hangovers, and, occasionally, induce slumber in the most restless of night owls.

"Park your pretty behind in the sauna," I instructed. "I'll straighten up in the den and fetch us some wine. There are towels in the cabinet next to the sauna."

I cleaned up the remains of dinner, put the dishes in the dishwasher, and iced a bottle of champagne. When I entered the sauna, Luci was stretched out facedown on a bath sheet taking up the entire bench.

"Stay there," I told her as she started to make room. She groaned with pleasure as I massaged her, working her muscles area by area and mixing in a little sexual molestation in the process.

"I'm yours," she admitted huskily. "Just keep me here, feed me occasionally, and I'll do anything you want. This is heaven."

After a few more minutes, we moved to the hot tub. She leaned back in the whirlpool and took my hand, allowing the hot water to ease what remained of her earlier tension. She had just tasted the champagne when her eyes widened suddenly. "Damn, with everything else, I forgot. Blooie won going away. I had just cashed the ticket when those goons grabbed me."

"What'd he pay?" I asked lazily.

"Twenty-six dollars! I've got over six thousand dollars in my purse."

Along with everything else, we were still winning.

"I think you're wrong about Cowboy," she said after a moment.

"Why's that?" I asked, surprised by this turn of conversation.

"Just think about it. If he intended to give us up, why would he go through all the trouble of renting a suite and a car? Why wouldn't he just have those same goons meet our flight?"

"Makes sense," I admitted, wanting to accept Cowboy's innocence. "But how else could they have found us?"

"How would I know?" she argued. "Maybe someone saw us at the airport or the hotel. Or maybe Cowboy let it slip to someone he trusted. Anything is possible. Why don't you call him and ask?"

Someone he trusted, I thought to myself. The odds were against our having been spotted at the airport or the hotel. The "boys" simply did not have that kind of manpower. But the last possibility she mentioned was likely and just as disturbing as the idea of Cowboy betraying us.

"It can wait until we get back," I told her finally. I still couldn't cope with the idea of betrayal. As I said the words, I wondered if the two of us would actually return together. More than ever, I hoped that we would.

15

Since we had only carry-on luggage, Peter T. led us directly from the gate to his "customer entertainment vehicle," a 1976 Cadillac Eldorado convertible, the last of the dinosaurs. Most of the time, Peter T. drove a truck, but for the sake of comfort for three, he brought out the immaculately preserved classic. The car was as perfect as the day it came off the Clark Street assembly line in southwest Detroit.

Luci was delighted, for big convertibles were a vague memory of her childhood rather than an indelible aspiration of the American Dream. She insisted that Peter T. put the top down and said that she felt like an old-time movie star. To Peter T. and me, a car built in 1976 may have been a classic, but was hardly ancient history—1976 was not all that long ago. I remembered when a car like this was an important symbol of the success Jenna and I had achieved so early in life. She had been killed driving a 1976 Cadillac Eldorado.

Even a few days ago, I comprehended quite suddenly, a ride in a car like this would have brought me almost unbearable melancholy. Now it brought back bittersweet memory and, perhaps, a pang of fear for the fragility of happiness. Uncomfortable but endurable.

Peter T. was a car collector, he explained. Along with the Eldorado, he had a 1961 Chevrolet "409" and a 1964 Corvette Sting Ray, both completely restored. "Next project is a fifty-seven Thunderbird, the two-seater," he told us. "I guess some of us never grow up."

Peter T. maneuvered the massive car through freeway traffic on an eastward heading. He gave no hint of our destination. At last he exited the expressway and parked the car alongside a plain-looking restaurant called "Ed and Bill's."

"A Texan needs his daily dosage of chicken-fried steak," he drawled. He led the way to a corner table in the clean but modestly appointed dining room.

"I see some things have changed since I left you two," Peter T. observed after we were seated.

"What are you talking about?" I asked, knowing what was coming.

The Texan laughed. "You think I have to be Sherlock Holmes? You two might as well be wearing a sign."

"That obvious?"

"Shit. Like high-school kids at homecoming. What're you blushing about?" he teased Luci. "Hell you're both adults.

"Well, darlin'," the Texan continued in a more serious tone, "looks like you're no worse for wear after meeting up with those Mafia folks."

Luci shuddered. "It scares me more now than it did at the time," she admitted. "I guess I never realized what could happen. Now I get the shakes just thinking about it."

"They say organized crime ain't as big down here," Peter T. mused. "The theory is that down here everyone owns a gun and knows how to use it so they ain't so intimidating as they are up North. My own opinion is that they just don't have 'tradition' in Texas . . . no Al Capones or guys in ol' cars blasting away with Tommy guns. You can still get a bet down or buy drugs—they're here, just less visible."

"They'll be here soon enough after Armand and Marcel," I put in. "If we don't get busy and find them first."

"Well, folks, we aren't doing so good right now," Peter T. admitted. "I thought this farm would be easy to find, but I've struck out so far. You're convinced Armand is down here too?"

"Yeah. I should have figured it. We agreed, the whole deal was too sophisticated for the Larrance brothers alone, so it makes sense that the 'money man' is someone who knows the Las Vegas scene well. Armand is most likely right where he fits in. He's a competent horse trainer, and someone is getting these horses ready to win."

"No ideas on the money man?"

"Not a clue." I explained about Lou Rubenstein's operation and the man Mosey had seen. " 'Just a guy,' was all Mosey could tell us. The best we can do is to find the training center and hope something turns up."

"I haven't been doing so hot on that job. None of the vets know of any thoroughbred farms that ain't supposed to be here."

"Any chance that they're blending in with an existing facility?" Luci asked.

"Maybe, but if they did that, too many people would know about them. I'd say it's more likely that they have a secret operation. I also checked with the farriers and came up blank. That one doesn't surprise me as much as the vets. We got a make on the truck that picked up Marcel. It's registered to an Octavio Melendez. Naturally Octavio had moved out of the address on the registration. The thing is, this Melendez used to work at the track in Juárez as a farrier. That's a switch, by the way. Ol' Octavio is a 'legal', born in Texas, but he crosses over to Mexico to work."

"Wait a minute," Luci interjected. "When Armand's Louisiana operation blew up, there was a vet who was tied in. The guy got suspended for life, lost his license, the whole works." She started shuffling through the case files.

"Dr. Vernon Mack," she announced finally, "whereabouts unknown. I'd say that Armand's put together a self-contained organization."

We digested this item as the bad news it was. We were back to the original task of locating a single horse farm in Texas, all 266,807 square miles of it.

"Everybody's got to believe in something" Peter T. declared. "I believe we should head for Longview."

"You're convinced the training center is in that area?" I asked.

"I'm not convinced of anything," Peter T. admitted, "but it makes the most sense to me. Marcel gets picked up in Dallas by Octavio Melendez. Octavio shoes horses for a living, and we know a training center needs a farrier. Ergo—how's that for professionalism—'ergo,' the training center is Marcel's destination." Peter T. paused for affirmation.

"Octavio uses a Harrison County address to renew his license tags," he continued. "Ergo, the training center is within, say, a fifty-mile radius of where he renewed his tags."

"Wait a minute," I protested as Peter T. beamed and Luci applauded. "You're really getting out in left field now. You already told us that the address is a fake. Now you two are ready to narrow down a search?"

"You got any better ideas?" Luci demanded defensively. I had to admit that I did not.

"It's not so farfetched when you consider available airports," Peter T. explained. "If you were going to Longview from Chicago, you'd fly into Dallas or, maybe, Shreveport."

"Why not Shreveport? It's closer," I argued.

"Airline connections. Chicago to Dallas is almost a shuttle. It's probably faster to fly here and drive than to connect to Shreveport. The point is, there are major airports all over the state—Houston, San Antonio, Austin, Amarillo, Corpus, Lubbock, El Paso—anywhere you need to go."

"He's right," Luci interjected. "We have Octavio Melendez in Harrison County and it's reasonable to fly here and drive to Harrison County. I'm not saying that we're right, but it's a place to start."

I had to admit the sense of their argument. Certainly Marcel and Melendez could have headed west from Dallas rather than east, but we did, indeed, have to start someplace. Still I continued to take the contrarian point of view.

"How do we know that Melendez isn't originally from Harrison County? Or that he drove over there to throw off a trace?"

"He's from El Paso," Peter T. said flatly. "Son, don't you think you're giving these guys a little too much credit? Octavio's just a hired hand. Our boys've been smart, but they can't think of everything."

"Let's check one more thing," Luci suggested. "Let's see if Mel's come up with anything yet."

Luci marched off in the direction of the nearest telephone, returning after about fifteen minutes, her eyes flashing. "Paydirt," she announced. "There were murders in both Chicago and L.A. at times when Marcel was in town with horses. I realize that those are big towns with lots of crazies, but here's the kicker. Six months ago a prostitute was murdered here in Texas. Take a guess where?''

"Longview," we chorused.

"Go to the head of the class," she told us with grim satisfaction.

"So what do we do when we get over there?" I asked. "We still have the problem of finding the training farm."

"Why don't we charter a plane?" Peter T. suggested. "There should be something we can see from the air, like a training track, maybe?"

We agreed that this was an excellent idea. To get his sleepers ready to win, even against the lowest level of competition, Armand Larrance would need at least a half-mile training track with rails, turns, and a starting gate. A facility like this should be visible from the air.

"Would they have to have a starting gate?" Luci asked.

"Maybe not," I answered. "But they'd be taking some serious risks without one. Some horses can run like hell, but hate the gate. Teaching a young horse to break 'in company' is one of the toughest jobs a trainer has. If they wait until the horses ship, they have to work them from the gate at the track. That takes some finagling just to set up, and the official 'clockers' and workout watchers pay more attention to gate workouts. Somebody is bound to notice a sharp-looking horse if they see enough of him.

"Look at it this way. If you're looking to bet a bundle and win a ton on a horse which has never raced, you're damn sure gonna get him 'gate ready' in plenty of time. They've got a starting gate."

"I've got another idea," Peter T. said. "Ned Burdine, who runs the Longview Texas Ranger station, is a friend of mine. I bet he'd be damn interested in hearing about ol' Marcel. He might even have some ideas on this ranch."

This time Peter T. excused himself to use the phone. Luci seemed distracted, and she stared absently out the window. At last she turned to me and spoke.

"Tennyson, do you think Marcel really killed those girls?" she asked, her voice full of insecurity. Her idea had borne fruit, but now she had doubts.

"I can't say about Chicago and L.A.," I answered. "As you said, there are plenty of crazies. But I'm ninety-nine percent sure he killed Leslie Pilarcik. You think so too."

"What about this Longview rape and murder? Are we on a wild-goose chase?"

I shrugged. "Who can say? We sure as hell don't have any better place to start."

"I'm starting to feel very scared, Tennyson," she admitted finally. "Mel told me what was done to those girls. The whole thing makes my flesh crawl."

"I wish I could tell you everything will be all right, but I'd be lying. I've seen Marcel, and he scares me too. If we find him, I hope Peter T. can call up lots of help."

Peter T. returned, a puzzled expression on his face. "There's something funny going on," he told us as he took his place at the table. "Ned Burdine's an ol' friend, like I said. When I told him what I wanted, he acted real strange. Put me on hold for a few minutes. When he came back, he asked me to meet him at Bubba's, that's a big barbecue joint in Longview. I asked him what's up, but he jus' said he'd explain later. Could be we've opened a can of worms."

Over Luci's objections, we put the top up on the Eldorado. Three hours of sun and wind, combined with Peter T.'s inexhaustible beer cooler, would have left us in poor condition for an interview with a Texas Ranger. The mood in the car was one of high anticipation. We all believed that we had once again picked up Marcel's trail.

The movies and television have conjured an image of a Texas Ranger that excluded the stocky Peter T. Westmoreland and cast the likes of Ned Burdine solidly in the role. Burdine was a few inches over six feet, and lean. He had the requisite lines around his eyes and mouth that seemed perfect for the icy stare of a gunfighter facing "Black Bart" on a dusty western street at high noon. The western-cut clothes, the boots, the white Stetson, the slightly drooping mustache, everything about the man seemed to fit the Hollywood productions I had loved as a boy.

"Good to see ya, Hawg," Burdine drawled as he and Peter T. attempted to grind each other's hand to hamburger. Luci and I exchanged grins as Peter T. grimaced, either from the grip or Burdine's use of an unattractive nickname.

We settled into a roomy booth, once the introductions had been completed, and ordered, at Burdine's suggestion, "Bubba's Special Bloody Mary." The drinks were strong and spicy with enough hint of smoky barbecue to give away Bubba's secret formula.

"What're you workin' on, Hawg?" Burdine asked, coming directly to the point.

"Ned, what the hell's goin' on here?" Peter T. shot back. "I call you with a simple piece of information about a six-month-old murder and you get all funny. Now I don't have but two swallows of this drink down and you start with cop questions."

The Ranger sighed and lit a cigarette. I found myself slightly disappointed that, instead of a Bull Durham roll-your-own, it was an extra-low-tar brand similar to my own. "We got us another dead girl, Hawg," Burdine explained on the exhale. "Dumb little no-count kid who worked at one of those massage parlors out in the county. We don't get many murders out here, and when we do, they're the usual kind. You know, husband-wife-girlfriend shit or more than three drunks in the men's room of a cantina on Saturday night. This one's bad, Hawg. Somebody tied this kid up, beat her, and strangled her to death, and used her sexually somewhere in the process, though we ain't sure if it was before, during, or after the strangling. The girl six months ago was just the same."

"Then I come along asking about rapes and murders. I get the picture." Peter T. glanced at Luci and me meaningfully. The malevolence that made my hackles rise at Frankie's was in the air in Longview, Texas.

Elizabeth Cline, known to her friends as "Lizzy," had been a local girl, a high-school dropout, nineteen years old. She lived in a rented mobile home with her three-year-old daughter born out of wedlock. With limited intelligence and no skills, Lizzy elected to market the only commodity she had to feed herself and her child.

The massage parlor, of course, was nothing more than a brothel, but it was far enough off the beaten track that it failed to offend the eyes of the righteous. Consequently, the law, represented by pragmatic types like Ned

Burdine and Sheriff John Kirts, took the position that a discreet whorehouse provided a useful outlet for highs spirits that might otherwise manifest themselves in drunkenness, fights, drag racing, and other potentially destructive pursuits. Since the place cost no votes for politicians and caused no embarrassment for law-enforcement officials, they left it alone.

Two nights before, on the day Marcel arrived in Texas to be exact, Lizzy Cline had accepted an "out-call" assignment at a motel along the interstate which catered to truck drivers and commercial travelers. Such an assignment was among the advertised services of the massage parlor, and the motel had always been a good source of business. Lizzy's body was discovered the next day in a ditch beside a seldom-traveled country road.

Tracing her movements, Burdine had learned that Lizzy had called the massage parlor from a pay phone near the motel to report that no one occupied the room designated for the assignation. More sophisticated out-call operations have callback systems to verify their customers' legitimacy. Lizzy's employer had no such procedure. Burdine learned from the motel manager that the room had not been rented on the fatal evening.

More sophisticated out-call services also have strict rules prohibiting girls from accepting "dates" who do not go through the system, and more sophisticated call girls never accept an alternative date when a caller has stood them up. Lizzy was not in the least sophisticated and had little regard for her employer's rules. Time was money and money was what she needed. A truck driver who had been checking in late seemed to recall a girl climbing into a pickup. He thought that the girl matched Lizzy's description, but he couldn't be certain. He was unable to describe the truck or the driver.

The proprietor of the massage parlor had been of little assistance. The customer requesting the out call had a rough voice and a bit of a rude manner.

"That's all we have, Hawg," Burdine concluded. "Now, if you know something that might help us, I'd be obliged if you'd tell me."

"Oh, I do believe we can help you, Ned," Peter T. allowed. "Let's order up another round of Bubba's Special. This may take a while."

Before Peter T. began his story, Luci asked for the keys to the car and excused herself. She returned a few minutes later with her working files, which she turned over to Peter T.

"I think we all agree that this is the man you're looking for, Ned." He handed the Ranger a photograph. "His name is Marcel Larrance. The computer printout here will give you the official line on him, so I'll just let you read for yourself."

The Ranger patted his pockets and extracted a pair of half-glasses before he read the printout, once again denting my Hollywood image. Of course, I conceded, John Wayne never had to read material produced on a dot-matrix printer. The Ranger scanned the data quickly, pausing only to attend to his drink and light another cigarette.

"I can see where you racing people don't like this fella very much, Miz DeGuerre," he said evenly, "but there's nothing here that says he beats up women or goes for kinky sex. Why do you folks think this is our man?"

I recounted the story Vanessa had told me at Frankie's, describing as best I could the aura of violence that surrounded the scar-faced man. "Keep in mind that this is a topless bar in the inner city. It's in a black neighborhood, and most of the customers were black. Marcel was openly, in fact aggressively, contemptuous of blacks, yet he thoroughly intimidated them. Lesle Pilarcik goes out with Marcel, according to my source, and a couple days later she's found dead."

"We checked Marcel's movements against similar murders," Luci added. "Chicago and Los Angeles had similar cases, one girl a dancer, the other a prostitute."

"And you think he's here?"

"He landed in Dallas around five-thirty P.M. on the day Lizzy Cline was killed," Peter T. said. "The guy who picked him up at the airport had a Harrison County sticker on his license plate. That's not all that much to go on, but we've got one sadistic crazy and you've got one dead girl."

Burdine studied the photo for a moment. "Two dead girls," he corrected softly, pausing to consider our revelations. "Tell me about this horse-training place."

I explained in detail the type of facility we were looking for. Burdine asked a few questions about acreage and water requirements. Texas has about every imaginable type of terrain, high plains, prairie, desert, swampland, the "Hill Country" south of Austin, the "Big Thicket" in East Texas, and even a chunk of the Continental Divide running through the southwestern part of the state. The area of northeast Texas where we were featured rolling grasslands quite similar to north-central Kentucky, ideal horse country.

"I've never seen anything like you're describing," Burdine said. "That don't surprise me. Out here they've got more horses than people, and I don't think I'd recognize a thoroughbred if he bit me on the ass. Tell me, how did you folks plan to find this place?"

Peter T. explained our intention to charter an airplane. "Say, Ned," he said speculatively, "the Rangers still have helicopters?"

"A few. Closest is based in Dallas, though."

"You suppose you could get one over here? I mean, seeing's how we may be looking for the same fella."

"You know, I believe that might just be possible, Hawg," Burdine answered. "Why don't you folks order up some food while I go make a couple phone calls."

There was really only one thing to order at Bubba's, the barbecue platter. For $12.95 per person, Bubba would deliver a tray heaped with ribs, chicken, beef brisket, and smoked sausage. When the tray was empty or if one of the entrées ran out, the tray would be refilled. The meats were accompanied by french-fried potatoes, pinto beans, and a tangy sweet-and-sour slaw, all served "family style" in bowls and baskets to be passed around the table. While we waited for the food and Burdine, we speculated on the possibility of Marcel going down on a murder rap. The idea had great appeal.

Burdine and dinner arrived at the same time. "We're all set," the Ranger informed us. "The chopper will fly over first thing in the morning. By the time they refuel, we should be airborne by nine or nine-thirty. They're sending over one of the bigger choppers, so we can all go up."

"Suppose we locate Marcel?" Luci speculated. "What are the chances of proving he killed Lizzy Cline?"

"If he did it, then he's ours," Burdine declared emphatically. "Used to be we had to rely on blood-typing or skin samples in cases like this. With no witnesses and no prior record, there would be some element of doubt. Now they got this DNA-typing and the courts are starting to accept its reliability. The semen samples will put this boy's ass in Huntsville to wait for the needle."

"The needle?"

"Lethal injection," the Ranger explained. "Personally I think hanging would better serve for a killing like this one, but the needle will do."

Just as I had learned to hate airplanes from the drudgery of business travel, I had developed a positive loathing for helicopters in Vietnam. To me helicopters were infernal devices designed by Torquemada and piloted by Evel Knievel for the express purpose of driving the innocent to the brink of insanity before dropping him into the chaos of a "hot LZ." There his sorry ass could be blasted at will by angry little patriots, not in the least in awe of the noisy flying machine or the high-tech firepower of the soldiers it spews forth. Many of the guys I fought with loved the helicopters for bringing them out. I was never able to get past the fact that the choppers brought us in to begin with.

At nine A.M. the sun was already warm with the promise of heat and humidity to come. I would almost have rather taken a beating from Marcel than to have boarded one more chopper in my lifetime. Luci, however, could not restrain her enthusiasm. Another "first," I thought ruefully. Peter T., though his time "in country" had not required jumping out of helicopters, guessed the source of my revulsion and looked on sympathetically.

I felt a heavy hand on my shoulder. "About a hundred years ago I swore I'd never again set foot on one o' those goddamn contraptions," Ned Burdine drawled philosophically.

"Marines?"

"Army," the Ranger grunted. Our eyes met with recognition of experience shared. "I reckon I can stand one more ride if you can."

"Let's go, dogface," I said with resignation.

"Up yours, jarhead," Burdine retorted with a grin.

By the end of the day we had seen hundreds of horses,

thousands of cows, a few oil wells, and dozens of ranch houses with outbuildings. We had seen not a single training track or starting gate. Even Luci was tired and irritable, the novelty of her first helicopter ride having worn off in the first hour of flying. We had underestimated the vastness of the country, for after a full six hours in the air, we had flown over less than a third of the area considered most likely to contain the training center.

The pilot, a friendly "urban cowboy" in his mid-twenties named Billy Jeff Holbrook, advised us that he could stay just one more day. He and the aircraft were scheduled to be in Austin for search-and-rescue training. Burdine and I exchanged glances in the unexpressed hope that the kid never had to learn the "true purpose of helicopter existence."

"Hope that boy can spend all his time saving asses rather than dropping 'em in the mud," Burdine noted dryly. "Guess there ain't nothing to do but come back tomorrow and try again. Maybe we'll get lucky."

"I need about six cold beers," Peter T. declared.

Burdine shook his head. "Six beers? You're getting old, Hawg. I remember the day when you woulda had six beers down already."

"Old my ass. I'm just exercising caution. Never a good idea to drink and drive."

The Ranger snorted. "Take note of the wisdom of a man who cracks open a 'traveler' to drive to the Seven-Eleven for cigarettes. If you folks don't mind, I'm gonna head home. Momma ain't seen much of me since this business began, so I better put in an appearance."

We agreed to meet the next morning at seven in the motel coffee shop. Peter T. used the ride to the motel to terrorize Billy Jeff with his driving, reasoning that the pilot had it coming. Tomorrow Peter T. had to put himself back in Billy Jeff's hands and the rest of us would pay. Terrific, I thought.

"Billy Jeff, if you try to get even with this maniac while we're up in the air, I'll kill you myself," Luci declared, taking the words out of my mouth. "And you, asshole," she warned Peter T., "if you don't get me to a shower, quickly and in one piece, I'll come back from the dead and haunt you forever." The Texan apparently believed her; his driving became downright sedate.

When we reached the motel, Luci bolted for the room. The three of us repaired to the bar, where Peter T. ordered cold beers two at a time. The waitress brought tortilla chips and a bowl of salsa with the drinks. We ate and munched while Peter T. and Billy Jeff exchanged high-school football stories. The two had discovered that they had played for arch rivals, the former in the early sixties, the latter in the late seventies. Billy Jeff, who could have been no more than an infant at the time, claimed to remember the feared nose guard "Hog" Westmoreland, all-conference, all-state. For his part, Peter T. allowed that he seemed to recall reading about a tailback named B.J. Holbrook gaining over fourteen hundred yards rushing his senior year. Were we anyplace but Texas, I would have suspected that one made up a story and the other swore it was true. Here people take high-school football very seriously.

Luci returned freshly scrubbed and hungry, just in time, by my thinking. We'd been through three decades of football rivalry already, with no end in sight.

"Go get your showers and make it fast," Luci instructed. "You guys are taking me out for Mexican food."

Peter T. grumbled about "bossy women," but after ordering three beers to go, he complied. Billy Jeff announced that he had other plans and would keep Luci company until we returned. Somehow the idea of leaving Luci alone with a six-foot, twenty-five-year-old pilot made me a big uneasy, and I was back in less than twenty minutes. Peter T. showed up shortly thereafter, minus the three beers.

"You sure you won't join us, son?" Peter T. inquired as we were leaving.

"No, thanks," the pilot answered. "I believe I'll run over to Goldie's 'n' see what's cookin'."

Peter T. smiled knowingly. "You can bet Goldie's is cookin'."

Two hours later, only Luci had room for fried ice cream. Armando's had fed us in the best Tex-Mex tradition, "plenty hot and plenty of it." We were tired, but not quite ready to cut the evening short.

"Let's go someplace where we can hear fiddles playing," Luci suggested.

"That sounds okay," Peter T. agreed, "but I don't know the town that well. We'll have to take our chances."

"What about that place Billy Jeff was going? Goldie's?"

"I don't think you want to go to Goldie's, darlin'," Peter T. replied, laughing. "Goldie's is one of the most famous go-go joints in Texas. You know, 'nekkid' women, that kind of thing."

I was laughing along with Peter T. at Luci's discomfort when the memory of Marcel's interest in the dumpy, tattooed dancers at Frankie's came back to me. Both of my companions, noticing my abrupt change of expression, waited expectantly.

"Boys and girls, luck may be swinging back in our direction," I announced. "I have a serious hunch we might find Goldie's more than interesting."

16

Goldie's, while in the same business as Frankie's, was markedly different from its Detroit counterpart. The saloon, located in the country, was in a barnlike steel building which could have just as easily been a factory or warehouse. The site included a spacious gravel parking lot, full of cars and, of course, pickup trucks.

The interior of the nightclub, which covered six to eight thousand square feet, made an attempt at western decor with rustic wood columns and, in a few strategic areas, plank flooring. Not much had been invested in decoration, however. Had the go-go business failed, a few hours' work would have turned the building back into a warehouse or a farm-implement dealership.

The entertainers, in various stages of undress, were spread out, with a main stage facing the long bar and three smaller satellite stages in the more remote corners of the room. Luci, Peter T., and I were later to learn that a dancer performed her main routine at center stage and, on completion, rotated from satellite to satellite, one dance at a time, until she reached the dressing room.

Another sharp contrast with Frankie's was that everyone seemed to be having a good time. Texans of all ages, in their boots and jeans, were stomping and whooping, and the dancers seemed to be caught up in their boisterousness, gyrating, if not artfully, at least with enthusiasm, to driving country-rock.

Behind the bar, two bartenders hustled to keep drinks flowing to the seated patrons, while a third concentrated on supplying the scantily clad waitresses who circulated among the tables. The overwhelming beverage of choice was beer, overpriced and served in cans rather than bottles or mugs. "Hard to break an aluminum can over someone's head," explained Peter T.

A bouncer with the height and girth of Boog attended the door, checking the ages of the suspiciously youthful and sullenly sizing up potential troublemakers. The entry was posted with several hand-painted signs delineating house rules: "You must be 21 to enter" . . . "Shirts must be worn at all times" . . . "No leathers or colors permitted" (no bikers, according to Peter T.). The last declared, "If you are offended by dancing and nudity, do not enter here." Someone had scratched out the "do not enter" and had written in "pack your ass."

The bouncer cast a curious glance at Luci as we entered. By custom, the only females at Goldie's were dancers and waitresses. Hookers were not permitted, so standard practice was to turn unescorted females away. Apparently a woman escorted by two males was beyond the bouncer's experience or instructions, so, with a speculative shrug, he let us pass.

"Come, babe!" Peter T. hooted as the search for a table led us past a satellite stage occupied by a six-foot blond wearing only three-inch heels. Luci, her eyes wide, poked him in the ribs to keep him moving.

I felt conspicuous as we meandered between tables. Luci and Peter T. had insisted we stop at a western-wear store just before it closed, and the two had outfitted me in a pair of medium brown Tony Lamas—I had refused the two-tone boots—a checked western-cut shirt with mother-of-pearl snaps rather than buttons, and a wide-brimmed "Texas straw" hat.

"If we run into Marcel, without the beard and dressed like this, he'll never notice you," Peter T. insisted.

"Dressed like this, my own mother wouldn't recognize me," I retorted.

"I think you look . . . well, rugged," Luci said, doing her best to suppress her amusement.

I owned several pairs of boots, and jeans were my preferred trousers, but I was self-conscious in this cowboy "costume." However, a confrontation with Marcel before we discovered the location of the training center would be disastrous. I went along with the disguise reluctantly. Though the costume blended with the crowd, it was foreign to me and I was certain that "real cowboys" would notice the imitation.

We selected a table for its view of the bar and the door, rather than its vantage point for watching the dancers. Across the room, Billy Jeff was seated next to one of the satellite stages, lustily stuffing a dollar bill into the ankle bracelet of a naked dancer. Alarmed at the prospect of going up in a hated helicopter with someone who had partied all night at the controls, I resolved to monitor the degree of drunkenness the pilot attained.

A waitress in short-shorts and an abbreviated halter top brought cold beer and flirted cheerfully with Peter T. The loud music made conversation next to impossible, so we sipped our beer and waited.

Marcel Larrance paused at the entrance, surveying the premises with apparent care. I noticed that the massive bouncer followed him into the room and eyed him from behind with obvious concern. Clearly Marcel was not unknown at Goldie's. Making his way to the bar, Marcel took a seat recently vacated by a young cowboy in need of the men's room and, brushing aside the half-finished beer and open pack of cigarettes, the scar-faced man sat down. The bartender served him a beer without comment, his motions displaying a hint of nervousness.

The young cowboy returned from the men's room and hesitated. Peter T. looked at me expectantly, for the elements of a salon brawl were firmly in place. The watchful bouncer moved closer to the bar, and the bartenders tensed visibly. The cowboy took in the fact that his recently vacated, but not abandoned stool was now occupied, and he considered whether his honor demanded that he reclaim it at all costs. If Marcel noticed him or recognized the tension building, he gave no indication.

The scene was right out of a Grade B western, the ruthless gunfighter provoking an inexperienced trail hand into slapping leather. I almost expected the music to stop and the customers around the bar to run for cover. The cowboy was clearly not happy with his options and he looked around furtively for a way to escape the confrontation while maintaining his self-respect.

The bouncer saved the day. Making his way along the bar, he grabbed the cowboy's cigarettes in a massive paw and continued past Marcel without so much as a glance.

He sidled up next to the hesitant cowboy and, with a friendly but insistent arm around the youth's shoulders, led him to an empty stool at the end of the bar. With a nod to the bartender, the bouncer bought the cowboy a beer and stayed, shooting the breeze in a friendly manner, until the tension passed. No bloodshed, no damage, the bouncer clapped the youth on the back and resumed his post at the door.

"Whatever they pay that guy, it isn't enough," Peter T. observed. The good-time momentum at Goldie's pounded on with no broken glass, no demolished furniture, no blood or broken heads, and no visit from the sheriff. The bouncer's cool-headed intervention had saved his employer hundreds of dollars in damage and aggravation.

All four stages at Goldie's featured tablelike appendages and chairs for those patrons who appreciated a truly close-up view of the dancers. Surprisingly, there were a few open seats at each stage, giving the impression that the patrons were maintaining an embarrassed distance from the objects of their attention. When the tall blond we had seen upon entering once again took center stage, Marcel left his stool at the bar and took a seat directly in front of the dancer. The blond, who had up to that point been enjoying the admiration of the crowd, suppressed a shudder and continued her act. Her expression changed from that of a star in full command of her audience to that of a novice dancer chilled and self-conscious at finding herself naked in front of a crowd of cheering men.

At Goldie's, dancers did not hustle drinks. They received numerous tips while they were dancing, and all wore an elastic ankle band or garter in lieu of pockets. They also performed what were known as "table dances," during which the dancer perched on a sturdy wooden box and soloed at tableside for the enjoyment of a specific patron. Tipping a dancer onstage involved a certain protocol. A bill was placed flat in front of the customer. Using slow, exaggerated movements, the dancer would then squat or bend to retrieve the currency in a manner that would provide the tipper with a "special show" of her various endowments.

The tall blond was richly endowed and she had a way

of making eye contact with her audience, making men reach deep into their pockets. On a good night she probably made three or four hundred dollars in tips. Even though Marcel's proximity had marred her performance, several bills were spread out on the stage.

The blond gradually recovered her composure, concentrating on retrieving her tips and on rewarding the tippers in her best style. To his chagrin, Marcel found himself studiously ignored, and as a countermeasure, he went to his own pocket. Pulling out a fat roll, Marcel peeled off what must have been a twenty or a fifty and placed the bill on the stage. The blond appeared not to see the offer and continued to pick up the customary singles and fives, thereby throwing Marcel into a serious rage.

When the music stopped, the blond continued to ignore the scar-faced man and moved quickly to the next satellite stage in the rotation. Marcel angrily picked up his tip and his beer and followed. The chairs surrounding the smaller stage were all occupied, and his growing frustration was visible. I thought for a moment that Marcel might appropriate a seat by force.

Once again the alert bouncer intervened. He had obviously been keeping an eye on Marcel, and when the music stopped again, he signaled another dancer to take the station next in rotation. Paying no overt attention to Marcel, he took the blond's arm and escorted her to the dressing room. The blond smiled gratefully while Marcel seethed.

"C'mon, let's go," Peter T. said urgently. With our quarry still on the scene, I was reluctant to follow, but Peter T. was insistent.

"The bouncer's gonna send the girl home," he explained when we reached the parking lot. "I'm betting that ol' Marcel has figured that out too. He'll either come out here and wait for her or, if he's smart, he'll figure he's attracted too much attention and take off. I'd guess he's not that smart."

We sat in Peter T.'s "dinosaur" with the top down, smoking and talking as though we were taking a breath of fresh air. We made no attempt to hide and paid no overt attention to Marcel when he came out. As Peter T. had predicted, Marcel did not drive away. The blond dancer followed about a half-hour later, dressed in jeans and a T-shirt, her hair pinned up under a hat advertising "Bow Wow Dog Food." Her appearance had been toned down, but her height and stride were unmistakable.

No interior light came on as Marcel eased out of his truck. Had we not been watching for movement, he would have been undetectable. I started to get out of the car when Peter T. reached across Luci to restrain me.

"We can't let him take her," I whispered urgently. "If he loses us on some back road, she's history."

"Wait," Peter T. shot back as he nodded in the direction of Goldie's back door. The bouncer had been watching out for the dancer after all, and he moved swiftly to catch up with her.

From where we sat, Marcel's ravaged features were invisible, but I could easily imagine his expression of hate and fury, having seen it twice before. The dancer finally noticed him and stopped in her tracks. Marcel seemed to be weighing his chances of dispatching the bouncer and taking the girl when a pickup truck full of whooping cowboys skidded into the lot and parked. Whether as potential reinforcements or witnesses, the cowboys forced Marcel to opt for discretion rather than aggression, and without a word he slammed the door of the truck and roared away in a shower of gravel.

The terrorized dancer hugged the massive bouncer, either in fear or in gratitude, as Peter T. started the Caddy and followed Marcel's truck at a discreet distance. "That man is truly scary," Luci said as we let out a collective sigh of relief.

"It's amazing he's stayed out of prison," Peter T. observed. "He's a goddamn BooHoo always lookin' to take somebody's head off."

"Shouldn't we stop and call Burdine?" Luci suggested.

"Can't. We'll lose him."

Peter T. was maintaining several hundred yards of distance from the truck. Marcel seemed to have no concern for pursuers, for he maintained a fast but not evasive pace. A vintage Cadillac convertible is much too noticeable to be an effective tail car, but Peter T. maneuvered skillfully, turning off and doubling back with his lights off and dropping back when the road ran straight.

The excitement level was high as Marcel led us farther into the country. There was an implicit understanding that Marcel was headed home to the much-sought-after training center. When the road we were on ended at a stop sign, Marcel turned east on a paved county highway. We were too close at the time to follow, and Peter T. turned in the opposite direction. Keeping the truck's taillights in sight, the Texan switched off his lights and turned around. The highway was straight, with no traffic in either direction except for the pickup. I estimated that we had come about twenty miles from Goldie's.

Marcel continued for another fifteen miles, and the straight road with recently painted white lines allowed Peter T. to follow with no lights. Peter T. showed no concern for the lack of visibility and easily maintained Marcel's speed with about a quarter-mile between the vehicles. In the distance, Marcel's brake lights flashed and Peter T. slowed the Cadillac to a coast.

"Shit," the Texan muttered. Marcel had turned onto a dirt-and-gravel lane. To complicate the problem, the terrain changed from relatively flat to rolling. The dirt road now curved to run between low hills. We passed through a section which had not been cleared of timber, and any light provided by the moon and stars disappeared in the tall pines. We were too close to use the lights, so progress slowed to a crawl.

The trees finally thinned out and, fearing that Marcel had gained too much ground, Peter T. switched on the headlights and increased his speed. If we came upon Marcel suddenly, we would certainly be spotted, for there was no reason for anyone but a resident to be on this road at night. The Cadillac bumped and groaned as if in protest for the abusive treatment, but the Texan pushed on.

We came over a rise and the road straightened. A flat stretch of farmland lay in front of us. There were no taillights to be seen.

"He couldn't be that far ahead," I said. Peter T. agreed that Marcel must have turned off. With considerable backing and spinning of the wheel, he reversed the big convertible and followed slowly in the opposite direction.

"Look, the training center has to be in this general

area," Luci observed. "Why don't we just go back to the motel and fly over this sector tomorrow?" She was right, of course, but Peter T. and I were caught up in the chase like hounds on the scent. Luci's entirely reasonable suggestion went unheeded.

We spotted the tire marks before the turnoff was visible. It was very easy to understand how we had missed it when we first passed. There was no mailbox or other markings, just a break in the pines. When we had passed earlier, our lights had been off and Marcel's tire tracks had been invisible. Peter T. doused the lights, pulled into the drive, and stopped.

Without a word, I jumped out of the convertible and jogged along the dirt road, mentally cursing the stiff new boots. About a quarter-mile later, the stand of pines ended and an old-fashioned barbed-wire fence enclosed pastures on each side of the road. About five hundred yards farther on, I could see scattered lights in the windows of buildings. I made my way back to the car and immediately began struggling to pull off the boots.

"What are you doing?" Luci demanded as I changed back into the athletic shoes I had been wearing before the stop at the western store.

"It's up there," I answered. "About a half-mile. I'm going in for a closer look."

"Don't be stupid," she insisted. "We've got them. All we have to do is get Burdine and come back in the morning." Continuing to lace up the shoes, I said nothing. Luci turned to Peter T. "Talk to him. This is dumb. There's nothing to be done except get hurt or worse."

"Look, goddammit," I said heatedly, unwilling to be denied with the quarry so close, "you want Armand so bad. We know Marcel's in there, but if Burdine comes busting in and Armand is somewhere else, we've lost him."

She refused to accept the argument and, had logic prevailed, I would have agreed with her. Once again she looked to Peter T. for support, but the Texan just shrugged. I was out of the car and running down the road before she could say any more.

Once the woods ended, the road was too exposed to approach the training center. I had no way of knowing if guards were posted, but I had to assume there would be some kind of watch. The fence presented little obstacle, and I went over in a vault, circling across the pasture away from the road.

I came to a higher wooden fence delineating a more formal paddock. From there I could make out a long horse barn, a utility shed, a low building I took to be a bunkhouse for the hands, and a main house. I paused, watching for signs of movement around the buildings. Moonlight, lights from the windows of the house and the bunkhouse, and a single bulb over the barn door cast an eerie glow over the barnyard. Though the evening had cooled off, my shirt clung to my back. Staying in the meager shadows provided by the paddock fence, I crept up to the barn, careful not to alert the sleeping horses. The barn had two rows of eight stalls facing each other, with a tack room at the far end. I couldn't tell how many of the stalls were occupied and I feared that a closer inspection would stir up a commotion.

Carefully, but quickly, I came around the rear of the barn and sprinted across an open stretch to the shadow of the shed. Inside were a tractor and a small flatbed truck. The bunkhouse was about fifty yards directly in front of me, the house another hundred yards ahead and to the right. About half of the bunkhouse was dark, but a section near the door was well-lit. As I tiptoed closer, I heard voices speaking Spanish and a radio playing Latin music.

Still staying in the shadows, I crossed to the dark portion of the bunkhouse and circled to the rear of the building. I was beginning to appreciate the validity of Luci's argument as the voices grew louder. Peering through a back window, I saw four men around a table playing cards and drinking. There were two half-empty bottles of tequila and several open beer bottles. One of the chairs was empty, but the presence of a shot glass and some loose bills and change gave testimony to its recent occupation. Where was the fifth man? I wondered anxiously.

I was about to circle around to the rear of the house when I smelled the cigarette smoke. The fifth man was not ten feet away, around the corner leaning against the building. Apparently he had folded his hand and opted for a breath of fresh air. A stream of obscenities flew through my mind as I flattened against the side of the bunkhouse, hardly daring to breathe.

After what seemed like an eternity, I saw the red glow of the cigarette butt fly into the night. The screen door slammed and a voice called out something in Spanish. Several men laughed as the smoker resumed his seat and growled a response. Giving the hands a few minutes to resume their game, I made another wide circle to the house.

The house was a one-story structure, fairly long, and with no wings or courts. The back was dark all the way around. As I came around the far side, I saw several vehicles parked in a haphazard manner, among them Marcel's pickup. In the front, a long porch ran the length of the house and lights glowed from what must have been the living room. I jumped as a central-air-conditioning unit cycled on, my heart pounding frantically.

Marcel is in there, wired and furious over the aborted abduction, I reminded myself. The utter foolishness of my situation loomed in my mind as I inched across the creaky wood decking of the porch to the lighted window. Because of the air conditioning, the house was closed up, but with every groan of the old boards, I winced at the prospect of discovery. Please, no dogs, I thought fervently.

Finally able to see inside, I observed Marcel pacing the room. His face was red and his features contorted in anger. A man I couldn't identify sat drinking in an armchair facing the window. The stranger had thinning dark hair with the puffy features and the red whiskey nose of a habitual drinker. He was studying the drink in his hand in a conscious effort to ignore the volatile Marcel.

The object of Marcel's apparent anger was seated in another armchair facing away from me. I could see the third man's hands gesturing, but I couldn't make out what was said. Marcel stopped his pacing long enough to snarl something at the unseen speaker. The argument raged for several minutes, but the third man remained out of view. Finally the third man rose from his chair, crossed the room, and stood toe-to-toe with Marcel. He was as tall as Marcel but not as muscular. The rolled-up sleeves of a denim workshirt revealed large hands and thick wrists as he stood facing the scar-faced man.

To my surprise, Marcel turned away first, marching angrily across the room to pour a drink from a bottle on a sideboard. At the moment of victory, the unidentified man let out a deep breath and turned back to his chair. I immediately recognized the man I had first met as Aaron Locklear . . . Armand Larrance in the flesh.

Having long since recognized the folly of this stealthy mission, and having seen what I had come to see, I knew the time was right to get out. There was no need to take the circuitous route I had followed coming in. The car was no more than a half-mile up the dirt lane. With the Larrance brothers occupied and the hands engrossed in their card game, the shortest distance seemed the most desirable.

Once a safe distance from the house, I covered the ground between the house and the woods in a sprint. Whether I had underestimated the distance or, more likely, had simply ignored the concept of pace, by the time I reached the trees, I was winded and had to slow down. I stopped to catch my breath and turned back to the cluster of buildings. No lights had come on, nor were there any signs of a general alert. Inhaling great gulps of air and cursing my recent lack of exercise, I started to jog on at a much slower pace.

I was within a couple hundred yards of the convertible when I saw a beam of light reflected off the pines—too small and too dim to be the car's headlamps. Several seconds elapsed before I recognized it and ducked off the road and into the trees. I waited until my breathing returned to normal and edged closer until the car came into view.

Peter T. had backed the Cadillac into the lane, anticipating the need for a quick exit. Luci and Peter T. were out of the car with their backs against the driver's side. I could see Peter T. talking and gesticulating to someone holding a flashlight and a gun.

There had been a guard after all, I thought, my mind racing. Only the accident of timing had allowed me to slip into the training center undetected. Had I not winded myself sprinting up the lane, I would have blundered right into the scene ahead. Having no illusions as to our collective fate had we fallen into the hands of the Larrance brothers, I cursed silently.

Drawing upon old skills, neglected but ingrained by the necessity of survival, I moved silently into the trees, circling to the rear of the guard. As I drew near, I could hear Peter T.'s voice explaining how he and Luci were lovers just searching for a place to park.

"No way, man," the guard responded in a Spanish accent. "You too old to be parkin' in de country."

Peter T. managed an embarrassed chuckle. "Ya see, pardner, we're both married. You know how it is."

I had drawn even with the guard and could see the shotgun the man had trained on Luci and Peter T. I took some consolation that the guard looked to be the size of a jockey, probably doing double duty as an exercise rider. I edged closer, searching for some kind of weapon.

"Look," Peter T. continued in a placating voice, "I know we can work something out. We didn't mean to trespass, and this whole thing could be real embarrassing to the lady and all."

Luci had taken up her role like a seasoned actress, trying to hide her face behind Peter T.'s shoulder. In the beam of the flashlight, I could see that she had her purse in her hand. I knew she was carrying a .32-caliber automatic in the purse, but I cared little for her chances against the shotgun.

"Now, I'm just gonna reach into my pocket," Peter T. was saying. The barrel of the shotgun followed his movement. "Don't get nervous. How about if I hand you a hundred-dollar bill and we'll forget this whole thing." Peter T. peeled off a bill and held it in front of him for the Mexican to see.

Unable to see the guard's face, I could easily imagine the man's range of thoughts. He could accept the hundred and walk away, or if he were smart, he could rob Peter T. outright. If the Texan's story were true, the victim would be unlikely to report the theft. The guard's mental calculations were almost palpable.

"I think we'll go up to the house now," the guard said finally. Apparently his fear of Marcel overcame his greed.

I was within striking distance and the time had come to act. I picked up a loose branch and tossed it to his left, where it rustled in the brush. The guard turned reflexively and the barrel of the gun followed just enough. By the time the guard could turn back to his captives, I had my left arm around the guard's throat and had twisted the shotgun away with my right. Peter T. had moved at the same time, kicking the Mexican solidly in the groin. The guard sagged with the blow and moaned as the breath went out of him. Luci shoved the little automatic in his face. The poor bastard hardly knew what had hit him.

"The next time he'll take the money," Peter T. observed dryly.

"Let's get out of here," I urged. "There no telling when he's due for relief."

"What do we do with him?" Luci asked.

"He goes with us," I answered.

We secured the guard in the trunk of the Cadillac and drove some distance down the road before using the lights. Once we hit the highway, Peter T. stopped long enough to put the top up, and then made some speed to get back to Longview. No one spoke for some time. To her credit, Luci refrained from pointing out that her warnings had been correct.

"Armand Larrance is there," I told them. "And you were right, that was a dumb thing to do." Luci said nothing, but she gripped my hand tightly. "I don't know what they're going to do when they find this guy missing. I think we'd better get to Burdine as soon as we can."

A general store came into view ahead, but it showed no lights. The clock on Peter T.'s dash read two-fifteen. We were about to drive past when the headlights picked up an older-style glass telephone booth. Peter T. quickly brought the dinosaur to a stop. Luck was with us. The phone worked.

Luci and I held each other while Peter T. worked on reaching Ned Burdine. "I got you into trouble again," I confessed. "I should have listened to you earlier."

"You got us out when it counted," she said.

"Pure luck. I almost got all three of us captured. Just plain stupid."

"Be quiet," she murmured, snuggling closer.

The effect of the late hour and repeated surges of adrenaline were beginning to hit me as Peter T. talked on the phone. The white leather seats of the big Eldorado were seductively comfortable, and with Luci tucked into the crook of my arm, I gave way to exhaustion and closed my eyes.

* * *

There was a shaft of moonlight through the trees. Tall trees with hanging vines. There were night sounds—not the familiar chirp of crickets or the buzz of cicadas, but sounds more exotic and sinister. I could smell the rotting tropical vegetation and something else. Blood? My sense of danger—"the nose"—shrieked its warning and I struggled to find cover. But I could not move. I strained against invisible bonds, but to no avail. The shaft of moonlight glinted off polished steel, and behind the blade, a huge form loomed closer. I knew it was Marcel without actually discerning the face. The form squatted next to me and I could make out the ravaged features, the leering grin, and I thrashed about in an effort to free myself. Useless. Hopeless.

I cried out in frustration and fear as Luci shook me gently. My head snapped up, my eyes wide and searching. My muscles tensed as I nearly lashed out in fear and desperation. She put a hand to my feverish forehead and spoke to me softly. Gradually I relaxed and shook my head to clear the sleep.

A glance at the dash clock told me that almost two hours had elapsed since we had arrived at the little country store, but the place was no longer empty. Ned Burdine's unmarked car was parked next to the Cadillac, along with two sheriff's cars and a highway-patrol cruiser. A third deputy arrived at that moment. All the lights were on in the old store, as Burdine had apparently aroused the owner and set up a command post.

"Are you awake?" Luci asked gently. "They need you inside."

"Jesus," I gasped weakly. The dream had been too real.

Luci watched with concern as I climbed out of the car. She winced as I leaned heavily on the railing to pull myself up the steps to the low porch which fronted the store. At the top I straightened and drew a deep breath, searching for reserves of energy. The light above illuminated Luci's face as she followed.

Inside the store, a grumbling old coot I took to be the owner rustled around making coffee while Burdine, Peter T., and a half-dozen officers gathered around the counter. I gratefully accepted coffee from the old man and smiled reassuringly at Luci as she came up and took my arm, the care etched on her face. We joined the circle of men crowding around to examine the county maps of the access road and the training center spread out on the counter.

"These maps just show the property lines and the terrain," Burdine explained after the introductions were completed. "Tennyson, here, has been inside, so I'll let him describe the place."

In as much detail as I could remember, I sketched in the buildings in pencil on the map. "If they've discovered the guard is missing, there may be all kinds of activity," I warned.

"What guard?" Burdine demanded, and I looked at Peter T.

"Shit. I forgot about that little guy."

Two deputies used Peter T.'s keys to retrieve the Mexican from the Cadillac's trunk. In the light, I could see that the guard was only in his late teens. He was bewildered and more than a little frightened to be in the hands of so many police.

"Hell, that's Billy Robles," one of the deputies observed with some surprise.

The young Mexican was somewhat relieved to see a familiar face, even if it belonged to the law, and he was suddenly eager to cooperate. He had done nothing wrong, he maintained. He had needed a job and had been hired to ride horses. The boss, Mr. Locklear, had promised to train him to be a jockey. He had taken his turn guarding—all the hands did—because Mr. Locklear said some of the horses were very valuable. Robles thought the guard duty was a waste of time, but did as he was told.

Under urging from the big Ranger, Billy Robles described the security measures, the number of hands, and the farm's routine schedule. Robles had begun his guard duty at midnight and was not scheduled for relief until six A.M. when the exercising and feeding activity began. There was no guard during the day.

"Weapons?" Burdine asked. There was a rifle rack in the house, but other than the shotgun, the hands had no firearms that Robles knew of.

Once all the intelligence had been assimilated, Burdine laid out a simple plan. Since Robles' absence was not likely to have been discovered, the officers would just drive in and arrest everyone. Four men would secure the bunkhouse and the rest would take the main house. The plan did not include the participation of Peter T., Luci, or me, a detail which Luci and Peter T. protested vigorously on the grounds that they were both trained investigators and entitled to be in on the bust.

"You're civilians," Burdine stated flatly. "I appreciate your argument, but I won't have a civilian getting hurt on an operation of mine."

After much wrangling, Burdine finally conceded that we "civilians" could advance past the tree line and take up positions blocking the lane in case anyone tried to escape. Once the center was secure, we could go in. The arrangement suited me fine, but Luci and Peter T. were clearly not happy with a secondary role.

"All right, then," Peter T. said. "What're we waiting for?"

The Ranger sighed patiently. "Warrants," he answered with an edge in his voice. "The Larrance brothers could be heading for the hills or building Fort Apache, but these days we wait for warrants. Your case and Tennyson's reconnoiter give us what might pass for probable cause to go in. Sheriff Kirts went to roust a friendly judge, so all we can do is hope it doesn't take too long."

The sunrise beat Sheriff Kirts about as easily as Secretariat won the Belmont. In the interest of doing something rather than nothing, the group had taken up positions on the dirt road at the entrance to the lane leading to the training center. The thick pines shielded us from the view of the house, and in the darkness everyone had been comfortable with the decision. Now the beginning of daylight left us feeling exposed and uneasy.

We had bought the old storekeeper out of his entire stock of the half-dozen thermos bottles he had allowed some sporting-goods salesman to sell him two years ago, along with the camping gear gathering dust on his shelves. The lawmen swilled cup after cup of coffee and then marched into the woods to get rid of it. Now and then someone would attempt to relieve the building tension by telling a joke or uttering one of those gems of folksy wisdom I've come to think of as "Texasisms."

However, any levity was quickly silenced by just a look from an intense Ned Burdine.

I noticed Billy Robles smoking in the back of one of the sheriff's cars. "What's he doing here?" I asked Burdine.

"What were we supposed to do with him? Leave him at the store?"

"Can we trust him?"

"How the hell should I know?" Burdine snapped. Then he seemed to think the idea over. "He ain't a bad kid. What have you got in mind?"

"It's almost six o'clock," I explained. "If he doesn't show up soon, somebody's liable to come looking for him. Suppose we send him on down there, that is if he's willing, to just take up his chores like everything's fine?"

Billy, anxious to exonerate himself through cooperation, quickly agreed to return to the center. Burdine struggled with the decision before finally allowing the kid to proceed.

"Don't do anything, Billy," the Ranger instructed. "Just go on watering the horses or shoveling shit, whatever it is you do. And, Billy, if you warn 'em, you'll spend some time protecting your ass in Huntsville, I guarantee."

The kid's eyes widened as he nodded his understanding. I watched him disappear down the road before I realized what was missing.

"The shotgun. We forgot the goddamn shotgun."

"Let's hope they don't notice," Burdine said with resignation.

Sheriff John Kirts arrived ten minutes after Robles made his trek down the lane, the warrants in hand and in order. Burdine took just long enough to apprise him of the plan before ordering the lawmen into their cars. Burdine led the way, with Sheriff Kirts right behind. Luci, Peter T., and I brought up the rear in the Cadillac. When we reached the end of the trees, the point at which we had been instructed to stop, Peter T. paused just long enough to snatch Billy's shotgun out of the backseat.

"Peter T. . . . ." I began.

"Fuck him." Peter T. grinned. " 'Scuse me, Luci." Luci just grinned back and dug around her purse for her gun.

"Terrific," I muttered.

The firepower proved to be unnecessary. When we

skidded to a stop in front of the main house, a group of deputies was already bursting into the bunkhouse. The hands filed out protesting in Spanish and gesticulating wildly. The group which hit the house emerged leading the slovenly, whiskey-nosed man I had seen the night before. The man, still in his underwear, staggered to the porch rail and puked in the bushes.

Dr. Vernon Mack, I assumed,—the veterinarian suspended in Armand's race-fixing scandal. I watched the man stagger. I watched one of the hands conversing with Burdine, pointing toward the training track and shaking his head in denial. Where the hell were the Larrance brothers? I wondered frantically.

"The boy says the Larrance brothers took off overland in a jeep," Burdine answered my unspoken question. To the sheriff he said, "John, we'll need your four-wheeler."

"Not with me driving," the sheriff said. "I can't handle that monster off the road." He looked around for one of his deputies. "Hey, Howard . . ."

"I'll drive it, Sheriff," Peter T. said calmly.

"Who the hell are you?"

"He's the best driver, drunk or sober, I've ever seen," Burdine explained, already on the run.

"Let's go, then," the sheriff agreed as two other deputies piled into the big utility vehicle.

The rest of the training center was secure. The hands, spread out to be searched, protested their innocence in a loud mixture of Spanish and English. Luci was questioning the now identified Dr. Vernon S. Mack, DVM.

They must have noticed the missing shotgun, I thought, in an attempt to account for the Larrance brothers' sudden flight. With a start I realized that Billy Robles was not among the hands.

"Oh no," I cried with a sinking feeling of despair. I vaulted the paddock fence in an instant and ran for the barn.

Luci broke off her questioning of the barely coherent veterinarian and followed in my tracks. She found me standing motionless over the broken and lifeless body of Billy Robles.

"Sonofabitch," I muttered vacantly. "Sonofabitch." I would be a long time forgetting that I had been the one who suggested the boy go back to the center. I had been the one to forget about the shotgun.

17

"The sonofabitch can't get away," Ned Burdine was saying to the group around a government-issue conference table adjacent to the Ranger's office. "Every lawman in Texas is looking for him, and, ugly as he is, he can't be too hard to spot."

While I looked around the table I didn't even notice the vile taste of the vending-machine coffee I was drinking. All of the county law-enforcement officials, representatives of the state and city police departments, Luci, and Peter T. looked on skeptically. Burdine was expressing frustration rather than confidence, because for two days since the raid on the training center, Marcel Larrance had eluded everything that Texas law enforcement could throw at him. Luci, Peter T., and I had been included in these official meetings because of the research we had done and because of the relationship Peter T. had with Burdine. I was beginning to think we were all wasting time.

Two days earlier, Peter T. had maneuvered the sheriff's big four-by-four on the trail of Marcel and Armand Larrance. The tire tracks had been fairly easy to follow and Peter T. was, indeed, a driver of considerable skill. While they bumped over the rolling pastureland, Burdine and the sheriff called for additional support from patrol cars, planes, and choppers. Unfortunately, the nearest helicopter had been grounded as its pilot recovered from a massive hangover. Burdine had vowed to have Billy Jeff's ass.

The single-vehicle "posse" had remained on the trail for several miles, passing through openings in fences which the jeep had broken in its flight. The lawmen had known that Marcel's options were becoming fewer as the forest loomed thicker to the north and Calvary Creek blocked the way directly east. Soon enough, the fugitives would have had to turn south in an effort to find a road. The nearest major highways, U.S. 59 and I-20, were soon to be well-covered by deputies and the highway patrol.

As they came over a rise, they saw the jeep. Marcel must have seen the ravine too late or had been moving too fast, for the jeep had come to rest, wheels up, at the bottom of the ravine. Armand Larrance was dead at the scene. Marcel, apparently thrown clear, was thought to have escaped on foot.

The group had speculated and dogs later had confirmed that Marcel had made his escape into the woods to the north. A full-scale search had been organized. The manhunt had taken on Rambo-like aspects as a trained jungle fighter was matched against inexperienced deputies and volunteer woodsmen. First dogs had disappeared in the chase, then two men. The media became involved in the drama and Marcel's ravaged features filled the television screens and the front pages of newspapers.

The media reports were further spiced when news of the race-fixing scheme leaked. Armand Larrance was dead, but Dr. Mack proved to be a cooperative and well-informed witness on the mechanics of the scam. Four rather bedraggled, dispirited nags were found tattooed with the same identification numbers as Picky Peaches, Calamatator, Winter Muffin, and Thurgood. Four other sleek, well-conditioned animals were housed in the barn. These matched up with horses currently establishing abysmal statistics at minor tracks. The racing community cringed as the media fed on the brilliance of the scheme and regurgitated details of careful planning and millions of dollars won.

To their embarrassment, Peter T. Westmoreland, "the renowned equine insurance investigator," and Lucinda DeGuerre, "the tenacious agent of the TPB," had become minor media stars for uncovering the scandal and tracking down the villains. Somehow the reporters had missed identifying me in the excitement. I was not unhappy at the oversight.

I stared out the window at the bright Texas morning, tuning out the official discussion around me. Marcel was not going to be found, I was certain. In the maniac's twisted mind, he was back on "recon," search and destroy, where he was totally at home. A bunch of cowboys and their hunting dogs were not about to catch him. He had slipped out of the search net easily and was now on his way to . . . wherever.

I found myself becoming impatient with these professionals who had become friends during the brief intensity of the raid and subsequent search. They were feeling the pressure, of course, and were grasping at any possibility to effect capture and avoid public embarrassment. However, I was too wrapped up in my own state of depression to muster much empathy.

Events here in Texas were drawing to a close as far as I was concerned. I had been completely exonerated in Las Vegas, Armand Larrance was dead, and the cheating scam was crushed. That was the good news, I thought sarcastically. Marcel Larrance was still on the loose and, of course, there was no clue to the identity of the mastermind who had orchestrated the affair and set me up to take the fall.

The matter of the senseless death of Billy Robles weighed heavily on my conscience. Lizzy Cline, Leslie Pilarcik, and unknown others had died at the hands of the escaped lunatic, and Kermit Golightly lingered, comatose. Marcel Larrance had much to account for by my reckoning, but I felt powerless to bring about that accounting by sitting in meetings and dispensing advice. I was outraged by the injustices left unsettled and I recognized that my world could never be completely set right while Marcel remained at large.

Tomorrow, Lucinda DeGuerre would return to Chicago to formulate her report to the racing establishment and accept her accolades. To me, this one fact overshadowed all other considerations. I had carefully constructed a life on my own terms, a life which demanded nothing of others. While the race-fixing scheme and its perpetrators had disrupted it beyond measure, the prospect of rebuilding my life and continuing without Luci was bleak, without joy. She had opened up something within me which I had thought was buried with Jenna. The wounds had scarred over and I had achieved, if not happiness, a certain sense of satisfaction and contentment. Now, simple resumption of my Las Vegas existence would never be enough.

The night before, Luci and I had engaged in one of those stupid conversations lovers hold during which a great many questions are asked and answered, though the important questions and the most-sought-after answers are carefully ignored. She revealed her intention to return to her job. I revealed my intention to return to Las Vegas. Neither of us could ask, "Do your plans include me?" Neither could say, "This is what I want you to do." Neither could declare, "I want you with me." These were my thoughts on a sunny Saturday morning in Texas, while dedicated lawmen worried about how to bring a psychotic killer to justice.

"What do you think, Tennyson?" Ned Burdine's voice snapped me out of my trance.

"What? I'm sorry, Ned. I was thinking about something else."

"We were just facing up to the possibility that Marcel has slipped out of the net," the Ranger explained. "Most of us were figuring he'd head south to Mexico. The bodies in Palestine would seem to confirm that theory."

The mutilated corpses of an old rancher and his wife had been found at their remote ranch outside of Palestine, Texas. The woman, in her seventies, had been raped. Their pickup truck was missing. Marcel's death toll continued to mount.

"Miz DeGuerre and Peter T. here were saying that he might double back north to hide out in the cities," Burdine continued. "What do you think?"

Las Vegas, I nearly answered aloud without thinking. Perhaps the thought had been in my subconscious for some time, but the realization formed without any mental process apparent. That's where the money is, I thought.

The group stared expectantly. Those closest to me—Luci, Peter T., and now Ned Burdine—had come to depend on me for insights which did not follow any investigative "book." In my mind, I rolled over the possibilities. The Larrance brothers were carrying guns and a briefcase when they took off, according to the hands and Dr. Mack. It was a fair bet the briefcase had money in it. But the big money was in Vegas, put on the street by Lou Rubenstein and collected by someone who had not been identified. Even if the actual cash had found its way to the Cayman bank, the key to the cash was the man Mosey had described as "just a guy." Marcel had worked all his life around racetracks and now he couldn't go near one. He'd need money to go underground, and that unidentified "just a guy" was holding his cut.

"I'm sorry, folks," I said finally. "I think Marcel's gone, but I don't have any better ideas on where he might be headed."

Having made this one dissembling contribution to the morning's strategy session, I picked up my cigarettes and left the room. No one asked a question or followed me out. I found a bench on the courthouse grounds and sat smoking, watching the pigeons.

A part of my consciousness was shocked by the fabrication. What are you thinking of? my mind railed. Haven't you done enough damage already? This man kills people.

But another part of me had made the resolution. I knew what I had to do. Sharing my theories with the police would not catch Marcel. Marcel was a guerrilla, an "irregular" like the Vietcong. Organized pursuit was almost powerless against him unless he made a serious judgment error. Too many people would die before that happened, I concluded.

Luci found me there a half-hour later after the meeting broke up. Taking a seat beside me, she said nothing. Her presence and her touch told me that the unspoken questions were not forgotten, just postponed. That she shared my thoughts and concerns somehow made a difference, and my mood brightened.

"Everybody's got to believe in something," Peter T. announced, coming up behind the bench. "I believe I'm gonna have some lunch and a drink or twelve."

We lunched on "competition-class" chicken-fried steak, accompanied by several margaritas. Peter T. was joined by Molly Wheeler, a deputy sheriff with whom he had struck up a friendship. The afternoon was spent drinking, swapping tales, and simply enjoying the company of friends.

At four-thirty P.M. Texas time, we watched Alysheba win the Preakness on the television in the hotel's bar, where we bought the house a few rounds in order to peacefully preempt Texas Rangers baseball.

"This has to be a new one, the Poet watching a Triple Crown race on TV," Peter T. observed ironically.

"Will he win the Belmont?" Luci asked, referring to Alysheba.

Caught up in the possibility of the first Triple Crown winner of the decade, I said, "He's gonna kill 'em." What the hell, nobody's perfect.

Postrace found us by the hotel's pool catching the last of the day's sunshine and attempting to shake off the effects of too much tequila. We were pleasantly but thoroughly wasted.

"Where shall we go for dinner?" Luci asked brightly.

"Darlin', I am dinner," Peter T. announced lewdly, taking Molly's hand.

Back in our room, after a shower and some prolonged lovemaking, Luci and I determined that we were, indeed, hungry. Luci dialed Peter T.'s room, where Molly answered.

" 'Dinner' has passed out," Molly informed us.

I slept poorly that night, my rest disrupted alternately by thoughts of Luci returning to Chicago and images of Marcel Larrance blazing a trail of blood, inexorably moving toward my home. I paced the floor and smoked, allowing my mind to range free, waiting for insight to strike.

Fearing I would wake Luci, I left the room and walked in the pleasantly cool early-morning air. I finally admitted to myself that I didn't know what to do about Luci. I loved her, but I had not told her so. I believed she returned the feeling, but she, too, had held back. I examined, inflated, and then ultimately discarded all of the obvious problems—the difference in our ages, diverse vocations, the problem of maintaining the relationship over the distance between us: real questions but problems with multiple options for solution.

My real cause for hesitation I had not yet articulated even in my mind. In my heart I knew we could make a start. The mutual desire, respect, friendship, and love were all present in our relationship. But if I had learned one thing in my life, it was that nothing is forever. People come together with great optimism and come apart with great pain. Some emotional defense mechanism—an irrational yet very real fear that I couldn't survive another lost love—afflicted me with excruciating indecision.

I couldn't continue walking. Collapsing on a nearby bench, I bent over and held my sides. The anguish gripped me, inside and out, and I felt temporarily paralyzed. Yet my mind raced on. My old life had been safe and comfortable; its only risks were those I chose to take. Should Luci and I decide to be together, all those carefully contrived sinecures would evaporate and I would be inviting fate to deal me disaster.

Slowly my thought process cleared and turned from the unknowable to the certain. I got up from the bench and moved on. With Marcel Larrance at large there was no future in any decision regarding Luci. Marcel would come to Las Vegas. This I knew. And after Marcel had claimed his reward, he would look for revenge. Marcel would not rest, would not simply disappear with his fortune, while I lived. Of this, too, I had no doubt.

As the sun was coming up, I came to an all-night restaurant. If my memory served, I was about a mile from the motel. Breakfast smells—hot coffee, frying bacon—proved irresistible and I went in. Except for two old men at the counter, the place was empty. I took a seat in a booth, where a tired waitress brought me coffee. I sat there for the next two hours, burning up a nearly full pack of cigarettes and communicating only with nods for more coffee and a negative shake to decline food.

At last I went to the pay phone and called Peter T.'s room. By the time I had walked the distance back to the motel, he was waiting for me in the coffee shop. His expression was purposeful and expectant. I came right to the point.

"I'm going after Marcel," I informed him. "I've thought about it and I can't do it alone."

"I take it you don't have much faith in the law's finding him," the Texan observed.

I shook my head. "He's a jungle fighter, an expert. The law has to play by the rules, but Marcel gets to make up his own. In the best of circumstances, he'd be difficult to catch. Once he gets the money, he'll be impossible."

"The money?"

"Millions of dollars were won on these horses. Marcel will be coming for his share. Maybe for all of it."

"Where do you think the money is?"

"Las Vegas. Or, at least, the guy who can get the money is in Las Vegas. Sooner or later, Marcel will end up there."

"Why didn't you tell this to Burdine?" Peter T. asked with a knowing half-smile on his face.

"What can Burdine do?" I shot back. "We don't know who the money man is. The cops can't stake out Las Vegas. Not the whole town."

"So what do you think you and I can do that the police can't?"

It was a good question with some big ifs. I wondered how much I could afford to reveal before Peter T. committed himself. I hesitated, but I really had no choice.

"I think I can find the money man," I declared at last. "We've been figuring all along that someone I know well is in this. In Vegas, there are only two or three possibilities."

"So you stake out the money man till Marcel comes to get his share," Peter T. surmised aloud. "That could take a long time. And again, once you find this money man, why not let the police handle it?"

"You're right, it could take months," I agreed, "but unless I'm out to lunch, patience is not one of Marcel's positive traits. I think he'll come as soon as the access is clear. The cops would only complicate things. There'd be too many people and too many procedures to follow. Marcel would spot the cops in a New York minute. Then all he has to do is wait them out. They'll always have other priorities, other crooks to catch."

"And you and me? We don't have 'other priorities'?"

I stared at him before answering. "I don't have anything I can plan for while that maniac's out there," I said emphatically. "You see, I believe that once Marcel has his money, he'll come after me."

Peter T. looked up sharply and stubbed out his cigarette. "Why?" he demanded flatly.

"I could say it's because I was the one who screwed up their plans or that he was bound to think I'm responsible for his brother's death. Both of those things are true, but that's not it. It's not based on facts, it's just something I know. I can feel it. When Marcel comes to Vegas for the money, he won't be able to leave without a settlement.

"That's why I have to go after him, Peter T.," I continued. "I can't pick up where I left off and I can't plan anything with Luci knowing that sometime, somehow, he'll be coming."

Peter T. didn't respond. He signaled the waitress for more coffee and lit another cigarette. For Peter T. to accept what I was proposing, he would have to ignore years of training and set himself against former associates like Ned Burdine. It was a lot to ask.

"You know, son," Peter T. began carefully, "back when I was a Ranger, down on the border, all we had to worry about was drugs and illegal aliens. Hadn't been for those two things, my sector would have been a decent place to retire. Working with the Border Patrol, we caught dozens of drug smugglers and shipped back hundreds of illegals. But I might as well've been pissing on a forest fire. They just kept coming.

"I've been investigating insurance fraud for almost ten years. Now I can catch the assholes and screw up their plans, but they don't hardly ever spend much time in jail." He paused and dragged hard on his cigarette. "The law will eventually get Marcel. He's burning out of control, and eventually he'll start to think of himself as superman, invulnerable. Then they'll get him."

My heart sank. I had guessed wrong. Peter T. would be unable to step out of the system.

"But I agree with you, Tennyson," he continued with an edge of anger in his voice, "a lot of people will die before Marcel self-destructs. Some of 'em might turn out to be friends of mine. I'm not sure this is the right decision, but if it can be done, I think we ought to go get him."

I felt like I had just won a long-shot daily double with my last ten-dollar bill. I wanted to shout, to dance around the table and fill the air with war whoops. Instead, I extended my hand across the table and Peter T. grasped it in his own.

I started to outline my thoughts on how we should proceed, when Peter T. interrupted.

"You better hold up a minute, son," he said. "Looks like you got another decision to make."

I turned in my chair to follow his eyes and saw Luci crossing the room. I could tell by the set of her jaw and her determined stride that she was not here for a leisurely breakfast. She took a chair between us, folded her hands, and looked first at Peter T. and then at me.

"I know what you're planning," she declared flatly, "and I want in."

My mouth opened to protest, but she cut me off.

"Don't bother, Tennyson," she said. "I knew when you left the meeting yesterday that you had your own agenda. I think you're right. They're not gonna catch him, and you think you can. If you believe it, so do I. I want in."

"No way," I responded. "It's too dangerous. I want you out of his reach."

"You're not listening," she insisted urgently. "I won't let you go after him without me. If I have to, I'll dog you wherever you go."

Flat refusal hadn't worked, so I tried reason. "Luci, we're about to violate the law, obstruct justice or whatever they want to call it. We could end up facing criminal charges. We could end up getting killed. I can't—we can't let you take the risk."

"Tennyson, I'm not about to try to argue logically with you. This has nothing to do with logic. I want Marcel Larrance as badly as you do. Have you forgotten about my brother? I've got a right." She held her head high, daring us to deny her. "Besides," she maintained less stridently, "you need me."

"She's got a point, Tennyson," Peter T. agreed. "There's a lot of ground between here and Vegas. We can use some help."

I didn't like it. I almost wished I had kept my plans to myself. But Luci was determined and Peter T. approved, at least tacitly.

"All right," I said with resignation, "if I can't talk you out of this, there is one thing that you have to understand and accept. Otherwise you get on that plane for Chicago and stay there until this is over." I took her hand and stared into her eyes. "If things go the way I think they will, we might . . . I repeat, we might . . .

get a shot at Marcel. We're not talking about a citizen's arrest here. If the chance comes, we're going to have to kill him. If we don't, we're dead."

She took a deep breath and returned my gaze. "I know," she said softly.

18

Luci and I returned to Las Vegas. She had little difficulty convincing Mel Gendler that she needed some time off. Peter T. drove south, first to Austin to exchange the Eldorado for his more durable truck, and then on to the Rio Grande. Our assumption was that Marcel would first escape into Mexico and then, when he sensed it was safe, double back north to Las Vegas. Peter T.'s first task was to confirm that Marcel had indeed crossed the border, and second, to gain some feel for the scar-faced man's movements. We had accepted the grim reality that Marcel would leave his own unique trail. Peter T.'s job was to find it.

On the morning after our return, while Peter T. made his way south from Austin, we set about making our Las Vegas preparations. Our most important task was locating the money man, "just a guy," whom Marcel would eventually seek out. Our most immediate need, however, was for weapons. We needed the kind of firepower which couldn't be purchased at the local sporting-goods store. While Luci looked for electronics and communications equipment, I went to see Jimmy DeMaria.

The obese superbookie seemed genuinely pleased to see me. His welcome was effusive as he led me through the sprawling house to the poolside table and insisted on serving refreshments appropriate for a morning meeting. A houseman returned in an instant with freshly squeezed orange juice, croissants still warm from the oven, and a rich aromatic coffee which I didn't immediately recognize.

"Jamaica Blue Mountain," DeMaria explained.

"There's nothing quite like it." The fat man beamed as I sipped appreciatively.

"Now, then, Mr. Poet," DeMaria got down to business, "as much as I enjoy your company, I realize you didn't come out here just for coffee and rolls. What can I do for you?"

I hesitated, suddenly fearful that DeMaria might find my request rude and out of line, or worse, that he might suspect my true purpose. "I need a favor, Jimmy," I answered after a moment. "Some equipment, actually."

DeMaria looked puzzled. Equipment was not exactly his line. "I'm in your debt, Tennyson," he said. "I'll help you if I can. What sort of equipment do you need?"

"Frankly, I'm embarrassed to ask," I replied. "My needs are way out of your field of endeavors, but I thought perhaps you might know someone . . ." The fat man smiled and nodded encouragement. I continued. "I need some 'hardware' of a military nature . . . weapons to be exact."

The fat man's expression hardened. This was not at all what he had expected.

"Don't misunderstand me, Tennyson," DeMaria said, his voice etched with concern. "I know someone who can help you. But on a strictly personal level, I have to ask you . . . why?"

I sighed. This was the question I was most uncomfortable with. Should DeMaria guess my true purpose, the fat man's people could be as burdensome and obstructive as the police.

"I have some concern about Marcel Larrance," I admitted, having decided to tell part of the truth. "As you know, he's still on the loose and, frankly, I can't shake the feeling that he might see me as being responsible for his brother's death. I know it's irrational, but I feel like I need some protection."

DeMaria sat back in his chair, regarding me carefully. "I can understand your concern," he said, "but why don't you let me have someone keep an eye on you? After all, we'd like to get our hands on this Larrance character 9too."

I shook my head. "I appreciate the offer, Jimmy, but it's a waste of manpower. My imagination may just be working overtime. Marcel is most likely in Mexico by now, and he'll probably stay lost forever. It's just that I would feel a little safer if I took some precautions."

Instead of offering obvious solutions like alarm systems or bodyguards, he elected to help. "All right. I have to say that you've got me worried, but I'll do what I can. Please excuse me for just a moment."

After an absence which stretched out to several minutes, DeMaria rejoined me on the patio. "The man I'm sending you to see will have what you want, short of guided missiles, tanks, and airplanes," the fat man explained. "His prices are high and not negotiable, and, of course, the terms are cash. He'll require a sizable deposit and will deliver the order within twenty-four hours."

"I appreciate your help, Jimmy," I said sincerely.

The fat man held up a hand to wave off the thanks. "It's nothing," he insisted. "I wish I could do more. Are you sure I can't have someone keep an eye on you for a while?"

"I'd be obliged if you wouldn't, Jimmy. You've done enough as it is. Like I said, the whole thing is probably just my imagination."

DeMaria eyed me skeptically. He was much too smart to accept my story at face value, and I realized that we would have to watch out for his people as well as Marcel. However, instead of voicing his growing suspicions, DeMaria nodded his agreement, smiling like an indulgent rich uncle.

The ever-present Al came out a few moments later and handed DeMaria a note.

"Thanks, Al," DeMaria said. "The man you're to see is known as Juan. He'll see you in an hour in room 718 at the Tropicana. Go directly to the room."

The fat man accepted my thanks with an airy wave of one massive paw. He sipped his coffee and thought for a moment.

"Tell me something, Tennyson," he said. "What do you think happened to the money? They didn't find any cash in Texas, correct?"

"I don't know, Jimmy," I answered carefully. "Maybe Marcel has it. Or maybe it's in some offshore bank. That was obviously what the Larrance brothers intended."

The fat man shook his head. "I have trouble seeing

the Larrance brothers as being sharp enough to pull this thing off," he said, reaching the same conclusion I had seen to when the scheme had come clear. "I think there's someone else involved, someone out here in Vegas." He peered at me over the tops of his glasses. "What do you think?"

"Anything's possible." I shrugged. "Armand Larrance was out here as Aaron Locklear. Maybe he was working with someone. Just the same, Armand was a race fixer in New Orleans and he had ten years to figure this deal out. We'll probably never know unless the cops catch up with Marcel."

DeMaria grunted, but whether the sound was one of assent or dismissal, I couldn't be sure. Claiming urgent business, I thanked him once more and left. I had the nagging feeling that DeMaria's interest was more than casual curiosity.

Twelve hours later, as night was falling over the empty desert, I handed Juan Parrada an envelope stuffed with cash and received in return a large heavy suitcase. I had ordered the weapons earlier in the day after viewing the incredible array of samples the Cuban had displayed in his hotel room. Parrada could have supplied virtually any weapon a man could carry into combat, including rockets and heavy machine guns. He did not count the cash in the envelope, nor did I examine the contents of the suitcase. We shook hands and parted company without exchanging more than a few words.

Luci was waiting at home with news.

"Peter T. just called a few minutes ago," she told me as I lugged the heavy suitcase down to the basement den. "He's in Del Rio, Texas. They found the truck Marcel stole from those two old people. They figure he crossed the border on foot. He said he'd call back in the morning when he knew more."

"At least we're right so far," I said without much enthusiasm. I was pleased that Peter T. had picked up the trail, but DeMaria's questioning still bothered me. I put the suitcase on the desk and opened it. Luci failed to suppress an astonished gasp before she moved closer to examine its contents.

I had opted for overkill. I sincerely hoped that all the

weaponry would not be needed and could later be destroyed. Just the same, I knew I couldn't go back for more equipment. If Parrada reported the exact nature of my purchases to DeMaria, the fat man's suspicions would be doubly aroused. The weapons Parrada supplied exceeded what would be required for personal defense; they were sufficient to arm a small assault team.

For close encounters, there were two police-style shotguns with short barrels and pistol grips. For long-range work there was a military-style sniper rifle complete with scope. I had purchased pistols of various shapes and calibers, with "hot load" ammunition for each. A stubby little Uzi submachine gun completed the inventory of firearms.

For explosives, I had selected a half-dozen grenades and a block of "plastique" with a variety of detonators. Luci recoiled at the sight of the edged weapons, a pair of combat survival knives and a wicked-looking stiletto. High-powered binoculars and a night-vision scope rounded out the array of hardware.

"What is all this stuff?" Luci exclaimed. "Are you planning to start a war?"

I took her arm and sat her down at the desk. "I want you to listen to me very carefully," I said earnestly. "It's not too late for you to get out. But if you stay, you have to understand the truth. If Marcel gets within ten feet of any or all of us, he's more than we can handle. Do you understand what I'm saying? When he comes, someone will die. I have to do everything I can to make sure that someone is Marcel and not one of us."

I reached into the suitcase and held up a combat knife. Its twelve-inch blade of blackened steel held her eyes hypnotically. "You can bet Marcel has weapons like these," I continued. I dropped the knife and picked up the Uzi. "Or this. And he knows how to use them. If we sent out a squad of combat veterans after him, the odds would still be on his side. He's that good."

I pulled her from the chair and took her in my arms. "Luci, our only chance is that he doesn't know we're expecting him. He won't anticipate that we have this kind of firepower. If we get the chance, I have to make sure Marcel goes down for good."

She held me tightly and I could feel her trembling.

"It's not too late to go home," I said softly, praying that she would agree but knowing she would not.

She squared her shoulders and looked me in the eye. "I guess you'd better show me how this stuff works," she said quietly.

Peter T. called at seven A.M. I had been up for an hour, but Luci was still sleeping.

"He crossed the river about ten miles west of Del Rio," Peter T. reported wearily. "He ran into a family of Mexicans, illegals with a 'coyote' all set to bring them across." He paused and I knew what was coming. "One of the men lived long enough to tell the Federales what happened. Marcel took the coyote's truck and a sixteen-year-old girl."

I cursed dejectedly, wondering if I could have prevented this had I told Burdine of my suspicions.

"They were all over the border," Peter T. went on as though reading my thoughts. "The cops, the Rangers, and the Border Patrol were on our side, with the Federales across the river. He just slipped through, Tennyson."

"And killed a bunch of people in the process," I finished grimly. "Christ, that poor girl."

"There were two little kids with that family." Peter T.'s voice was like ice. "Just three and four years old. Marcel has got to pay, Tennyson.

"I'm gonna cross the border and follow for a while," he went on. "By the time the Federales decide what to do, Marcel'll be long gone."

"If you catch up to him, don't get close," I cautioned. I was concerned about the emotion I heard in the Texan's voice. "Don't try to take him on yourself. Just stay with him if you can."

"I doubt I'll catch up with him," Peter T. sighed with resignation. "He's at least a day ahead of me. The best I can do is find out when he changes course."

When I hung up the phone, Luci was standing next to me. I hadn't heard her come down. She could read the expression on my face, and I made no attempt to keep from her the fate of the Mexican family. Her eyes clouded and she turned abruptly and went back upstairs. I gave her a few minutes alone and then followed. I found her staring out the window, brushing tears from her eyes.

"That poor girl," she whispered tearfully.

I led her to the bed and held her for a while. In time we made love with an urgency born of uncertainty and fear. Marcel would be coming soon.

An hour later we were on our way to the Athletic Club. We would have plenty of time to play racquetball and dress before Cowboy joined us for lunch.

Luci still maintained that Cowboy could not be the betrayer. I wanted to accept her reasoning, but I suspected her feelings were based in part on her affection for the congenial poker player. I shared her affection, but reminded myself sternly that there were few other possibilities. After much discussion we decided that the best course of action was direct confrontation.

"There's something that's been bothering me," I told Cowboy as the three of us relaxed over a glass of California Chardonnay. "Something that came up the last time we saw you. I guess there's nothing to do but come out with it." I related the events of our capture and wondered, rhetorically, how DeMaria and the bookies could have learned of our presence in Las Vegas.

"I'll be goddamned," Cowboy swore when I had finished. "Do you really think I'd blow the whistle on you, or anyone else for that matter? An' if I did, why'd I go to the trouble of rentin' a hotel suite or meetin' your flight? Why not jus' tell the boys where you could be found?"

"I confess, those very questions have occurred to us. Luci keeps reminding me of those facts. Still, how could they have known? I mean, these guys had to have been following us all day. Are you sure you didn't let something slip by accident? Maybe here, or at the Turf Club?"

"Tennyson, I'm a professional poker player," he insisted indignantly, "I don't let things 'slip,' Hell, I knew there were people lookin' for you. Remember, it was me who gave you that gun. The only person I told I'd seen you was Buck, but, shit, he wouldn't say nuthin.' He was just worried about you."

"You told Buck?"

"Yeah, but, hell, Buck wouldn't know who to blow the whistle to. Ol' Buck is lucky he knows the way between his apartment and the Tiara. Why would Buck want to hand you over to the mob?"

Why indeed? I thought to myself. But all of a sudden, things were beginning to make sense. Buck had met Kermit Golightly during Kermit's one and only visit to Las Vegas. We had all become fairly drunk one night at my place and Kermit had told the story of how I had taken him to the hospital and had made certain that his bill was paid. Buck had also known about Kermit's custom of calling me with hot tips as a means of repaying the debt he still believed he owed. Cowboy had been out of town on the poker circuit at the time and had never actually met Kermit.

It suddenly became painfully clear. Buck had not only delivered Luci and me to the bookies, but he had been involved in the setup from the beginning.

"You look strange, son," Cowboy observed. "You don't think that Buck would have turned you in, do ya?"

I said nothing for a moment. "Cowboy, I apologize. I had to ask questions for reasons which should be obvious. You've been a good friend when I needed help. I've treated you badly. I'm sorry."

He held out his hand and we shook. "Apology accepted," he said simply. "But, Buck? I still don't believe it."

"I'd appreciate it if you would keep this conversation among the three of us for the time being. There's a small chance I could be wrong or that Buck made an innocent mistake. Either way, Luci and I were placed in a situation where we could have been killed. If Buck had something to do with it, I mean to find out."

I parked the Corvette in the lot serving Buck's apartment complex. Buck Brewster lived simply in a two-bedroom second-floor flat in a large complex off Paradise. The complex featured medium-priced apartments with little in the way of extras beyond a good-sized swimming pool. Its principal redeeming feature was its proximity to the Strip, which accounted for its popularity among casino employees. Buck liked it because its location allowed him to walk to the Tiara.

If Buck followed his usual habit, he would be home anytime now. The last West Coast post time had passed about an hour ago, leaving ample time for Buck to walk home after a stop at his favorite deli to pick up his evening meal.

Luci was smoking her second cigarette in the ten minutes we had been waiting. "You're sure it's this guy?" she asked again.

"Positive. It had to be either Cowboy or Buck."

"I'm glad I was right about Cowboy."

"Me too."

"Do you think Buck will own up to it?"

"We'll see." Actually, I was certain that I could get the truth out of Buck, but I was in no mood to answer questions. Buck's appearance on the walk in front of us interrupted Luci's nervous chatter. He didn't see us as we followed him into the building and up to his second-floor apartment.

"Hello, Buck," I said.

He started at the sound of my voice and turned in our direction. In a split second his face registered recognition, fear, and then a false camaraderie.

"Poet!" Buck exclaimed jovially. "This is a surprise. I haven't seen you since . . . well, since you left the club. Well, come in, come in. Excuse the mess. I wasn't expecting company."

He scurried around nervously, picking up dirty dishes and old copies of the *Racing Form*. He stowed them in the small kitchen and stood nervously waiting to be introduced to Luci. It was obvious that I was just about the last person he wanted to see.

"This isn't a social call, Buck," I said instead of making introductions. "I want to know everything about how you set me up and why you did it."

Buck seemed to sag all over. He must have known when he saw us that I suspected the truth. Still, he tried to bluff it out.

"I don't know what you're talking about, Poet," he said weakly.

"Don't waste time bullshitting me, Buck. I know it was you."

Buck shook his head and walked into the living room. He looked at the drab rented furniture and the bare walls as though, finding a reflection of his life in them, he were seeing their shabbiness for the first time. "I'm sorry,

Tennyson. I never wanted you to get hurt," he said sorrowfully. "He made me work with them. I had no choice."

"Who, Buck?" I demanded.

Another pang of fear seemed to grip Buck and he hesitated. "He'll kill me if I tell you," he pleaded. "He'll send that maniac after me."

I shrugged. "Maybe," I agreed, "maybe not. What you can be sure of, though, is that if you don't tell me, I'm gonna pick up this phone and call Jimmy DeMaria. What do you think I'll tell him, Buck? What do you think he'll do when he finds out Buck Brewster helped some assholes rip him off for a few million dollars? I'll ask you one more time . . . who, Buck?"

"Bellisari. Mike Bellisari." Buck went to the nearest armchair and sat down heavily.

I stood there dumbfounded. Bellisari had demonstrated such righteous indignation when he barred me from the Turf Club. An act! A goddamn act.

Luci understood none of this revelation and stood by watching my confusion. She went to Buck's small portable bar, found reasonably clean glasses, and poured two shots of bourbon. As an afterthought, she poured a third for herself and handed one each to Buck and me.

Slowly and with many protestations of benign intent and rambling apology, Buck told what little he knew about the scheme. After the Texas raid and the ensuing publicity, he realized that Bellisari had originaly considered Buck himself for the role of fall guy, but Buck's normal conservative betting pattern did not fit the part. To make the scenario believable, Bellisari needed someone who routinely made large bets on long shots. Buck willingly suggested me. Bellisari wanted to know how I made my selections. Buck told him that most of my selections were the product of my own handicapping but that, once or twice, I received a tip from a friend. As soon as Bellisari had the story of Kermit's long-distance touting, he knew he had found the perfect fall guy.

As to how the scheme was to operate or the identity of any other participant beyond Bellisari and Marcel Larrance, Buck had no clue until after the Texas raid. He knew that when I was called into Bellisari's office and barred from the Tiara, the scheme had started to unfold.

Buck swore he had expected that, once I had been barred from the Turf Club, I would simply shift my operations to another casino and go on as before. He never dreamed that I would be in danger.

The parts Buck didn't know were easy to fill in. The conspirators had tipped Kermit through Pierre LeBlanc and then had killed LeBlanc and attempted to kill Kermit to cover their trail. I would stand out as an obvious participant to the bookies and would have no way to correct that impression. Had I been captured by Ratface and Neanderthal that first day, Bellisari and the Larrance brothers would have been free to bring in a few more ringers before the bookies realized they had dispatched the wrong guy.

As I thoughtfully sipped the bourbon, I recalled almost every word of my encounter with Michael Bellisari, from the man's smooth arrogance to his self-righteous anger. In retrospect, I could see that Bellisari had enjoyed throwing me to the wolves.

"Why, Buck?" I asked finally.

Buck fumbled for a cigarette. Luci gave him one and lit it for him.

"He had me, Tennyson," Buck said after he got the cigarette going. "You know how I bet, small amounts on lots of horses. It's not very elegant, but it works, you know? I could never really understand why they invited me to join the Turf Club. I thought at first it was overall volume of action. Maybe they just saw me cashing a lot of tickets and thought they could turn a profit on what I was doing. I guess I'd have been better off if they'd never asked, you know.

"A little more than six months ago, I got called into Bellisari's office. That little weasel Lou Fine was there. Everybody's buddy, fuckin' Lou. Bellisari says that the club—meaning him, of course—is concerned. They analyzed my action and couldn't find any way to lay off at a profit. I was soaking up the perks and not giving them anything. He said that the club was considering not renewing my membership.

He paused to stub out his smoke. "Not renew, who was he trying to kid? I shoulda told him to stick his fancy club up his ass. But, you know, I was hooked. I mean, hanging out with guys like Friedman and Cowboy, you

... it was like the big time." Buck's eyes pleaded for understanding. "It was like for the first time in my life I was important, a shooter. I was even a goddamn TV expert, for Chrissakes.

"So I tried to give them some big winners," Buck continued forlornly. "I tried to change a style that made money for more than twenty years. But I was no good at it, you know? It just wasn't me. Oh, I still crunched the numbers, as you call it, and sometimes I would catch you or Cowboy talking about a horse and I'd win with it. But I always lost more than I won.

"Things kept getting worse, and then I signed a couple of markers. Yeah, I know it was stupid, but I was desperate. I got to thinking that the club was all I had, you know? If I got kicked out of the club, I'd lose the *Vegasline* job, everything. Well, Bellisari had me then. When he offered me a deal where my markers would be torn up and, as he put it, my 'status would be assured,' I jumped at it. But believe me, Tennyson, I never thought this kinda shit would happen. Never."

There was nothing to be said. Buck was hungry for some kind of absolution, but I could give him none. Now that I had the story, I didn't know what to do about Buck. I couldn't give him to DeMaria without messing up our plans, but I feared that, left on his own, he would eventually go to Bellisari.

"Get out of town, Buck," I said abruptly. Even Luci recoiled at the coldness in my voice. "Pack your bags and go. A month, maybe two months."

Buck sat in his chair, neither moving nor comprehending.

"Now, Buck!" I shouted. "This minute. We'll take you to the airport."

"But . . . where, Poet? Where can I go?"

In two strides I crossed the room. I grabbed Buck by his shirt and dragged him out of his chair. "I don't give a shit where you go, Buck," I snarled bitterly. "But if you stay here, you're a dead man. In a month or two this'll be over and then you're on your own. Now, move it!"

The telephone was ringing when we got back to the condo. Peter T. was in Torreón in North Central Mexico.

Fighting a terrible connection, he explained that Marcel had turned southwest at Monclova. The coyote's truck had been found abandoned outside of Torreón. Inside was the body of the sixteen-year-old Mexican girl.

Peter T. sounded exhausted. Gone was his usual lighthearted banter and inexhaustible optimism. There was a hard edge in his voice as he described Marcel's most recent savagery. The scar-faced man was clearly growing more and more out of control. From our standpoint, the raging insanity made him all the more unpredictable and dangerous.

Marcel's trail had disappeared at Torreón, Peter T. reported. From that intersection of highways, he could head south into the interior of Mexico, southwest to Mazatlán and the coast, or back north to the U.S. border. Our original theories and projections suggested north, but Peter T. could not be certain. Marcel's agenda was his own, fueled by his surging mania.

"He's got to be headed north," I told Peter T. "We have to assume that Marcel is still following a plan."

Peter T. mumbled his assent. He was tired and dispirited, with more than eight hundred miles of bad Mexican highway and one raging maniac between him and the border.

"Never mind trying to pick up his trail," I continued. "Just get to Las Vegas as fast as you can. We've found the money man."

Peter T.'s spirits rose as I related the details of our discovery. We now knew Marcel's ultimate target. We just had to wait for him to show.

I couldn't sleep that night. Neither the tenderness of Luci's touch nor the soothing warmth of her body next to mine could bring me rest. The nightmare I'd had in Texas, in which I lay helpless before Marcel's snarling dementia, kept coming back like a portent of doom. Hours before dawn, I gave up the effort to sleep and eased myself out of bed.

In the kitchen I made coffee and sat smoking, wondering whether every move I made was compounding the danger. I tried to convince myself that Marcel would be coming no matter what I did. The knowledge of that certainty fed the fear, but in that knowledge was hope for survival.

Luci must leave, I decided without knowing how to implement the decision. Peter T., too, should go home. I had no right to put my friends in danger and I had no firm idea of how to trap Marcel without putting them at risk.

Frustrated and exhausted, I knew I had to calm myself, to take control of my own thought process. There was time. Marcel would have to move cautiously. The border crossing was a major obstacle. It would be several days before he could reach Las Vegas. I had to think, to plan. Our lives depended on it.

Wearily I searched for distraction. I was concentrating too hard. The *Racing Form*, my faithful refuge, my books and periodicals, all required too much mental effort. I turned on the television in the hope that some mindless gibberish would bore me to sleep.

On the screen, Barry Sheline's face appeared as *Vegasline* went on the air. I suddenly realized that Buck Brewster would be absent from his usual slot and I wondered what Barry would do. I sat through twenty minutes of a boring Hoops Farb monolgue on the NBA playoffs before I learned the answer.

"We'll be back at the Tiara Las Vegas with the horse racing segment of *Vegasline* in just a few moments," Sheline announced. "Buck Brewster is under the weather this morning but we have with us two of the most famous handicappers in Las Vegas, Toby "Cowboy" Waltham and Aaron Friedman. So stay tuned."

Marcel forgotten momentarily, I laughed out loud at what was to come. Sheline must have been desperate when Buck failed to show for the program. I raced upstairs, snapped on the television in the bedroom, and shook Luci awake.

"You've gotta see this," I insisted as she rubbed the sleep from her eyes. She looked at me like I had finally cracked under the strain as a commercial for mail-order Mario Lanza records filled the screen.

"My God, that's Cowboy," she exclaimed as *Vegasline* returned live. "Who's the other guy?"

"That's Aaron Friedman. He's even more daft than Cowboy. This is gonna be good."

The two horseplayers looked terrible. Cowboy had insisted on wearing his Stetson, and as a result, the shadows from the lights obscured the top half of his face. Both men had obviously refused makeup, and Friedman, especially, looked like an escapee from Dachau.

Instead of responding verbally to Sheline's introduction, Cowboy touched his hat and grinned broadly at the camera while Friedman simply nodded nervously. Sheline was left with dead air.

"Okay," Sheline continued bravely, "we have nine races on the Belmont program today. The first race is one and one-sixteenth miles for fillies and mares with a fifteen-thousand-dollar claiming price. Let's turn first to Aaron Friedman. Aaron, who do you like in the first?"

"Nobody," came the one-word response.

Sheline paled, but pushed on brightly. "Yes, it's a tough race, but if you had to pick a winner, Aaron, which horse would you go for."

"Are you deaf?" Aaron answered tersely. "Nobody. Anybody who bets this bunch of fleabags deserves to lose their ass."

In an effort to save the segment, Sheline turned to Cowboy, who was audibly cackling over Friedman's comment.

"Don't look at me," Cowboy said with the same wide grin, "I agree with Aaron. Anybody who would—"

Sheline was unwilling to hear the rest, and he cut Cowboy off. "Our handicapping experts are passing," Sheline announced, his professional smile looking all the more fragile. "Let's move on to the second race, a twenty-four-thousand-dollar Allowance contest for nonwinners of two races, at six furlongs. Cowboy Waltham, your choice."

"Well, Barry," Cowboy drawled, "this ain't exactly my kinda race, but I sorta like Slewfoot Slew . . ."

"Hah!" Friedman barked derisively.

"What're you hootin' about, you old fart" Cowboy retorted. "You ain't got any better idea."

"Slewfoot Slew is a dog with fleas."

"You lookin' for Man o' War in these're nonwinners of two, Aaron?"

By this time we could hear the laughter of a small crowd off-camera. The antics of the two irrepressible horseplayers promised to make this installment of *Vegasline* most entertaining. Sheline was losing any pretense of control over the show and I could see visions of canceling sponsors rolling through his mind. The two handicappers argued, oblivious of the camera, for nearly a minute before Sheline could restore decorum.

Luci and I watched for the next half-hour of broadcasting chaos, holding our sides with laughter. The early-rising horseplayers who persevered through the squabbling, without being caught up in the hilarity of live programming gone amok, were treated to two or three golden insights worth many dollars at the mutuel windows. On the rare occasions when Cowboy and Aaron agreed, a bettor could go to the bank. By the time Sheline signed off, his professionalism was gone, his composure crushed. He managed only the weakest of smiles with his promise to return tomorrow with another installment. He was so distracted that he didn't notice the uncontrolled applause from the makeshift live audience or the bows his two newly discovered stars took in accepting their accolades. *Vegasline* had just put on the best handicapping presentation in the show's history.

For me the laughter was a catharsis. I shook off my depression and accepted the new day with a renewed sense of purpose. Luci noticed the difference immediately, and with a blend of humor and tenderness, induced me into bed for a prolonged interlude of playful lovemaking. Afterward I slept. Deeply.

19

Keeping track of Michael Bellisari proved to be more difficult than any of us expected. The casino executive's office, above the Turf Club and overlooking the Tiaradome, offered limited access. We could hardly monitor his comings and goings while waiting in his secretary's anteroom. The Tiaradome itself was as close as we could get, and from that location, the sheer vastness of the Tiara worked against us.

Bellisari's residence was almost as bad. He lived in a tenth-floor penthouse apartment at the Grosvenor Club on the Strip. The Grosvenor Club had been financed by the pension fund of a well-known though somewhat disreputable labor union and was designed and built to be the ultimate in resort condominiums in Las Vegas. Some of its apartments were owned by permanent Las Vegas residents like Michael Bellisari. Others were maintained by corporations for entertainment purposes. Still others were owned as investments to be rented out for shorter periods, from one week to several months, to discriminating visitors who demanded luxury and services but wished to avoid the crowds and the visibility of the large hotels.

The Grosvenor Club also had excellent security. The system was not so tight that it couldn't be penetrated by a determined intruder with a good cover story, but an observer hoping to keep a resident under surveillance was bound to be noticed and discouraged. To make matters worse, the Grosvenor Club had its own underground parking with a security gate activated by a resident's own magnetic card. The same card provided access to the building elevators.

As a further complication, Bellisari maintained a fast-and-furious life-style. Along with meeting the demands of his job, he did more than his share of entertaining important guests and show-business personalities. Bellisari considered complete enjoyment of the Las Vegas nightlife to be one of the perquisites of his position, and he had become a well-known man-about-town.

On the first day of surveillance, I found out just how difficult our task would be. I was waiting when Bellisari drove his own car, a sleek Jaguar, from the garage of the Grosvenor Club to the Tiara, less than a half-mile away. He left his car with the hotel valet and went directly to his office, arriving at approximately eight-thirty. The problem of maintaining the surveillance at the Tiara became immediately apparent when, between the main entrance of the hotel and the Tiaradome, I ran into a half-dozen people I knew. In any other hotel on the Strip, I could have blended in with the crowds in the race book or the casino, but I was too well-known at the Tiara. I made a hasty retreat and spent a hot and exhausting day in the parking lot keeping an eye on Bellisari's car.

At six P.M. Bellisari summoned his car and returned to his apartment. An hour later one of the hotel's limousines picked him up and brought him back to the Tiara, where he was joined by a well-known Hollywood agent and two spectacular-looking young women. The limo transported the foursome downtown for dinner at the gourmet restaurant on the second floor of the Union Plaza. The cocktail show at Caesar's Palace, where one of the agents' famous clients was performing, was the next stop, followed by a return to the Tiara for an hour of baccarat. At three A.M. the limo deposited Bellisari and one of the women in front of the Grosvenor Club.

As Luci was quick to point out, we had to find a better way. The hours of the surveillance were impossible for one person to maintain for any length of time. Plus there had been too many opportunities to lose sight of the target. I had been watching for the Jaguar when the limousine had picked Bellisari up at the Grosvenor Club, but luckily I noticed the Tiara's special license tags. I realized that Bellisari could have left the Tiara using alternate transportation at any time and I would have been totally unaware he had gone. What had sounded like a reasonable idea—watching the casino executive until Marcel showed up—was beginning to look like an exercise in futility.

Peter T. arrived from Mexico late that evening. Eight hundred miles of Mexican highway had depleted both his patience and stamina. He had left his truck in Tucson and flew the rest of the way to Vegas, arriving too exhausted to do much more than bathe and sleep. He was up and ready to go the next morning, with no lingering damage beyond a mild case of Montezuma's Revenge.

Peter T. estimated that Marcel could be expected anytime within the next five days, but that his arrival before tomorrow was unlikely.

"The border is tight," Peter T. told us. "Texas, New Mexico, Arizona, even California. His chances of slipping in at one of the official entry points is about nil. He'll have to figure out an informal crossing and then find transportation on this side of the border."

"Any new signs of him?" I asked.

"You mean bodies?" he responded grimly. "Nothing so far."

I explained the problems I had encountered during the previous day's surveillance. Peter T. listened thoughtfully and came up with a masterstroke.

"What're the chances of renting a penthouse in that Grosvenor place?" he asked.

"Damn! I never thought of that."

Luci placed a call and in a matter of hours she had rented, on behalf of a "visiting Texas oilman," a two-bedroom apartment on the same floor as Bellisari's. While Peter T. and Luci moved in, I resumed the watch outside the Tiara. I parked where I could keep Bellisari's car in sight, but as a steady parade of taxis and limos pulled up to the main entrance of the hotel, I realized that there was still a big margin of error.

When I followed Bellisari back to the Grosvenor Club, I found that Luci and Peter T. had been busy. They had rented two very ordinary-looking late-model cars and had equipped them with CB radios. The two investigators had set up a base station in the penthouse and had worked out a simple communications code. They had also purchased clothing, wigs, and accessory props so that we could change our appearances as often as necessary.

The crowning touch was the surveillance equipment Peter T. had rented from a local detective agency. He had attached a small directional transmitter to Bellisari's car that would send out a signal over an effective range of several miles. A receiver had already been placed in each of the rented cars, and a third was in the penthouse. In addition, Peter T. had made a surreptitious entry to Bellisari's apartment and had installed a bug on his telephone and transmitters in his bedroom and living room. Should Marcel contact his partner prior to his arrival, we would know, unless, of course, he called Bellisari at his office. The system wasn't perfect, but it was a good deal more professional than anything I had thought possible.

Peter T. and Luci dressed for an evening on the town. They were prepared to keep up with the high-living Bellisari wherever he went. Reservations and show tickets would not be a problem; Peter T. was equipped with the universal Las Vegas passport, a pocket full of hundred-dollar bills.

Both investigators were armed with unregistered pistols from our arsenal. One shotgun had been installed, within easy reach, in each of the rental cars. The balance of the equipment was in reserve in the penthouse. Our agreement was that, when Marcel appeared, the one who spotted him would summon the others immediately. We would then keep Marcel in sight until the opportunity arose to take him.

After Peter T. and Luci had left, I reflected on the vulnerabilities of our tentative plan. We would have to locate Marcel before we could devise a means of taking him out. In effect, our target's actions would dictate our own. This was hardly the best of circumstances.

There was also the possibility that Marcel might spot one of us before we saw him. In fact, should Marcel even suspect that Bellisari was under surveillance, we could be in deep trouble. We were trying to be clever about the surveillance, but we were far from undetectable if someone were looking for us.

Finally, we were uncertain as to the relationship between Marcel and Bellisari, at least as it existed in Marcel's mind. Were they still partners and allies as we were assuming? Had Marcel already contacted Bellisari and set up a meeting? Or was Marcel planning to "terminate" the partnership in his own unique manner? Did Bellisari have the money in Las Vegas, or would arrangements have to be made to retrieve it?

There were too many things we didn't know. Any one of them could be fatal to us. I was expecting that the element of surprise would be ours to exploit, but that slight edge could be reversed too easily.

Nothing much happened for two days. As we diligently followed Michael Bellisari through his normal routine, we could only marvel at the man's incredible energy. Bellisari ran the streets until two or three in the morning, often bringing home an overnight guest, yet he always reported to work on time. In none of his activities did he show signs of fear or abnormal tension.

On the third day, Saturday, Bellisari left his apartment dressed in casual clothes. This in itself was a break in procedure, for we had never seen him without a suit and tie. In one of the rental cars, I followed as he drove past the Tiara, east on Flamingo, and entered the short U.S. 95 expressway which became the main thoroughfare through Henderson. In Henderson he headed east on the state highway which ran along the shore of Lake Mead.

Peter T.'s transmitter enabled me to follow at a distance beyond Bellisari's line of sight. As the Lake Mead shore became less and less populated, I became concerned that a meeting had been arranged without our knowledge. I attempted to radio Peter T. and Luci, but I had driven beyond the base station's range. The only way I could reach them was by telephone, and I couldn't risk losing the transmitter's signal.

Bellisari turned off the highway onto a dirt lane which ran back to the lake.

"Shit," I cursed out loud. There was no way I could follow without knowing what was back there. I could run right into Bellisari and blow the surveillance with one dumb move.

I drove a little farther on the highway and pulled off to the side. The receiver emitted a strong and steady signal, which indicated that the target was stationary and less than a half-mile away. I backed up to within a hundred yards of the turnoff, stuffed a pistol into the waistband of my jeans, and followed on foot.

The dirt road ran between two low sandstone formations and then dropped down to a flat, treeless strip of ground next to the lake. A faded sign read "Echo Beach Resort." A handful of weathered trailer homes fronted the lake.

Bellisari's Jaguar was parked next to the most distant trailer. There were no other vehicles nearby. No cover existed along the direct approach to the trailer, but I thought I could climb the sandstone formation near where I had parked the car and reach the few scrubby trees on the opposite side of the "resort."

From the top of the rocks, I surveyed the site through the binoculars. There was no indication that Bellisari had company. Still, a house trailer at Echo Beach was hardly the casino executive's style. I decided to wait to see if Marcel showed up.

Less than an hour later, Bellisari came out of the trailer and drove away. I was torn between checking out the trailer and following my target. After a moment's hesitation, I went back to the car and followed Bellisari's signal back toward Vegas. Peter T. and I could check out the trailer later.

I stayed about a half-mile behind Bellisari all the way back to town. The curious little hideaway at Echo Beach Resort had me puzzled. Bellisari was no outdoorsman and he'd never consider such a place as a weekend retreat. He had to be planning to hide there, or hide someone else. The trailer would be an ideal spot for Marcel to conceal himself.

Bellisari returned to his apartment and remained there for the rest of the afternoon. The three of us welcomed the chance to put our feet up and relax. We were excited about the discovery of the trailer, but were puzzled by its very existence and Bellisari's mysterious trip.

"If you have a partner who's a homicidal maniac, whose picture's been in the papers and on TV, you'd need a place to keep him out of sight," I speculated.

"If you had a partner like that, you might want a place to keep yourself out of sight," Peter T. countered.

"So which is it?

"Damn if I know."

"I think we should talk to the police," Luci said with conviction. Peter T. and I stared at her in disbelief. "I'm serious," she continued. "Michael Bellisari is a criminal and he should be prosecuted. Marcel is out there someplace, but we don't have the slightest idea where he is or what he's doing. For all we know, he could be watching us. Let's face it, guys, we're in over our heads."

She was right, but I didn't want to hear it. "The police will lose him," I insisted. "They'll throw manpower at the problem for a week or two and then move on to something else. As soon as they do, Marcel and Bellisari will bolt for the Caymans and spend their millions on a beach somewhere."

"You can't be sure of that, Tennyson," Luci argued. "At least the police have enough manpower to stake out Bellisari properly. The only advantage we have is that you may have anticipated what Marcel will do, and you two tough guys will keep up this watch as long as it takes."

I started to answer, but she cut me off.

"We haven't even figured out what happens when Marcel does show," she accused. "What do we do then? Are you planning to shoot him down on the street? In Bellisari's apartment? I mean, suppose we get lucky and Marcel doesn't get us first, do we spend the rest of our lives in prison just to take this guy out?"

"Of course not," I snapped. I was about to remind her about her brother, about her own crusade against Marcel and Armand Larrance, but I stopped myself and turned away in frustration. I was infected with the zeal of a crusader, unwilling to listen to practical advice or criticism.

The ringing of the telephone interrupted the debate. We had automatically been forwarding calls from my condo to the penthouse. Luci went to answer.

"She's right, you know," Peter T. said softly.

"About the cops?" I shot back, disbelieving.

"No, about the lack of a plan. I agree with you about the cops, but I agree with Luci on the rest."

Before I could respond, Luci called me to the telephone. "It's somebody named Boog," she said.

The balcony of the penthouse offered a spectacular view of the Las Vegas Strip. After dark, it was like a private fireworks show with flamingos, crowns, carousels, and starbursts blazing their colors into the sky. Huge billboards advertised products and shows and the names of stars beckoned from the marquee lights. Blackjack! Roulette! Craps! Keno! Slots! The promise of riches underscored with dollar signs and long strings of zeros.

"The best thing in life is to gamble and win," the disciples of Tallyrand proclaimed. "The second best thing is to gamble and lose."

"This is life," Las Vegas boasted to both the awed and the jaded. "Anywhere else is just existence." The awed looked on in wonder and decided it must be true. The jaded smiled wryly and decided it was close enough.

Kermit Golightly had died that morning. He never regained consciousness. He was just an anonymous little man who loved to solve the mysteries presented by groups of horses racing over distances of ground. Just an anonymous little man who supported a widowed sister and did his best to look after a handful of friends by passing on his most treasured secrets. There is a saying among gamblers and horseplayers that if you give a man a fish, you feed him for a day. If you teach him how to fish, you feed him for a lifetime. Boog Wilson. Johnny Lanchek. Tennyson Wilder. How many others? I wondered. An anonymous little man, perhaps, but Kermit had not lived without impact on the lives of others.

There had been no more discussion about going to the police.

Luci came out onto the balcony and took my arm as I watched the light show on the Strip. Peter T. was following Bellisari on his nightly carouse. Ordinarily this interlude would have been welcome; Luci and I had so little time to ourselves. Unfortunately, I wasn't very good company that night.

"I'm really sorry about your friend," she said with an understanding in her eyes which told me she was sorry for my sadness, for my rage, and for the cruelty of the loss.

I lit a cigarette and watched the lights. When someone close dies so senselessly at the hands of a stranger, there are no words to ease the passing. I had become an old hand at such things, I thought bitterly. I reflected on the argument Boog's call had interrupted. The Russians who killed my father and the drunk driver who ended Jenna's life might go beyond my reach, but Marcel Larrance was another matter.

"Let's assume that everything goes well," Luci speculated, "I mean, that we get Marcel and none of us ends up dead or in jail. What then, Tennyson? Have you thought about it?"

Had I thought about it? Aside from the practicalities of our current venture, I'd thought of little else.

"Not long ago, I guess I figured you'd go back to Chicago and catch race fixers and I'd go on here trying to pick winners. Then we'd see how things went. I don't think that's such a good idea now, do you?"

"No, I guess not."

"I was in love once," I said slowly. "It ended tragically."

"Jenna Sonnier." She nodded and then noticed my startled look. "I read your dossier, remember."

I remembered and was relieved that I wouldn't have to tell the story. "For many years I believed that I couldn't live through that kind of loss again. I protected myself, behaving rationally and never letting myself get too involved." I laughed. "I actually thought that I had made a conscious decision with proper justifications."

I turned away from the lights of the Strip to face her. She waited patiently for me to go on.

"That was all bullshit," I said flatly. "I just never met anyone special. Does this make any sense?"

"I think so," she answered with an enigmatic smile.

"What I'm trying to tell you, Lucinda DeGuerre, is that you've changed my thinking. Sure, it's true . . . if somehow I lost you, if you were taken from me the way Jenna was, I don't think I could handle it. But right now I can't bear the idea of life without you."

I took a deep breath and pulled her a little bit closer. I touched her face and her hair and marveled at how wonderful she looked in the gaudy artificial glow of Vegas.

"When this is over," I went on, "I want you to stay with me. That is, if you want to."

She tossed her hair back and brushed a tear out of the corner of her eye. "Yes, I think I want to," she said softly. "I don't know how to work it out and I don't know what I'll do out here. The whole idea scares the hell out of me, to be honest. But I know I don't want to leave you and I don't want to try to carry on a love affair with two thousand miles between us. So, yes. I think I want to stay."

We held each other, not talking, but savoring the implications of our pact like the luxurious afterglow of fine brandy. We would be together. The rest would sort itself out.

"I want you to promise me something," Luci said seriously.

"What's that?"

"I want you to promise me that you won't let yourself get killed in this mess. If Marcel shows up here and we can't figure out a way to take him, I want you to promise me we'll go to the police. Will you promise me that?"

Loving a woman does strange things to other resolutions. Quests for wealth, power, fame, even revenge, however highly motivated, seem to fade ever so slightly. I wanted to avenge Kermit and all the others. I felt a responsibility, a duty, to eradicate this maniac from the planet. But I wanted a future with Luci most of all.

"Yes, I can promise you that," I agreed finally.

Bellisari slept late the next morning. He had returned home alone at an unusually early hour and placed a call to a woman, who showed up at his place an hour later. Our bugs picked up clearly the business transaction which took place shortly after her arrival.

"Why would a guy who runs every night with 'show dogs' need to bring in a hooker on Saturday night?" Peter T. had wondered.

"Maybe they're all business deals," I speculated. Peter T. allowed that I was probably right.

"Maybe he needs to remind himself that he's a stud," Luci remarked with her usual insight.

While Luci monitored our various electronic devices, Peter T. and I checked out the trailer at Lake Mead. We approached from the opposite side of the scruffy "resort" and kept our weapons at ready. We had both agreed that Marcel might possibly be holed up there.

There was no sign that anyone, Bellisari or Marcel,

had recently occupied the trailer house. The furniture was covered with a layer of dust, the cabinets were barren, and the refrigerator was empty. What Bellisari had done there for forty-five minutes the day before remained a mystery. We drove back to the Grosvenor Club with the uneasy feeling that we were missing something.

Late in the afternoon, Bellisari made preparations to go out. It was my turn to follow, so I donned what I called my "cowboy suit," complete with blond wig and false mustache. I thought I looked ridiculous, but I had covered three days at the Tiara in the disguise without being recognized.

The Tiara turned out to be Bellisari's destination. He went directly to his office. I watched the feature race at Hollywood Park in the Tiaradome without making a wager and then took a seat in one of the bars to keep watch for my target.

The bar soon bored me and I took a stroll through the casino. I found an empty twenty-five-dollar blackjack table along the route Bellisari would follow to exit and sat down. The dealer was a pretty Oriental lady who seemed genuinely pleased to have a player at her table. We traded money back and forth without much conversation. After about forty minutes, I was down about one hundred dollars and the cute little dealer was relieved by a scowling Cuban. One of the very strict rules I apply in the casinos is that, if a dealer's looks or demeanor bother me, I leave. Gambling requires concentration, and with the rules favoring the house the way they do, I won't allow any distraction. I picked up my chips and left the table.

I was looking for another table when I heard a voice at my side. "Can I buy you a drink, Tennyson?"

I stopped short and turned. The voice belonged to Al, Jimmy DeMaria's right-hand man. He seemed to have seen through my disguise with no effort and I knew this was no accidental encounter. I felt foolish and embarrassed to be recognized in this getup, as though I had been caught in some illicit or kinky act.

We found a table in one of the cocktail lounges and ordered drinks. I did my best to act as though my appearance and behavior were perfectly normal. Al carried on idle conversation with a slight smile of faint amusement. Since that first encounter with Al in the coffee shop where Luci and I met with Mosey, he had always conducted himself in this quiet, friendly manner, but beneath his easygoing mien lay a restrained confidence and athletic strength. Al did not have the look of "mob muscle" like his two confederates, Mickey and Bobby. He was a different sort and, while not sinister, he seemed infinitely more dangerous.

Jimmy's been worried about you, Tennyson," Al said lightly after the drinks had arrived.

"Worried? Why would Jimmy be worried?"

"It's probably just his imagination," he replied sarcastically. That he had paraphrased my excuse to DeMaria about Marcel was not lost on me. "First you buy enough weapons and explosives to start a small war." He held up a hand to stave off my interruption. "Then you drop out of sight. You haven't been to the Frontier, the Athletic Club, hell, you haven't been home for several days. And now, here you are at the Tiara dressed like the Sundance Kid. Yeah, it's probably just Jimmy's imagination."

There was nothing to be said to refute Al's accusations. I remained silent.

Al sighed elaborately and continued. "What are you up to, Tennyson?" he demanded.

There was no point in protesting innocence. The disguise, which now seemed even more ludicrous to me, spoke for itself. "Al, with no disrespect intended, I don't have to explain my activities to you or Jimmy. Let's just say I'm doing some private research."

Al sat up straight in his chair and leaned closer to me. His expression grew intense. "Let's quit fencing, okay?" he said. "You've been watching Michael Bellisari." I started to protest. "Don't bother to deny it. Bellisari hasn't noticed, but we have. Since you don't seem to want to tell us what your interest is, let me just speculate out loud for a minute.

"Given the nature of this recent 'business,' we surmise that you think Bellisari is involved. Mike Bellisari is hardly a man of action, so it follows that he must be the money man. Are you with me so far?"

I nodded, feeling an ominous sense of dread.

"Now, this is all speculation, you understand," Al continued. "But since there was no money found in

Texas, it's reasonable to conclude that the proceeds of this enterprise are still around. Someone who had the brains to figure out Bellisari's involvement might be tempted to keep an eye on Bellisari in the hope of finding the money. Five or six million dollars is a lot of dough for anyone, even a big-time horseplayer."

I had to do something to buy some time. DeMaria and his cohorts were about to screw up everything.

"Would it make any difference to you or Jimmy if I told you I had no interest in the money?" I asked.

Al shrugged. "Maybe," he agreed. "Depends on what you are interested in."

"Okay, I'll level with you," I told him. "I think Bellisari might be the money man." Al grinned, satisfied that his speculation had been correct. "I'm not sure yet," I lied. "I'm just going on some loose gossip, a few half-ass descriptions, and a hunch. I should know for sure in a couple of days."

"Then what?"

"Then I don't give a shit. You get him, the law gets him, it makes no difference to me. I just want a couple more days to make sure."

Al seemed to be thinking this over. "Okay," he said decisively, "you got two days. Then we get together and you tell us everything. Mike Bellisari is well-regarded in this town. We wouldn't want to be too hasty."

I knew that "well-regarded" meant that Bellisari had organized-crime connections. The Nevada Gaming Commission's official position was that the mob had long since been run out of the Nevada casinos. Las Vegas had been built by the likes of Bugsy Siegel, Moe Dalitz, and Ed Levinson. While the licenses were in the names of international corporations, everyone knew that the "boys" were still very much around. Whatever connections Bellisari had would keep DeMaria's people at bay until they were sure.

Al left a bill on the table to cover the drinks and stood up to leave. "Jimmy likes you, Tennyson," he said. "Except for that bullshit about the weapons, he feels like you've been straight with us. Don't fuck with us on this one, okay?"

I sat at the table and slowly finished my drink as Al disappeared into the casino. Al hadn't just picked me out of a crowd of gamblers, I thought to myself. DeMaria's people had been watching all along. They had obviously figured out Bellisari's role and could have moved against him at any time. Instead they were squeezing me for more information. Bellisari's connections must be very heavy indeed.

An hour later, I followed Bellisari home to the Grosvenor Club. As I walked into our rented penthouse, I found a celebration in progress. Luci and Peter T. were drinking champagne, with a second bottle on ice. Both investigators were beaming with pleasure. Luci came to me immediately and threw her arms around my neck.

"Ned Burdine called about an hour ago," she said joyfully. "They caught Marcel Larrance."

Peter T. lifted his glass and nodded in confirmation. "Crazy sonofabitch tried to cross the border at El Paso. Had a phony West German passport."

"When?" I demanded, confused. "Marcel is just now crossing the border? At El Paso?"

"This morning. Tried to come through when all the day-workers were moving. Like he wouldn't stand out in a crowd of Mexicans, for Christ's sake."

I sat down in the nearest chair as Luci handed me a glass of champagne. "What did Ned say? I mean, is he sure?"

Peter T. shrugged. "He's going over there to make sure, but the description fits—six-foot-four, muscular, bald, scarred features. How many of 'em can there be? The clincher is that the West German passport is a forgery. Ned says it's gotta be Marcel."

I slumped in the chair, feeling an overwhelming sense of relief. The encounter with Al, followed by this unbelievable news, was too much to handle all at once. Could it really be over? I thought. Could Marcel have been so stupid as to try to cross over at such a well-guarded point of entry? In Texas, of all places?

Could I have been so far wrong? That was the question that nagged me as my partners celebrated. By this time, Marcel should have been well across the border and working his way to Las Vegas. According to the trail Peter T. followed in Mexico, Juárez and El Paso could have been Marcel's destination, but it seemed inconsistent with his flight from Texas and retreat into Mexico.

"Get dressed, get rid of that horrible wig," Luci ordered. "You two handsome men are taking me out on the town."

I sipped my champagne and suppressed my feeling of unease. As Peter T. had said, how many huge, bald, scarred maniacs can there be? I could decide what to do about Bellisari tomorrow. Tonight we would go dancing.

20

We decided to make our celebration a memorable event. I gave Luci and Peter T. first shots at the penthouse's two bathrooms and spent the next half-hour on the telephone. By the time Luci had finished her shower and started to put on her makeup, I had made dinner reservations at Villa D'Este, booked a table for the Pointer Sisters' cocktail show at Caesar's, hired a limousine, and found a date for Peter T. Linda Slaney, a pit boss at the Desert Inn and an old friend, was more than happy to put aside her plans for a hot bath and a good book for a night on the town in style.

We ate, gambled, told jokes, danced, and consumed enough alcohol that even Peter T. was reeling. Sometime after three A.M. the limousine dropped Luci and me off at my condominium, leaving Peter T. with the car, the penthouse, and Linda. The penthouse at the Grosvenor Club had felt like camping out. Being "home" had the same feel as slipping into a favorite sweater or a well-worn pair of jeans.

Despite the late hour, we took time to warm up the spa. We drank huge glasses of diet soft drinks, loaded down with ice, and let the combination of sauna and whirlpool dispel what could have been serious hangovers. We went to bed, made love, and vowed to sleep till noon.

The telephone awakened me at eight A.M. Luci mumbled something unintelligible and went back to sleep as I scrambled to answer. I lifted the receiver, but got no sound. I had forgotten to take off the call-forwarding. I made the necessary changes and dialed the penthouse. A busy signal. Five minutes later Peter T. answered. I could tell from his voice that we had trouble.

"That was Burdine," he explained grimly. "The guy in El Paso wasn't Marcel."

"Jesus, how the hell could they make a mistake like that?"

"You're not gonna believe this. The guy they caught was an ex-Nazi."

"A what?"

"An ex-Nazi. Been living in Mexico since after World War II. He fitted the description perfectly, burn scars and all. Only trouble is, the guy is sixty-four years old."

"Goddammit! In the meantime, Marcel's probably breathing down our necks. Christ, we gotta locate Bellisari."

"Yeah, well, it's Monday morning. His car's gone. I turned on the receiver and there's no signal."

"Shit!"

"Look, get dressed," Peter T. instructed. "I'll take Linda home and pick you up."

"I'll just meet you someplace."

"All the cars are here, remember. I'll be there within a half-hour."

When I put down the phone, Luci was staring at me, her eyes wide. I told her about the El Paso debacle and she put her face in her hands and shook her head in denial. The nightmare wasn't over.

Peter T. arrived on schedule, bearing Styrofoam cups of coffee and a sack of doughnuts. Luci and I accepted the coffee gratefully. The receiver in the car was turned on, but there were no telltale beeps from the transmitter on Bellisari's car.

"I've been by the Tiara," Peter T. reported. "No signal."

"We'll have to try to locate the signal," I suggested, lacking any better ideas. "Let's go back to the Grosvenor Club and get the other cars. That way we can split up and cover more ground."

At the Grosvenor Club I had another thought and went up to the penthouse for the suitcase containing the remainder of our arsenal. Bellisari's failure to report to the Tiara was an ominous sign. I cursed myself for accepting the unconfirmed and erroneous report of Marcel's capture despite my misgivings about its credibility. Sometime during the twelve-hour period since we abandoned our surveillance, our target had disappeared.

The range of the tracking transmitter was between three-quarters mile and two miles, depending on atmospheric conditions and physical obstructions. The trailer house at Echo Beach was our target's known hideout, but not necessarily his expected avenue of retreat. We had to attempt to locate a signal closer in and work our way to Lake Mead after eliminating other possibilities.

We set up a search pattern with Luci and Peter T. in each of the rental cars and me in the Corvette with the third receiver from the penthouse. With the radio equipment Peter T. had acquired, we could maintain constant communication. According to the plan, we would cruise the city from west to east, converging in Henderson. Should any of us pick up a signal, he was to radio the others before investigating. In the absence of a signal by the time we converged, we would leave one of the vehicles in Henderson and proceed to Echo Beach.

The search was tedious, and through it I chafed impatiently at the prospect that, at this moment, Marcel and Bellisari could be meeting, dividing their loot, and making their respective escapes. I was convinced that the trailer house was the rendezvous point simply because I could divine no other reason for its existence. Still, I restrained my impulse to rush to Echo Beach in favor of a more systematic approach.

The radio crackled. "Signal," Peter T.'s distorted voice reported, along with his location. I heard Luci's voice acknowledge, and follow suit.

"I'm headed east on Tropicana, just crossing the Strip," Peter T. called. "The signal seems to be stationary, maybe a mile from here."

"Shit," I muttered, guessing the location of the target. Peter T. was heading straight for McCarran Airport. The possibility that Bellisari had bolted loomed large.

"Long-term parking, McCarran Airport," Peter T.'s voice confirmed my fears. I found him parked in an empty row and pulled up alongside. One hundred feet ahead of us, in a full row of parked cars, was the Jaguar. Luci drove in a few minutes later.

"Go find a phone and call Bellisari's office," Peter T. told Luci. "Find out if they know he's left town."

As soon as she had driven off, he motioned me to join him. Using the tail of his shirt, he tried the door and found it unlocked. The keys were underneath the seat.

"I was afraid of this," he said as he closed the door with his hip. Still using his shirttail, he opened the trunk.

"Holy shit," I gasped, turning away. Bellisari's naked body was covered with cuts, bruises, abrasions, and what looked like burns. It didn't take a pathologist to determine that the casino executive had been tortured.

Peter T. stood stoically, making his visual examination as thorough as possible. "Look at the hands," he ordered. "Recognize it?"

With some effort I forced myself to return my view to the gory sight. The hand Peter T. had referred to had parts of each finger missing, neatly amputated at a knuckle. I had seen this type of torture before.

"Vietnam," I rasped, barely recognizing my own voice. "Marcel."

Peter T. nodded and slammed the trunk lid. He removed the keys and put them back where he found them, careful to leave no fingerprints of his own.

"We might want to get into Bellisari's apartment," I cautioned.

"I've been in there twice," Peter T. advised. "We don't need keys. Let's get the fuck out of here."

I followed Peter T. to the parking lot of a nearby fast-food restaurant. On the way I heard him radio Luci to advise our destination. She was waiting when he pulled in, having completed Peter T.'s made-up errand.

"Bellisari's office doesn't know where he is," she reported.

"We do," Peter T. said bluntly, and told her what we had found. She choked back her revulsion with obvious effort and closed her eyes. I took her hand lightly in mine and received a light squeeze of acknowledgment. Her expression never changed.

"So much for the 'partners' idea," I observed with resignation. "At least we've learned something."

"What's that," Luci inquired.

"The money is in Las Vegas. Marcel would never have 'dissolved the partnership' if the money had to be retrieved from the Caymans. Also, it's safe to assume that Marcel either has it or knows where it is."

"Bellisari must have held out a long time, judging from the condition of his body," Peter T. noted.

I shook my head. "I'd guess Bellisari gave in easily. He wasn't a hard case. Marcel did all the rest for fun."

Luci shuddered and Peter T. nodded grimly. "So what do we do now?" he asked.

"The way I see it, we have a couple of choices. We can hole up somewhere and wait for Marcel to come." Luci grimaced and Peter T. grunted in distaste for that option. "Or we can take the one chance we have to pick up his trail."

"What's that?" Luci asked.

"The trailer house at Lake Mead. There's a possibility Marcel doesn't even know about it, but there's an equal possibility that Bellisari cached the money there."

"Why do you say that?" Peter T. asked, his tone hinting surprise.

"Ever since I saw the place, I've been trying to figure out why Bellisari would go there. Before, I assumed the money was safely offshore and the two 'partners' would have to go to the Caymans to get it. That was just one of several wrong assumptions I made.

"I think Bellisari intended to screw the Larrance brothers. He stashed all or most of the money here and probably planned to betray the Larrance brothers sometime after their last betting coup."

"How could he hope to get away with it?" Luci asked. "He must have known Marcel would come after him."

Peter T. answered for me. "A guy like Bellisari thinks because he's smart, everyone else is stupid. It's easy to disappear with the kind cash he was figuring to bolt with. He probably had it all figured out, passports, IDs, the works."

"Then why didn't he just go? Why wait for Marcel to catch up with him?"

"A combination of arrogance and calculated risk," I told her. "We've seen the way he lives, or lived. He was probably gambling that Marcel would self-destruct, that the police manhunt would either get him killed or keep him out of the country forever. Then Bellisari would've been free to keep up what he considered the good life with a five-million-dollar cushion. He could launder the money through the Caymans, bring it back in the form of legitimate investments and, by his definition, have it all."

"Bad bet," Peter T. said philosophically. "Clever man, fatal greed." He looked at me with a wry smile. "I don't think much of waiting around for Marcel. Let's check out that trailer house."

Peter T. drove one of the rental cars with Luci in the front seat beside him. I rode in back with our entire arsenal. As we rode, I studied Luci's expression. I had made a feeble attempt to suggest she stay behind, but she cut me off short with a look that defied protest. Besides, I knew that, with Marcel at large, her only real safety was on a plane to Chicago. Short of that, I didn't really want her out of my sight.

We rode in silence, each of us past the point of indecision. While logic might dictate that Marcel could be anywhere, intuition had taken over. We knew that Marcel waited at the tawdry Echo Beach Resort. By the same independent thought processes, we knew that the afternoon would end in death; Marcel's or our own. There existed a curious air of acceptance.

The afternoon was reaching its hottest period as we turned east from Henderson. The temperature on the rocks overlooking the Echo Beach Resort would be approaching 120 degrees. The car whispered along the narrow highway at a sedate speed, the air conditioning holding the desert's ferocity at bay. We might have been on a sightseeing expedition, except for the murderous collection of military hardware.

As we passed the entrance to the Echo Beach Resort, Peter T. allowed the car to coast to a stop. We looked at each other expectantly, waiting for someone to take the lead. I handed out weapons. Peter T. and Luci each had their unregistered pistols. I handed Peter T. one of the shotguns and passed the Uzi to Luci, along with an extra clip. I stuffed a nine-millimeter Beretta, a mate to the one Cowboy had loaned me, into the waistband of my jeans. Two extra clips went into a back pocket. As we got out of the car, I slung the sniper rifle over my shoulder and picked up the other shotgun. I started to close the door, and stopped. I didn't need the extra weight of grenades, but they would be handy if Marcel barricaded himself in the trailer. I grabbed two and tossed one to Peter T.

Loaded down, the climb over the rocks was difficult. The rock formation wasn't particularly high, but it seemed so with the heat and the weight of our weapons. We worked our way east, keeping the rocks between us and the resort, following a narrow trail in single file. Once Peter T. put out a hand and stopped Luci in her tracks. From the rear I looked over Luci's shoulder to where the Texan was pointing. A rattlesnake, lying in the shade under an outcropping of rock, buzzed an angry warning. After a moment it surrendered its shelter and slithered away.

I hate those goddamn things," Luci whispered, cringing with disgust.

"Just watch out for the shady places," Peter T. warned. "These rocks are like luxury condominiums for rattlers."

Luci's eyes widened and I gave Peter T. an evil look.

We pushed on without further incident until we reached a point where we could overlook all of Echo Beach. Bellisari's trailer was about a hundred yards ahead. Luci handed me the binoculars and I straightened up to scrutinize the ramshackle collection of trailers.

"Any people?" Peter T. asked.

"No," I answered. "Looks like Echo Beach is strictly a weekend retreat."

"Yeah, second prize in the Miss Cleveland contest," the Texan snorted. "How about Marcel? Any sign?"

"No."

"Cars?"

"Just an old van about three trailers down. I think it was there the last time we were here. Take a look."

I dropped down and Peter T. took the glasses.

"You're right," he said. "Damn thing's pretty dirty, like it hasn't moved for a while." He dropped down out of sight. Luci took the binoculars and made her own inspection.

"There's no sign of life," she agreed as she settled down beside us. "What do we do if Marcel's not here?"

"Depends," I answered. "If he's been and gone, we

go back to town. If there's no sign he's been here, we wait." I handed the sniper rifle to Peter T. "I'm going down to check things out. Cover me from up here."

Luci reached out and intercepted the rifle. "You work your way around and cover his flank," she told Peter T. as she handed him the Uzi. "I'll cover you both from up here."

The Texan regarded her skeptically. "Can you hit anything with that?" he asked her.

She raised an eyebrow and sniffed indignantly.

" 'Scuse me," he drawled, and started moving out. "Watch out for those rattlesnakes." He grinned over his shoulder. Luci gave him the finger.

She put a hand on my arm as I started to move off. "Be careful," she whispered insistently. "Remember your promise."

I put a hand on her cheek. Neither of us noticed it was a grimy hand and sweaty cheek. "Love you," I said, and scuttled down the narrow trail.

There was a hundred yards between me and the trailer. Instead of lush jungle, there was a complete absence of vegetation, and the air was hot and dry rather than oppressively humid. Still, I was reminded of years ago when my squad had to make an approach to what appeared to be an unoccupied Vietnamese village. The potential for ambush and booby traps had been at a gut-wrenching maximum then. If Marcel was waiting in the dilapidated trailer camp, I was in serious trouble.

I dashed about twenty yards and dived flat on my stomach. To my right I heard the scuffling of running feet. Peter T. scampered across an open stretch and flattened himself against the side of a trailer. He trained the stubby submachine gun on Bellisari's trailer.

I scrambled forward another twenty yards and covered as Peter T. edged closer. There were no challenging fire, no signs of movement from the trailer. I zigzagged the rest of the way to the corner of the mobile home, keeping out of the line of sight from the windows. Cautiously I crept closer and peeked in the nearest window. There was no one in sight.

I ducked underneath the windows and peeked in from the other angle. Still nothing. I tried the doorknob and it turned easily. Signaling to Peter T. what I intended, I went in.

Someone had been inside . . . recently. There were large areas where the layer of dust had been disturbed. I tiptoed the length of the trailer to the bedroom. A large section of the floor had been torn out. I sagged against the wall in disappointment. Bellisari had hidden the cash in the crawl space, I surmised, and now Marcel had it.

Outside I heard a thump and a crash. I tensed and brought the shotgun to bear, but relaxed immediately. Peter T. must have tripped over something, I guessed. Marcel was certainly long gone.

I was about to call out to Peter T. when a burst of machine-gun fire ripped across the facade of the trailer. In the living room in front of me and in the bedroom behind, bullets penetrated the thin siding as if it were cardboard. I had been in the kitchen, where the heavy appliances had sheltered me from the burst.

"Wilder!" a voice that gave me chills shouted. "C'mon out, Wilder."

Shoot the fucker, my mind screamed for Luci's benefit. Another quick burst of fire sent me to the floor. I crawled to the nearest window, pushing a chair in front of me. The well-worn armchair wasn't much protection, but it was better than the thin walls of the trailer.

I looked out the lowest corner of the window and my heart sank. Marcel was standing arrogantly in front of the trailer. Slung over his shoulder like a sack of potatoes was the unconscious form of Peter T. Westmoreland. Marcel bore the two-hundred-plus pounds of the detective effortlessly. He had a large-caliber revolver stuffed in his belt and he aimed Peter T.'s Uzi at the trailer.

Luci had undoubtedly held her fire for fear of hitting Peter T. My shotgun was of less value than Luci's rifle. I could blow Marcel away at this distance, but Peter T. could not escape the shot pattern. I took out the pistol and aimed, but lowered it. An expert might, just might, make the shot. I wasn't an expert.

"C'mon out, Wilder," Marcel commanded. "I got your buddy here. I'm gonna blow his head off and then I'm comin' after you. You ready to die, railbird?" The thought amused him greatly, and he laughed with sadistic mirth.

"Thought you'd sneak up on me, did you, Wilder?" he continued to rage. "I've been watchin' you assholes for two days."

I scuttled across the floor and eased open the back door. Maybe, if I could get him to turn, Luci might get a shot. Marcel seemed unaware of her presence. I wondered just how good a shot she was.

"Too bad you didn't bring your little girlfriend, Wilder," Marcel jeered. "I'd keep you alive long enough to see what I do to her." He laughed obscenely. "Don't worry, Wilder. When I'm done with you, I'm gonna look her up. I wouldn't want her to miss the experience of a lifetime."

Good, I thought as I edged along the back side of the trailer, he doesn't know Luci's up there. Marcel's depravity was working for us. Having anticipated our coming, he could easily have set up a foolproof ambush and killed us with no difficulty or risk. Instead, he was controlled by his warped desire to smell our fear, to see us in pain and agony.

"Here I am, motherfucker," I snarled as I stepped around the corner and fired the pistol. I still had no clear shot so I aimed at the ground at his feet.

Marcel whirled and sprayed a burst of fire in my direction. He jumped reflexively to dodge my shot, and Peter T.'s weight threw him off-balance enough to cause most of the bullets to go high. I felt a searing pain in my side as a bullet passed cleanly through the corner of the trailer and raked my rib cage.

Marcel flung Peter T. to the ground and opened fire on my position. Bullets thudded through the siding as I scrambled for cover. I heard the sharp report of the sniper rifle as Luci opened fire. Marcel howled in pain as Luci's first shot took him in the thigh. He spun around and dropped to one knee, but his prodigious strength kept him from going down all the way. Luci's second shot passed over his head, and he hustled between two trailers, dragging his injured leg behind him.

Luci fired twice more, but her angle was wrong to reach the maniac. I let loose two quick blasts with the shotgun, which tore up the corner of one of the trailers but did no damage to Marcel.

"Wilder!" came the rasping snarl. "Very good, Wilder. You almost got me. Must be your little girlfriend after all. I appreciate that. Too bad she don't shoot so good." He laughed and fired a short burst. The dust kicked up all around Peter T.'s inert form. "See that, Wilder," he chortled gleefully. "Your buddy's about to be dead meat."

He fired another short burst, this time even closer. "There ain't nothin' you can do, railbird," he taunted. "Next burst stitches him a new zipper. Then you. Then the girl."

The sniper rifle cracked again. Luci had moved to adjust her angle of fire. Marcel had moved deeper between the trailers and was well-concealed. Still, the shots had distracted him momentarily from the helpless Peter T.

I had one chance to save the Texan. The single grenade made a tight bulge in my pocket and I struggled to free it. I needed to lob the grenade between the two trailers. Too short or too far and the grenade would blow out the roof of one of the trailers before any of the shrapnel reached Marcel. There was about a ten-foot gap between the buildings where the psychopath lurked.

Just one toss, maybe thirty feet with enough arc to clear the first trailer. I pulled the pin, counted the requisite seconds, lobbed, and prayed. The projectile arched over the first trailer, struck the second below the roof line, dropped between them, and exploded. Marcel screamed and fell silent.

There were no shots in Peter T.'s direction and no sound from between the buildings. I saw Luci moving in the rocks and waved to her to remain under cover. There was no way to tell how badly Marcel was hurt. He could be dead or barely wounded, waiting for me to come and investigate.

The last thing on earth I wanted to do was check out what lay between those trailers, but it was also the only thing I could do. I scurried along the front of the first trailer, hesitated at the corner, and then whirled into the gap, firing the shotgun. The shots went high, as Marcel's body lay facedown on the ground, bleeding profusely from a multitude of wounds. I could tell from the blast pattern and blood on the walls of the trailers that the grenade must have dropped almost on top of him. I'd seen enough men "fragged" in Vietnam to know that Marcel was a goner.

I watched for nearly a minute, and Marcel didn't move. I ran to Peter T. and turned him over. He was till unconscious but breathing. I dropped the shotgun and started to drag him into the shade of the trailers, then froze as a bloodcurdling scream rang out from behind me. I turned, astonished, to see Marcel struggling to his knees, the Uzi in hand. Too late I snatched for the Beretta. The snub nose of the submachine gun trained on me; it looked like the gaping bore of a cannon. Operating on total reflex, my body twisted in a futile effort to make itself smaller. The Uzi clattered harmlessly on an empty magazine.

Luci fired from two hundred feet away. The bullet passed close enough to me that I could swear I felt it go by. Her shot struck Marcel chest-high. Luci's shot must have killed him, exploding his heart, but still he struggled to fight, his depraved instinct to shed blood controlling him to the end.

I had a fleeting image of Kermit Golightly, Lizzy Cline, Billy Robles, and even the mutilated corpse of Michael Bellisari. Without an ounce of remorse, I leveled the pistol and shot him between the eyes.

21

I parked the Corvette in the circular drive in front of Jimmy DeMaria's sprawling ranchero. Al answered my ring sporting his usual gold jewelry and flashy tailoring. He greeted me with a handshake and a sardonic half-smile. His eyes flickered to the large suitcase I carried with me, but he made no mention of it. Instead, he ushered me through the house to the patio where DeMaria customarily held court.

The obese superbookie seemed a bit preoccupied as he sorted through some paper on the table before him. When he saw me, he shook off his concern for business matters and greeted me warmly. A houseman appeared a moment later with refreshments.

Al started to leave, but DeMaria motioned him to sit. The fat man, swathed in a voluminous terry-cloth robe over his swim trunks, poured coffee for all of us.

"I love the mornings out here," he rhapsodized. "Early mornings and nights make this furnace of a place more than livable. When I was a kid in Brooklyn, I didn't know there was air like this, air that didn't smell like something. You know what I mean, Tennyson?"

I nodded. "I grew up in Detroit, Jimmy."

"Yeah, right. I forgot. Al, here, is from North Jersey. He grew up with so many chemicals his blood probably looks like motor oil." Al smiled his half-smile at his boss's joke. "So what brings you out here this morning, Tennyson?" the fat man inquired, abandoning his reminiscence.

"It's about the Bellisari thing."

"Ah, yes." He shook his head sadly. "Bad business."

"I promised Al I'd bring you up-to-date. Here I am."

DeMaria's eyes narrowed and he leaned closer in his chair. "I take it you know something about the unfortunate Mr. Bellisari?" He glanced at Al meaningfully. "Please go on. Bring us up-to-date."

Bellisari's body had been found just the day before, thanks to an anonymous tip to the police. The police and the papers had speculated that the murder was drug-related.

"Bellisari was the brains behind the Larrance brothers," I said without inflection. "I know now without a doubt that he was the money man."

DeMaria seemed unimpressed by this disclosure, as I expected. "So who killed him?" he demanded bluntly.

"Marcel Larrance."

This time I had their attention. "You know this?" DeMaria asked. I nodded.

"And where is Marcel Larrance now?"

"Let's just say Marcel Larrance is no longer with us."

DeMaria and Al looked at each other with surprise. Abruptly the superbookie laughed. What started as a short, forced bark of surprise and disbelief exploded into a prolonged seizure of uncontrolled mirth. Even Al joined in with a low chuckle of appreciation.

Finally DeMaria wiped his eyes and shook his head. "Tennyson, Tennyson," he exclaimed. "I've always had a high regard for your abilities, but still, sometimes you amaze me. I guess I'm safe in assuming that Juan's 'merchandise' was put to good use?" He held up his bearlike paw to stave off my response. "Never mind," he said seriously, "the details are unimportant. Tell me, does Marcel Larrance's, ah, 'disappearance' mean that all the participants in this scheme are now accounted for?"

"Yes," I answered. "But there is one other thing."

"Oh?" DeMaria again glanced at Al and their attention was drawn involuntarily to the suitcase beside my chair.

I stood and cleared a space on the table before lifting the heavy bag to its surface. I unzipped the suitcase and displayed its contents. Jimmy DeMaria and his organization handled millions of dollars but the sight of $2.8 million in cash left him speechless.

"How much did these guys take you for? You and your associates?" I asked.

DeMaria thought for a moment. "Three million, maybe a little more."

I nodded, satisfied. "This represents almost all of your loss," I said, indicating the cash in front of us.

The fat man eyed me speculatively. "Altogether there had to be at least five million," he observed with just a hint of accusation.

"Perhaps," I agreed noncommittally. "Nevertheless, this is what we recovered, less deductions for expenses and what my partners and I considered to be token compensation for a few of the victims." DeMaria raised an eyebrow skeptically, but said nothing. "My partners and I want nothing for ourselves," I declared, "We deducted our out-of-pocket expenses for this recovery and nothing more."

DeMaria looked at Al, who shrugged. The fat man stared thoughtfully for what seemed like several minutes before speaking. "Very well," he pronounced almost officiously, "we'll accept your accounting. At the same time, I wonder if you aren't entitled to some sort of finder's fee."

"Nothing, Jimmy," I insisted with finality. "We're satisfied with the final outcome." I sat back down and sipped my coffee.

"Remarkable," DeMaria commented, "I can't think of anyone I know who wouldn't have gone south. So much cash is simply irresistible. We had no idea you had 'settled' with Marcel Larrance. You were in the clear. Why would you . . . ?"

"C'mon, Jimmy," I sighed impatiently. "You knew my partners and I were watching Mike Bellisari and you had a good idea why. How long would it have been before you or your associates came around asking questions? The simple fact is, we don't want the money, you do. We just want the whole thing to be over."

The fat man nodded his agreement with an air of finality. "Then that's it," he declared. "I'll advise my associates that the matter is resolved satisfactorily." He paused to regard me with a certain amount of respect. "People are very strange, Tennyson," he mused. "At my age, I shouldn't be surprised at what they do. These guys—Bellisari and the Larrance brothers—had one helluva scheme. They could have run in their ringers, say, once every six months or so, and no one would have noticed them. Instead, they tried to pull off one every few weeks. Stupid. Greedy.

"Then they made the mistake of trying to pin the whole thing on you." He shook his head in wonder. "A loose cannon, 'double zero,' the fall guy takes them apart. They could've been home-free.

"All this aside, Tennyson," he said seriously, "I feel we owe you. I hope you understand, that's not a statement people in my profession use lightly. If ever you need a favor, I'd be most distressed if you failed to come to me."

We shook hands and Al escorted me out. "You're a piece of work, horseplayer," he said, offering his hand as I was leaving. "What Jimmy said back there, about owing you, that goes for me too." He still wore his peculiar half-smile, as though he were mildly astonished that I had survived everything that had transpired. Still, I caught a trace of admiration in his tone and I was, strangely, pleased.

Once out on the highway headed back to Vegas, I breathed a huge sigh of relief. I was confident that DeMaria and his people would take no further action.

The cash I had given DeMaria was a little over half of what we recovered. There had been two suitcases stored in the battered old van. After we had gotten Peter T. on his feet, the Texan displayed no sustained damage beyond a pounding headache. We did our best to remove traces of our presence at the scene. Only after we picked up shell casings and obliterated potential fingerprints and tracks did we think about what could have happened to the cash.

Luci was the one who first noticed the Arizona tags on the battered van. Peter T. and I had been correct that the van had been parked in the same spot the day before the shoot-out. Marcel must have been watching us even then.

We found an old aluminum fishing boat behind one of the trailers and a paint-stained plastic tarpaulin in a makeshift shed. We wrapped Marcel's body, along with the remains of our arsenal, in the tarp, and, about three hundred yards offshore, we weighted the gruesome parcel with enough rock to send it to the bottom of Lake Mead.

We cleaned up bloodstains, but we could do little about the damage to the trailer houses. With no better ideas, we left packets of cash in the damaged weekend retreats with which the unfortunate Echo Beach residents could either repair their "slices of paradise" or, more likely, abandon the tacky dumps and seek another refuge.

All that remained, as I parked behind my condominium, was the disposition of the balance of the cash. I had not misled Jimmy DeMaria when I said that Luci, Peter T., and I wanted nothing for ourselves. The thought of keeping any of the proceeds that had caused so many to die made me nauseous. Even so, we couldn't reconcile turning all the money over to DeMaria. DeMaria's business, the National Sports Book, was so lucrative it almost manufactured money. The suitcase I delivered that morning was intended, as I had stated, to put the matter to rest in the eyes of the bookies. There were other victims of the Larrance brothers and Bellisari who deserved compensation.

When I descended to the den, Luci and Peter T. were hard at work. Spread before them on my desk were neat parcels of cash wrapped in plain brown paper. Both of the investigators were wearing thin surgical gloves to avoid leaving fingerprints. They were nearly finished and I detected an air of conspiracy in their laughter when I entered the room.

"How'd it go?" Peter T. asked.

"No problem," I rejoined. "It's over."

Luci got up from her chair and hugged me. Peter T. beamed with delight. When Luci disengaged, Peter T. handed me a single sheet of plain paper. In the nondescript type of my dot-matrix printer it read:

> To put your mind at rest, Marcel Larrance is dead. The enclosed funds should serve as small compensation to the families of his victims. We trust you will do us the service of delivering them.

I nodded approval and Luci enclosed the unsigned note in the last package of cash. She affixed a typed label bearing Ned Burdine's office address. Perhaps Burdine might divine the source of the note and the money, but we doubted that he would ever mention it.

We sent a similar package to Kermit Golightly's sister in New Orleans and another to Boog for delivery to the dancer Vanessa in Detroit. To Kermit's sister we wrote that the money was Kermit's, held for safekeeping by an anonymous friend. Our instruction to Boog was to deliver the package only if Vanessa agreed to leave her present occupation and pursue her education. Should she refuse, he was to donate the money to a charity of his choice. I had no doubt Boog would honor the instructions.

These "bequests" covered the survivors of victims of Marcel's violence as we knew them, with a little license applied to classify Vanessa as the beneficiary of Leslie Pilarcik. With the balance of the cash we made a few donations—to a local priest who ran a shelter for the homeless and a refuge for tapped-out gamblers; to an agency which provided free counseling services to compulsive gamblers and their families; to the fund administered by the Jockey's Guild for families of riders injured or killed in the course of their hazardous career; and to a program in Kentucky which provided a retirement of sorts for old race horses, geldings mainly, who had no commercial value after their racing days were over.

We had no way of returning money to bettors who had lost money in the races fixed by Bellisari and the Larrance brothers. Our arbitrary donations to worthy causes were as close as we could come.

There remained two parcels that needed to be delivered in person, for we had no addresses for the recipients. These two bequests could not be considered recompense, nor could they be conceived as going to worthy causes. We designated them for people who had been of peripheral benefit to us in the course of events, people who, for once in their life, could use a windfall.

Satisfied with our preparations, we loaded one of the rental cars and set out. After dropping all but two of the parcels at the post office, we headed downtown.

We found Mosey on a bench in front of the Fremont Social Center. Peter T., who was unknown to the old horseplayer, made the delivery. Luci and I watched from a distance. If I gave Mosey a packet of money, word would be out all over town.

"Daft ol' buzzard," Peter T. said when he returned to

the car. "I couldn't get 'im to take the package. First he thought I was out to mug him. Then, when I told him to go home before he opened the package, he decided I was a spy. Crazy."

I smiled at the observation. "He'll probably blow it all on the horses inside a month," I predicted. "Even so, he'll have the time of his life for a while."

Slot Rat Rosie proved more difficult to locate than Mosey. We had to search through several of her favorite casinos before we found her at the Stardust. This time Luci made the approach.

"Wha'd'ya think I am, a bag lady?" Rosie protested when Luci attempted to press the parcel on her. The old woman backed away suspiciously. "I don't need no care package," she insisted haughtily.

Luci looked at me for assistance. "It's from one of your longtime admirers, Rosie," I told her. "We're just making the delivery."

"Oh. That's different," Rosie said, and touched her hair coquettishly. We could sense her mind searching her distant memory for the possible donor. "It must be from . . . No, not him. Perhaps . . . No, he would never . . ." We watched her puzzled expression as she sorted through the gamblers and gangsters she had known forty years ago. They were long dead, victims of violence or time, their glitter and glitz only a fading recollection of their aging paramour.

With an absent gesture, Rosie dropped the package, unopened, into her shopping bag. Carrying a hundred thousand dollars in neatly wrapped cash in her tote bag, and the shimmering memories of happier times in her mind, she resumed her endless search for the special slot machine she'd been dreaming of for so many years.

We burst out of the artificial environment of the casino into the early-afternoon sun, laughing together with the pure joy of having unloaded an onerous burden. Standing on the garish Strip, we breathed the combined heat and exhaust fumes as though it were a magic, life-sustaining elixir. Victors, conquerors, survivors . . . we believed, for that moment at least, that there was nothing we couldn't accomplish.

"Do you suppose she'll put it all back through the one-arm bandits?" Luci asked thoughtfully, thinking of Rosie. "I mean, it seems like such a waste."

"Maybe," I allowed. "I don't think Rosie will go crazy like Mosey. The slots are a bad bet, but she makes it according to her own rules."

"I guess that makes her a professional," Peter T. observed lightly.

I smiled. With sound rules and disciplined behavior, despite a flawed game, perhaps Rosie was a professional.

In the distance, a siren sounded and an ambulance threaded its way through the traffic of Las Vegas Boulevard, drawing closer. Inside the casino there was a flurry of activity.

"What's going on?" Luci asked a bellman as the ambulance braked to a stop in front of the Stardust.

"Some old lady," the bellman answered disdainfully. "Hit a quarter slot for fifty grand and fainted right there on the floor. She's okay."

By the time we eased past a small crowd of onlookers, Rosie was sitting up and acidly shooing the paramedics away. She glanced up when we approached, and showed us the glowing smile of a winner who had always known her time would come.

"Just like I always tell the boys, Poet," she advised us, "the secret is stayin' in the game long enough to get lucky."